All I Want for Christmas

Jon Jeffrey

Chris Kenry

William J. Mann

Ben Tyler

KENSINGTON BOOKS
http://www.kensingtonbooks.com

KENSINGTON BOOKS are published by

Kensington Publishing Corp.
850 Third Avenue
New York, NY 10022

All Kensington titles, imprints, and distributed lines are available at special quantity discounts for bulk purchases for sales promotions, premiums, fund-raising, educational or institutional use.

Special book excerpts or customized printings can also be created to fit specific needs. For details, write or phone the office of the Kensington Special Sales Manager: Kensington Publishing Corp., 850 Third Avenue, New York, NY 10022. Attn. Special Sales Department. Phone: 1-800-221-2647.

Kensington and the K logo Reg. U.S. Pat. & TM Off.

ISBN 0-7582-0310-1

First Kensington Trade Paperback Printing: October 2003
10 9 8 7 6 5 4 3 2 1

Printed in the United States of America

Contents

He'll Be Mine By Christmas Morning

Jon Jeffrey

In Memory and Tribute to
Ruma Haque
1962–2002

I want a man who's kind and understanding.
Is that too much to ask of a millionaire?

—Zsa Zsa Gabor

Chapter One

Things to Do Before Christmas

1. Stop chasing straight guys

"Where did you learn to give head like that?" Freddie Michel asked.

"At a Holiday Inn in Beverly Hills," Carson St. John said, rising up to allow Freddie the freedom to put himself back together. "It was a Frankly Speaking Sexuality seminar, but we spent most of the time practicing fellatio on big dildos attached to cheap salad plates with suction cups."

Freddie stretched lazily, a move which emphasized his impressive stomach muscles. "You must've been at the top of your class."

A cell phone jingled.

In perfect synchronization, Carson and Freddie reached for their respective third ears, which were casually slung onto the bedside table.

Freddie's killer green eyes flashed victory. "It's mine." He checked the ID screen, grinning. "You won't believe who it is."

"A spokesperson for the Heterosexual Society? They probably want to revoke your membership."

Freddie for Fun metamorphosed into Freddie for Business. "It's Brad Pitt."

"Yeah, right. That guy can be such a pest."

"I'm serious," Freddie insisted, his focus total, his every synapse on fire. He raised the sleek instrument for Carson's benefit. It was the new Sony Ericsson number—less than three ounces, vibrant color screen, digital camera attachment that popped up people's faces when they called—an expensive toy to be envied.

Sure enough, there flashed *Mr.* Jennifer Aniston.

"Brad! What's up?"

For a moment, Carson merely stared. Seconds after an orgasm and Brad Fucking Pitt is ringing Freddie on speed dial. It just wasn't fair.

Freddie lit up a Marlboro Light. "It's all sorted out. Fifty bottles? Consider it done." With a chuckle, he signed off. "Brad's throwing a surprise party for Dermot Mulroney and Catherine Keener."

Carson buttoned up his shirt. "Oh, really? Where?" He tried for a cool, detached tone, even though, deep down, he wanted to shake the smug bastard and scream, "Tell me, goddammit!"

"Sorry," Freddie chirped. "Secret venue."

Carson shrugged. "It's not like I intend to crash."

Freddie Michel was Manhattan's go-to guy for delicate social fixes— locations for celebrity events, trustworthy bodyguards, discreet holiday travel arrangements, etc. His personal database included hotel door- men, club bouncers, PR flaks, maitre d's, boutique sales associates, spa managers—virtually every A-list foot soldier who could get something done in a hurry.

"You know what they say," Freddie trilled, dragging deep and then killing his barely smoked cigarette. "Loose lips sink ships."

"They say that?" Carson asked.

"Did I ever tell you about the P. Diddy incident?"

"No, but let's pretend that you did."

Freddie gave him a quizzical look.

"P. Diddy, Puff Daddy, Sean Combs—they *all* bore me," Carson said, fastening his Gucci belt and slipping back into his Prada half-boots. As he thought about it, he had to admit that Freddie Michel was creeping close to a flatline on the who-gives-a-shit meter as well. He didn't kiss, he didn't fuck, and he didn't offer up any work-related gossip. Just an- other straight guy who closed his eyes during oral sex and still consid- ered himself to be on the family values side of the fence.

Carson had been here before. Same story, different cast. But Freddie really did it for him. He was movie-star handsome, had a body built by a strict Zone diet and punishing sessions at the gym, possessed a certain guileless charm, and engaged in just enough ambiguous flirtation to hold Carson's hope and interest.

Staying tuned to that channel had led him to this—occasional mid-morning romps at the SoHo Grand. Hardly a root canal, but going nowhere just the same.

"I need it bad," Freddie had groaned into his cellular, dispensing with the more obvious hello and how are you. "And you're the best, man. Come on. Break away. I'm dying here."

Each time Carson had promised himself *never again*, and yet he continued to oblige Freddie's pleas for attention. Jesus, the way the man carried on, he made it sound like community service. If only he were a fireman or a rescue worker, then it would be.

"Okay," Freddie relented, breaking the silence. "But don't breathe a word of this to anyone."

Carson gazed at him expectantly.

"It's at Chateau. In the VVIP room."

Carson had heard of it. Fourth level. L-shaped. Impossible to get into if you weren't a regular fixture with Us magazine. Apparently the regular VIP room was now nothing more than a human lint tray for B-listers like the Baldwin brothers, Carmen Electra, and the reality show star of the moment. He smiled at Freddie. "Should I bring a gift?"

Freddie's cell phone buzzed to life. He held up a halting finger, then just as quickly forgot that Carson was in the room. Apparently, a Mrs. R needed to see hair stylist Paul Podlucky on the double. Freddie promised to make it happen and signed off. "Why the fuck did I tell her that? Paul's on a photo shoot all day."

"What about Super Cuts? They take walk-ins. I'm sure Mrs. R won't mind."

But Freddie didn't hear him. He was already burning up the wire with Crystal, Paul's assistant, negotiating for a block of time that didn't exist. But obviously he said all the right things, because Mrs. R got in at three o'clock. Crisis averted.

"Let's get back to this little school you went to," Freddie began, scratching his chin, grinning. "There's something that you do that makes me come really fast. Drives me crazy. What is it?"

"That would be the Penis Samba."

Intrigued, Freddie's brows shot up. *"The . . . Penis . . . Samba,"* he murmured slowly, dramatically, as if it were a covert operation directly under Homeland Security.

"And no," Carson put in quickly, "I'm not going to explain what it is or how to do it."

"Why not?"

"Because you'll pass it on to that junior socialite you're stringing along and delete me from your Palm Pilot." Carson stepped into the bathroom and finger-combed his hair into place. "I much prefer me getting tired of you first."

Freddie appeared in the doorway. "Lovers never get sick of me. I'm twenty-eight. Do you have any idea how many I've broken up with?"

Carson gargled with Scope. "Hundreds, I imagine."

"I'm no rock star . . . but it's a lot."

"Is there a point here? Beyond the fact that checking your ego at the door would require an airport hangar."

Freddie shrugged. "If there was, I've forgotten. But about the Penis Samba . . . don't get me wrong, it feels great, but ease up next time. That taffy pull thing you do makes me shoot too quickly."

"Listen, I've got a schedule to maintain. I mastered that art, so I wouldn't have to pack a lunch before going down there." Carson checked his watch. He was really pushing it to get to his appointment on time. "I have to run." Grabbing his Burberry coat and Marc Jacobs messenger bag, he halted, remembering that Freddie usually kept a rented Ford Expedition and driver stationed at curbside. "Can your guy run me to Harlem?"

Freddie shook his head. "Sorry. We're off to pick up two strippers at the airport. They're flying in from Vegas for Zyler Brillstein's birthday party at Bungalow 8."

Carson knew the name. The Upper East Side kid was just turning eighteen, and his first novel, *Rich Brats*, a seedy account of the way he and his peers lived, had been perched on the bestseller lists for weeks. The little shit. "Whatever. I'll take a cab." He started out.

"Not so fast," Freddie said. "I've got more for you today than just my big, beautiful cock." He crouched down, reached underneath the bed, and pulled out a long antique bottle with what looked like a parchment scroll stuffed inside. Proudly, he presented it to Carson, as if it were a passport to enter the gates of heaven.

With great curiosity, Carson took the object. "Is this an old prop from that terrible Kevin Costner movie?"

Freddie grinned. "Open it up and see."

Carson tapped the paper from its prison and rolled it out. The words HOSTED BY RUMA SINDI captured his attention first. The name was legendary. She gave great parties and possessed super-human social adrenaline. By comparison, Freddie might as well be saddled with Chronic Fatigue Syndrome.

Ruma's family had ties to Iraqi royalty, and her family had fled Baghdad for America to escape violent revolutionaries. She'd flourished at Brown and established herself as an It Girl upon moving to Manhattan, when she boldly turned down offers from platinum PR companies to start her own boutique firm. Benefit parties were her calling card. Memorial Sloan-Kettering and the New York City Ballet had the balance sheets to prove it.

"Merry Christmas," Freddie said.

Carson stood there, speechless. What he held in his hands was an invitation to attend Ruma Sindi's Blue Lagoon Party. It was a costumed affair playing cheeky homage to that dreadful Brooke Shields/Christopher Atkins vehicle. Everybody was required to show up in their shipwrecked best. The still-secret location would be remixed, remade, and remodeled into a tropical paradise. A tough order considering the current brutal winter conditions, but if ever there was a woman who could pull it off and not disappoint, then that woman was Ruma Sindi.

Buzz on her Blue Lagoon bash was already deafening. Where would it be? Who would turn out? The only certain fact was that all proceeds benefited the Robin Hood Foundation, which funded projects for New York's most troubled neighborhoods. Before his death, John Kennedy, Jr. had been part of the board. Carson realized that, besides those endless hours of Court TV coverage on the creepy cousin's rape trial, this was the closest he'd ever come to a Kennedy.

"Bring someone classy," Freddie said. "No bar trash, okay?"

Carson pulled a disappointed face. "Oh, well, that leaves *you* out."

Freddie made a playful move to take back the invitation.

But Carson shifted too fast for him. "I'm insulted that you even said that. Like I'm going to bring just anyone."

"Do you have someone in mind?"

"Not yet," Carson murmured, concentrating hard on the possibilities. "But he has to be someone of merit. You know, he should've at least earned a mention in Page Six. And it can't be for multiple rehab visits or fighting with J. Lo's hypersensitive security detail."

"Have you ever met Ruma?"

Carson shook his head. "No, but I feel like I have. That profile in W was very intimate. I loved what she said about getting through that period of conformity where you just have to have the right Gucci shoes. She's so evolved." He looked down at his Prada feet. "I'm not quite there yet."

"You'll love her," Freddie assured him. "And I really think she's going to outdo herself with this Blue Lagoon theme."

Carson secured the delicate paper back into the bottle. "So everyone will be wearing swimwear in December?"

Freddie arched an eyebrow. "Apparently."

"I better give up all carbs until then. That includes ejaculate. I know it's only about twelve calories, but every little cutback adds up. So that's the last time I swallow until New Year's."

Freddie made a pantomime out of being wounded. "You're killing me."

"You'll survive. Have fun with the strippers. I hope you loaded up on antibiotics." And then Carson darted out the door, down to the lobby, and into a taxi on West Broadway.

The cabin reeked of cigarettes, curry, and body odor. No matter the freezing, whipping wind, Carson cracked the window a quarter of the way and braved the cold. He sat fitfully as a garbage truck impeded their progress for long, excruciating minutes. Finally, he stopped watching the gridlock and snatched his cellular to check in at the office.

Four rings. No answer. Then voice mail. Where the hell was Plum? He hung up, popped two chicklets of Dentyne Ice, and took out his aggression on the gum, chewing hard, thinking fast. Jesus, his life was insane. Being editor of *BFM*, formerly known as *Throb*, still the gay man's answer to *Cosmopolitan*, only smarter, sexier, and, alas, one-tenth of the circulation, gobbled up at least a million hours a week. And then there were his *BFM* lifestyle segments for *Manhattan Morning*, hosted by Mike and Manzie, the poor man's Regis and Kelly, but great exposure just the same. Somehow he managed to do it all. Of course, being single, childless, petless, and having no immediate family within a five hundred mile radius helped.

He rang Keri, his field producer for the TV spots.

"I'm here, Cruz is here, our subject is waiting patiently in his office. Where the fuck are you?"

The taxi picked up speed.

"In traffic hell. But I'm almost there." Tiny lie. Okay, a big one. But Keri could be so high-strung at times. No need to push her into upping the ante on her daily Paxil dosage. Those pills caused sexual side effects, and dating was hard enough for girls in New York.

"Did you get the press kit I messengered over?" Keri asked.

"Yes." Carson grabbed the sleek black portfolio from his bag. "It's right here."

"Did you *read* it?" Huffy.

"*Yes.*" More huffy.

"It's not a stupid question. It took seven takes to get the name of our last bachelor right."

"What kind of parent calls their son *Sandy*? I was doing him a favor by calling him Sam."

"I believe you also referred to him as *Richard*."

"That's still better than Sandy." Carson peered out as the streets flashed by. They were flying now. "I'll be there soon. If Mr. Wonderful gets impatient, tell Cruz to take off his shirt. That should happily distract him."

He signed off and began flipping through the material on today's subject. All the other *BFM* Hot Bachelor Profiles for *Manhattan Morning* had been young, buff, beautiful, and entrenched in glamour careers like club promotion, fashion, media, and publishing. But the time had come to play the diversity card.

Enter Callum Fox. He was British, a total stranger to sunbathing or Mystic Tan, fighting a weight problem, and past the age of thirty-five. Luckily, his resume looked better than his glossy. He owned The Crystal Group, a successful consulting firm that forecasted trends and advised corporate clients on next-big-things in consumer culture. Already huge in London, the company's first stateside office had just opened in the same trendy Harlem building that housed Bill Clinton's professional digs.

Carson's attention zeroed in on the press clippings. Something clicked as he read about the savvy prognosticator's rapid rise to the top. Callum Fox was a true visionary. Too bad he looked like Louie Anderson a few months after gastric bypass surgery.

Carson tried his office again. This time he got an answer.

"Plum Kinsella's office."

"Not to be a stickler for details, but it's *my* office, and you're my *assistant* with your own *cubicle*."

An exasperated sigh. "Are you finished? You know, lots of clubs have open-mike nights for this problem."

Plum was a reject from *Teen People*, desperate for anything at *Vogue*, and generally worthless. But Carson kept her on anyway. She showed up, rarely complained about her salary, and knew more of his personal secrets than he cared to acknowledge.

"Any calls?"

"Some man named Paul Easton has phoned twice," Plum remarked casually.

Carson jolted. "Who?"

"Paul Easton. As in Sheena. 'My baby takes the morn—' "

"Yes," he cut in. "I know who Paul Easton is. What time did he call?"

"I don't know," Plum said vaguely. "Twice in the last two hours I guess."

Carson's mind was spinning. What did the CEO of Harlequin Vamp want with him? This man presided over a fashion dynasty rivaled only by Gucci, LVMH, and Prada. "Why didn't you call my cell?"

Plum paused a beat. "Because you were with Freddie Michel, and it's not polite to talk with your mouth full."

Chapter Two

Things to Do Before Christmas

1. Stop chasing straight guys
2. Cancel subscription to *Us* and start reading books

Keri was chain-smoking outside the building when Carson's cab pulled up to the curb. She killed her cigarette with a Nine West heel and folded her arms, scowling.

Carson threw money at the driver and tumbled out.

She shook her head, checking her watch, a cheap digital. "We've still got fifteen minutes if we're lucky. This man *does* run an international business."

Carson grinned. "A bachelor with a schedule? What a switch. We've profiled so many club sluts whose days don't get started until four o'clock."

In the elevator, Keri announced that the intro package would have to be reworked. That meant an extra trip to the station. Carson gave her an annoyed look. "Why?"

"Because Callum Fox has pulled a fucking Sandy from *Grease*. He's not in leather, but just wait until you see him."

Carson merely stared. He knew better than to trust a woman's opinion about a man. After all, they got excited over Russell Crowe. "What did he do? Go on Slim Fast and apply a bronzer?"

"Let me put it this way: If he were a movie star, he could be openly gay, because I'd still want to see him making out with other women. The man is that sexy."

Carson had never heard Keri go on like this about any guy, and together they had been up close and personal with some pretty hot numbers. He kept an open mind as the elevator doors opened.

Keri led him through a Kartell-crazy foyer and into an expansive office with a picture-window view of Manhattan.

Carson stopped. He looked. He looked again. He salivated.

Even with all her hyperbole, Keri had completely undersold this hunk. Carson tried to reconcile the man in front of him from the publicity photo in the press kit. To say there had been a transformation was the understatement of the century. This went beyond Sandy from *Grease*. Or Sandra Bullock's airport hangar switcheroo in *Miss Congeniality*.

Carson heard an apology jumble out of his own mouth. He had no idea what he was saying.

Callum Fox smiled. Ultra Brite. Infinitely welcoming. "No problem. This beats an ad in the personals. Should be worth the wait." He offered a strong manicured hand. It was attached to a lean forearm. Where there had once been excess flesh was now tightly coiled muscle.

Carson shook firm and fast, drinking in every detail.

Callum spoke posh English, his accent all mellifluous vowels and dentilingual consonants. He looked younger, the weight loss prominent everywhere, especially his face, sporting sculpted cheekbones now instead of fleshy jowls. The moussed spiked chestnut hair, gleaming jade eyes, and sex-bomb tan (courtesy of the Portofino Sun Center, no doubt) made for an incredible package.

Carson glanced down to see two masking tape Xs on the floor.

Callum was on his mark.

Carson was not. And every cell in his body was alive with the ardent need to stop this segment. Why ruin his chances at a great find by alerting the masses? It would be like announcing a secret liquidation sale at Barney's to the city at large. Just . . . stupid.

"Maybe we should reschedule," Carson said. "This is so rushed. You deserve more time."

Callum's perfectly balmed lips parted in surprise, but he seemed open to the idea.

Until Keri spoke up. "Not a chance. We need this segment for tomorrow's show, and the promos are already running." She gave Carson that what-the-fuck-is-your-problem look, then pressed the mike into his hand.

"Anytime you're ready, Carson," Cruz said, holding the shoulder cam steady.

Usually, Carson felt the urge to bed down the Latin dream, but right now he simply wanted to push him out the window.

Callum smiled. "I'm all yours."

Not after this airs, Carson wanted to say. But instead he launched into a series of cliched bachelor questions. What qualities do you look for in a potential mate? Do you believe in love at first sight? When will you be ready to settle down? By the end of the interview, Carson felt like Mary Hart after a one-on-one with George Clooney.

Even worse, Callum had been infuriating, answering everything with great charm, cleverness, and just the right level of self-deprecation. Damn! Why couldn't he be a hopelessly boring interview like, say, Tom Cruise?

"That was fantastic," Keri gushed. Five minutes ago she had been three-quarters in love with this man. She was all the way there now.

Callum fixed an uncertain gaze on her. "You're sure this won't backfire in my face? Most interviews turn out humiliating."

Keri rushed over as if Callum needed emergency medical attention. She touched his arm. "Why? You were brilliant."

Callum glanced at Carson for confirmation.

He gave him a nod. "And we're part of the friendly press. You must have battle scars from the British tabloids."

"They once reprinted an entire month's worth of grocery receipts. I was binge-eating at the time. It wasn't pretty."

Keri waved off the unfortunate mention of pre-stud Callum. "That's all in the past. Look at you now."

"I know," Carson chimed in. "You're like the male version of Carnie Wilson."

Keri's eyes blazed with disapproval.

Callum smirked in response, but there was still a question in his gaze.

"Without the Beach Boy father and unfortunate pop music career of your own, of course," Carson said.

"I didn't invite a film crew to document the procedure, but I did have gastric bypass surgery. I hope the similarities with Carnie end there."

Cruz announced his exit with a short wave and left the office.

Callum extended a hand to Keri. "It was a pleasure."

"No, thank *you*," Keri cooed.

He turned to Carson curiously. "Can you stick around for a few minutes?"

"You should know that I like my eggs scrambled."

Callum drew back a bit, smiling broadly, almost blushing.

Keri looked appalled.

"Did I say that out loud?" Carson asked. He really hadn't meant to, but, ultimately, he was happy that he did. Why not get to the point and just let it be known that staying over for breakfast was perfectly within reason? They were single adults.

"I'll make a note of that for the future," Callum said cheekily, then smiled graciously at Keri as he began walking her toward the door.

"We'll messenger over a tape of the final edit in the morning," she was saying.

"That would be lovely," Callum said. "Let's hope the blind dates will be as painless as this interview."

Keri's brow furrowed. "You should have someone on your staff do guerrilla screening. There's no point in wasting your valuable time with losers . . . or liars. People might make up anything to get a date with you."

Callum raised his perfectly tended brows in faux alarm. "That sounds frightening."

Keri stared back, like a fan meeting her favorite star for the first time. "You smell better than any man I've ever met in my life."

"It's called bathing regularly. I highly recommend it."

Keri's face turned pink.

"I'm kidding," Callum went on. "I wear a scent created especially for me by Angela Flanders. She's on Columbia Road in London. Wonderful perfume maker. She put together ingredients that work with my specific body chemistry. I'll have an assortment of her fragrances sent over to you." He retrieved an Hermes notepad from his rear pocket and scribbled down the thought. "Earl Grey is a favorite of mine. It makes me think of high tea on a beautiful lawn on a summer afternoon. You'll adore it."

"You don't have to do that," Keri said unconvincingly.

"Not at all. Consider it done. And know that I'm trusting you to edit this in a way that doesn't make me look like a total imbecile."

"Impossible. Even George Lucas couldn't do that," Keri said, starting out.

"You're too kind." Callum turned around and fixed a smile on Carson that smacked of a secret agenda. "Have you spoken to Paul yet?"

"Paul Easton?" Carson asked, stunned.

Callum nodded.

"We're playing phone tag. How did you know?"

"I suggested that he call you." Callum slipped his new and improved ass onto the edge of his desk and gestured for Carson to sit down.

"About what?"

"A job," Callum said simply.

"Really? Any day now I might be firing my assistant. That position could be available. Does Paul mind fetching coffee and the occasional Krispy Kreme?"

"Does that job come with a multi-million dollar salary, stock options and unlimited use of a private plane?"

"No, but every Friday is dress casual."

Callum beamed. "I think you just poached the CEO of the fourth largest fashion dynasty. How could he turn that down?"

"He would have to be completely insane. Of course, I read that he's backing Lulu McQueen, so at the very least he must be on the wrong medication."

Lulu McQueen was the wild child daughter of rock icon Simon McQueen, former lead singer of Tantrum, a solo success in his own right, famous for screwing scores of high-profile women, and miraculously still alive given his never-ending appetite for drugs and booze.

Lulu was his neglected twentysomething daughter, a girl desperate to pull off a Stella McCartney in the world of fashion.

"I was a bit surprised by that announcement myself," Callum admitted. "But Paul must see something we don't. He has vision."

"In her case, I think it's blurry."

"I don't know. People are going mad for her new T-shirts."

Carson raided his brain files and came up empty. He prided himself on being up to speed on useless information like this, and Callum had trumped him. "Fill me in."

Callum ran a hand across his impressively defined chest. "Picture a tattered white cotton tee."

"As in *Flashdance* ripped?"

Callum shook his head. "Think your brother's old high school football T-shirt. More ratty than strategically scissored."

"I'm with you."

"Pink felt block letters are sewn across the front to read, 'I LIKE BIG DICKS AND I CANNOT LIE.' "

Carson was floored. "That is fucking brilliant. Sir Mix-A-Lot should sue, but it's still brilliant."

Callum grinned.

"Why don't I know about this? You must think I'm Baby Jessica and that I've been trapped in a well."

"It's all just taken off in the last two weeks or so."

"Don't ask me who the Secretary of Defense is, but I should be well-versed on Lulu McQueen's latest shenanigans." Suddenly, it dawned on Carson that there was a larger point to reach. "We've digressed a bit. What does Paul Easton want with me?"

"How happy are you at *BFM*?" Callum countered.

"Very. But someone could always make me happier. I'm fickle that way."

Callum's desk phone jingled. He ignored it, forming a tent with his fingers as he leaned in to speak.

Carson couldn't stop admiring the impossible golden glow of Callum's tan. On closer inspection, he had never witnessed a solarium-produced color this gorgeous. It was perfect. More perfect than Ursula Andress's hue when she walked up on the beach in *Dr. No*. "Excuse me, but I have to know where you got that amazing tan before we get down to business."

"Canouan. It's my favorite spot in the Caribbean."

Carson decided that he hated this man, who lived like Catherine Zeta-Jones. "Okay, go on. What's the story with Paul?"

"You're well aware that Harlequin Vamp rules British fashion. Now they want to conquer America. That's one of the reasons why I opened a New York office."

"What does this have to do with me?" Carson asked.

"Paul needs an image director. It makes sense to raid a magazine creative. You're a proven trendspotter. You know the youth market."

Carson paused a beat, allowing the possibility to sink in. Image Director for Harlequin Vamp, Inc.? This was *huge*.

"Interested?" Callum asked.

"I don't know," Carson murmured. "I'm . . . I'm still processing it." He gave Callum a raygun gaze, half expecting a punch line to come. "That would be an enormous undertaking. Are you sure he wants me?"

"You've been an observer, a commentator, the very nature of your experience up to now gives you a different perspective that's very valuable." Callum tilted his head. "I didn't take you for a self-doubter."

"I'm not," Carson said quickly. "Generally. It's just . . . I've only been in charge of things I can wrap my arms around. A magazine. Short segments like the one we just shot. But this is an entire *corporation*. That's terrifying."

"Fear is good," Callum remarked easily. "I get the sense that you've peaked at *BFM*. It's probably diminishing returns from now on. When a challenge like this falls into your lap . . ."

Carson said nothing. He could sense his blood humming in a hyperglycemic rush, as if he'd just chugged down a can of Red Bull. "But what if I fail?"

Callum's stare was hard. He didn't deal in failure. "So what? This is the major leagues. Even if you do fail, you fail upward. The exposure alone would nail you a great job someplace else. But I've got a strong record when it comes to matching people with organizations. I haven't been wrong yet. I don't think I'm wrong now."

"Can I get that motivational speech on tape?"

"If that's what it takes to get a yes out of you."

"What am I saying yes to?"

Callum shrugged. "Good point. But that's where Paul comes in. You know, you should try being in your office occasionally. He's been trying to call."

"So I've heard."

"I think you'll be pleased with the package he's planning to offer."

Carson gasped in mock shock. "That sounds suspiciously like sexual harassment. Paul's in his late fifties. I'd feel much better if you were making the offer."

Callum's eyes sparkled with mischief. "I can't make this one, I'm afraid. But I do have you in mind for other things."

Chapter Three

Things to Do Before Christmas

1. Stop chasing straight guys
2. Cancel subscription to *Us* and start reading books
3. Switch from Kiehl's Hair Gel to Frederick Fekkai

Balthazar was vacuum-packed with scene seekers.

"What the fuck? Has there been a Matt Damon sighting?" Stella Moon stood up from the cramped table and peeled off yet another layer of clothing. "And it's so goddamn hot in here." She stopped a passing waitress. "Honey, can you do something about this heat? I'm ready to strip down to my bra."

The waitress took notice of Stella's Lulu McQueen I LIKE BIG DICKS AND I CANNOT LIE T-shirt. "Please do. The manager thanks you in advance," the girl snapped before disappearing into the crowd.

"When did you get that?" Carson demanded.

"A few weeks ago," Stella said. "Isn't it great?"

Carson had to admit that the crass declaration was a perfect fit for Stella Moon, an infamous shock artist best known for her popular series of paintings depicting mutant fruit and vegetables with large phallic shapes protruding from them. She was a bonafide *personality* as well, turning up in *Vogue*, on Page Six (her every move chronicled thanks in large part to a budding relationship with Eurotrash stud Prince Alessandro Imperiali), and, most recently, in a glossy pictorial for December's *Playboy*, (doing very naughty things with a paintbrush).

"Did I tell you about my in-store appearance at Tower? I signed over five hundred copies of the magazine. I never realized that I had such a strong butch lesbian following." Stella sipped her wine. "Very sweet girls. Sometimes I envy them. I mean, they don't have to worry about a colorist or getting their nails done every week. It must be so liberating to be a bull dyke."

"I hear membership numbers are up for that reason alone," Carson said.

Stella glanced up and waved excitedly to someone seated several tables away, then blew him a kiss. The smile on her face appeared forced. Under her breath she murmured, "I can't believe he's here tonight. That's the guy I was fucking before I met Prince Alessandro. He liked me to draw things on his dick when it got hard. And honey, I'm used to working on a much bigger canvas, if you know what I mean."

Carson laughed. "So how are things with the prince?"

"Amazing. The sex is great, we have lots to talk about, and he makes me laugh."

"Sounds like it could be serious."

Stella leaned forward to whisper, "He told me that he had something very important to ask me. Do you think . . ."

"That he's going to propose?" Carson jumped in. "I don't know. Are things that intense?" His mind raced. Stella married? Jesus, that was just too much. "Would you say yes?"

She nodded demurely. "I think I would. Let's face it, he's everything I want, plus he's a goddamn prince. I mean, what the fuck am I waiting for?"

Carson finished his wine and just sat there for a moment, factoring all the serious relationships in his personal orbit. Stella was having Vera Wang dreams about the heir-to-nothing prince, and all three of his best friends were in love—Danny with Tommy Hilfiger model Joel, Nathan with personal trainer Christian, and Rob with advertising executive David. Yet here he remained, alone and facing down a past littered with ridiculous hook-ups. Even worse, it was the fucking Christmas season, which, at the very least, heightened the yearning for something more than blowing Freddie Michel.

"I have no idea what to get Prince Alessandro for Christmas, and it's driving me crazy. I even had a panic attack at Bergdorf Goodman. Luckily, half a dozen shoppers offered me a Xanax." Stella sighed. "Any ideas?"

Carson looked around for their waiter. More wine. *Please.* He'd already faced this question from Danny and Rob and knew for a fact that Nathan would be asking soon.

"We're at that stage where the gift has to be something substantial. I mean, I can't get him a sweater. You know?"

Actually, Carson didn't know. He'd never been in a relationship over the holidays that didn't involve sleeping with someone for their retail discount. Suddenly, the delicious image of Callum Fox flashed into his mind. "I think I met a guy."

"Where? In the steamroom at the gym?" Stella laughed at her own joke.

"No," Carson replied hotly.

"Another straight guy, I take it. Honey, when are you going to—"

"He's gay, Stella. And he's smart and incredibly successful, too."

"And *you're* interested in him? Why?"

"What's that supposed to mean?" Carson demanded.

"Honey, come on, everybody knows that you've never been involved with anyone worth mentioning."

Carson felt a flush of defensive anger. "Gil Bellak is a highly sought-after media consultant and certainly *worthy of mention.*"

Stella shook her head. "Doesn't count. He's married."

"You've been with married men."

"Who hasn't? But I don't count them as real ex-boyfriends. I file them under *unfortunate lovers.*" She regarded him for a moment. "Now your last legitimate relationship was Roger, the pizza delivery guy, right?"

Carson flailed at the waitress and impatiently raised his empty wine glass. "His name was Rocco, and he was a DJ. I've only slept with one delivery guy, and at least he worked for FedEx. Give me some credit."

"Pardon me."

"Seriously, this guy is different. And he's British. I've never been wild about British men, but he's definitely an exception."

The waitress swooped in with another glass of merlot, and Carson wondered why they hadn't just ordered a whole bottle.

Stella fished through her purse, pulled out her cellular, and began scrolling through the stored phone log. "Okay, honey, if you're serious about this guy, then there's someone I want you to call before you fuck it all up." She peered at the tiny screen as her thumb worked overtime to move the data forward. "Here we go. Write this down." She called out a number.

Carson pretended to commit it to memory.

"I'm serious," Stella said fiercely. "Write it down."

Frustrated, Carson scribbled it onto the back of an old receipt. "Who does this belong to anyway?"

"Matt Yorn. He's a dating coach. And he's brilliant."

Carson pulled a disgusted face. "A *dating* coach?"

"Don't sound so smug. He's very talented. I have a friend who's extremely insecure, and he worked with her to the point where she started going out on blind dates and even put in an application to be on *The Bachelor*."

Carson stared at the menu and said, "Are you forgetting that I write a sex column for *BFM*, that I do relationship segments for *Manhattan Morning*, and that people usually ask *me* for dating advice?"

"Are you forgetting that my last orgasm lasted longer than your last relationship?"

Carson glanced up, smiling. "Well, you must be still coming as we sit here, because I'm with Freddie Michel."

This time Stella zeroed in on the menu. "I have it on good authority that Freddie has sought treatment for sex addiction. His weakness is head, and I know of at least two people, not including you, who blow him on a regular basis. In fact, my friend Talisa sucked him off at about two o'clock today." She closed the menu and looked up. "I think I'll have the veal."

Carson blanched. A meaningless affair was one thing, but enabling a sickness like that was quite another. If Freddie was a true addict, then he would think nothing of sticking his dick through one of those

glory holes for a quick fix. The realization left Carson feeling unset-
tled. Not to mention dirty.

"All you have to do is call Matt and set up a time and place to meet.
The two of you will go on a simulated date and then he'll assess your
strengths and weaknesses." Stella paused. "On the issues of dating, of
course."

Carson could hardly believe it. "A *simulated* date?"

Stella gave him an upbeat nod. "It only costs three hundred dollars,
and he gets right to the point. Very efficient. My friend who saw him
could just kill herself for wasting all that money on a therapist. She
was two years in, and they were just getting to her high school slut
phase. How is digging that up going to help her find a husband?"

"Maybe there's a story here," Carson murmured.

Stella shook her head no. "Matt's not a media whore. He doesn't
need publicity, and he's not interested in it. Besides, you just want to
expense this to the magazine. Write the check yourself. It'll mean
more."

Carson found himself reluctantly intrigued. After all, he usually
ended up sampling the latest therapist and psychic to come along. Why
not add a dating coach to the mix?

After dinner, he begged off Stella's pleas to hit a few gay bars and
opted to go home. The phone was ringing when he pushed open the
door, and he raced to answer before voice mail clicked on. "Hello?"

"Finally my persistence has paid off." A distinguished English voice.
But not Callum's. This man was older.

Carson swallowed hard. It had to be Paul Easton.

"I can only assume that I'm speaking with Carson St. John."

"You are," Carson said, laughing a little. "And Mr. Easton, I must
say, this has been one sinister game of phone tag we've been playing."

"Callum mentioned that the two of you talked," Paul said, shifting
down to all business. "So you know why I'm calling."

Carson took a deep breath. "I do, and I'm quite flattered that you
even thought of me, but—"

"We need someone with a gimlet eye for what's hot. That's you. We
want you on board as creative director for Harlequin Vamp's American
launch."

The declaration stunned Carson into silence. The truth was, he hadn't thought this far ahead. Paul was flat out offering him the job! Carson darted into his tiny kitchen and, with nervous hands, poured himself a shot of bourbon. This was crazy. He'd merely imagined that he and Paul would eventually make contact, that a vague conversation would take place, that aerial castles would be built regarding a huge contract and a dramatic exit from *BFM*, and, as with so many things new and exciting and potentially life altering, that nothing would ever come of it.

"Whatever your salary is at *BFM*, I'll double it," Paul said matter-of-factly. "I can offer you a full benefits package, stock options, and an annual bonus as well."

Carson drank up fast, and the bourbon nearly burned a hole in his chest.

"Of course, we want you to start right away."

Carson stood there, more quiet than George Clooney must have been after hearing the first week's box office returns for *Solaris*.

"Is that a problem?" Paul asked.

"Actually, if I did decide to leave, I would want to give my publisher—"

"There's a twenty-five thousand dollar signing bonus."

Something clicked in Carson. "As I was saying, I would want to give my publisher a call tonight and let him know that I'll be cleaning out my office in the morning."

Chapter Four

Things to Do Before Christmas

1. Stop chasing straight guys
2. Cancel subscription to *Us* and start reading books
3. Switch from Kiehl's Hair Gel to Frederick Fekkai
4. Apologize to old woman down the hall for forgetting to feed her cat

Telling the *BFM* staff was easier than Carson had imagined. Deep down, he realized that the last few months had been auto pilot at best, no real passion for the work. Even crafting the catchy headline copy (example of a keeper that became a hot newsstand seller (SEX WITH MARRIED MEN—ARE YOU A NEW MILLENNIUM MISTRESS?) had become a chore. The sizzle was all gone.

Everyone appeared to take his announcement with the appropriate degree of self-involvement, either seeing it as an opportunity for advancement or as a chance to reinvent themselves in the eyes of a new editor.

But Plum, of course, had serious issues. For example, being dispatched to find a large box to pack up his personal things infuriated her. She returned with a flimsy cardboard number that had once held five hundred envelopes, insisting that it was all she could find.

Carson sighed. "Plum, there has to be a better box around here. This is your last official act as my so-called assistant. Try performing a miracle."

Plum settled into an empty chair and watched Carson struggle with the packing handicap. "Any idea who's in line for your job?"

Carson stopped and regarded her seriously. The truth was, he had no idea at all. In fact, he'd hardly considered the situation. "I don't know." His brain ticked through a quick WWMD—What Would Matthew Do. The brash publisher of *BFM* had kept any future plans under wraps during Carson's call last night to announce his exit. "Maybe he'll poach from another magazine. Or he might promote from within."

Plum inspected her nails. "Hopefully, the next editor will see me as more than a glorified secretary."

"I've never seen you that way, Plum," Carson said earnestly. "A glorified secretary? Don't be ridiculous."

Plum gazed back at him warily.

"I've always viewed you as completely useless."

She pursed her lips into a fuck-you smile. "Until it's time to break up with one of your loser boyfriends. Then I'm more than competent."

"Remind me to mention that in the letter of recommendation you want for *Vogue*."

Plum snarled. "Don't bother. That job went to some bitch who grew up on the Upper East Side. Figures. No girl without a trust fund to dip into could live on that shitty salary."

Carson regarded his subordinate nemesis with something close to genuine affection. He would actually miss her surly attitude and horrible work habits. "Seriously, if you don't like how the situation here pans out, let me know. I'll do what I can to help you find something else."

Plum rolled her eyes. "What can *you* do? It's not like I'm dying to get on at *Genre* or *Out*. People already think I'm a lesbian for working here."

"Well, aren't you?"

Plum shot up her rudest finger. "An isolated three-way in college doesn't make me a dyke. Besides, I was really drunk."

Carson glanced around. He had the essentials gathered. The rest could be left behind. "Please tell me there's not a surprise going-away party planned."

Plum laughed. "Get over yourself. Everyone thinks you're a dick for leaving without notice, and everyone thinks you're a bigger dick for getting a ten thousand dollar signing bonus."

"Actually, it's twenty-five, but who's counting?"

"You make me sick."

Carson grabbed his belongings. "Well, I guess this is it. I'll send you a Christmas card."

Plum moved in for an awkward, half-hearted hug. "Please don't. I prefer gifts. Anything Louis Vuitton or Chanel would be nice."

"I'll keep that in mind." He glanced at his watch and started out. "I better run. Early lunch with my new bosses. Remember, you're my personal wire service for what goes on, and while I move on to enormous success, I want to hear things like, 'the new editor sucks' and 'the magazine is falling apart.'"

This made even the dour Plum smile. "How mature. And if I can't get you on the phone, I'll just leave an update taped to your locker."

Carson jumped into a cab and screamed his address. He had just enough time to drop off his *BFM* baggage and change into a suit for his power lunch with Paul Easton and Callum Fox.

The car whizzed by a bus advertising *Manhattan Morning*. The show's co-hosts, Mike and Manzie, were beaming Ultra Brite smiles. And then it dawned on him that the segment on Callum had run this morning. The British bastard would be overrun with suitors by lunch. Shit.

Following up on this train of thought, Carson fumbled for his cell and called the executive producer of *Manhattan Morning* to announce his immediate departure. She took it well. After a full month of promotional hype, Liza Minnelli had just canceled for tomorrow, so his news was hardly devastating.

Rushing into his cramped walk-up apartment, Carson's spirits soared at the realization that he could now afford to buy a place of his own—one with a full bath, kitchen, decent-sized closet, and maybe even a cute doorman to receive packages. He made a mental note to ask around about good realtors, then dressed quickly into a Gucci suit just back from the cleaners and still drowning in Visa interest charges.

Carson hit the door of Le Cirque 2000 fifteen minutes late, received an arched brow from the stiff maitre d', and was coolly escorted toward the table where Paul Easton and Callum Fox sat waiting.

Callum was nestled into the banquette. A man stood over the table, talking animatedly to Callum, ignoring Paul outright. The stranger looked vaguely familiar. As Carson approached, he tried to make the connection. And then it hit him over the head.

Sawyer Collins. Brainchild of M4M Television, the new pay channel that was a runaway hit on cable and satellite systems nationwide, even though its programming was for shit. Nothing but crudely edited gay porn flicks, reruns of *Queer As Folk*, a talk show hosted by a drag queen that drew C-list celebs, and endless airings of the original reality series *Circuit Party Boys Gone Wild* and the movie *Broken Hearts Club*. But it was a chance for the curious and the closeted to watch a bad actor/good gymrat dolled up in butch construction gear recite lines like, "Take that big cock, man. You know you want it."

Back to Sawyer Collins, though. After a string of failures (junior agent at William Morris, manager of a Britney clone who went nowhere, independent producer of two dead-on-arrival slasher flicks), his success with M4M had catapulted him to gay media mogul status and sent his ego into orbit, triggering a series of incidents that made Eminem seem like a third Olsen twin.

When Carson reached the table, Sawyer had just made Callum laugh. Instantly, Carson felt a stab of jealousy. Whatever. It couldn't have been that funny. Certainly a man like Sawyer was too in love with himself to be clever.

"You made it," Callum said.

Carson sighed and made up a story about an insane cab driver who couldn't find Madison Avenue.

Callum and Paul laughed, but Sawyer was a tougher audience. He merely stared, a chilly smile frozen on a borderline handsome face. The man was aging about as gracefully as Patrick Swayze.

Carson traded firm handshakes with Callum and Paul, and then extended his arm to Sawyer. "We haven't met, but I'm familiar with your work. Congratulations on the success of M4M."

Sawyer's grip just dangled there like a dead fish.

Carson noticed that he bit his nails.

"I was just telling Callum that I saw *Manhattan Morning*. I suppose I owe you some thanks for sharing this amazing import with the rest of us." One beat. "A smart man would've kept the secret to himself." He put a hand on Callum's shoulder and squeezed. "So we're on for dinner? I'll have my assistant call your office."

"Oh, you have a new one already?" Carson cut in with equal parts bite and innocence. "I just read in Page Six that your assistant quit. Something about an assault charge against you?"

Sawyer shrugged off the bad PR. "There's nothing to it. Just a bottom feeder looking for a quick pay day." He sized up Carson and then dismissed him. "Good to meet you, gentlemen. I better return to my party before my manners come into question."

Carson wanted to vomit. P. Diddy's security goons had better manners than Sawyer Collins.

"Very ambitious man," Paul said. "I hear he's launching a lesbian channel, too—W4W."

Surreptitiously, Callum clocked Sawyer from afar. "He possesses a great deal of charisma, and there's a crudeness about him that's rather appealing. He reminds me of a young James Caan, the Sonny Corleone era. What do you think, Carson?"

"I think I'm lucky not to be his assistant."

Callum's grin revealed a mild appreciation for gossipy humor.

But it was Paul who laughed the hardest and pressed for more. "Is this true about the assistant?"

Carson fingered a space just above his left eyebrow. "Six stitches right here. Sawyer threw a stapler at her."

Both Callum and Paul appeared visibly stunned.

Carson couldn't resist more character assassination. "And there's a pending suit from another assistant. A guy this time. Apparently, Sawyer's into water sports. When the guy refused to let Sawyer pee into his mouth, he fired him. The guy who cuts my hair also cuts the hair of a paralegal who was there for the deposition."

Paul, obviously still recovering from the image of Sawyer pissing into another man's mouth, said nothing.

Callum seemed unfazed. "That's hardly a first-hand account. Certainly there's more to this man than what you get from the *New York Post* and a hair stylist."

Carson bristled at the rebuke. Any minute now Callum might start singing Tammy Wynette's signature anthem.

The waiter arrived to inquire about Carson's drink order.

A quick glance told him that Callum and Paul were sticking to iced tea and water. Damn. He needed something stronger, but he couldn't be the only Suellen Ewing at the table. Gesturing to their glasses for the same, he buried his face in the menu until the subject changed. Enough about Sawyer Collins. What a pig. Basically, the gay Harvey Weinstein, only less talented and with fewer famous friends.

There was a jingle, and the entire table felt for their third ear.

"It's me," Carson said, embarrassed. Why didn't he turn that stupid thing off? He read the ID screen. It was Plum. Sheepishly, he stood up. "Please excuse me. I'll only be a moment." Moving out of earshot, he hissed, "This better be good. I'm in a meeting, and I've already shown up late and offended my future ex-husband. Now I'm on a call. What is it?"

"Gil Bellak is leading the editor search," Plum said. "He's flying in tonight."

Gil was a hot media consultant, married with three kids, and a former lover, but this bulletin on his imminent return was generating no central nervous system response. Definite sign of being completely over a guy. Carson sighed. "You know what? This information is of no interest to me. Anything else?"

"I booked him a room at the Hudson. That should save you a call later."

"Plum, I don't care where he's staying."

"Oh, please. You're going to end up there if only to prove to him and yourself that you've moved on. This isn't some twit you're talking to. I read *Elle* cover to cover."

Carson, still walking, passed by Sawyer's table.

"If you want your Christmas bonus, then find me an assistant by the end of the day." And then Sawyer shut his little phone and cackled to the group at his table.

"Maybe I should just quit before Gil turns me into his office bitch," Plum said.

That's when the idea hit Carson. "You know, I just heard about an opening for a job with a major television executive."

"What kind of job?"

"Personal assistant. And he wants to fill the position right away. Maybe it could tide you over until something better comes along. You should know in advance that it's for the M4M Channel."

"Of course. What else?"

"I'd take your work history with *BFM* off your resume, though. It's better that we not be connected."

"I've always felt that way, too, but why in this case?" Plum asked.

Carson fell silent for a moment.

"Wait a minute. What are *you* getting out of this?"

He decided to come clean. If Plum got the job, she would be lucky to last a few days, and he didn't want her unemployment on his conscience. "The man you'd be working for is Sawyer Collins. He's—"

"A fucking psychopath! I read about him in the *Post*. He gave his last assistant a concussion."

"Stop exaggerating. Granted, she needed a few stitches, but there was no concussion."

"You're sick. I'm hanging up."

"Plum, wait. Please. This won't be for long. I need you on the inside to keep tabs on Sawyer. We're interested in the same guy, and I need an inside edge."

"Christ!" Plum screamed. "I'm so tired of dealing with your gay love dramas!"

"This time there's a big reward in it for you."

"I'm listening. And it better be good."

Carson thought fast. "A job. A real job in fashion with Harlequin Vamp, Inc."

"I want to be a vice president," Plum said.

Carson quickly agreed. After all, corporations gave out those titles as easily as free pens. "Call me when you're on the inside. God, this feels like an episode of *Charlie's Angels*. Let's pretend like you're Sabrina. And I'm Kelly."

"No, I want to be Kelly."

Carson huffed. "Fine, I'll be Sabrina." He signed off and speed-walked back to the table. "Sorry about that. Some last minute business with the magazine."

Paul cleared his throat. "We're just beginning to map out a strategy for Harlequin Vamp's American launch—"

"I've been thinking about that," Carson cut in, "and my idea on how to approach it is pretty radical."

Callum and Paul exchanged curious looks.

Carson took a deep breath. "Harlequin Vamp is known for luxury—two hundred dollar T-shirts and thousand dollar handbags, but if you want to break into the American market in a big way, then go for the fash consumer. Cheap chic. Everybody loves it. The rich and the not so rich. Harlequin Vamp is too much of a mouthful. Call it HV. Find a fierce designer to create an HV logo and slap it on every product from underwear to handbags. Open a few stores in major markets. Create an online presence. Design a campaign with cool celebrities who have serious street appeal. Trust me. This will be so much more fun than opening up a stuffy boutique where a bitchy salesgirl named Victoria just stands there and tries to convince people who've never heard of Harlequin Vamp how *fabulous* it is in London. Nobody's going to argue about a fifteen dollar fake alligator bag. They'll be lined up around the block. God, I'm starving. Has anyone seen our waiter?"

Chapter Five

Things to Do Before Christmas

1. Stop chasing straight guys
2. Cancel subscription to *Us* and start reading books
3. Switch from Kiehl's Hair Gel to Frederick Fekkai
4. Apologize to old woman down the hall for forgetting to feed her cat
5. Find out exactly what a mutual fund is

Sex with Prince Alessandro had hit an off-night. Stella Moon could feel it, and she knew that he could feel it, too. Suddenly itchy and hot, she bolted from the bed and opened a window, letting in a blast of cold air which felt better to her body than whatever he had just done.

"Baby, please, it's freezing."

Stella ignored him. It was too soon for their bedroom life to fizzle. They should have at least been married for three months before that happened. Given this new wrinkle, the ring had better be a goddamn rock, something that would stop Elizabeth Taylor dead in her tracks.

She heard the flick of a match and turned to see her prince lighting up a joint. One thing about royalty—even B-list royalty—they only dealt in the very best drugs. Alessandro's pot was primo. Leaving the

window open, she dashed back, dipped under the covers, and took a
long, deep drag, feeling it almost immediately. She grinned.

"Good stuff, isn't it?"

"Mmmm. I needed that."

His hand reached out and stroked her inner thigh. "Oh, yeah?"

"*Yeah.* That was some weak-ass sex we just had. I was bored out of
my mind. At one point I just zoned out and started making a mental
list of all the errands I have to run tomorrow."

Alessandro removed one hand from her leg and repossessed the
joint with his other. "A relationship can't survive without honesty. Tell
me how you really feel."

Stella laughed and spooned into him. "Maybe I'm overreacting. But
only a little. I mean, honey, it *was* uninspired."

He smiled, seemingly unaffected. "Now might be a good time to
talk about my Christmas present."

Stella squealed and raised up to straddle him. "You have my full attention." She shut her eyes for a moment, praying for a pink diamond.

He rose up to kiss the tip of her nose. "Tell me what *you* want, and
I'll tell you what *I* want."

Stella just looked at him. This was no fun. *Asking* for an engagement ring? Pretending to be surprised when she got it was the best
part! "You go first."

His lips curled into a sexy grin. "I want to take you to a special
party."

Stella trailed a hand down Alessandro's sculpted chest, stopping at
his navel. "Will I need a special dress for this special party?"

"That's up to you. But I wouldn't put too much into something like
that. No one will notice. Not at this kind of party."

Who doesn't notice the bride's dress? Suddenly, Stella got a sick
feeling that this had nothing to do with a wedding. Her eyes blazed
into Alessandro's. "What the fuck are you talking about?"

"An orgy."

"An *orgy*?" Stella reeled back, almost losing her balance, coming
close to tumbling off the bed.

Alessandro reached out to steady her.

Stella flicked his hands away. "You want me to fuck other guys while
you watch? That's what you want for Christmas?"

"Not just men. There will be women there, too. Don't worry. Everybody plays safe. And the guest list is prescreened for erotic appeal. This isn't the bridge-and-tunnel crowd that frequents Check-mates and Le Trapeze."

Stella had heard of those swinger clubs. They charged a hundred dollar cover and played to fat and ugly losers from New Jersey. An artist friend had gone, eaten something bad off the buffet, and thrown up in the middle of a blow job.

"Everything is first class," Alessandro went on. He sensed her reluctance and called out the name of a famous actress who had turned up at the last gathering.

Stella just stared at him as if he were insane. "Honey, what makes you believe that I would ever want to be in a room where a bunch of strangers are fucking and sucking each other?"

Alessandro seemed genuinely stunned. "Because it's hot."

"Honey, I might draw cocks for a living, take drugs, and act like a whore in the bedroom, but get this straight—I'm an old-fashioned girl from Alabama!"

"You were brilliant!" Callum said.

"Are you sure?" Carson asked. "He barely said a word."

"Believe me. When Paul Easton is silent, then that means he's blown away. In fact, I've never heard him so quiet. It never dawned on me to take Harlequin Vamp in a fash direction. But you bloody well convinced me."

They were back at The Crystal Group offices in Harlem, ostensibly to continue brainstorming, but it'd turned into nothing more than a play-by-play of the lunch meeting.

"How did this come to you? I'm always fascinated by the origin of good ideas."

"It's quite simple, really," Carson said. "I saw a picture of Ben Affleck in Us magazine, and I noticed that he was wearing Old Navy briefs."

Callum laughed. "That's it?"

Carson nodded. "Basically. The concept of fash is very democratic—big stars, the guy at Pizza Hut. Name a hot actor that you've got a crush on."

Callum wavered. "I generally don't get crushes on celebrities."

"There has to be someone. Brad Pitt?"

Callum shook his head. "Overexposed. I do find Josh Hartnett quite attractive."

"Picture him in HV underwear."

Callum shut his eyes. "I'm getting an image."

"All we have to do to make that dream come true is litter the next Sundance festival with HV gift bags. Same goes for all the big awards shows and major events. It's sick. These bastards are making twenty million a picture, but what really makes them feel important is a free pair of sunglasses." Carson hesitated a moment. "Are you really into this concept? You're not just humoring me?"

Callum grinned. "Trust me. Paul is paying a ridiculous amount of money for my services. It's worth hurting feelings over. I would never humor anyone."

"Good. Because the more I think about it, the more I'm convinced that fash is the direction to go. I mean, you could take the high-end route, say, open a few stores in New York and Los Angeles. But you'd have to be in the right location. Next door to Hermes. Nothing less. And then you could open up some mini boutiques in Neiman Marcus and Saks Fifth Avenue. But that's a bit boring, don't you think? It might work in the short run, but everybody goes back to the luxury main stays—Louis Vuitton, Chanel, Gucci, Prada. Who's to say Harlequin Vamp would have legs in that arena?"

"It's a risk either way," Callum put in.

"But fash is sexier. Something new and hip and shockingly affordable. That's fashion Viagra, don't you think?"

Callum laughed. "Fashion Viagra. I like that."

Carson's cell phone jingled. He took a peek and recognized Plum's number. He turned to Callum apologetically. "It's the magazine again. Is there someplace I can take this?"

"The outer office is all yours. My assistant's out today."

"Thanks. Just give me one minute." He rushed out to escape Callum's earshot. "This better be good. He thinks I'm smart as a whip, and I don't want to give him any extra time to analyze what I've said and possibly change his mind."

"I got the job," Plum said without preamble.

"Already?"

"It's obviously the occupational equivalent of *Fear Factor*. I'm the only one who stepped up to eat the big gross bug."

"When do you start?"

"Forty-five minutes ago. I just made dinner reservations at Daniel. I'm supposed to call Callum Fox to confirm."

"What time?"

"Seven."

Carson thought fast. "Okay, tell Callum that the reservation is for *seven-thirty* at *Town*."

"You must want me to get stitches, too."

"Just hide the stapler."

"That's the first thing I did."

Carson sighed. "How can I keep that pig from getting in touch with Callum?"

"Easy. I have to hot-link tomorrow's schedule changes onto his Palm Pilot. I'll invert the last two numbers of Callum's cell phone."

Carson whistled. "Truly wicked. I'm impressed."

Plum giggled. "And you thought I was incompetent. This girl will go to great lengths to avoid work and cause problems for people she despises."

"Less than an hour on the job and you already hate Sawyer?"

"That son of a bitch expects me to eat at my desk so I won't miss his calls. I'll show him. I've already forgotten to give him a message from Barry Diller."

Carson smiled at the fact that Plum was someone else's nightmare right now. "Keep up the good work." He hung up and returned to Callum, who in a matter of seconds had turned out a trick worthy of Penn and Teller.

On the British wonder's desk was a gleaming silver ice bucket and two champagne flutes. *Pop!* Callum was just releasing the cork on a bottle of Cristal. "I thought we should celebrate your new career." He poured without spilling a drop and offered Carson a glass, raising his own in a toast. "To an exciting new beginning."

Carson accepted the bubbly and moved in closer. "It's customary in America to take the first sip like this," he said, invading personal space and interlocking his champagne arm with Callum's.

The trend forecaster played along, smiling.

Carson bumped his crystal flute against Callum's. *Clink*. In unison, they sipped slow and deep, eyes locked on each other, bodies closer than manners allowed.

"So this is how American men celebrate new deals?" Callum asked.

"Okay, maybe just Siegfried and Roy. But it's nice, don't you think?"

Callum sipped again, swallowing hard. "Indeed."

Carson noticed a tiny bubble of champagne on Callum's lower lip. Suddenly, the overwhelming urge to kiss him rose up from within. He hesitated, then decided to just go for it.

At first, Callum's eyes were moving like a trapped animal looking for the way out. But soon his mouth relaxed, and the kiss picked up speed and intensity.

Carson leaned against him, panting almost, hungering for more. He heard his crystal flute slide off the desk and break quietly on the carpet. And just as their tongues met in a violent, lusty clash, he felt Callum withdraw.

"I'm not sure this is . . . a good idea," Callum whispered, his face hot and flushed, his voice thick.

Carson could feel Callum's erection pressing against his trousers. "I hear a dissenting opinion from the guy in your pants."

"It's just that we're working together . . ."

"So? You're a colleague, not a boss. The only person who should be telling me these things is Paul, and I have no intention of making out with him."

Callum smiled at this. "We're going to be joined at the hip on this project—"

"I'd prefer to be joined at the—"

"Stop," Callum pleaded, laughing a little. "I'm serious. If things don't work out, it could get very—"

"Don't think that way. Besides, gay relationships rarely last, so there's no point in having expectations."

"I know several couples back in London who've been together for years."

"They must be homely."

Callum's expression turned serious. "Are you really that shallow?"

"Yes," Carson said.

Callum's face failed to register any amusement.

"That was a trick question," Carson argued. "I'm maybe a tiny bit shallow."

"Do you mean to imply that unattractive people stay together because no one else wants them?"

"I'm going to say yes, but this feels like another trick question."

Callum shook his head. "You know, it wasn't that long ago that I would get dressed up and go out to a party or a club in London, and no one would pay any attention to me at all. Sometimes I would go home and eat myself sick or just cry in front of the television."

Carson merely stared. He'd never faced inner fat child baggage before and didn't know how to proceed. "Is it too late to change my answers?"

Callum's desk phone rang and he picked it up right away, as if grateful for the interruption. "Callum Fox . . . Yes, go ahead . . . Seventhirty at Town . . . Where is that exactly? . . . The Chambers Hotel, got it . . . Thank you." He twisted away to scribble it all down onto a yellow Post-It.

"What a coincidence," Carson said.

Callum looked up, his stare alarmingly cool. "How's that?"

"I'm meeting someone for dinner there tonight as well."

"Small world." He tossed a vague look at his desk. "Look, I should really get some work done before my date." Callum gestured to the champagne on the floor and then to Carson and himself. "Can we just forget that this happened?"

"Forget what?" Carson asked pointedly. And then he turned for the door.

Chapter Six

Things to Do Before Christmas

1. Stop chasing straight guys
2. Cancel subscription to *Us* and start reading books
3. Switch from Kiehl's Hair Gel to Frederick Fekkai
4. Apologize to old woman down the hall for forgetting to feed her cat
5. Find out exactly what a mutual fund is
6. Write letter of support to Whitney Houston

Carson considered dashing over to Apollo Express on 125th Street to console himself with a new Fendi item, then quickly disregarded the idea. No time for shopping. He had to make a comeback and fast. The situation was deep-in-a-ditch bad. Something along the lines of Mariah Carey after the *Glitter* debacle.

He jumped into a taxi and begged the driver to take him anywhere in midtown. For some reason Harlem blocked his clear-thinking skills. Safe in the smelly cab, he fished through his wallet until he found the scribbled receipt with Matt Yorn's number on it. Tapping in the digits, he chanted, "Please no voice mail, please no voice mail . . ."

"Good afternoon, Matt Yorn."

Thank God. No recording. Carson felt instantly comforted by the pleasant voice. He sounded kind, probably around forty, with a penchant for navy blazers, khakis, and sensible shoes, perhaps Rockports. "Hi, this is Carson St. John. I was referred to you by Stella Moon."

"Yes, the artist." Matt's voice went up an octave.

"Well, okay. I think of her more as a cultural wrecking ball. But whatever."

Matt fell silent.

"Listen, I need to see you right away. I have sort of a . . . *dating emergency*, I guess."

"How soon were you thinking?"

"Now. Or at least before seven-thirty."

Matt chuckled. "Carson, I'm not a relationship ambulance. There's a process to the way that I work. Why don't you give me your fax number or e-mail address. There's a questionnaire I'd like you to fill out first."

Carson stifled the urge to throw his cell phone out the window of the speeding cab. "I don't have time for that. I'll double your fee."

"I'm sorry. That wouldn't be appropriate."

"Come on. If you're like me, there's an American Express bill due in a few days. Six hundred dollars for an hour, and you don't have to take off your clothes? This isn't Sophie's choice."

"You're obviously dealing with a lot of anxiety. I can tell you right now that this would color the analysis."

"Let me worry about that. Just do what you do." Carson paused a beat. "Exactly what do you do anyway?"

"We meet in a comfortable, public place as if we're on a blind date. After about forty-five minutes to an hour of date simulation, we separate to write down our assessments. Then we regroup to share."

"Is that the part where you tell me how to act, so men will fall in love with me?"

Matt chuckled again. "Not exactly. A positive outcome would be making you aware of certain blindspots that might hinder your success as it applies to dating. Hopefully, I can suggest some behavior modification. We all have room for improvement when it comes to relationships."

"How does five o'clock sound? I'm meeting the man I might want to spend the rest of my life with at seven-thirty, so that should give me plenty of time to learn what my problems are and change them."

Matt agreed to the meeting, and they settled on a Dean & Deluca location close to the Chambers Hotel before signing off. Carson had just enough time to shower and change clothes before heading out again. No way could he dazzle Callum Fox in this Gucci suit that screamed stylish banker.

Carson rushed up to his cramped digs, stripping on his way to the tiny bathroom. He stood in front of the mirror. A shadow was already forming on his face. To shave or not to shave? Definitely not. He figured the rougher look gave him a Colin Farrell vibe and jumped into the shower, lathering up with Space.nk's Laughter shampoo and body wash.

The moment he stepped out, dripping as wet as Tobey Maguire and Kirsten Dunst during their rain-soaked kiss in *Spiderman*, the telephone rang.

Maybe it was Callum calling to profess his infatuation and apologize for being so prickly.

Carson wrapped a towel around his waist and nearly froze his ass off on his way to grab the receiver before the answering machine revved up. "Hello?"

"Thank God you're there. I'm having a nervous breakdown." It was Stella Moon.

"Get in line. I'm having one, too."

"No, honey, I'm serious. I'm about to pull a Courtney Love and go sit on the sidewalk buck naked."

Carson listened patiently while Stella bashed Prince Alessandro for wanting an orgy for Christmas. Finally, he cut her off. "I'm going to have to call you back. I'm meeting Matt Yorn for coffee."

"You called him! Oh, honey, I'm so proud of you. Shit. Now he's going to turn you into Cinderfella, and you'll meet the perfect guy, and I'll still be stuck with my Eurotrash pervert."

Carson laughed. "I'll call you later."

"Quick," Stella blurted. "Tell me what I should do."

"Well, off the top of my head I think settling for an orgy when you want an engagement ring would be very Jenna Jameson."

"Is that a good or bad thing?"

Carson sighed. "This is the kind of adventure you're either into or not. So if you have to psych yourself up, maybe it's not the best idea."

"Why can't he just ask for a three-way like normal guys? Or a simple mate swap with another couple? His friend Benjamin is hot. I'd agree to that in a minute. You know, I never should've let him put that blindfold on me and do it to me in the butt with no condom. That let him think he could push the envelope."

"Stella, I really have to go. Take a few Ambien, and I'll call to wake you up when I get home."

"Okay. But I'm going to take enough to totally knock me out, so just let the phone ring until I answer."

Carson hung up and headed into his closet. On the floor were little piles of perfect designer pieces that were wrinkled, stained, and waiting to be dry cleaned. He spied two crisp pair of khakis. One was Versace and had cost almost three hundred dollars, the other from the Gap and only about forty. How cruel. He couldn't tell which was which. Still, he hunted for the Versace label, because if his pants happened to come off tonight, then that would certainly be a more impressive garment to sling over a chair.

Pant drama over, his hands flew to release the Burberry Prorsum print shirt he'd never worn. It clung to his chest just enough to be sexy, more see-the-work-I'm-doing-at-the-gym than International Male catalog sleazy see-the-imprint-of-my-nipple. Then he slipped on some shiny Paul Smith boots, grabbed his black coat, and prayed that he wouldn't have to wait long for a cab.

The freezing temp outside went straight to Carson's head. His hair was still slightly damp and all over the place. He liked to think of it as his maybe-I-just-had-sex-with-Ashton-Kutcher look. Very young Hollywood. Women wore open-toe Manolo Blahniks in this weather, so he figured he could go out with wet hair and no knit hat.

The taxi ride to Dean & Deluca took forever. What the hell was going on? And then it dawned on him. Rush hour. Christmas season. New York City. The cab had inched along to the point where Carson could make a run for it and get there quicker. He was already ten minutes late, which meant Matt Yorn had just earned ten dollars for cooling his heels with a cup of coffee. Shit! Leaning forward to tell the driver this was it, he suddenly reconsidered. His boots were freshly polished, and a street sprint would likely cause a scuff. No way could he show up at Town like that.

Traffic picked up a bit. Carson took a deep breath and relaxed. He eyed the meter and busied himself with his wallet, counting out the cash to cover the ride and a decent tip since the driver didn't stink or play Middle Eastern music.

He spotted Matt instantly. Tweed sportcoat, black denim jeans, cheap shoes, vaguely handsome in a daytime soap actor who never gets a main storyline kind of way. Tentatively, he approached him. "Matt?"

Big smile. Bad teeth. One front tooth was slightly chipped, and it's not like there weren't a million whitening products at CVS. "Carson! It's a pleasure to meet you. Sit down. Get warmed up. I'll grab a hot drink for you. What's your poison?"

Carson didn't like the game show host eagerness or the limp handshake. "A peppermint hot chocolate sounds good. Sorry I'm late. Traffic was a fucking nightmare."

"Not a problem. Be right back." Matt's parting gesture was the thumbs-up sign, a double with both hands.

Carson couldn't believe he was about to pay this schmuck six hundred dollars for dating advice. He was entertaining the idea of canceling altogether when Matt returned.

"So, Carson, tell me about yourself." Another bad smile.

"This already feels like a campus job interview."

Matt gave an optimistic shrug. "Would you like to hear about me?"

"Not really," Carson said. "That would kind of be a waste of time, and this is costing me a lot of money. Okay, I'll tell you about me." He launched into a mini E! True Hollywood Story, telling Matt about how long he'd been in New York, his stints at Throb! and BFM, his new job at Harlequin Vamp, his short-lived relationship with Rocco, his even shorter lived affair with family man Gil Bellak, his crush on Matthew McConaughey, and his thoughts on reality television, Tom and Nicole's marriage, America's obesity problem, the sex appeal of President Bush, stars who whore products on QVC, the scrumptious aging of Jon Bon Jovi, and Britney Spears.

Matt checked his Fossil watch.

"What do you think?" Carson asked. "Does Britney have enough iconic status to continually reinvent herself like Madonna?"

"I'm not familiar enough with her work to speculate."

"But what's your gut feeling?"

"I don't have one." Matt leaned forward. "I'm a classical man myself. My favorite composer is—"

"I've never met anyone who didn't have an opinion on Britney," Carson cut in. "I mean, she's like the cultural equivalent to the abortion issue. You're not one of those people who doesn't own a television, are you? I hate those people. I just want to say, 'Get over yourself! You know deep down that you want to watch *The Bachelor.*' " He laughed. "I mean, come on!"

Matt cleared his throat. "We should probably stop at this point and spend some time alone writing our individual assessments."

Carson glanced at the new Rado Sintra watch he *borrowed* from the last *BFM* cover shoot. "God, we've been talking for almost forty minutes. I can't believe it."

Matt slid a yellow legal pad and black pilot pen over to Carson's side of the table. "I'm going to move to that table in the corner. Let's give ourselves about fifteen minutes." He stood up quickly.

"Wait. Am I critiquing you or myself?"

"The latter," Matt said. "I'm writing one, too, so we'll see how they compare." He settled in several tables away and started to write.

Carson finished his part in five minutes and wondered if Matt would spring for another peppermint hot chocolate. It's the least he could do since he was earning a double fee. Glancing over at the so-called dating expert, Carson noticed that he was already on a second sheet of paper and showed no sign of slowing down. This went on for ten more minutes. Finally, he wrapped it up and returned to his original seat.

"I think I'll have another one of these," Carson said, pointing to his empty cup. "Do you mind?"

Matt gave him a strange look. "Not at all."

"Good," Carson said, smiling. "And don't worry. I promise not to peek at your notes while you're waiting in line." He tried to focus on his own notes, but the longer it took Matt to fill the order, the stronger the urge to glance at Matt's scribblings became.

Unable to stand it another second, Carson attempted to read up-side down and managed to make out: DISCLOSED MORE PERSONAL INFO THAN APPROPRIATE. Okay, maybe the story about Gil's semen tasting so clean on account of his macrobiotic diet had crossed the line. But what else? Hmm. Perhaps all the talk about his new salary and amazing signing bonus had been too much?

Carson squinted to get more.

"Liar," Matt said. "You promised not to peek." He slid back into his seat, smiling.

"Actually, my exact words were no peeking while you were *waiting in line*, so technically, once you reached the counter, those notes were fair game."

Matt managed a weary grin. "Why don't you go first. How do you think the last half hour went?"

"Amazing. First of all, being late was a good move. You know, start the date off with a little suspense. Is he coming? Am I being stood up? Nothing like keeping a guy guessing. Then I arrive in this—okay, I'm just going to say it—a kick-ass ensemble. Burberry, Versace, Paul Smith—inspired separates from classic lines. Head-to-toe designer looks are so lazy. I thought I was entertaining—fresh, funny, occasionally revealing, didn't stay on one subject too long. Saved a near crash and burn when you started droning on about classical music. That was skillful. I managed to get it back on point about Britney without offending you." Carson took a deep breath. "I forgot to mention that oral sex class I took in Beverly Hills. People should know that. It makes me sound like someone who is actively expanding his horizons."

"Any constructive criticism?"

Carson thought about it. "Well, maybe I shouldn't have told that story about Rocco's mother being arrested for shoplifting at Blooming-dales. Ultimately, I made the choice to be with him, so the fact that he comes from such a disturbing family could possibly shed negative light on me."

"Is that it?"

"I probably look a little pale. If I hadn't been in such a rush, I would've applied a bronzer."

Matt took a deep breath. "I have a general checklist of behaviors that I consider date napalm."

Carson laughed. "I bet some serious relationship losers have come your way."

Matt clasped his hands together and gazed at Carson with grave seriousness. "You're guilty of just about every one of them."

Carson blanched. "What?" He fought the urge to snatch Matt's legal pad. "Well, what are they? Besides *disclosed more personal info than appropriate*. I saw that one."

"Some of your opinions were very dogmatic. That can be a turn off."

"Look, if you get me talking about that stupid *Joe Millionaire*, I'm not going to hold back."

"You were very critical of me."

"I'm sorry, but if you can't name at least five *Real World* cities, then I have to classify you as being out of touch."

Matt soldiered on. "In discussion of your high credit card balances, you portrayed yourself as a victim of . . ." He glanced down to scan his notes. "Bloodsucking bank bastards who employ more evil tricks than the tobacco companies."

Carson gave a diffident shrug. "I stand by that statement."

Matt shook his head. "You talked about money on a first date. Dangerous move. It's too toxic a subject. Especially in the area of salaries." He stared at Carson with a mixture of kindness and amazement. "At the risk of sounding cruel, if this had actually been a first date, it would probably also be the last." There was a brief sigh. "Frankly, Carson, you might need more help than this one short hour can provide."

Carson looked at his watch again. "Listen, I'm not falling for some sales maneuver to get me to sign on for more services. I have a date in thirty minutes, so just give me the Cliff's Notes version on how to impress him, and I'll write you a check."

Chapter Seven

Things to Do Before Christmas

1. Stop chasing straight guys
2. Cancel subscription to *Us* and start reading books
3. Switch from Kiehl's Hair Gel to Frederick Fekkai
4. Apologize to old woman down the hall for forgetting to feed her cat
5. Find out exactly what a mutual fund is
6. Write letter of support to Whitney Houston
7. Complete application for the next *Survivor*

Plum Kinsella was still at her desk, printing out reams of Internet research on Harlequin Vamp, Inc. If Carson thought he could offer payback for her torture with just any position, then he better get ready for a rude awakening.

"I want a plum assignment," she whispered aloud, giggling to herself at the play on words. What intrigued her most was Lulu McQueen, the edgy, fast-rising designer with the rock-and-roll pedigree. Maybe she would insist on something in that division.

Her desk phone began a series of short rings in fast succession. "Sawyer Collins's office."

"Are you sure Callum Fox got the message to meet me at Daniel?" It was Sawyer, sounding rude, testy, and short fused.

Plum smiled. "Absolutely, Mr. Collins." She glanced at the wall clock. "And it's almost seven-thirty. This must be so embarrassing for you."

"It's not embarrassing," he snapped. "It's annoying. I've fired people for being this late. Punctuality is king in my world."

"Don't you mean *queen?*"

"What did you just say?"

"Never mind. Everyone in the restaurant must know you've been stood up. Maybe you can sneak out through the kitchen. I'd hate for Page Six to get word of this." Plum made a mental note to call in this tip as soon as she hung up.

"I didn't get stood up," Sawyer hissed. "There's a screw-up some-where, and I think you made it. That cell phone number you trans-ferred to my PDA is wrong. I got some parking attendant who could barely speak English. Find Callum's original business card and double-check it for me."

"Oh, I tossed that out already. You know, to avoid clutter."

Sawyer seethed in silence. "What about his office number?"

"I posted that."

"It's not here."

"Oops."

"Plum, the only reason I'm not firing you right now is because you've only been on the job for half a day. Tomorrow we'll have a meet-ing about what I expect from you."

"Does that mean you're taking me to lunch?" Plum asked excitedly. "Should I make a reservation at the Four Seasons?"

"No. We'll do it over coffee first thing in the morning."

"Okay. I'll make muffins. Blueberry or strawberry?"

"Don't bother. I'm on a low-carb diet." He let out a frustrated sigh. "Chances are this tight-ass Brit isn't going to show. Call Chelsea Escorts and get me a guy for later tonight. Make it for eleven o'clock. Ask for a college wrestler-type. Big muscles. Huge dick. No one over twenty-five."

"Consider it done, Mr. Collins," Plum said. "I'll make up for today's mistakes and arrange for the perfect guy." And then she hung up, fully intending to find this pig the skinniest twink in town.

Carson floated through the enormous doors of the Chambers Hotel with equal parts daring and self consciousness. He tried to keep Matt's suggestions top of mind, even though most—if not all—of the *behavior modification* would require a personality transplant.

He approached the maitre d'. "St. John. Reservation for two at seven-thirty."

The dead ringer for Matt Lauer (before the unfortunate buzz cut) beamed a welcoming smile. "The other member of your party hasn't arrived yet. May I suggest a drink in our lounge?"

Carson played along. What the maitre d' didn't know was that no *other party* existed. He found Callum in the balcony lounge, kicked back on a liquid leather settee, waiting for his *other party*. "You look familiar. Have we met?"

Callum glanced up and smiled weakly, not thrilled to see him but not repulsed either. It was a start. "I believe we have."

Carson ordered a bottled beer from the bartender and boldly joined Callum. "My date must be taking his sweet time."

"Same here."

He allowed a few beats to pass, occupying himself with his beer. "I want to apologize for this afternoon. Things felt really awkward when I left, and it's been bothering me a lot."

Callum gazed at him with forgiving eyes. "I might have been a smidge uptight."

"Just a smidge?"

Callum smiled. "I'm not used to this." He put down his Smirnoff Blue and splayed open his hands. "This new body, this appearance. I imagine that, deep down, I'm still that unattractive fat guy. If only I'd been straight, I would've met a nice plain girl and saved myself a great deal of torment. Gay men are merciless when it comes to looks."

"I know," Carson agreed. "I have no sympathy for women in Hollywood. They should try going to a gay dance club. Now *that's* pressure."

"Precisely!" Callum exclaimed.

Carson didn't know why exactly, but he found it infinitely adorable that Callum had just uttered the word *precisely*.

"I remember my official coming out after the surgery and all the other minor transformations I paid a small fortune for. I splurged to join The Sweet Suite. It's a members-only club in London that revels in general fabulousness. Rupert Everett is a founding member. Graham Norton and Neil Tennant of the Pet Shop Boys are as well. So I'm finally feeling good enough about myself to venture out on a hunt, I suppose it was. For a man. Any man would do, providing he was young and appropriately gorgeous."

Carson gulped down more beer and sat, wide-eyed, thoroughly captivated.

"I arrived in a pink and black designer shorts ensemble. Criminally queeny, I know, but I'd endured so much torture at the hands of a vicious personal trainer that I was nothing short of belligerent in my desire to show off my newly toned legs and arms. The whole scene was excruciatingly intimidating. Yet to my almost paralyzing astonishment, I was cruised by an actor from *Footballer's Wives*. Not my favorite cast member, but definitely a close second or third. I actually cried while we were having sex. It was all just so unbelievable and lovely that my emotions ran away from me."

Carson laughed. "Being hit on by a TV star your first time out? That's worth crying over!"

"As I remember, he found it quite frightening. Anyway, I went back later in the week, took home a cute bar boy, and didn't shed a single tear. So bloody good for me." He downed the rest of his drink and glanced at his watch. "I think I'm being stood up. How appalling."

Carson made a show out of checking his timepiece and looking around. "I know how it feels. If we're both still stranded in fifteen minutes, I say we have dinner together."

Callum gestured to the bartender for another Smirnoff Blue. "I hope our wires didn't get crossed. I'm quite certain that Sawyer's assistant told me seven-thirty at Town."

"And that's exactly where you are."

Callum shrugged. "What about your missing person?"

"My friend Danny," Carson lied. "He's an entertainment attorney and sometimes gets caught up. This wouldn't be the first time he's missed dinner plans. Usually, it pisses me off, but tonight I'm kind of hoping he doesn't make it." He gave Callum the benefit of his best smoldering stare.

"I can imagine worse scenarios."

Carson raised his Michelob Lite. "To worse scenarios."

"Indeed," Callum said, drinking up. "I feel like I owe you an apology, Carson. I was too quick to call you shallow earlier today."

"But I am shallow," Carson said without a trace of shame. "With occasional moments of depth. And therein lies the key. It's what separates a Christy Turlington from, say, a Naomi Campbell."

"So you've given this matter a great deal of thought," Callum observed wryly.

"Yes, I have. It's all about balance. I might shock my therapist with a keen insight, obsess over a pair of jeans at Helmut Lang, ponder the plight of a former eighties pop star who hasn't been seen in years, and read a chapter of an Anna Quindlen book before bed. All in the same day."

"Share with me your most shallow thought of the day."

Carson concentrated hard. "Okay. I was running late for an appointment but refused to get out of my cab in the middle of a total traffic fuck because it might have sullied my Paul Smith boots. See." He wriggled his left foot. "Perfect."

"That's not shallow," Callum said. "That's simply practical."

Carson raised his bottle once more. "I think you're right. I'm being too hard on myself. Let me think of a truer shallow moment . . . I've got it. This morning I turned the channel from a breaking international news story to a cable rerun of *Lois and Clark*. Why? Because I knew that this was an episode where Dean Cain takes his shirt off."

"Bravo!" Callum said. "I must say that is quite shallow. What was the nature of the news story that didn't hold your interest?"

"I can't remember. Something about a bomb going off in one of those troubled countries that you would never visit."

"*Exceedingly* shallow. You've outdone yourself."

"Thank you."

"What about deep thoughts? Certainly you've had at least one today."

Carson finished the last of his beer. "I did. I walked by a Christmas tree in a store window and felt sad."

"Why's that?"

"I don't know. It just made me feel lonely, I guess. All my friends are in serious relationships and bombarding me for advice on Christmas gifts. And here I am—alone. There's not a single decoration displayed in my apartment. I have one Christmas CD—Barbara Streisand. But I can't find the disc. All I have is the jewel case. Anyway, it's pathetic. I have no one to buy for and no one to think about. Except me. So I charged a new stereo at Sharper Image. Are you going back to London for the holidays?"

"No," Callum said. "But I will be away."

Carson felt a pang of disappointment. "When do you leave?"

"Not until Christmas Eve."

His spirits perked up. "You know, I have an invitation to an amazing party. We should go. You'll meet everyone worth meeting in the city at the same time. And some not worth it. But no social situation is perfect."

Callum's grin appeared to be all knowing. "You must be talking about Ruma Sindi's party."

"How did you know?"

"I received my invitation before I left London."

"I take it you didn't need kneepads for yours."

"What do you mean?"

"It's not important."

"Are you suggesting that we go together?"

"Well . . . yes . . . assuming you don't have other plans."

"I don't. It's a date."

Carson breathed a sigh of relief. *Finally*. A step forward that didn't require a high-tech spy operation. "I say we forget these idiots who stood us up and eat dinner. I'm starving."

Callum stood up and left his half-finished drink on the bar with a twenty dollar tip. "I'm amazed. You're simply bursting with brilliant ideas today."

They were on their way to the dining room when Carson's cell phone rang. He stole a glance at the screen. It was Plum. "Go on ahead. I'll join you in just a moment." Once Callum had walked a comfortable distance ahead, Carson answered. "As usual, your timing is terrible."

"Without me, you wouldn't even be on this date," Plum said.

"I'll thank you in about twelve hours. But only if he's asking me how I like my eggs."

"Enough about you. I need a new job. Starting tomorrow."

"You lasted half a day? That's it? Are you that bad, or am I that tolerant? How long did I keep you on? Two years?"

"Listen, I've sabotaged a date, erased his schedule for the rest of the year, told Barry Diller he didn't want to talk to him, hung up on David Geffen, and screwed up his escort request for later tonight. I'll be lucky to get out of here with all of my teeth."

Carson gasped with naughty glee. "He asked you to book an escort?"

"Yes," Plum hissed. "Isn't that disgusting? He wanted a wrestler-type with big muscles and a bigger you-know-what. Well, I say it's rude to order people like a menu item, so I found the most effeminate nineteen year old. His name's Yancy. Skinny, bird chest, pale as a ghost, no mention at all about his endowment. In this case, I don't think no news is good news. Oh, and for an extra fifty dollars he'll dress up like Kylie Minogue."

Carson was laughing so hard that his sides ached. "This could get you killed. You might want to think about the Witness Protection Program."

"Luckily, the only thing truthful on my application was my last name. If Sawyer tries to find me at home, he'll come face-to-face with Matthew. He didn't offer me so much as a penny in severance. I figure he deserves the aggravation."

"Don't worry. I'll honor my promise about the job."

"I want to work in whatever division handles Lulu McQueen."

"I'll see what I can do."

"No," Plum said. "Make it happen, or I'll fuck up *your* life next."

Carson felt a nagging sense of responsibility for unleashing this monster upon society.

Chapter Eight

Things to Do Before Christmas

1. Stop chasing straight guys
2. Cancel subscription to *Us* and start reading books
3. Switch from Kiehl's Hair Gel to Frederick Fekkai
4. Apologize to old woman down the hall for forgetting to feed her cat
5. Find out exactly what a mutual fund is
6. Write letter of support to Whitney Houston
7. Complete application for the next *Survivor*
8. Visit Ellis Island

"Do you know how Paul feels about hiring incompetent people for meaningless jobs with glorified vice president titles?" Carson asked.

Callum didn't pause so much as a beat. "He has a large extended family and runs a major corporation, so I would imagine that he's quite comfortable with it. Why? Do you have a cousin who's out of work?"

"No. A former assistant who's driving me crazy."

Callum took a sip of wine. "I assume she's not nearly as ridiculous as your former President's brother. Roger Clinton, I believe it was?"

Carson shook his head. "No, not that bad. I mean, she doesn't sing in public or anything like that."

"Then you should be able to tuck her away in the bowels of Harlequin Vamp. Explain to Paul that it's a nuisance hire. He'll give you latitude for a few of those."

"She mentioned something about working with the Lulu McQueen line," Carson said.

"That could be tricky," Callum murmured, finishing up the last bite of escargot risotto in black truffle broth. "Lulu is the daughter of a rock star, which means a much higher nuisance hire ratio. Can you imagine having other rock-star children friends? How frightful. It's quite a blow to our insurance carrier as well." He leaned in to whisper. "Multiple rehab visits."

Carson knew his smile was mega-watt as he sat back in his chair, more enamored with Callum than ever. He took a moment to admire the Austrian crystal beads cascading from the twenty-four foot high ceiling.

For dessert they ordered tea and an exotic cheese collection with apple and maple strudel on the side. The Hugo Boss outfitted waiter arrived with it straight away, and they lingered lazily, commenting on the food, the atmosphere, the sight of Quincy Jones at one table, the spectacle of *New York Post* columnist Cindy Adams at another.

Carson experienced that strange stirring of feeling totally at ease with a man yet still being wildly attracted to him. He sensed Callum was an instant best friend, but he wanted to rip off his clothes just the same.

"I need to find an apartment," Callum announced.

"Me, too. I can finally afford to buy one. Where are you staying now?"

"Paul has been generous enough to let me use one of his corporate units on Central Park West. It's quite lovely, but I'm a nester and love to decorate." Callum arched his brow. "Tomorrow a realtor is showing me something in the same building where Ricky Martin lives."

"If you see him in the elevator, ask him if needs a house boy who's almost thirty."

Callum laughed. "Wouldn't it—"

Carson's cell phone cut him off. He glanced at the screen. It was

Plum again. *Jesus Christ.* "I'm going to take this call, and then I'm going to turn off this fucking thing. I promise." Slipping out of his seat and speed-walking toward the lounges, he answered. "I had to deal with you less when you actually were my assistant. Maybe I should just rehire you."

"Stop, Shecky, you're killing me."

"What is it?"

"When do I start?"

Carson couldn't believe this. "Plum, I just spoke with you an hour ago. I'm working on it. Honestly, I am. The job won't be a problem at all. Getting you in with Lulu McQueen could be. That's more complicated."

"I don't care," Plum hissed. "I'm not going to stand by and have some lame position in human resources shoved down my throat. I've always wanted to be in fashion. Fashion, fashion, fashion. Those bitches at *Vogue* have ignored me for years. I even got turned down for a weekend job at the Anna Sui boutique. They said I didn't have enough piercings. I want to work with Lulu McQueen! But not as her assistant. I read that she likes to drink Tab, and I'm not going to spend the rest of my life running around trying to find that stupid soda."

"Are you finished?"

"For now. I want an offer by tomorrow morning. Salary plus benefits. And there better be a dental plan."

"Look, if you're dead set on Lulu McQueen, it could take longer."

"Completely unacceptable."

Carson sighed. "Well, I'm not going to promise something that I can't deliver. It's as simple as that."

"Is it now?" Plum said, her tone threatening. "You seem to be able to work wonders when it comes to setting yourself up nicely, so I strongly suggest that you perform some of that same magic on my behalf."

"I'll try," Carson said, trying to sound assuring. "Really, I will."

"Just to keep you on your toes, I'm going to fire a warning shot tonight. Know that it's only a hint of what I'm capable of." *Click.*

"Plum?" But the line was dead. Carson had a terrible feeling about this. Things with Callum were in a very delicate place. Almost anything could upset the balance. Paranoid, he swept the dining room with a circular glance. Plum might've been calling from the restaurant! Wait a minute. What a crazy notion. She could never afford Town's prices.

Carson turned off his phone and headed back to the table. No more threats. No more interruptions. The rest of the night would be dedicated exclusively to Callum. "I'm sorry. Believe me when I say that all of this is not a ridiculous attempt to impress you with how important I am."

"I do feel grossly upstaged," Callum joked. "I run a business here and one overseas and have received no calls tonight."

Carson looked at Callum, *really* looked at him for perhaps the first time. "I can't remember the last time I had such a wonderful time with someone over dinner."

Callum raised his water. "At the very least we should toast Sawyer Collins and Danny for the very bad manners that led to this."

Carson clinked his glass against Callum's. "To social pigs."

Callum sipped, sighed, and smiled.

"Are you up for going out? I could take you around to a few bars, show you the better part of Manhattan's gay scene."

"I'd much rather stay here and have you all to myself." Callum's gaze hinted that the possibility for this date to last until the morning was there.

Carson pounced. "May I suggest something decadent?"

Callum seemed intrigued. "Fire away."

"I hear the rooms at the Chambers are amazing. Each one is different."

"Are you suggesting that we stay here tonight?"

Carson hesitated. "Maybe. How do you feel about it?"

"I feel like this isn't even an official date. It's only by coincidence that we ended up together."

Carson opened his mouth to backtrack until he noticed the teasing glint in Callum's eyes.

"I should proceed cautiously." Callum grinned. "Otherwise you might think I'm a slut."

"You told me about that actor from *EastEnders*. I already know you're a slut."

"I take great offense to that. He was from *Footballer's Wives*. The people on *EastEnders* are much too common."

"I stand corrected. And I won't even mind if you cry a little, but I would prefer that you not do it during sex. Wait until we watch *Imitation of Life* together."

"I promise to try." Callum glanced around for the waiter. "Let's order another drink, shall we? I'm only sort of drunk, and I might as well be properly drunk before a shag on the first accidental date."

More wine arrived. They went on talking and laughing, the animated energy of flirtation and inevitable sex crackling between them.

And then came a voice from the past. "No fair. Looks like you're several shots ahead of me."

Carson recognized that laconic drawl immediately. He cringed, then turned to see Gil Bellak standing over the table, looking better than ever, actually. Damn him. For a moment, Carson merely stared back, stunned. "Gil . . . hi . . . how did you know I was here?"

Gil's brow creased with uncertainty. "Plum called me. I was under the impression that we were meeting here for drinks."

"Plum?" Callum inquired. "That's the name of Sawyer's assistant. How odd to hear of two Plums in one day."

Gil looked at Callum and extended his hand. "Gil Bellak."

Callum shook firm and fast. "Callum Fox. Don't you head up Full Picture Associates?"

Gil smiled. "That's me. And you're with The Crystal Group, right? Congratulations on the New York office."

"Thank you. It's going very well. No complaints."

"Okay, boys, save it for the next chamber of commerce luncheon," Carson cut in, unable to stomach another stroke of perfunctory business chatter. He dropped his napkin on the table and stood up. "Callum, would you mind settling the tab and meeting me in the lobby? I need a moment with Gil." Before he could answer, Carson grabbed Gil's arm, and pulled him away from the table.

"That was rude," Gil said.

"No more rude than you showing up here like we're high school sweethearts."

"Plum called—"

"Plum *lied*. That bitch is trying to drive me crazy, and it's working."

"How was I supposed to know—"

"Gil, you're married, and your wife is insane. She could easily be the next Clara Harris, so I hope she doesn't drive an SUV. Look into that. You wouldn't stand a chance."

"This is between you and me. Leave my wife out of it."

Carson just stood there, mouth agape. "I can't believe you just said that. It might be the dumbest thing I've ever heard anyone say. And that includes all direct quotes from *The Anna Nicole Show*."

Gil's nostrils flared.

God, he was sexy when angry, but Carson tried not to notice.

"Plum didn't lie," Gil said. "That's bullshit. You just wanted to humiliate me."

"Okay, you don't have to unleash all the stupid talk at the same time. Save some for later."

An annoyed waiter tried to maneuver around them with a tray of drinks.

Carson suddenly realized that he was co-starring in a minor restaurant scene. Even Quincy Jones was looking on with lurid interest. God, on any other night he would've marched right up to the music legend's table and demanded to know what he really thought of Michael Jackson's *Invincible* album. But instead Carson made a beeline for the men's room.

Gil followed in hot pursuit.

The place was empty, save for an older man drying his hands. Gramps offered two friendly nods and shuffled out.

Carson took a deep breath. "I didn't want to see you, Gil. This is a stunt that Plum pulled. Seriously. Besides, we haven't had any contact for months, and our last conversation was nothing Hallmark might try to steal. What were you thinking?"

Gil turned pink with embarrassment. "I just thought—"

"What? That you could blow into town, and that maybe I'd blow *you* for old time's sake? I'm so over that. By the way, don't talk to Freddie Michel if you try to verify that statement."

Gil looked confused. "Who's Freddie Michel?"

"That's not important."

Gil stepped over to the urinal and zipped down his pants. "So are you with this Callum guy?"

Carson checked his teeth for stray food particles in the mirror. "I'm trying to be. There are no wife and kids that I know about yet. That's a plus."

Gil flushed and stepped over to the sink to wash his hands. He laughed a little. "Plum really did a number on me."

"She's very talented that way," Carson said.

"Good luck . . . with everything—the new job, the new guy. I mean it."

Carson believed him. "Thanks."

Gil started to pull the door but hesitated. "Is there a back way out of here?"

"No. You're officially a drama queen now. Walk proud."

Gil laughed and sauntered out.

Carson found Callum slumped in one of the oversized chairs near the front window in the Chambers lobby, his body language talking disappointment. "What's wrong? Are they completely booked?"

Callum looked up, his face guarded. "I haven't asked yet."

"Listen, that was not a clever ruse to weasel out of the bill. I had no idea—"

"Are you involved with him?" Callum cut in.

"No, of course not." Carson paused. "I was. But it's ancient history. Trust me. What happened tonight was a complete misunderstanding."

Callum's mood seemed to instantly levitate. He rose up, smiling.

Carson tossed a glance to the front desk. "Are you still game?"

Callum wavered teasingly. "I'm not sure. How do I know that you won't close your eyes and think of this Gil chap?"

"Listen, if I have to close my eyes and think of someone else, then it's going to be Matthew McConaughey, not Gil Bellak."

"I suppose that's comforting."

"Come on. We can raid the mini bar, lounge around in white terry cloth robes, order insanely expensive room service. It'll be fun."

"What about sex?" Callum asked.

"On the first night? Never."

Callum slipped a hand under Carson's waist band and tugged playfully at his pants. "Oh, there *will* be sex. I just spent three hundred
dollars on dinner, and I imagine these rooms are quite pricey."

"That sounds like date rape. I feel just like Tracey Gold in a bad
Lifetime movie."

"I'm going over there to book us a room but only if you promise
never to bring up a cast member from *Growing Pains* within minutes
of possible amorous activity. It's a definite mood killer."

"Kirk Cameron." Carson covered his mouth. "That's it. I'm done.
Sorry. Couldn't resist. Get the room. I'll be quiet."

Chapter Nine

Things to Do Before Christmas

1. Stop chasing straight guys
2. Cancel subscription to *Us* and start reading books
3. Switch from Kiehl's Hair Gel to Frederick Fekkai
4. Apologize to old woman down the hall for forgetting to feed her cat
5. Find out exactly what a mutual fund is
6. Write letter of support to Whitney Houston
7. Complete application for the next *Survivor*
8. Visit Ellis Island
9. Send group E-mail to all former *Real World* alumni to break the news that they are not actually stars

"My wife and I want to take turns eating your pussy."

Stella Moon glared at the former big-name action star turned straight-to-video has-been. "Honey, as my grandma always used to say, 'You can want in one hand and shit in the other. See which one fills up the fastest.' "

Prince Alessandro took Stella firmly by the arm and half escorted, half pushed her into a corner. Right next to a console table littered with condoms and Astroglide. "Why did you even agree to come? You'll never get any action with that kind of attitude."

Stella scowled at him, turning away. Her gaze fell upon two nude women making out across the room. They were acting out a lesbian scene from the porn movie going strong on a large plasma TV.

Alessandro brought up a good point. Why had she agreed to this?

"Just keep an open mind. Go with the flow." He stroked her arm, sliding his hand down her side, into the back of her jeans, and through her panties, cupping her ass possessively. "They say it's like a drug. Once you indulge, that's it. You're addicted."

Somebody turned up the techno music, ostensibly to drown out a man groaning too loud over a double-mouth blow job.

"Don't tell me it's not a turn-on to know that every man here wants to fuck you."

Stella couldn't hear him. She was reading lips now. Glancing upward, she noticed that they were standing directly under a speaker. Pointing to it, she pulled him away to a spot where she might actually have a slim chance of hearing the son of a bitch. "Big deal. Everywhere I go there are men who want to fuck me. Does that mean I should get turned on at the post office?"

But Alessandro was barely listening. He was too busy staring lasers into a fivesome going at it next to the chiffon drapes. "I'm surprised that you don't want to explore this," he said, unable to take his eyes off the three women and two men bumping and grinding.

Stella recognized a junior socialite somewhere near the bottom of the pile. There were about thirty people here, all of them steadily engaged in a carnal activity, or at least earnestly moving in that direction. She and Alessandro were the only ones gawking like passing motorists at a fifty car pile-up.

Who knew that this fancy triplex on a tree-lined block just off Ninth Avenue could be the site of *Caligula 2003?* "Nipple ring" had been the password to get through the bolted door. And for what? To watch people have sex? If Stella wanted to do that, then she could have just rented a movie and watched better-looking people who actually got paid to fuck professionally show her how it was supposed to be done.

A Wall Street-type with a so-so body sauntered by and told

Alessandro, "You need to get your girl out of those clothes, so we can see her tits." Then he snatched a fried lobster tail from the hot buffet and bulldozed his way into an ongoing threesome.

Alessandro looked at Stella expectantly.

"Forget it," she snapped.

"Why don't we just act like nobody's here but you and me, baby. We'll do our thing. And if somebody wants to join in, we'll just ride the wave."

Stella realized that if Alessandro was just some guy she'd been fooling around with, coming here might've been a kick. Hell, right now she'd probably be stripped down to her La Perla undies and chasing after that lobster-hogging bastard. But Stella loved this oversexed asshole. Christ, she wanted to *marry* him. That took everything to a higher level of play. And, honey, this wasn't it.

God, if only she hadn't answered the phone when it rang just seconds after she'd hung up with Carson. Alessandro had gotten to her before she had a chance to load up on the Ambien. Then came the sweet talk and seductive manipulation. And suddenly Stella found herself here . . . in this . . . *place.*

Alessandro moved in to kiss her on the lips.

Stella rebuked him.

"Baby, come on! I wrote an essay to get us in here tonight!"

She laughed in his face. "You wrote an *essay?* Is this an Ivy League orgy?" She surveyed the scene with obvious derision. "Looks very junior college to me."

"I wrote an essay because you have to prove that you're sexual enough to hang with this crowd."

"You're an idiot."

"I did it for us. Give this a fucking chance!"

Stella, blinded by frustration and anger, slapped Alessandro across the face so hard that the imprint of her hand remained on his cheek.

"Hey," a voice reprimanded from the stairwell. "Rough sex will get you thrown out of here."

Alessandro's eyes were flashing fire, a potent mixture of shock and hurt. "Why did you hit me?"

"Because! I thought you were going to propose! I thought I was getting a ring for Christmas! And all you want is for me to fuck a bunch of

strangers while you watch! Well, shit! Let's just get this over with."
She unbelted her Burberry coat and began to unzip her Seven jeans.
"Okay, listen up, freaks!" Stella screamed. "I'm ready to party! Who
wants some of this?"

A senior partner from a major advertising firm came running.

Alessandro stepped in to block his path. "Put your coat back on.
We're going home."

"No!" Stella said, fury and adrenaline surging through her veins.
"I'm going to fuck this man, and you're going to watch." Her blood felt
like it was boiling. "So pull up a chair and grab some lobster before it's
all gone. The show's about to start." She gave the eager ad exec an up
and down glance.

"How do you like it, baby?"

"Dog—"

Alessandro shoved the creep several steps backward and spun angrily on Stella. "Put your goddamn coat on. We're leaving. Right now."

She just stood there, defiant as hell.

"I mean it, Stella," Alessandro warned.

A muscular guy in a classic Adidas track suit moved in on the com-
motion. "I'm going to have to ask the two of—"

"Fuck you!" Alessandro shouted. "We're out of here!" He reached
for Stella's hand and pulled her through the door, down the stairs, and
onto the sidewalk.

"Jesus, slow down," Stella cried. "I can't walk that fast in these
shoes!"

Alessandro relented, then turned on her. "You really want to get
married?"

Stella just stared at him for one long, pissed-off second. "Not after
tonight!"

"I didn't think you were the marrying kind."

"Honey, what the fuck is that supposed to mean?"

"I don't know."

"You don't know." She looked at the lamppost as if it held the answer. "Well, you thought I was the *orgy* kind, but I'm obviously not
that, so you don't know shit!"

"I just . . ." He stopped himself, shaking his head. "We've never talked about marriage. Not even once. I just thought you weren't interested in settling down."

Stella glared at him. "Like I said, you don't know shit. How many times have I made you watch the scene in *Sweet Home Alabama* where Patrick Dempsey closes down Tiffany's and lets Reese Witherspoon pick out any ring she wants? Memo: That's called a hint."

Alessandro leaned in and kissed Stella's forehead. "Let's go." He took her hand again, this time practically dragging her down the street to the corner, where he hailed a cab and ushered her inside the warm cabin.

"Where are you taking me?"

"Tiffany's."

Stella's heart picked up speed. "They're closed."

"I know that," Alessandro said. "But you can look through the window and pick out any ring you want."

Instantly, she felt her eyes fill with tears.

"I don't have the connections to get in the store after hours, which means you're marrying a prince with no pull. Are you okay with that?"

Stella smiled at him. "I can live with it."

"Merry Christmas, baby." Alessandro leaned in to shout at the driver. "Fifth Avenue!"

"What do you call that again?" Callum asked, slightly out of breath and totally spent.

"The Penis Samba," Carson repeated. "I took a class. I'm certified."

"As well you should be. Quite frankly, that is the most intense pleasure from oral sex that I've ever experienced."

"See, I was worth dinner and a room." Carson tumbled out of bed to grab a bottled water from the mini bar. He turned back to Callum. "Do you want anything?"

"Gummi Bears."

Carson snatched a pack and pitched it back.

Callum caught the bag with one hand.

Carson twisted off the Evian cap and guzzled half the bottle. "I drank too much tonight. I'm going to be worthless tomorrow. Who do I call in sick to?"

"I guess that would be Paul. And you've only been on the job one day. Impressive."

"Thank you. I always manage to do as little as possible." Carson halted. "Please tell me you're not a workaholic."

"I'm not a workaholic."

"Are you lying?"

"Absolutely."

"I'll just have to become one, too, I guess."

"Whether you want to or not. Do you have any idea how much work will be involved in being image director for this American launch?"

"You make it sound like I'll actually be earning my salary."

Callum ripped open the candy and popped a few into his mouth. "So much that you'll feel underpaid."

"How long do I have to stay on the job to keep the signing bonus? A day?" He crawled back into bed, moaning with pleasure as Callum spooned into him, interlocking their legs.

"But we'll be working together. Just think. We can fight all bloody day at the office and have make-up sex once we get home."

Carson sighed. "You know, I've been thinking about a cool face to launch the HV campaign, someone not too obvious but with edge appeal."

Callum tucked his chin over Carson's shoulder. "This is why we hired you."

"I'm thinking Eminem before soccer moms started singing along to his hits. A true maverick. Stirrer of controversy. But in a sexy, provocative way."

"I'm stumped."

"Zyler Brillstein."

"Now I'm blank. Who's he?"

"An eighteen year-old author. He wrote a novel called *Rich Brats* about Upper East Side teen depravity. Kids love him for telling the truth, and parents hate him for doing the same. They're scared to death and protesting his signings and calling his book rubbish. So of course he's a bigger star than he ever would've been. Now teens in Oklahoma have heard of him. They're scrambling to their local Barnes & Noble as we lie here."

"Is he attractive?"

"Very. A high school swimmer, too. Great body."

"You should approach him before someone else does. Maybe we can tie him up with an exclusive contract before he pitches for Taco Bell and signs on for celebrity *Fear Factor.*"

"Sometimes I think you're the British version of me, only older, richer, and with a stronger work ethic."

Callum took in a deep breath. "Speaking of work ethics, I should check my messages at the office." He extricated himself from Carson and twisted around to use the phone on the bedside table.

Carson stretched, making a mental note to call Freddie Michel for Zyler's contact information. Hopefully, the little shit didn't have a swarm of handlers already. He glanced over at Callum, whose face was a masterpiece of disbelief as he held the receiver to his ear.

"You'll never guess what happened," Callum said.

"They found a fifth Baldwin brother!"

"No. I was supposed to meet Sawyer Collins at a restaurant called Daniel tonight. He waited there for an hour."

Carson did his best to look bewildered. "But I thought his assistant called and told you to meet him at Town."

Callum returned the receiver to the cradle, distracted. "She did. And I'm absolutely certain that's what she said. How bizarre. I feel dreadful about this. I should call him."

"But it's so late."

Callum moved to see the clock. "Eleven o'clock for a single man in Manhattan is late?" He didn't wait for an answer. "People like Sawyer don't give in to a lot of sleep. Can you believe it? There are at least two Plums in this city, and both of them have fucked up royally today. He should get a laugh out of that." Callum reached for the phone.

Carson practically dove on top of it. "Don't call."

"Why not?"

"Because I'm ready to do the Penis Samba again."

"You'll get nowhere with it. I just climaxed a few minutes ago, and I've had far too much to drink. Who do you think I am? Zyler Brillstein?" Callum laughed and tried for the phone again.

Reluctantly, Carson released his grip, speed-searching his brain for a way to come clean without seeming like a lying, scheming, manipulating rat in desperate need of therapy.

Callum was dialing.

Carson was dying.

"Ah, it's ringing."

"Hang up."

"Give him time to answer."

"*Please*. Hang up. There's something I have to tell you."

Callum put down the receiver. "I hope he doesn't have star sixty-nine. In addition to a deserter, he'll think I'm a prankster."

Carson drew in a calming breath and slowly revealed everything about Plum's one day stint as a double agent in Sawyer's office. When he finished, Callum just looked at him as if his head carried the snakes of Medusa.

"Let me get this straight," Callum began, finally, with equal parts amazement and amusement. "You dispatched your former assistant to take a job in Sawyer Collins' office?"

Carson nodded.

"This same person purposefully gave me erroneous dinner plans and has made it her goal to drive Sawyer as mad as possible in a single day?"

Carson nodded again.

"And for her efforts, you've promised this girl—who's named after a fruit and has no identifiable skills—an executive position at Harlequin Vamp with expanded benefits?"

Carson shut his eyes. "Yes."

"I dare say that I'm quite flattered. Bring on the Penis Samba."

Chapter Ten

Things to Do Before Christmas

1. Stop chasing straight guys
2. Cancel subscription to *Us* and start reading books
3. Switch from Kiehl's Hair Gel to Frederick Fekkai
4. Apologize to old woman down the hall for forgetting to feed her cat
5. Find out exactly what a mutual fund is
6. Write letter of support to Whitney Houston
7. Complete application for the next *Survivor*
8. Visit Ellis Island
9. Send group E-mail to all former *Real World* alumni to break the news that they are not actually stars
10. Confess to Stella that I lost our Cher concert tickets

Ruma Sindi's Blue Lagoon party rocked.

A warehouse in the meat packing district had been transformed Hollywood style—artificial sand, sun, and beach, authentic palm trees, even wind and humidity machines. Costumed islanders straight out of casting central were strolling about with halved coconuts brimming with a concoction called Shipwreck. The contents were unknown to

Carson, but after two of these, he was feeling no pain, and suddenly Cindy Adams (her again!) was starting to look a lot like Tina Louise.

Sugar Ray tore loose on a raised dais, lead singer Mark McGrath thrilling the girls and certain boys with his tattooed, spike-haired, face of Adonis bad boy rocker act.

Freddie Michel danced up to Carson. Badly. For a man who primarily made his living in night crawling, he should have had better moves. By comparison, Elaine's herky-jerky choreography on *Seinfeld* was the stuff of Martha Graham. "Having a good time?"

"Don't do that," Carson said.

"Do what?"

"Dance. This is a benefit. You'll scare away the big spenders."

Freddie stopped and downed the better part of his Shipwreck. "How come you don't return my calls anymore?"

"Because I'm in a real relationship."

"There's no such thing. You'll learn."

Carson's lips curled into an ambiguous smile. After all, he needed this fool to get to Zyler Brillstein once the holiday crush was over.

It did the trick, filling up Freddie's ego tank with the notion that things might start up again. And then the cocky social fixer disappeared into the swimwear-clad crowd.

Stella rushed up to Carson and grabbed his arm. "Honey, you're not going to believe what Prince Alessandro saw in the bathroom!"

"Please tell me it has nothing to do with Lance Bass and Joey Fatone."

Stella yanked Alessandro's arm, pulling him closer. "Sawyer Collins was snorting coke like there was no tomorrow! Tell him!"

Alessandro confirmed this with a nod, then added, "It was like a scene out of *Scarface*. He didn't even try to hide it."

Carson spotted the minor cable player across the room, looking more wired than Tara Reid at the opening of anything. Shadowing him was a muscle-bound steroid case who should've just gone the distance and stamped RENT ME BY THE HOUR on his forehead. Sawyer passed Callum without acknowledgment and began chatting up designer and Swell mastermind Cynthia Rowley, while boy toy fidgeted in the background, awkward as hell.

"Honey, I'm madly in love with Callum," Stella announced. "If you fuck this up, then I'm dumping you for him. I just thought you should know that." She waved, flashing an impressive rock from Tiffany's on her most important finger. "Play your cards right, and you might get one of these."

"Does this mean he's only after me for my money?" Callum joined in, sidling up to them with a fresh Shipwreck in hand.

Carson, Stella, and Alessandro traded secret looks and then answered in perfect unison, "Yes."

Everybody roared.

The island fever raged a few more hours, and then the crowd began to thin out. Carson thought of the days ahead and felt a cloud of sadness creep around him. Christmas was staring them dead in the face, and Callum had mentioned nothing about plans.

"You look pensive," Callum said. "At a time like this a shallow boy should only be factoring a list of the best and worst plastic surgery cases of the night."

Carson smiled wanly. "I was just wondering about Christmas."

"Stop wondering about that and start wondering about this: How long will it take you to pack sunscreen and a thong?"

They took a flight from New York to Barbados, then a fifty minute puddle jumper ride that made one stop in Mustique, where all the passengers except Carson and Callum departed. From there they flew to the island of Canouan. The sky view revealed nothing but virgin greenery and postcard-perfect beaches.

A soft-spoken French woman named Isabel was their official greeter at the one shack airport, then she escorted them by van to the Carenage Bay Resort.

Carson was unprepared for the sight of the breathtaking luxury, and Callum seemed to delight in just watching his mouth gape open wider and wider.

Isabel settled them into their waterfront villa, and Carson listened in wonder as she and Callum enjoyed a long conversation in her native language. For a moment, he felt like an imbecile, as the only French he knew was *bon jour*, *oui*, brie cheese, and disco producer Cerrone.

The trip had been exhausting. They took turns showering, slipped into fluffy Frette bathrobes, and alternated long naps with lazy love-making until the brilliant sun rose over the villa the next morning.

It was total Vistavision. The crescent-shaped miracle blue infinity pool that matched the ocean just yards away. The white sand. The gabled South American feel of the villas.

Carson and Callum lost themselves in chaise-lounge idyll on a tiny plot of grass that sloped all the way down to the beach.

"Can you believe it's Christmas morning?" Callum asked.

Carson breathed in the perfect air. He savored the perfect moment. "You've set the bar pretty high. What are we doing for New Year's?"

An Extra-Large Christmas

Chris Kenry

Chapter One

"You're here! Oh, thank God!" Gerald cried, descending the steps from his office. He was a small, wiry man, completely bald, with oversized black-framed eyeglasses. As he approached with open arms, Rodya couldn't help thinking that he looked like some sort of tree frog, or exotic beetle.

"I was so worried you wouldn't be able to come," Gerald said, "what with the holidays and all. I've gone through a whole roll of Tums and it's not even noon. It's all a big mess, I'm sure you've heard."

Rodya had heard. The telephone call from Gerald's secretary had woken him up. At first she had been reluctant to release the details, afraid that Rodya would demand more money if he caught the scent of trouble, but Rodya knew as soon as he heard her voice, that there must be something wrong. They only called him when there was trouble: when someone stormed off the set in a fit of arrogant pique, or got a case of nerves that Viagra couldn't cure. At those times the secretary would always call and Rodya would always oblige. He was the pinch-hitter, the reliable temp, the first runner-up who could always step in if the reigning queen proved unable to fulfill her obligations. He was, as Gerald liked to refer to him, "Old Faithful".

Occasionally, he was still offered a cameo—usually a jackoff scene in which he could show off the most famous part of himself for the nostalgic segment of the audience. Or, sometimes he was brought in to teach the newest twink sensation how to handle a piece of heavy equipment, but more often than not they called him only when they were in trouble.

It had not always been so. Once, he, too, had been one of the bright stars and been offered all of the good parts. Once there were several studios bidding for his services and wooing him with offers. But, like all stars, his period of brightness had a definite life span. It had lit up the night sky for a while but then began to collapse in on itself and fade. His fame was still glowing, probably would continue to glow for a few more years, but eventually, he knew, it would exist only as a faint memory in aging videotape collections.

The project the secretary called him about this time (working title: A *Handful of Lust*), was behind schedule, over-budget and plagued with equipment troubles—cameras that had recorded hours of nothing, and some badly wired lights that were burning through bulbs like flashcubes. Troubles that had caused a two-day delay in filming, during which the film's principal ingénues had salved their ennui by visiting some of the rowdier dance bars and after-hours clubs. As a result, one of them (the one who was to perform as Top, of course) was in detox recovering from Ecstasy poisoning, and the other was so worn down and haggard-looking that even the artful application of make-up and use of subtle-lighting (if indeed the lights could be made to work at all) would barely conceal the harm done.

The film was, Rodya learned soon after his arrival, to be on the theme of "size," so he knew he possessed all the talent necessary to step in as an understudy. In his heyday he'd been given the nickname "The Tripod" and it was a name that still applied. There were few men better endowed than he and for that reason, he had to admit, he was bothered by the fact that he had not been considered for the cast in the first place. Bothered but, again, not surprised. He knew he was getting too old for the work. He saw the evidence of time's passage around his eyes and in his hair. His once soft looks had begun to harden and there was nothing he could do about it. This transformation from boy to man was not, he knew, unattractive, but most of his fans, like irresponsible pet owners, had lost interest in the puppy as soon as it grew into a dog.

It was time to get out of the business, that much he knew. Time to get out before he became pathetic. Before too many hastily thrown-together, problem-plagued ventures like this one spoiled the higher quality canon of work he had made. And yet, between the knowing and the doing there is a wide yawning gap and Rodya had not been entirely successful in crossing it. His attempts to reform himself into something more legitimate had not been entirely successful.

The majority of his porn contemporaries had, he'd observed, followed one of two routes: they had either capitalized on their fame by becoming prostitutes (which again, was limited by age), or they had found rich, usually elderly husbands to finance their lives of leisure. Rodya had taken short journeys down each of those paths, but lacked the fawning nature necessary to succeed in either one. He had tried to find legitimate work but did not have any skills or the language necessary to do them. So, like many people his age, he sought solace in the ivory tower of academia and enrolled in some classes at the community college. For three years, he had been studying photography, first in school and then, for the last year, on his own. He had learned the technical side of it, had developed his own style and aesthetic, and had assembled a rather impressive portfolio. But something was missing. Money and jobs, of course, but there was also a knowledge—a level of experience—that he just could gain on his own. With that in mind, he had been trying to get some sort of internship with a more established photographer, but his attempt had, so far, met with little success. The queries he sent out were answered with polite rejection letters or, more often, not answered at all. And for those reasons he continued to take on porn work.

In the first scene, Rodya was cast as an assistant baseball coach, holding a special "batting practice" for one of his players. Casting him in this role had taken some thought. He was not, Gerald observed, old enough to be the coach but he was too old to be one of the players so they had compromised and made him the assistant coach. It was, Rodya knew, better than being cast as the equipment manager, or worse, the custodian (which were all possibilities that had been discussed) but he was still offended by it. He was further offended when, five minutes into filming, Gerald stopped the camera and asked him to speak as little as possible since his accent, which, once upon a time, had been a major selling point, was not really in sync with America's pastime.

Rodya took several deep breaths to contain his annoyance, closed his eyes and imagined the paycheck, and then smiled and nodded his agreement.

When they finished the scene, Gerald summoned him off the set.

"That was beautiful!" he said, handing Rodya a robe and patting him on the back. "Just great! I don't know why we didn't use you in the first place. You'll be at the top of the list next time, believe me."

Rodya smiled at this lie and said a meager "Thank you." He wiped his brow, put on the robe, and was just turning towards the bathroom to go take a shower when Gerald grabbed him by the sleeve.

"Listen," he said, pulling him close and speaking in a whisper. "Do me a favor and talk to this friend of mine?"

Rodya followed Gerald's eyes to the other side of the set where a man was standing. He was dressed conservatively in a navy blue suit and was busy chatting on a cell phone. The part in his hair was so precise and defined Rodya thought he must have done it with a ruler.

"Sure," Rodya agreed. "Who is he?"

"He's sort of helping to finance this picture," Gerald said, "so . . ."

"So he's not happy," Rodya said, comprehending the situation.

"Uh, no, he isn't. He's much happier now that you're here. He's a big fan of yours. He watched the shoot and he'd really like to meet you."

Rodya nodded. He looked over at the man and smiled. Then he followed Gerald across the set and waited for the man to finish his phone call. When he had, Gerald introduced them.

"Rodya, this is Evan. He's seen all of your movies."

Rodya gave a slight nod and shook Evan's hand.

"I sure have!" Evan replied. "I love them all. I own the box set of *Crime and Punishment* and I've watched *Cream of Tartar* so many times I wore out the tape. What a great movie!"

Again, Rodya smiled and gave a polite bow of thanks.

"Why don't you make some more like that?" Evan asked, addressing the question first to Rodya and then shifting his gaze to Gerald. Gerald felt the sting and tried to shift some of the blame back to Rodya.

"Uh, er, Rodya is in retirement from porn. It is very seldom we can get him to make a movie."

This was a lie, but Rodya let it slide. Maybe he could use it as leverage later.

"Retirement?" Evan asked.

"Uh, yes," Rodya said, glaring at Gerald. "My days in movies are not many more."

"Rodya's going to be a photographer," Gerald said. "He's quite good. He takes all of our publicity photos, don't you?"

Another lie. Rodya was about to protest but Gerald stopped him. "He does beautiful work, you'll see."

"But I do mostly other type of work," Rodya said. "I do real photos. I want to be real photographer."

"Really?" Evan said.

"Yes, I do art, some portraits, fashion. All kind. I have portfolio. I show you sometime."

"I'd like that," Evan said, blushing. "My, uh, next door neighbor, Frank Molloy, is a photographer. You must have heard of him."

Rodya started at the mention of the man's name and his eyes widened. "You . . . know him?" he asked.

"Frank? Oh sure. He's been my neighbor for years. I watch his house sometimes when he's away. Do you know him?" Evan asked.

"No, sir, I do not," Rodya said gravely. "But I would like to. Very much."

"Well, you look very much like the guys who appear in his books. I'm sure he'd love to have you model for one of them."

Rodya felt his anger simmering in response to this insult, but he smothered it as best he could and said, "No, I don't want to model. I want to be—how you say?—apprentice for him. I send him letters but he never answer me."

And in truth, Rodya had lobbied hard to that end, writing to Frank Molloy and any other famous photographer he could think of, but to no avail. A few had sent him polite, tritely encouraging rejection letters, but most of them, Molloy included, had not bothered to respond at all.

"Yes," Evan assented. "That Frank's an odd one. Terribly private person."

"Do you think maybe—" Rodya began, but then coyly stopped himself and shook his head as if ashamed to have entertained such an idea. "No, no. Is too much to ask."

"What? Could I introduce you?" Evan said. "Is that what you wanted to ask?"

Rodya looked down at the floor and nodded humbly. When he spoke it was in a low, reverent tone.

"Molloy is idol to me. His work mean so much when I was young man in Russia. I would be so grateful just to meet the man."

"Don't be silly. Frank would be glad to meet you," Evan said. "And I'd be thrilled to introduce you."

"Come," Rodya said, taking Evan by the hand and leading him toward a more secluded area of the set. "I give you my phone number. I will be so grateful."

Although Rodya could no longer qualify as a young rising star, he still possessed the arrogance that went along with youth, beauty and a big dick. Even at the over-ripe age of thirty-five he had no real reason to be humble since he had yet to meet the gay man he could not sway with at least one of his three charms. And Frank Molloy was one he definitely wanted to sway. Frank Molloy, famous for his slick coffee-table books, was just the kind of photographer that Rodya hoped to learn from and eventually become. However, since the traditional, legitimate route of obtaining an apprenticeship—sending a formal letter and some of the best samples of his work—had failed, he decided, after meeting this neighbor of Frank Molloy's, to try a less traditional approach.

Rodya's interest in photography began with one of Frank Molloy's books. When he was sixteen he was given a copy of *Sandy Surfers* as a gift by a foreign man he'd "escorted" around Leningrad. A consolation prize for not being allowed to return with him to the West.

To Rodya, raised behind the Iron Curtain by two drab, elderly aunts, the all-male world he saw photographed in the book was nothing short of amazing. It was erotic, of course, but more important, it showed him an ever-sunny, colorful and clean world, populated with well-fed, robust men who seemed to be having a lot of fun. He used to lie awake at night staring at his chipped and stained ceiling and imagine himself amongst the *Sandy Surfers*, and he fantasized, too, about the man who had taken the pictures, imagining him as a strapping, broad-shouldered, golden-haired man, holding the camera in his giant, capable hands.

A year later Rodya met another tourist, this one a photographer, who asked him if he might like to have some pictures taken. Rodya said he would and they went back to the man's hotel room. The pictures the man took were destined for a less . . . artistic type of publication than *Sandy Surfers*, but it was, Rodya thought, a start, and he was thrilled. Not half as thrilled, however, as the photographer who, once he saw the size of what was in Rodya's pants, knew that he had something of real value.

When the wall came down, Rodya had just turned twenty. His pictures had been selling well on the wealthier side of the planet and the photographer returned, this time with bigger cameras and a crew, and asked Rodya if he wanted to be in a movie. He said he did, and thus began the wildly popular series of Russian films that would, for better or worse, make him famous. He was brought to the U.S., married a woman to get citizenship, and became an all-American commodity.

For Rodya, pornography was a springboard out of poverty. It had given him modest fame, and a very modest fortune, but he soon saw the transitory nature of it. In porn the goal was to make it appear that the participants were enjoying themselves, and Rodya was very good at it. He could disregard the cameraman and crew and focus all his attention on the one he was fucking. More importantly, he made it appear that he was enjoying what he did more than he'd ever enjoyed anything before, and that enjoyment was something that came through on film.

That the erotic world he was starring in was an illusion, had always been clear to Rodya. That the world created by Frank Molloy was just as artificial took him a little longer to realize. But, realize it he did one morning while on the set waiting for them to rig the lights for his next scene. He picked up a fashion magazine that had been sitting on the table and it fell open to the page near the beginning on which the biographical information of the contributors is given. There, above the caption "Frank Molloy at work" was a picture of the photographer himself. Rodya looked at the photo and then again at the caption and thought that surely there had been some mistake. The short, bespectacled man with a body lacking any discernible muscular definition could not possibly be the same man Rodya had so vividly fantasized about. Could not be the man who had created the worlds of *Sandy Surfers, Dude Ranch,* and *Crew Team.*

After he got over the shock, Rodya's next reaction was a feeling of betrayal. A feeling that somehow he'd been tricked. How could someone so absolutely ordinary-looking create a world that was to him so extraordinary? The contradiction was too much.

He brooded over it for a while, but, in time, as the shock faded, he found that he was more intrigued than offended by the contradiction. Rodya knew, from his own experience, that there was real power in being beautiful, but he also knew, again from his own experience, that there was more power in being able to create beauty. Soon after that epiphany, Rodya decided he would make the gradual move away from porn and begin studying photography.

Chapter Two

"If it ain't broke, why fix it? That's my motto. Your books sell. You make money. What's the problem?"

"Look, Chapman, you owe me this one," Frank argued, although he knew it wasn't true. "It's not that big of a deal. I already have most of the pictures so it will hardly cost you anything; a small advance to cover my expenses, maybe pay an assistant, and in two months I'll deliver a book you'll absolutely love."

"I don't want a book I'll absolutely love. I don't even really like books. What I want's a book that'll sell. Sell and sell and line my pockets with those green paper bills we all love so much, and I don't think a book with artsy photos of crumbling buildings is going to do that."

Frank groaned.

"If you had some boys in it," Chapman continued. "Now that's another story! Maybe you could get that NSync, or the guys from one of those reality shows, or if you're so set on Italy, how about some Italian soccer players? Yeah, that's it. There we go. I can see it now. Soccer's big all over the world, right? Imagine the market!"

And imagine it Frank did. A book of shirtless Italian soccer players would certainly make more money than a book of architectural photos, but that didn't make him feel any better. He pushed his glasses up onto his forehead and rubbed his eyes. He knew Chapman would go on and on in that whiney voice of his and would not give in. Why, after all these years, Frank was even trying to persuade him, he did not know. He set the phone down on the kitchen counter, poured out a glass of scotch and took a large sip. No matter how much he argued his point the discussion always returned to the topic of boys and how they should be the subject of every one of Frank's books. Boys, boys, boys, that's all Chapman ever wanted. Boys water-skiing with Golden Retrievers; boys playing leapfrog atop Mount Kilimanjaro; boys going over Niagara Falls in a barrel. Whatever. As long as ridiculously handsome, ridiculously well-toned eighteen to twenty-five-year-old men in various states of undress were front and foremost the books sold well and Chapman was happy.

If there is any truth to conventional wisdom then Frank should have been happy, too. His books were successful. Wildly successful, as those things go. His seventh book of "boy photos" (this one featuring semi-nude, buffed and coifed Argentinean boys playing a shirtless game of polo while perched on white Palominos) had just come out in a "limited edition" glossy hardback, wisely shrink-wrapped in Mylar to prevent bookstore perverts and thrifty window shoppers from sneaking a peak sans purchase. The book was the Christmas gift of choice this season and was flying off the shelves of bookstores and landing on the coffee tables of almost every gay man in the Western World. And that was precisely Chapman's goal: a book a year, one to replace the next, almost before they had a chance to collect dust.

So Frank kept coming up with ideas and new models, and he kept taking pictures. The locations and the concepts and the boys were always different, but lately Frank's lack of interest in the subject matter had been noted by some of his usually fawning critics. His shots, all from similar angles, with similar lighting and effects, were justly labeled "lazy and uninspired," and despite the exotic locales and high concepts, his last two books had been called "boring," "predictable," and "repetitious." One particularly snide (and insightful) critic even went so far as to say, "any muse Frank Molloy may have had is surely dead. He hasn't taken a decent photo since the early nineties." The criticism stung, but it hadn't phased Chapman a bit.

"Critics!" he'd said when Frank had presented him with the reviews. "Who the hell reads criticism of books like yours anyway?" He then presented Frank with a copy of the last royalty statement and said,

"Look here, the numbers don't lie. Those bitches are just jealous, that's all. Sour grapes if you ask me."

But Frank knew better. He knew there was truth in what he read. Of course his models were always different, and many were so handsome they could have reanimated even the deadest muse, but for Frank they did nothing. To him they were one set of smooth, sculpted abs after another, and none looked all that different from the one that came before. In rare moments of self-honesty, he could admit that he was not, nor had he ever been, excited by the sight of a flat stomach. He did not care about slender waists, hard, perfectly proportioned pecs, or the circumference of the *biceps brachii*. If anything, such perfection left him feeling cold, or, to be more accurate, limp. It was an ennui he thought he had been able to conceal in his work, but the last batch of criticism had made him realize that it was apparent to others.

Frank took another large gulp from his drink and picked up the phone. Chapman was still talking.

"How about collages?" Chapman asked, rhetorically. "Then you could have both boys and buildings! You could airbrush out their little jimmywangers and paste in some obelisk or tower, maybe even the Eiffel tower! That would be a good one, eh, Frank?"

Chapman was laughing now, thoroughly enjoying his own comic scenario.

"Now come on," Frank said, trying to hide his frustration. "You know that's not the kind of book I want to do."

"*Yes*," Chapman hissed, "so you persist in telling me. But it could be that kind of book." He paused to laugh some more and then continued. "Oh sweet Jesus, I can just see it. You could take down those little statues on top of St. Peter's. You know, the ones in front of that big domey thing . . ."

"Chapman."

". . . and replace them with boys!"

"Chapman, no."

"Maybe put some bowls of flame between 'em."

"Okay. Very funny. You can stop now."

"What's the matter Frank? You don't think they'd let you do that?"

"No, somehow I think John Paul himself might pull the plug on that one."

"Not even if they were Catholic boys?" Chapman cackled.

"Especially if they were Catholic boys."

"Well, then, my friend," Chapman said, signaling that the discussion of the subject was coming to an end, "I guess we won't be doing your little architecture book, will we?"

Frank couldn't argue. Or rather, he could have but he knew he didn't really have the courage to push the issue to a definite conclusion. The contract with his publisher was a good one and he knew just how lucky he was. More importantly, he knew there were hundreds, possibly thousands, of other young photographers who would give one of their kidneys to have a contract even half as good as his, and Frank's fear was that if he pushed too hard, Chapman just might abandon him and scoop up one of the newbies.

Frank hung up the phone and returned to his study, closing the French doors behind him. He lowered the window blinds and sat down at his desk, opening the large bottom drawer and removing a stash of Christmas catalogues. They were not fancy—no Neiman Marcus Wish Book, The Sharper Image or even Pottery Barn. These were small catalogues printed on cheap paper, from folksy companies based in Omaha and Osh Kosh—Miles Kimball, Swiss Colony, Harriet Carter. Frank flipped through them, absently selecting a few items and marking the pages he wanted to return to with Post-It notes. When he finished, he began filling out the order forms.

In the past four months Frank had ordered a set of pencils with his name on them, some Christmas tea towels, an electronic card shuffler, a stuffed Jackalope, countless boxes of waxy holiday cheese and "beef" sticks, a blackhead vacuum, and various other knickknacks, gewgaws and gimcracks. There was nothing in the catalogues that he needed, nothing he even wanted, to which the pile of unopened boxes in the closet behind him could attest, but he ordered anyway, always trying to space his orders so that at least one item would arrive each day.

In Japan, Frank had heard, they had a topsy-turvy philosophy when it comes to gift giving: the content of the gift is not nearly as important as the delivery. It had seemed stupid to him at first, but in the past few months it was a philosophy Frank had come to understand very well, and one which easily explained his catalogue ordering. For him, the content of the packages was superfluous and the delivery was all he cared about. Or, to be more specific, the person doing the delivering—a chunk of a man (not to be confused with a hunk) named Al. Or so Frank concluded from the embroidered patch on the left breast of his shirt. The small "L" looked a little bit like a "1" and to Frank that seemed more appropriate. To him, Al was A-1, so perfect did the man appear. And yet, Perfection, like its sister Beauty, was (despite what the avenues of Madison and 7th try to tell the world to the contrary) in the eye of the beholder, and in the tight-abs-hollow-cheek-large-pec-obsessed world in which Frank lived, there were few who would paste the label "perfect" on Al. He was, to be blunt, fat: a large, barrel-chested man with a belly like a beach ball. A belly that, whenever Frank saw it, encased in its brown uniform, made his heart race and gave him a little below-the-belt "chubby" of his own.

Frank had come to anticipate the daily arrival of Al the way most children anticipate the arrival of Santa Claus or the Easter Bunny, and he would run back and forth to the window all morning waiting for the brown truck to arrive. When it did, he would flee to the kitchen like a giddy teenage girl and wait for the doorbell to ring. Then, casually, oh so very casually, he would walk back down the hall to the front door, take a deep breath, and open it. In spite of his nervousness—nervousness that often left him speechless or stuttering—he always invited Al inside and sometimes even managed to squeak out a banal comment about the weather or how busy Al must be. More often than not his nervousness got the best of him. His ability to make small talk would evaporate and he'd just stand there staring, his mouth agape and lust clouding his eyes, unable to say anything. Verbally paralyzed, he would sign for the package and then watch forlornly as Al descended the front steps and drove away, apparently ignorant of Frank's secret crush. As soon as the truck rounded the corner and went out of sight, Frank would return to his study, close the door behind him, and slowly, sensuously, remove the brown paper from the package Al had just delivered, imagining it to be the tight brown uniform instead.

But his surreptitious unwrapping was not the only vice in which Frank indulged in the privacy of his study. Nor was Al the only man of girth for whom Frank carried a torch. In another desk drawer he maintained a fantasy file of pictures he had over the years clipped from various magazines. Pictures of celebrities mostly: John Goodman, Jack

Black, The King of Queens. It was a silly file, full of the kind of pictures a boy-crazy teenage girl might have snipped from the pages of *Tiger Beat* or *YM* and plastered on the inside of her locker at school, with one large exception, of course.

Frank's fetish for fat men had been with him as long as he could remember, his first inkling of it coming in kindergarten when he sat behind portly Kenny Mcmillan, whose green Toughskins were always sliding down, affording a tantalizing view of his ass crack. And yet, forty years later, Frank's fetish remained a private thing, something he never indulged outside the walls of his study. There, alone in the blue glow from his computer screen, he gave nightly thanks for the Internet, which enabled him to ogle the lurid photos of large, naked men on the Chubnet and BulkMale web sites, all in the privacy of his own home. Usually he just browsed these sights, but some nights, fortified with a few scotches, he would chat and flirt in the veiled world of the Chubby Chasers chat room, always too afraid to do anything more than chat and exchange headless pictures, afraid that if his true identity was discovered his reputation would be ruined.

To those on the outside it would appear that one of the enviable perks of Frank's success was that he was always at the center of a circle of beautiful, ambitious young men, all of whom were well acquainted with his books. Beautiful ambitious young men who were more than willing to offer themselves bodily to him with the hope of being picked as a model. Beautiful ambitious young men in whom Frank had not the slightest interest. Even more ironic was the fact that his disinterest was grossly misinterpreted by nearly everyone as an indication of his incredibly high standards. It was confusion that, he had to admit, he cultivated. He enjoyed the reputation it had given him, both professionally and personally, and it was a reputation he did not particularly want to tarnish. For that reason, it was imperative that his sizable fantasies remain locked behind the study door.

The doorbell rang. Frank quickly stashed the catalogues back in the drawer and shut off the computer. He got up, checked his appearance in the mirror and took a deep breath before heading down the hallway. He opened the door, saw Al, and the butterflies in his stomach beat their wings.

"Afternoon, Mr. Molloy," Al said.

"Um, hello Al," Frank replied timidly. He was suddenly afraid Al might smell the scotch on his breath. He glanced down at his watch. It was only three-thirty.

"Just got one for you today," Al said, "but it's a big one. "It's COD, too, so I'm afraid you're gonna have to pay this time."

Frank didn't really hear him. He was too busy staring at the stubble on Al's chins, at his huge, hairy forearms, at the large, chubby hands with dimples where the knuckles should have been. And then there was that belly! It hung pendulously over Al's belt, encased in the tight brown fabric of his shirt. Fabric that was stretched so tightly across the expanse that it strained the buttons. Buttons that Frank longed to pop one by one with his teeth, opening the wide terrain to further exploration.

"Uh, Mr. Molloy," Al repeated, tapping his pen on the clipboard so that Frank could see the figure. "It's COD. See right here. I need seventeen dollars and ninety-eight cents."

"Wha—?" Frank said, his voice quaky. "Oh, yes. How much?"

"Seventeen ninety-eight."

"Okay, thank you. I'll just get my checkbook."

Frank turned and headed down the hallway. He stopped suddenly and scolded himself. He had left Al standing on the porch. Emboldened by the scotch, he turned and said, "Why don't you come in. I'll just be a minute. Do you want to sit down? What about something to drink? Would you like some coffee? I mean, I don't know if you drink it or not, or if you're allowed to stop like this on your shift, but I've got some if you want it. Or a soda. Anything you like!"

Al smiled and raised an eyebrow. He stepped inside and closed the door.

"A glass of water would be great."

After Frank had gone, Al chuckled to himself. Lust was difficult to hide, and Al could see it plainly in Frank's eyes. In his twenty-five years on the planet he had met a lot of guys like Frank—guys whose repressed desire for his large body bubbled like lava just below the surface of their buff exteriors. He could tell when they wanted to sleep with him (and there were always quite a few who did), but he also knew that they rarely, if ever, wanted him for anything else. It was never anything more than sexual desire and, once they'd satisfied it, they'd slink away like straight men going back to their wives, ashamed of what they'd done and usually vowing that it would never happen again.

What Al wanted was a man willing to do more than just have sex with him, a man to hold hands with at the movies, a man he could date, and who would take him to meet his parents, or even just his friends. But so far that guy had never come along. The guys in Al's life savored him in secret, much the way alcoholics and ex-smokers savor their respective substances when they fall off the wagon. In short, he was seen as a vice, an indulgence, which is ultimately a one-sided pleasure.

Al recognized Frank from his books and had, like everybody else, judged him by his cover. This was, after all, a guy who made his living photographing buffed twinks. The same guy who was out every weekend with a different young guy on his arm. Al had seen his picture in the papers and in magazines and he was never with the same one twice.

The first time he caught Frank looking at him *"that way"* he could hardly believe it. The possibility that Frank found him attractive seemed to defy all logic, but Al knew he wasn't wrong. And, as his deliveries to Frank's address multiplied, he grew certain of it. He saw it in Frank's eyes, yes, but also in his nervous stuttering, and by the slight bulge in Frank's pants—a bulge that was always a bit more pronounced toward the end of his delivery. From there it was only a short step of logic for Al to realize that the guy's catalogue ordering was a ruse.

Initially Al was flattered. It was good for his ego, but he knew that Frank was probably just like all the rest. They were all hypocrites, to a degree, denying what they were attracted to because of the social taboo attached to it. But this one, this Frank Famous Photographer, was perhaps the biggest hypocrite so far. He had erected a huge public facade and it was a facade that Al didn't want to get pulled behind. He knew that if he ever did give in and do some sheet wrestling with Frank he would probably be spurned when it was over like he'd never been spurned before. Frank's shame would usher Al right back out the facade door. This would be the kind of guy who would ask him when it was over to "please not say anything about it to anyone else," like he had a wife or lover whose feelings he was trying to spare.

For that reason, Al did nothing to encourage Frank. No toying little cat and mouse games, no flirtatious looks or double *entendre comments.* He dropped off the packages, smiled, made polite small talk, but then went on with the rest of his deliveries and tried not to give it another thought. Or at least that's what he knew he *should* have done. As they say, the spirit was willing but . . . when you've been fat all your life and teased and taunted mercilessly, it is difficult to pass up the opportunity for a little harmless revenge when such an opportunity presents itself. So, Al toyed with Frank on a daily basis. Not really like a cat toys with a mouse, more the way a child with a coveted piece of candy teases another child who is without.

When Frank returned with his checkbook, Al was studying a series of three framed photographs on the wall of the foyer.

"Those are my photos," Frank said proudly, but then frowned, afraid that maybe his sentence was misunderstood. He backpedaled. "I took them. I mean, with my camera. I didn't mean that I own them. I mean, of course I do own them, but I didn't mean for it to sound like you couldn't look at them. You didn't think that, did you?"

Al looked at him blankly for a moment and then went back to studying the photos.

"I took them in Italy," Frank added, hoping to move the topic away from his blunder.

"Yes, I can see that," Al said, a cunning grin on his face. He made a grand gesture with his arm. "There's Italy," he said, "and there's your name down in the corner."

"Yes," Frank said with a nervous chuckle.

"Yes."

"Yes. Well, um . . ."

"Yes?"

"Um, have you ever been there?" Frank asked. "To Italy, I mean. I mean, you seem to recognize it."

"Yes, well," Al said, tipping his head at a photograph of the leaning tower of Pisa. "I think most people would."

Frank scolded himself again for saying something so stupid.

"I'm sorry, I didn't me—"

"No," Al said, grinning, "I'm just being a smart-ass. I haven't been there, at least not yet, but I am hoping to go this spring."

"Ahhhh," Frank said. "A little vacation? Well, as hard as you work, you certainly deser—"

"No," Al said, cutting him short. "Not a vacation. If I go, it will be to study."

"To study!" Frank cried.

Al did not reply but lowered his brows and gave Frank a frosty glare. "Yes, to study," he said, his expression cold.

Frank sensed that he'd made another faux pas and again started backpedaling. "Architecture?" Frank asked, hopefully.

"Uh, no," Al replied, cocking his head. "I'm a singer."

Frank's eyes widened.

"An opera singer."

"Ahhh," Frank nodded.

"If I get accepted into the program I applied to—and that's a big "if"—it will be to study. In Milan." Then he added, in a voice mocking Frank's, "Have you been there?" But Frank missed the jab.

"An opera singer," Frank said, and then began to laugh.

Again Al lowered his brow and the frosty gaze returned. Again Frank backpedaled, even more frantically this time.

"I didn't mean anything bad," Frank said. "Of course I didn't. I'm just, well, I'm surprised, that's all. Shocked, really. I wouldn't think someone like, er, I mean, you seem so . . . It doesn't seem like something most guys wou . . ."

Rather than dig himself in deeper, Frank stopped speaking. Al continued staring at him. The checkbook trembled in Frank's hand and his eye began to twitch.

"I, uh, have some," Frank said. When he didn't elaborate, Al changed his look to one of impatient incomprehension.

"Opera," Frank said, blushing. "CDs, I mean. I, uh, would you like to see them?"

"I'd like that," Al said, and followed as Frank led him into the living room. Frank gestured for him to sit on the sofa and then skipped over to the cabinet in which he kept his CDs, his heart full of bluebirds, as he considered which ones to show Al.

It was unfortunate that on his way across the room he failed to notice the electrical cord he'd stretched across the floor that morning to give extra power to his Christmas tree. In an ideal world the cord would have come unplugged when his foot slid under it, but in an ideal world Frank's condominium would also have had an electrical outlet in the exact spot he wanted to place the tree, which it did not. In his too-real world, Frank had been forced to rely on an extension cord to reach the outlet in the other room. A cord that followed a labyrinthine path, under carpets and around sofa legs, so that when he caught his foot the cord did not give and come unplugged, but instead stretched itself taut and sent him face down to the floor. Before he even had a chance to realize what had happened, before Al had a chance to react, before anyone, had they been so inclined, had the chance to yell "timber!" the tree fell on top of him.

Al ran over and dug his way through the chaotic mess of branches and garland and ornaments, until he found the trunk of the tree and was able to right the thing again. Frank feebly lifted his tinsel-covered head and spit pine needles out of his mouth. He wasn't hurt, at least not physically, but he couldn't help wishing that the tree would fall again so that he would have somewhere to hide. Al bent down next to him.

"Are you . . . hrmp!" he began, stifling a laugh. "Are you all right?" and then he erupted in giggles, his belly shaking when he laughed like a bowl full of, well, you know.

Frank groaned and shook his head from side to side on the floor, wishing he could dissolve into it. Still chuckling, Al got up and went over to Frank's stereo. He perused the CDs, selected one, and put it in the player. Frank was getting up and was just about to speak, but was silenced by Al, who put a finger up to his lips. The music began to play. It was the overture from Rossini's *Barber of Seville* and Al hummed along to it. He reached under Frank's arms and lifted him to his feet. When he was standing, Al lifted him from the waist, threw him over his shoulder and carried him to the bedroom.

Three hours later they were still in the bedroom, although much more tired.

"How often do you get to Italy?" Al asked, encircling Frank in his large arms.

"Not often enough." Frank sighed. "At least not as often as I'd like. I'm trying to get a new book together."

He told Al about the book and about his argument with his publisher.

"Well, he is right, you know," Al said. "It doesn't seem like it would sell as well as your other books."

Frank looked at him, surprised.

"So you've seen my books?" he asked.

Al nodded.

"And?"

"And . . . what?"

"What did you think?"

Al paused. "Hmmm. Now don't get me wrong," he said. "Your books are great for what they are but if I compare them to what I saw in the hallway I'd say you can probably do better."

Frank turned away again. He wasn't really offended so much as he was saddened by what Al had said.

"So why don't you?" Al asked, kissing the back of his neck.

"Why don't I what?" Frank asked.

"Do better."

Frank thought about this. It was the same question he'd asked himself a hundred times. It wasn't that he didn't know the answer so much as that he didn't want to admit it.

"I don't know," he said. "I guess maybe I'm afraid."

"Of?"

"That's a good question. Afraid it won't get published. Afraid that if it does, it won't sell and I won't make any money. Afraid that people won't like it. I'm also afraid I'll lose my contract with my publisher."

"That's a lot to be afraid of," Al said. "Are you that hard-up for money that you can't afford the risk?"

"No, nothing like that. Money's not really the problem."

"Well, what then?"

Frank was silent. Al sat up on one elbow. He turned Frank's face toward his, and kissed him.

"Won't you be in trouble?" Frank asked, when the kiss was finished. Al looked at the clock on the bedside table and rolled his eyes.

"Probably," he said, pulling himself out of the bed and picking up his uniform. "But some chances are worth taking."

Humming the Puccini aria, Al finished dressing and then he and Frank walked back down the hallway. When they were about halfway there, Al grabbed Frank from behind, lifted him up and set Frank down so that his feet were standing on his. He held each of Frank's hands and they did an exaggerated walk down the hall, both laughing as they went. Once they reached the front door, Frank stepped down, turned and kissed him again.

"I guess I'll see you tomorrow," he said, giving a shy smile. Al smiled back and nodded. Then, like so many days before, he lumbered down the front walk to the waiting brown truck.

Every day for the next week when Al arrived he was led from the front door directly to the bedroom. After the third day he started coming back in the evenings after work and one night the two stayed up so late talking and listening to music that they fell asleep and did not wake until morning. After that it was an unspoken assumption that Al would spend the night and Frank started planning and cooking dinners accordingly.

Whenever Frank was out during the day he started noticing and then buying things he thought Al might like—a shirt that would look good on him, a copy of *A Room with a View*, a box of *Bacci* chocolates. For his part, Al would arrive bearing flowers and a different opera disk or an Italian movie he'd rented for them to watch. They listened to the music during dinner while Al recounted the plot of the opera and taught Frank some Italian phrases.

As the morning dawned on the two-week anniversary of the consummation of their affair, Frank stood at the door and watched Al drive away. When he had turned the corner and was out of sight, Frank, still naked except for Al's brown knit cap, sighed contentedly and walked back into the living room. It was still dark outside so Frank lay down on the couch and covered himself in a blanket. He closed his eyes and thought about the night before, running his hands over his chest as he did so. He had always enjoyed sex, but never had he found it more satisfying. It was like Al had reached an itch in the center of his back that no one else had ever been able to scratch. As he drifted off to sleep he thought about Christmas and wondered how he and Al could spend it together without anyone finding out.

Hours later, Frank woke to the sound of the phone. The room was sunny and he squinted. He sat up and it took him a minute to realize that he wasn't in the bedroom. He fumbled for the receiver.

"Frank?"

"Uh huh."

"Frank, it's me, Evan."

"Oh, hello," Frank sighed. "What can I do for you?"

Evan was one of those neighbors who seldom called unless he wanted to complain about something: leaves from Frank's trees blowing into his pool, or to "remind" him to bring in his unsightly garbage cans, the kind of neighbor who is endured rather than enjoyed.

"It's the other way around, Frankie," Evan said. "I am the one in a position to do something for you. I know it's rare, but this time it's true. And believe me, when you hear it you're going to be a very happy man."

Frank looked at himself in the mirror, still wearing nothing but Al's hat, and he smiled.

"You're gonna thank me, buddy," Evan added. "Really."

"I'll bet," Frank scoffed. "It sounds like you're going to tell me about the life-changing and money-making possibilities of selling Herbalife."

"Ha, ha," Evan laughed, with all the genuineness of a used car salesman. "You slay me! But really, I know you. I know how you are. I know what you like. And I've got one that you won't want to pass up."

Suddenly Frank understood. He had heard this preface before. Hundreds of times. Evan didn't want something from him, at least not directly. No, someone else wanted something from Evan, or he owed them a favor, so now he was using his connection with Frank to get that someone, or that someone's little boyfriend, an opportunity to be in one of Frank's books.

"You didn't promise him anything, did you?" Frank asked, wearily.

"I'm telling you, you're going to freak when you hear who it is."

"Mmmmm," Frank said. "I doubt it."

"He really wants to meet you," Evan went on. "He's a big fan of your work and he's done quite a bit of work in front of the camera himself.

He's got, uh, a big body of work, heh, heh. A big body of work and a body that's big in the most important place. That's what's made him famous. And he is famous, Frank, almost as famous as you. Everywhere. The world over. Men want him, covet him, would pay a small fortune just to be with him, but he, for some reason that's beyond my comprehension, has set his sights on you."

"Look," Frank said, idly winding a piece of tinsel around his dick, "I'm too busy for this right now, so either tell me what you want and who it is or I'm hanging up."

"Oh, all right," Evan sighed. "I'm talking about someone you and I, and every pink-blooded male-loving male knows (in the psuedo-biblical sense) and loves (in as much as love can express itself in the stroke of a hand), and admires, nay, envies, every time they gaze down into their own underwear."

"Oh, Christ!" Frank cried.

"Not quite, but close, Frank, very close."

"Just tell me who it is."

"Rodya."

"Rodya?" Frank repeated. The name sounded vaguely familiar to him.

"That's what I said. Can you believe it!"

"No, I can't!" Frank said, mocking Evan's excitement. "But only because I don't know who the hell you're talking about."

"What!" Evan shrieked. "Come on! You are kidding. I know you are."

"No, I don't think so."

"You mean to say you've never seen *Vronsky's Boys*, *Slavixxx Summer* or *Slavixxx Summer II*?"

"Never seen 'em. What are they?"

"Other than a sizeable gap in your sexual education?"

"Oh, very funny," Frank snapped.

"They happen to be the new classics of porn," Evan said. "*Slavixxx Summer* is like the gay adult version of *Citizen Kane*. And Rodya, the thirteen-inch wonder, is the star!"

"Oh," Frank said, and then allowed himself the indulgence of imagining a naked Orson Welles. "So what does he want with me? I don't make movies, and especially not that kind. Granted, my books aren't

art but there are levels of junk and I fancy myself at least one level, al-
beit a thin one at times, above pornography. My publisher would go for
the idea but I don't think I will," he declared, adjusting Al's hat on his
head. "I am moving on to better things."

"Uh huh," Evan said. "Great. Whatever. That will probably make
him like you even more."

Frank was confused.

"It seems," Evan continued, "that in addition to his performing skills,
young Rodya is also an amateur shutter bug and wants, unlike seemingly everyone else in the world, to move from in front of the camera
to behind it, although it will be a loss for all of us, his adoring fans. In
short, Frankie, he wants you, and your expertise, and I gather he'll do
just about anything to get it. Ironic, isn't it? He's chased and wooed by
some of the world's most prestigious and wealthy men but you're the
one he wants—the one least likely to be interested in him at all."

"Hey, wait a minute!" Frank cried. "What's that supposed to mean?"

Evan laughed heartily. "Now, come on, Frank, you do have a reputation of being . . . how shall I say it? Something less than a tiger in the
bedroom."

"What!" Frank cried, leaping up from the sofa.

"Hmmm, maybe that didn't come out quite right. How to say this?"
Evan pondered. "Let's just say that you are (or at least so I've heard
from more than one of your castoffs), disinterested. Or, to quote one
of them, 'Frank Molloy is more finicky than an overfed cat when it
comes to sex.' "

"But—"

"And while we're on the subject of pussy . . . some have even wondered, myself not included of course, if you are really gay at all, or if you're
just pretending to be because it's trendy and helps to sell your books."

"Wha—! But I am gay!" Frank cried, pulling the hat off his head. "I
am gay!" Then, sensing the ridiculousness of his outburst he picked
the hat up and sat back down.

"Of course I know that," Evan said. "No straight man would ever
have chosen your window coverings, but you know how people like to
talk."

"But I—" Frank sputtered. "I mean, just because I don't bed down
every dick that pops up!"

"No, you certainly don't do that. You don't seem to use the bed for anything other than sleep. You're a one-man monastery, Frank. The Lone Brother of Perpetual Denial."

Evan chuckled to himself and let his words sink in. Frank was too surprised to speak. He looked in the mirror and suddenly was not quite sure who was staring back.

"So can I tell Rodya that you'll meet him?" Evan asked. There was silence while he waited for an answer. "That would be the best way to counteract the rumors, you know. Unless of course you're not interested in beautiful, young foreign men with great big dicks."

Frank's thoughts divided, and for a long time he remained unable to respond. On the one hand he knew that beautiful, young foreign men with great big dicks did not really excite him all that much and, more importantly, that Al did. The sex between them had been great, there was no denying it, but there was more to it than that. He had enjoyed the relatively small amount of time they'd spent together outside of the bedroom. Time spent talking or listening to music or plotting out the futures they each hoped to have. Time he wanted more of.

But, on the other, more public, hand, Frank was terrified of discovery. Terrified of what the world would think if they knew about his perversion.

The dichotomy between these two conflicting emotions—intense satisfaction and extreme shame—was difficult for him to reconcile. For decades he'd imagined his desire as something that he alone could see. A secret that he could keep. But suddenly he saw that it was the other way around; his desire was not invisible, but, rather, the cloak he'd imagined was covering it. He was the emperor in his new clothes. All eyes were on him and people were laughing. And if Evan was to be believed, they had been laughing for quite some time.

"All right," Frank said. "Bring him to the party tomorrow night."

"Excellent! Oh, and Frank, make sure you get plenty of rest tonight. You're going to need it."

Frank rolled his eyes and hung up. He had extended the invitation in a moment of panic, but as the day went on he found that he could not stop thinking about it. He was haunted by the feeling that somehow this meeting with the star of *Slavixxx Summer Parts I and II* was not quite right. That it was something Al might not like.

Chapter Three

Frank's annual Christmas party was always held the first weekend in December. Over the years it had become known as a notorious place to ogle, meet, and possibly pick up the models from his books, as well as a place for the model wannabes to display and sell themselves. For those reasons, invitations to the event were highly coveted.

Frank had not seriously considered inviting Al to the party. He had thought about it but every time he did, the butterflies in his stomach reawakened and began to beat their wings with such ferocity that Frank thought he might be sick. He was falling in love with Al, he knew, but he just could not imagine bringing him into his public world. At least not yet.

Someday, Frank thought, he might have the courage to do it, but that someday was off in the future and when it arrived well, maybe then Al would be thin! Yes, that would solve everything. The next time they got together Frank would suggest, ever so gently, that Al join a gym. Frank would help him, make him over, and by the time of his next party Al would be presentable! (In his frenzied, butterfly state, Frank had forgotten, of course, that Al's most attractive physical attribute was his weight, and were he to lose it Frank might also lose his desire).

Not knowing how to handle the party dilemma, and not having much time to consider it, Frank lied to Al and said they could not get

together that evening because he was having some "publishing associates" over for dinner.

"I wish I could get out of it," he said, as he kissed Al goodbye the
day before the party. "But I really can't. You understand, don't you?"

"I understand," Al said, and kissed the top of Frank's head. "I'll just
have to keep myself entertained for one night."

Preparations for the party had been going on since late October but,
due to his daily dalliances with Al, Frank had fallen behind schedule.
On the morning of the party he still had nothing to wear, so as soon as
the caterers arrived, he left them with a long list of instructions and
went out shopping for clothes. When he returned, late that afternoon,
laden with bags, one of the caterers—a young, blond brown-nosing
nuisance named Jason—came running down the driveway toward him.

"Everything's ready Mr. Molloy," Jason said, taking one of the bags
from Frank and carrying it inside. "No worries at all. We've just been
doing some last minute stuff, but it's pretty much all set. It should be
a cool party."

"Glad to hear it," Frank said, entering the house and heading down
the hall to his bedroom.

"Do you need any help with anything?" Jason asked, running ahead
of him to open the bedroom door.

"No," Frank said, squeezing past and setting his bags down on the
bed. "I think all I've got left to do is cut some tags and get dressed.
Thanks."

He went and got a pair of scissors from his desk drawer and when he
returned Jason was still standing in the doorway, staring at him. Frank
gave him a questioning look.

"Oh, I'm sorry," Jason said, grinning and shuffling his feet. "I didn't
mean to stare, it's just—it's just that I think you're really great. I mean,
I'm sort of in awe, you know. I love your books."

Frank gave an inward groan but smiled and tried to be gracious. As
much as he despised the type of work he was doing he still enjoyed
having it validated as something other than expensive masturbation
material.

"Yes, well, thank you for saying so. Remind me to give you a copy of
the latest one when the party's over."

"Wow!" Jason said. "That'd be so awesome."

"Don't mention it," Frank said, slowly pushing the door closed. "It will be my pleasure."

"Um, Mr. Molloy," Jason said, blocking the door with his broad, tuxedoed shoulder. Frank gave him the questioning look again, this time clouded with impatience.

"I don't really know how to say this."

Again, Frank stifled a groan.

"Um, but if you're ever looking for models. I mean, I have some experience and I'd love to work for you."

Yes, Frank thought to himself, *you'd love to work for me in every capacity except the one I've hired you for tonight.*

"Well, you're certainly a very handsome young man," Frank said, as diplomatically as he could. "Maybe we'll talk after the party. How's that sound?"

"You mean it?"

"Sure. But listen," Frank said, pushing more insistently on the bedroom door, "I've really got to get dressed now."

Jason took a step back and let the door close. A second later it popped open again and Jason stepped into the room.

"I'm sorry," the boy said, smiling and digging in his pocket. "But I forgot this." He removed a yellow Post-It note and handed it to Frank. It was a UPS delivery slip. The kind the driver leaves behind when the recipient isn't home. "Some fat guy dropped it off," Jason said, "but there was no package or anything."

Frank felt his hands go cold and sweat break out on his forehead. He unfolded the Post-It and looked at it. In red pen Al had drawn a heart around the words "Sorry you weren't home to receive your delivery." The note trembled in his hand and Frank was aware of Jason watching him.

Frank looked up at Jason. Had he been smirking like that before? Frank knew he needed to say something, but his mouth was dry. Panic began to run through his veins. The boy knew, didn't he. That was why he had brought up the modeling. Yes of course! That was it. Jason was trying to blackmail him.

"Oh, that must have been my cousin," Frank said, scrunching up the yellow paper and shoving it in his pocket. He tried very hard to look indifferent but was aware he was failing.

"Your . . . cousin?" Jason said. He was still smirking, but he had also raised one of his brows. Did he look doubtful, or just confused? Frank couldn't really tell, his expression was so vacant.

"My cousin," Frank repeated, pushing the door shut and turning the key. He stood for a moment, looking at the knob, and then took two steps back, turned, and walked into the bathroom. He closed the door behind him, locked it, took the note out of his pocket and without reading it again, ripped it in pieces. He lifted the lid of the toilet to deposit the scraps, but then stopped himself and reconsidered.

This is ridiculous, he thought. *Stupid! Paranoid!* But then he remembered that brow and the tone of Jason's voice and without any further hesitation he dropped the pieces in the bowl and flushed.

As he watched them swirl down—and indeed he did watch to make sure they all went down—he did not think about Al. Nor did he think about how foolish he was being. No, the only thought in his panicked head at that moment was how he would possibly fit the very blond Jason into a book of swarthy, Italian soccer players.

Twenty minutes (and a shot of brandy) later, Frank emerged from his bedroom. He put on a brave face and went into the kitchen to give the caterers their final instructions. Then he spoke to the maid doing the final cleaning and met with the bartender to go over the alcohol list, wondering all the while if Jason had shown them the note. The bartender went to retrieve some things from the kitchen and Frank was left in the dining room alone. From where he stood, he could see straight into the living room where the woman from the cleaning service was doing some last minute vacuuming. She was using the crevice tool to get into all the nooks and crannies of the sofa and Frank saw her almost unconsciously, peripherally, as he continued checking his list. It must have been the change in tone of the vacuum—the change from low hum to high-pitched whine—that made him look up. It was the kind of sound the vacuum made when it had grabbed onto something that would not go down the tube or let any air pass through. Not a troubling sound but one that made him look up from what he was doing, and over at the maid. Her head was down low and he saw only her ass peaking over the back of the sofa, like an undulating setting sun. He continued looking at her and then suddenly she popped up, holding the wand of the vacuum. Attached to the end of it Frank saw the thing that was responsible for the high-pitched whine. It was a magazine. The woman looked at it, a confused expression on her face, and then over at Frank. Frank looked at her, then again at the magazine and his knees nearly collapsed. It was not, Frank realized, just any magazine. Not *Time*, or *Newsweek*, or *People*, not *Vanity Fair*, not even *Freshman* or *Playgirl*. No, the magazine on the end of the vacuum wand was none other than *Bulk Male*. He must have carelessly shoved it under the sofa one day and forgotten about it.

Almost without thinking, Frank took two strident leaps across the dining room floor and then launched himself over the back of the sofa, snatching the offending periodical as he passed. He landed, ear-first, on the floor, and then somersaulted into a body slam on his back. For a moment neither he nor the woman moved or said anything. The vacuum ran on and was loud enough that the other cater waiters had not heard his tumble or the startled cry the maid emitted as he flew past her. When Frank had recovered, he hopped up, stuffed the magazine under his sweater, and tried to regain his balance. He smiled at the bewildered woman, as if to say "carry on" and then walked, as casually as he could, back to his bedroom, closing and locking the door.

Oh please God, he begged, leaning his back against the door and sliding down onto the floor. Please let her not speak English. Please don't let any of the cater waiters speak Spanish. Please God, please!

Maybe, he thought, he should pay her off. Yes. Summon her into the bedroom and offer her money to keep quiet. That would do it. Oh, but if she didn't speak English how would he explain? And besides, she'd just seen him dive like a crazy man after a porno magazine. Beckoning her to his bedroom would probably send her screaming for the front door.

The magazine was still under his sweater and its glossy cover now glued to his stomach with perspiration. He peeled it off and looked around the room for some safe place to hide it. Under the bed was too obvious, surely someone would look there first and he'd seen enough detective shows to know that nothing was safe between the mattress and box springs. No, not even inside the fabric of the mattress. He went to the closet and stepped inside, but the pathetic irony of that struck him almost immediately and he stepped back out. He thought of ripping the magazine into tiny shreds and then flushing them as he'd done with the note, but no, there wasn't time. People would be arriving any minute and what if it backed up the toilet? Imagine explaining that to the plumber! No, not the toilet, but where? After a few more minutes of frantic pacing, he returned to the closet and ripped a small hole in the lining of one of his coats. He rolled the magazine into a tight cylinder, slipped it through the hole, and then let it unroll, manipulating it until it lay flat between the lining and the outer fabric. When he was satisfied, he straightened the coats and closed the closet door.

Again, for a moment he paused and thought how ridiculous he was being. How stupid it all was. He was about to laugh—or cry, when the doorbell rang. He rolled his shoulders and took a series of deep breaths (and another shot of brandy). Then he checked his appearance in the mirror, practiced his happy party smile a few times, and stepped out the door to greet his guests.

In half an hour the house was full of people and the party was progressing nicely. Frank was glad to have his duties as host to take his mind off his troubles. He greeted everyone enthusiastically as they arrived and made sure they got a drink and some food. When the stream of new arrivals began to slow, Frank grabbed two bottles of champagne and made his way around the room, refilling glasses and chatting as he went. When the bottles ran out he approached the bar to get two more, but the bartender was so busy Frank couldn't get his attention. He remembered that there were extra bottles in the kitchen refrigerator so he headed that way. He pushed open the door and saw a group of waiters all huddled in a circle listening intently to Jason. Frank was far enough away that they couldn't see him, but he was also too far to hear what they were saying. Suddenly, they all started laughing, as if at the punchline of a joke. One of them noticed Frank and nudged another. The nudging went on until four of the five caterers had been nudged and were all looking back at him with guilty grins. The last to see him was the joketeller himself: Jason. He turned slowly, and gave what Frank interpreted as a defiant look. Frank turned and left the kitchen.

Of course he's told them! Frank thought, a blush suffusing his face and his panic returning. Yes, they'd all had a good laugh about it! Soon it would undoubtedly be the talk of the party. It would spread through the crowd like food poisoning, infecting everyone faster than a plate of rotten hors d'oeuvres and there was nothing he could do about it. Or was there . . . He opened his wallet and counted the bills. He'd have to tip all of the waiters an astronomical amount to keep their mouths shut, that much was certain. Either that, or find a way to fit them all into the soccer-player book, which he supposed he could do if he absolutely had to.

Frank's paranoid mind ran on, leaping from one wild thought to the next. He set down the bottles and stood against the wall, wringing his hands in a cinematic gesture of despair. Everyone seemed to be staring at him. He dropped his arms to his sides and tried to regain his composure by taking deep breaths and smiling. It didn't work so he grabbed two glasses of champagne from the tray of a passing waiter and quickly gulped one down. Then he inched into the shadow of the Christmas tree so that he was out of sight and could consider his position. After a few minutes he concluded that he would just have to do another book, that's all there was to it. A book of cater waiters. He looked around at the black-suited men carrying trays and tried to imagine them shirtless. No, that wasn't enough. They would have to be clad in nothing but small aprons, their biceps and shoulders flexing as they held trays of glasses aloft. No, that would never work. It was too mundane, too banal. It lacked exoticism. He might as well do a book of accountants or retail staff. He moved farther into the shadows and tried to think of some other solution. This time, all he came up with was defiance. He resolved that he would not give in to their blackmail (for in Frank's feverish mind that is what it had become). He would counteract the rumors and show them that the gossip wasn't true, make them see that Jason had lied, or at the very least, exaggerated. And he would do it publicly. Right that very evening. He scanned the crowd from his post behind the Christmas tree, looking over the young men and trying to select the most fabulous one. He knew he should go after Jason, the ringleader, and seduce him into silence, but in the long run that probably wouldn't work. Jason would give in, he was sure, but he would still expect some modeling work in exchange, and if he didn't get it then the threats and snickering would start up again and he'd be ruined.

* * *

Rodya arrived at Evan's forty-five minutes late. He had been dressed and ready to go for over three hours but made himself wait until nearly seven o'clock before leaving. When he finally did arrive, his stalling tactics continued; he lingered over the pre-party cocktail Evan gave him, asked at length about the furnishings and pictures. Finally, Evan said, "As much as I'm enjoying this we really better walk on over to Frank's if we want to get any food at all."

Rodya looked at his watch. "Five more minutes."

Evan grumbled.

"Is it okay?" Rodya asked.

"Sure," Evan said. "But I don't get it. You were begging me to introduce you to Frank and now you don't seem to want to go to the party at all."

Rodya smiled. "No, I want to go, but I have plan."

"I don't understand," Evan said.

"Is okay. You don't have to understand. I have plan," he said, tapping the side of his head with his index finger.

"Hmmm," Evan said, sitting down again. "Don't you think that if you want to make a good impression as a potential apprentice it would make sense to arrive early?"

"No."

"No?"

"No. That is wrong way. I have reason," Rodya repeated, and then asked Evan about the upholstery on the sofa.

Rodya's reason was, as so much in his life, a matter of size. He wanted to make a big, rather than a favorable, first impression when he entered the party and the best way to do that, he reasoned, was to arrive when it was half over. At that point everyone that was going to arrive would have done so and no one would have left yet. Rodya's audience—a house full of liquor-lubricated gay men, most of whom were familiar with his movies—was sure to be a friendly one, and one that had, Evan assured him, been well-informed of his possible arrival. Heads were going to turn when he walked in and if enough of them did, then maybe Frank would take notice.

When Rodya and Evan finally did ring Frank's doorbell, it was nearly nine-thirty. There was no answer and they were just about to let themselves in when a breathless Jason whipped open the door, apologizing and asking them for their coats. When he recognized Rodya, he stopped speaking and became flustered. Rodya smiled with an inward feeling of satisfaction. He gave Jason his coat and, without waiting for Evan, walked down the hall toward the party noise. Just as he predicted, heads did turn when he walked into the room. Soon, several men were openly staring at him, but he was miffed that Frank did not appear to be among them.

"I hope he hasn't passed out already," Evan said, standing next to Rodya and scanning the crowd. "That wasn't really in your plan, was it?"

Rodya sneered.

A moment later Rodya spied Frank, standing by himself in the shadow of the Christmas tree.

"Is that him?" Rodya asked, nodding toward the tree.

"Where?"

"Over by the tree."

Evan squinted. "Yes, that's him, the little weirdo. What's he doing back there? Come on."

He took Rodya by the hand and approached the tree.

"Frank? That you back there?" Evan called.

"Uh, yes," Frank said, emerging and pretending to dust off his hands. "I was just, um, adjusting the lights."

"Uh huh, well, it looks great," Evan said. "Beautiful tree. And it seems like a very successful party."

"Thanks."

"Oh, no, thank *you*. We've been looking forward to it all day."

Evan put his arm around Rodya.

"Frank, I'd like you to meet my newest friend and your biggest admirer, Rodya. Rodya, this is our host, Frank Molloy."

Rodya locked eyes with Frank, and fixed him with his best smoldering gaze. He could tell by Frank's glassy expression that he was slightly drunk, but he seemed very interested.

"Evan's told me a lot about you," Frank said, extending his hand, "and from the way everyone is staring at us, I'd say your reputation precedes you."

Rodya looked out at the crowd with feigned indifference and then turned his attention back to Frank.

"Sir," Rodya said, clicking his heels together and making a formal bow. "Mine is pleasure. I am great admirer of your work. It has meant so much to me in my life."

Frank eyed him skeptically.

"You don't believe me, I can tell, but it is truth. As a boy growing up I loved your books. *Sandy Surfers* is what made me want to be photographer myself."

Frank gave him a polite smile.

Rodya then launched into the story about the young boy in dismal Russia discovering one of Frank's books, and how it changed his life. His flattery seemed to be working and Rodya assumed that surely it was because his brand of flattery was just different enough from the flattery Frank received from the legions of ambitious young men who wanted to appear in his books. Legions of ambitious young men who were, Rodya could tell from the hostile glares thrown his way, in abundance that night. Even that waiter, the one who had let them in the door earlier that evening, was hovering close to them, his mouth bent down in an envious frown. Rodya scowled at him, and then turned back to Frank, who was also looking at the waiter.

"There are many what want your attention tonight," Rodya said.

"Yes," Frank agreed, "it looks that way. And since it's my party I suppose I better spread myself around."

Then, instead of leaving, Frank linked arms with Rodya, grabbed a bottle of champagne from Jason, and marched into the crowd, leaving Evan and the bewildered waiter behind.

For the rest of the evening, Frank adhered himself to Rodya and paraded him around the house, introducing him to everybody. He gave hearty, exaggerated laughs in response to all of Rodya's jokes, and seemed to listen intently to everything Rodya had to say. Even better was the fact that again and again throughout the evening Frank led Rodya over to the doorframe from which he had hung the mistletoe, and then waited to be kissed. At first, Rodya knew, it was a joke, but as the night went on, the trips to the doorframe grew more numerous and the kisses more sensual. More alcohol was consumed and soon they gave up the pretense of mistletoe and circulated the room like some grotesque pair of Siamese twins joined at the mouth. About the only time Frank seemed to want to come up for air was to beckon Jason to bring them another bottle of champagne.

Things were going so well from Rodya's point of view that when Frank sauntered off to the bathroom, Rodya took the opportunity to approach Evan and whisper, "Don't wait for me. I don't think I'll be going home with you tonight."

"No," Evan sighed. "I didn't figure you would be. Go on, have fun."

The hour got later and the guests began to disperse, moving on to bars or dance clubs or home to their beds, until there was only the wait staff and a few very drunk people waiting for their cabs to arrive. As the host, Frank probably should have been up and about, saying goodbye to his guests, or thanking the caterers and giving them final instructions on the clean up. Instead, he was sitting on the couch, Rodya's legs intertwined with his, as they continued to explore the inner workings of each other's mouths. Guests came to say their goodbyes, saw the spectacle, and decided not to interrupt. Most of the waiters, too, kept a respectable distance, except for Jason, of course, who flitted about the room, pesky as a moth, collecting glasses and emptying ashtrays, peppering Frank with whispered questions about what he would like done with the leftovers, and with offers to stay on after the others had left and help push the furniture back into place. Without removing his face from Rodya's, Frank answered Jason's questions and patiently declined his offers of help. Then, seemingly annoyed by the intrusions, Frank turned to Rodya and whispered in his ear, just loudly enough for it to be heard by Jason. "Why don't we go up to my room?"

Rodya nodded. "I would like to, yes." He smiled at both men and then stood up, making no attempt to hide the large tent that was pitching in his trousers. Jason's eyes grew wide, but Frank's, Rodya noticed, were not even focused on his crotch but, rather, on Jason again. Rodya frowned. He pulled Frank up from the sofa and nudged him toward the stairwell, then he turned and narrowed his eyes at Jason.

As Frank followed Rodya up the stairs, Jason called out to him.

"Excuse me, um, Mr. Molloy."

Frank, his face in the shadows, turned and looked down at him. Rodya stopped and turned as well.

"Sorry to bother you, it's just, well, it's just that you said earlier tonight that you'd sign one of your books for me."

Frank smiled but did not descend into the light. "Oh yes, I did," he said, his voice full of faux forgetfulness. "Look, why don't you, well, hmm, why don't you leave your address downstairs by the phone. Yes, that'll work. I'll have my secretary send one over to you first thing on Monday morning. How does that sound?"

"Uh, okay, I guess," Jason replied, unable to mask his disappointment.

It was a disappointment that was, Rodya knew, entirely justified, since there was no secretary. He knew as much from his many attempts to contact Frank. He watched the boy head mournfully back to the kitchen (probably with the intent of spitting in the leftovers) and couldn't help feeling a little bit sorry for him.

The next morning, Frank was again awakened by ringing, although this time it was the doorbell and not the phone. He opened one eye and looked at the clock on the nightstand. Ten o'clock. He sat up and looked at the empty space next to him. Someone *had* been there, that much he could tell from the indentation in the pillow, but whoever it had been wasn't there now, and for that Frank was relieved. He scanned the bedroom floor for strange clothes, but didn't see any. Nor was there anyone in his bathroom, the door of which was wide open. He shook his head, and tried to collate the events from the night before. Had the trick said good/bye? Frank tried to remember. He could feel the tightness in the middle of his head, a forewarning, like clouds on the horizon, of the headache and misery that were sure to come.

The doorbell rang again. He got up, put on his robe, and then did notice an unfamiliar-looking pile of clothes on the floor. They were black, which is the color he'd been wearing last night, but then everyone had been wearing black. He picked them up and examined them and saw that, yes, they were his clothes but had looked foreign because he had just purchased them the day before. The doorbell rang again. Maybe it was Robby or Roger or whatever his name was. Maybe he'd forgotten something. Oh, God, he hoped not. Frank knew he'd probably have to face him eventually but hopefully not until this hangover was gone. A thought occurred to him and his pulse increased. He looked at his watch. It was ten o'clock—the time Al usually arrived. But it was Saturday. There wasn't any UPS delivery on Saturday. No, it couldn't be Al. But maybe . . . As he made his way down the hallway, a hopeful spring in his step, he felt just the tiniest pang of guilt for what had happened last night. Strangely, he did not feel at all guilty for having enticed Rodya (yes, that had been his name) into bed because, once there, the encounter had been, so far as he could remember, fairly innocuous. Frank had not been attracted to him so once he had satisfied his curiosity and seen the sight that everyone had been talking about, he had turned over and pretended to pass out. It had been interesting to see, no denying that, so big and vast, but to him it had seemed like the Grand Canyon or Mount Everest: big, and impressive, but somehow stupid and unmanageable.

No, Frank did not really feel guilty about the sex, but he was ashamed of all the lies he had told and enacted to get it, and of the vehement and very public denial of all of his feelings for Al. Feelings that were, his remorse told him, very real and true. As more details from the night before came trickling back to him, Frank's shame increased. With the morning-after clarity only a hangover can give, he saw how paranoid and stupid he had been, and he wondered where all the panic of the previous evening had come from. Could it really have been from that note and the magazine? Both incidents seemed remote and silly to him; so trivial when compared to the giddy, contented way he felt just then, as he peered through the peephole and saw that it *was* Al who had been ringing the bell.

Frank opened the door. Since it was the weekend, Al was out of uniform, but his Saturday stubble and flannel shirt made him look even more burly and attractive. The dainty basket he held in one hand seemed somehow out of place.

"Good morning," Al said, grabbing Frank with his free arm and pulling him into an embrace. Al gave him several rapid kisses and then one long, slow one, before releasing him. He took a step back and looked Frank up and down.

"I've brought some breakfast," Al said, pointing to the basket. "Can I come in?"

"Yes, please!" Frank said, grabbing his hand and pulling him inside.

They kissed in the foyer and Frank grew almost feverish with excitement as he felt Al's large body press into him, and his rough hands as they traveled up and under his sweatshirt.

"Maybe we'd better slow down," Al said, pulling away. "We've got all day to do this and we'd better fortify ourselves first."

Frank sighed, gave Al another kiss, and then another and another. Laughing, Al pushed him away and headed down the hallway to the kitchen, Frank following like an eager puppy.

"Must have been a big dinner party," Al said, gesturing at the rows of clean glasses on the counter, waiting to be put away.

"Uh, yes," Frank said, scanning the scene for any damning evidence, a guilty feeling coming over him again. "It was a work thing. I do it every year. Have a little party, that is. For the people I work with."

Al nodded.

"And was it a success? Did everyone go home happy?"

"Uh, yes. I think so. To tell you the truth I had too much to drink so I'm not feeling all that great this morning."

Al came up behind him and encircled him in his arms.

"You feel alright to me," he said, running his hands up and down Frank's chest.

Frank turned and kissed him again.

"You just sit down," Al said, leading him over to one of the kitchen chairs. "I'll unpack the breakfast, we'll eat it, and then we can spend the whole afternoon in bed."

While Frank sat and watched, Al set the table and then began pulling food out of the basket, humming as he did so. There were toasted slices of panetone, melon wrapped in prosciutto, and a thermos full of fresh-squeezed orange juice. Al had just finished setting everything out when the door of the hall bathroom opened and Rodya emerged. He was showered and dressed and smiling the same naughty, feline smile he'd exercised so much the night before. But this time, Frank didn't see it. In fact, Frank didn't see or hear Rodya at all. His back was to the hallway, and his adoring gaze was on Al, so by the time he saw Al's expression change and turned to see what had caused it, it was too late. Rodya had pounced. He seized Frank's head in both his hands and kissed him on the mouth, firmly, in the manner the French are purported to do. Then he released him, smiled at them both, sat down in Al's seat and put Al's napkin on his lap.

"This looks like one of best morning-after breakfasts I ever have," he said, picking up the knife and fork and cutting into a piece of the ham-wrapped melon. "I didn't know you had house man." Then, addressing Al, Rodya said, "It all looks great, my friend, but is there some coffee?"

Frank couldn't speak. Indeed, what could he have said? He rose slowly from his chair and stared, open-mouthed at both of them. Initially, Al's expression as he watched Rodya eating had been one of perplexity. But then he looked over at Frank, saw the guilty expression on his face and his shoulders fell. He shook his head and just looked away.

In a panic, Frank tried to think of something to say, some way to explain or deny the situation, but before he could say anything Al spoke: "It seems you've still got a guest from last night," he said, putting his coat back on and picking up his keys. "I'm sorry I intruded."

Calmly, he left the kitchen and walked down the hall. Frank followed after him. When they reached the front door, Frank blocked it and said, "Wait! I can explain!" He couldn't, of course, but wasn't that what one was supposed to say in situations like this?

"Don't," Al said, picking him up by the shoulders and moving him to the side. "Don't you even try." Then, as he'd done so many times before, he opened the door and went down the walkway. The ground was covered in snow and Frank had nothing on his feet. Nevertheless, he ran down the walk toward Al's rusting Subaru parked next to the curb. Al got in the driver's side but Frank wouldn't let him close the door. He stood there looking down at him, not wanting to let him go but unable to say anything that would make him reconsider. He was still in his underwear and he knew he must look ridiculous, hopping from one foot to the other, trying to keep his feet from freezing. Al started the car.

"Look, I'm sorry!" Frank whined. "It was stupid. I was stupid."

"I'll grant you that much."

"Can't we talk it over?"

Al gave a bitter laugh. "No, we can't. And what could you possibly say?"

Frank said nothing. Al pushed his sunglasses up on his forehead and glared at Frank.

"I'll talk now. You listen," Al said, his voice reedy with sarcastic sincerity. "I really want to thank you. Thank you for all the wasted afternoons together. Thank you for pretending to listen to all I had to say and for pretending to take an interest in me. Thank you for making me fall in love with you and then fucking with my heart. Thank you for making me think you were different from all the other assholes out there. Oh, you had me fooled for a while but you're no different. No, wait a minute, that's not true. You're probably worse. Maybe the worst ever. But most of all I really want to thank you for having such shitty, shitty timing! If that boy in there needs a job, other than the kind that involves blowing, you should think of hiring him as your secretary because you have got some serious scheduling problems. In addition to all of your many, many other problems, that is. Merry fucking Christmas."

Al then put the car in gear and pulled away.

Late the following afternoon, Frank sat by the window, impatiently waiting for Al to arrive. He'd been waiting all day and had lain awake all night, thinking about what he would say. Frank was certain that Al *would* come today. He'd made sure of it by calling UPS that morning and telling them he had a package that he needed to have picked up to be overnighted. Al would have to come. Frank had also been ordering a lot lately, and he usually received most of his deliveries on Mondays. Al might be able to avoid delivering them for a day or two but eventually he'd have to come and when he did, well, Frank would probably still not know what to say. He'd tried and tried to think up excuses for his behavior, but, somewhere around three A.M., he'd realized the futility of it. Lying and denying the facts had gotten him into the mess. More lying would probably just make it worse. He resolved to try to explain about the note and the magazine and the gossiping catering waiters; he would tell him that he'd had too much to drink and explain his fears of having his desires come to light. Maybe Al would understand.

As the sun was setting, Frank heard the truck arrive. He checked his appearance in the mirror, did one final silent rehearsal of what he would say, and then waited for the doorbell to ring. When it did, he opened the door. The brown packages were there, and so was the brown uniform, but in it was not big, dark-haired Al, but a fair and slender girl! Frank was too shocked to speak.

"Got some packages here for you to sign for," the girl said, setting them down on the porch and handing him the electronics board she'd had wedged under her arm.

"But, um, you're not the usual delivery ma—, uh, person," Frank said.

"No," she replied. "I just got assigned this route this morning. Kind of a pain in the ass so close to Christmas. I've got a full load and not much idea where I'm going with it." She took the board back from him. "It says here you've got an overnighter, too, that right?"

"Where's Al? He's not sick, is he?"

"Huh?"

"Al," Frank repeated. "The guy who used to have this route."

"Don't know. I've got this route till at least after Christmas. That's all I know. Look, I don't mean to rush you but if you've got that overnighter . . ."

Realizing that she either didn't know, or wasn't going to say anything, Frank told her the package wasn't ready and sent her on her way. He closed the door and left all of his packages on the porch. Then he went straight to the phone in his office and called UPS to find out what had happened to Al. The call was a waste of time since, as the woman on the other end of the line told him, they "don't give out confidential information about employees, especially not to someone who doesn't even know the last name of the good friend he's asking about."

Frank was about to argue further when the doorbell rang again. It was probably that girl, bringing yet another package of his junk that she'd found lodged in one of the recesses of the truck, but maybe it was Al. He hung up the phone and ran down the hall to the front door. It was Rodya.

Frank had sent him home as soon as he'd returned to the house from his street scene with Al. By comparison the scene with Rodya had been anticlimactic. Frank told him calmly, but firmly, that something had come up and that he'd better leave. He promised he would call him later. Rodya had nodded, seemingly unfazed. He took a business

card from his wallet, handed it to Frank, and then left. Frank hadn't
called, didn't even remember what he'd done with the card. Rodya had
called him several times that day, but Frank had put him off each
time, saying he was waiting for a call and would call him back. Now
there he was, standing on the front porch, looking gravely at Frank.

"I'm sorry," Frank started. "I was going to call you back bu—"

"No, you weren't," Rodya interrupted. "Don't say that lie. You were
never going to call me back so I came to you. I'm coming in. Do you
want me to bring boxes with me, or leave them here."

Too depressed to even argue, Frank shrugged, turned and walked
down the hall to the kitchen. Rodya brought the boxes in and followed
him. Frank poured himself a scotch and offered one to Rodya, who declined it with a wave of his hand.

"I was confused at first," Rodya said, "but I thinked it over last night
and now it make sense. I mean, I was there at party and saw everything, but it took me time to put it all together."

"I don't know what you mean," Frank said, taking a big sip of his
drink. Rodya smiled, and narrowed his eyes.

"I mean," he said, "that you were not interested in me the night of
the party."

Frank groaned and stared at the boy. Could he really be concerned
about that? Was he that vain?

"It was late," Frank sighed. "I was tired."

"Please!" Rodya scoffed. "No one, even no one your age, is too tired
for sex with porn star."

Frank laughed. "Maybe you're just not my type."

"I am everybody's type. At least everybody your age. And everybody
except those people what like women, or what like . . . other things."

A little electrical surge of anxiety ran through Frank's body at the
mention of "other things," but he hid it well and turned to refill his
glass. They were silent, Rodya staring at him intently.

"Then there was way you acted at party . . ." Rodya said.

"The way I acted?"

"Yes. You don't know me but you grab me and take me all around
like your own little dog. Something happened during party and you
changed your mind. What happened? I asked myself that question last
night and I think I finally figure it out. I have lots of, how you say when

you are knowing and seeing things that the other people aren't knowing and seeing?"

"Perception?"

"Perception," Rodya repeated, trying out the new word. "Perception.
Yes, I have perception for you and what happened. I figure out what
was going on."

Frank didn't believe, or for that matter, really understand him, so he
sipped his drink calmly and waited to see what else the boy would say.
He was probably just fishing, bluffing, trying to get him to slip up and
confess. Well, he wasn't going to do that. Not yet.

"Why don't we go into the other room," Frank said, hopping off the
counter and heading for the door. "The light's nicer. We can plug in
the tree and turn on the fire."

Again, Rodya followed, taking the bottle of scotch with him. They
sat on the couch, the same couch on which they'd made a spectacle of
themselves less than forty-eight hours before, but this time they sat
farther apart.

"Then I see man at breakfast yesterday," Rodya said, continuing the
conversation from the kitchen. Again the nervous electricity shot
through Frank, although this time it was followed by a wave of sadness
as he remembered Al's expression.

"And I know that something is strange. Something is upset."

"I thought you'd left," Frank said, unsure if he should sound ac-
cusatory or apologetic.

"Yes, that much I knowed. But I didn't leave. I was standing in bathroom rehearsing what I was going to say to you."

"Rehearsing?"

"Yes."

"But why? For what?"

"I was rehearsing how to ask you for job. Rehearsing to ask you to let
me be your helper. Your apprentice."

"Look, I don't ne—"

"I know. I know. We already talked about it, but you were too drunk
to remember. You said 'no.' You said 'I work alone, like wolf. I don't
want apprentice.' I hear you. But I want to be one. I want to be yours.
I want you to teach me. So I decide I would try one more time. I would
seduce you and make you want me. Then I could get what I wanted,

but when I came out and kissed you that morning I knew something was wrong. Something was wrong even night before when you pretended to be too drunk, but I was little drunk myself and I didn't see it so clearly then."

Frank remained expressionless, but got up from the sofa and went and stood by the mantel. It was as if they were playing that childhood game of picking some object in the room and telling the other person they were either getting warmer or colder depending on how close they got to it. Rodya was definitely getting warmer and the heat was making Frank uncomfortable.

"That big man," Rodya said, making a circle in front of him with his arms, "he was your lover?"

Frank blanched, and then lied.

"No, of course not."

"You are still lying again," Rodya said. "That doesn't make sense. He made you wonderful breakfast and got mad because we slept together. Only other people who might do both those things is your dad or your mom, and he wasn't them."

Frank said nothing. Rodya stared at him, smiling.

"I told you I have it all figured out, didn't I? Do I have to do this?"

Still, Frank said nothing. Rodya got up, grabbed the scotch bottle, and refilled Frank's glass.

"The party was good," Rodya said, easing back into the sofa. "Everybody enjoy themself, I think. Even Evan got lucky. Can you believe? He picked up catering waiter. The blond one, Jason."

Frank dropped his glass. Rodya got up calmly and walked to the kitchen. Frank did not move. He stared down at the puddle around his feet and watched as a rivulet of scotch went across the floor and into the fireplace. His one hope just then was that the alcohol was undiluted enough to ignite and burn him up before Rodya returned. It did not. Rodya returned with a roll of paper towels and knelt down to clean it up.

"You like fat men, Frank," Rodya said, collecting the pieces of ice and putting them back in the glass. "Is not important. In my country many people are that way. Big, I mean. Some people love them, some people don't. Who knows why or why not. Who cares?"

Frank was still unable to say anything. Rodya stood up again and took the wad of paper towels to the kitchen. When he returned, it was with a glass full of water. He sat on the sofa, patted the cushion next to him and beckoned Frank over.

"How old are you?" Rodya asked.

"Why?" Frank asked.

"Just tell me."

"I'm in my forties."

"Uh huh. Well that's about halfway, yes? Probably more than half." Frank ran his finger nervously around the rim of the glass.

"What I wonder, Frank, is how long you going to wait. I feel like I already wasted too much time and I'm younger than you. When do you start to get what you want?"

"I have what I want," Frank protested, but then to his dismay his eyes filled with tears and his face grew hot. He knew he was turning red again but this time it was not from embarrassment but from a rush of emotion. Again his body was betraying him, the same way it had with his desires. Why was he still trying to hide what he really felt and wanted? The only one there was the boy and he knew everything. Who was he trying to fool?

As he sat crying, Frank was reminded of a time as a child when he was accused of stealing some chocolates from a box destined for an ailing relative. The chocolate was all over his face and hands but still he attempted to deny it.

Rodya handed him a tissue. "In Russia we have expression for right now. 'The ice have thawed and the river is starting to flow.' "

For the next half-hour, Frank drank more scotch and confided in Rodya. He told him all about his long crush on Al and the months of superfluous catalogue ordering leading up to the spectacular sexual consummation. Then he told him about the relationship that had developed in the weeks following their first encounter and all the things he liked about Al—his opera singing and knowledge of music and art and architecture. He told him about how they used to lie in bed in the afternoons and plot out their Italian adventures—the lives they would lead when they had enough money and courage, and how slowly, those plots had begun to intertwine and they had imagined having adventures together. Then he told him about the note and the magazine, and explained how he had panicked. How in an instant he had forgotten about all the good things and rushed back to prop up the façade he'd felt sure was about to topple over on him.

"Oh, if only I hadn't been so stupid!" Frank cried, smacking his forehead with his palm and pacing the room. "Just stupid! I know now how much he means to me and I don't even know where to find him so that I can tell him. If I could, I'd beg for another chance, I'd tell him I love him. Hell, I'd tell the world that I love him and not be a bit embarrassed about it. At least I think I would. I'd try to anyway. Then we'd both go to Italy. He could study and sing and I could do my work. Real work! Not this shit I've been grinding out. Yes, I could start over. I could really start living. It's not too late yet, is it? I'm not too old. Am I too old? Maybe it is too late."

"Look, your work is not shit and it's not too late," Rodya assured him. "Is never too late."

"Oh but it is," Frank sighed and fell drunkenly into a chair. "And it's my own fault. I've made my lonely bed and now I have to lie in it."

They sat in silence for a moment. Rodya leaned to the edge of his chair and rubbed his hands together, staring into the fire. An idea perched in his brain.

"What if . . . ?" he started, and then stopped himself.

"What if what?"

"What if I could find him?" Rodya asked.

Frank looked up, an annoyed expression on his face.

"Don't look at me with that voice," Rodya said. "I'm serious. What if I play like detective and find him. Then I explain for you, tell him what you just said, how you feel; tell him why you did what you did. Would that be good thing?"

"Oh, that would be a very good thing," Frank concurred, "but it's not going to happen. I told you I tried to find him already. I don't even know his last name. How bad is that? I didn't even bother to find out his last name."

"But what if I could find him for you? You'd be pretty grateful, yes?"

"Yes," Frank replied softly, imagining what it would be like to have him back. "Yes, I would be very grateful."

"Then I will try," Rodya said. "I will try and find him for you, Frank, and if I do, will you promise to do something for me?"

Frank knew what this was leading up to.

"You want me to hire you."

"That is it, yes. I want to learn from you. You don't even have to pay me. Well, maybe a little, but not that much. Most of the work I would do for free. What do you have to lose? I find him, you have me as cheap labor. I don't find him, you don't hire me, and I never bother you again. No joking."

Frank considered it. He really did not want, or need, an assistant. He would gladly give Rodya a job as a model, but teach him what he knew? That was something else. He had seen *All About Eve*, he knew to mistrust fawning protégés, and this one seemed especially conniving, but really, what were the boy's chances of finding Al? Slim, at best, but if he did, well, then he'd have a new boyfriend and a new assistant. And maybe that wouldn't be so bad.

"All right," Frank said, "bring him back so I can have a second chance, and I'll give you a job."

The next morning Rodya got up, got dressed, and stepped out of his apartment ready to begin sleuthing. Like all good gumshoe detectives, at the beginning of a search he did not have a lot to go on and as he waited in line at the coffee shop he wondered what he had gotten himself into.

Earlier that morning he had, in spite of what Frank had told him, called UPS and inquired about the man that had the route delivering to Frank's address. He was hoping, if nothing else, to get Al's last name. Then it would be as simple as entering it in Google or going down to the driver's license office and finding his address. Like Frank, he was hampered by the fact that UPS employees in the week before Christmas do not have a lot of time to answer the vague and seemingly frivolous questions of amateur detectives. His accent, too, with its Boris and Natasha connotations, aroused suspicion, and made people even more reluctant to release any information they might have had.

"Listen," the impatient woman in the UPS personnel department told him, "you call me up asking a lot of questions about someone you don't even really know yourself, what do you expect?"

"Please. It's important. He's not in trouble. I will make him happy. I will make three people happy if I can find him. Can't you tell me anything?"

The woman paused before responding.

"I can tell you that the man I think you're asking about doesn't work for UPS anymore, but that's about all I can tell you."

"Can't you even tell me his last name?" Rodya begged.

"I'm afraid I can't release that information, sir. It's company policy."

"Please!"

"I'm sorry, sir. It's company policy."

Next, Rodya had turned to the Yellow Pages to pursue the professional angle. He looked up music schools, and narrowed them down to those that taught opera, but his search was even more fruitless than UPS. None of the proprietresses or instructors recognized Al from the WANTED poster he had made up, and Al was not, because of his size, one that was easy to miss or forget.

"He certainly looks like an opera singer," clucked one dowdy teacher after examining the poster, "but I haven't seen him. Maybe you should try the Opera Companies. It's worth a shot."

It was indeed, so Rodya went to one of the opera companies to see if anyone there had seen Al. As he drove up he smiled as he read on the marquee that they were doing *The Magic Flute*. Smiled because that had also been the title of one of his earliest cinematic efforts and he hoped it was a good omen. It was not. He spoke to one of the stage managers, showed him the picture, but the man shook his head.

"Why are you asking so many questions?" he demanded. "He in some kind of trouble?"

"No, no," Rodya assured him, "nothing like that."

"Well, it seems strange you coming around here with that accent and all, showing his picture around and asking a lot of questions."

As Rodya left, he smiled again. He was beginning to like the idea of himself as an international spy, especially when he imagined the man's reaction if he had told him the real story:

"Not to worry, comrade, he's in no trouble. No, he has chubby chaser

photographer who is in love with him. I have to find him—fat guy in pic-
ture—so that photographer will give me job. We have bargain, you see: if
I find fat man, photographer will have chance to fix for being such an
asshole and I'll get to be apprentice. It doesn't sound like great job, I
know, but I really want it because I'm getting too old for pornography
and want to have stability. 'Why do I want to leave porn?' you ask. Well,
porn was good to me while it lasted. It was. But I can't do it forever, you
know? So that's why I got to find him."

In the evenings, Rodya and Evan went around to various bars in
town and passed out the WANTED posters. Most guys didn't recognize
him. Some said he looked familiar but further probing revealed that
they were thinking of Fred Flintstone or James Gandolfini.

At one of the last bars, the bartender, like most of the others, said he
hadn't seen him but suggested they return on Tuesday evening because "that's when they all meet here."

"They?" Rodya queried.

"The Girth and Mirths."

"The what?"

"It's a club. Sort of brings together fat guys and guys who like fat
guys. They meet here once a month. Maybe the guy you're looking for
will be there."

"Tuesday night, eh?"

"Yeah. I think they're having a Christmas party this week."

At the appointed hour on Tuesday, Rodya and Evan planned to re-
turn to the bar. Rodya would have preferred to go without Evan but he
persisted, saying, "Are you kidding? I wouldn't miss this for anything.
There really is a little subculture for everything. It's all research,
Rodya. Someday I'll use this little hunt as part of a doctoral thesis in
Queer Studies."

Evan was pokey about choosing an outfit and, as Rodya sat on the
bed waiting for him, he had to listen to several feeble jokes.

"I usually wear black to parties because it's so slimming but I guess

I really don't need to worry about that tonight. In fact, maybe I'll wear these pants precisely because they *do* make my butt look big. What do you think about that?"

"I think we're going to be late," Rodya said, tapping the face of his watch.

"You're probably right. I bet there won't be a thing left on the buffet table."

When they arrived at the bar, they were greeted by a heavy-set older man in a Santa Claus outfit around whom a host of skinny elves were twittering like parakeets. In fact, the room was full of Santas and elves, most of whom were out on the dance floor.

"I know who *you* are," Santa said, giving a knowing wink to Rodya, but then he turned to Evan, sized him up and down and said, "but you look like a new boy."

Evan blushed. Rodya pulled out the picture of Al and showed it to the Doorman Santa.

"Have you ever seen this guy? Does he come here? Is he here now?" Rodya asked hopefully.

Santa lifted his glasses and brought the photograph close to his face, studying it and thinking. "I've never seen him," he said, "but then I don't usually notice the other chubs. Ask some of the chasers, they'd probably be able to tell you more. Try talking to Truck and Trailer."

Rodya and Evan looked confused.

"They're over there," the Santa said, "by the bar."

Rodya's eyes followed where the man was pointing. Next to the bar stood a tall, muscular, heavily tattooed man. In one hand, he held a drink, and his free arm was around the shoulder of a man of girth who was staring, gape-mouthed, at Rodya. He nudged the tattooed one in the arm and pointed in their direction. Rodya approached.

"Are you . . . Truck?" he asked. The tattooed one lit a cigarette and looked at him suspiciously.

"Yes, he is," the heavy-set man replied, then he turned to Truck and said. "Relax, honey, he's not the police. But he did play one very convincingly in *Nightstick Interrogation*. I still love that movie!" he said, bringing his hand to his chest. "I love all your movies. I own every one on DVD."

Rodya smiled, as graciously as he could. He felt like telling the man that he wasn't getting a cent of royalties from DVD sales since he had stupidly taken a one-time payment, but then reconsidered and thanked him instead.

"The name's Truck," the tattooed one interjected, sticking his cigarette between his teeth and thrusting one of his large, calloused hands at Rodya. Then, nodding at the other man, he said, "And this here's Trailer."

"Pleased to meet you," Trailer said, giggling shyly. "Are you a fan of big men?"

Rodya hesitated.

"Answer the man," Evan prodded.

"Uh, I am fan of men with big . . . hearts," he said, and then quickly changed the subject. "Tell me how you get your names?"

Truck took a drag of his cigarette and then stubbed it out.

"Truck's my real name," he said, thumping his chest. "We call him Trailer on account of his size, and 'cause when we first met we were always hitched together, if you know what I mean." Truck snorted, giving a wink and a thrust of his hips. "At least that's what we like to tell people. Makes for a nice story."

"Charming," Evan added.

"But the truth is," Truck said, cupping his hand around his mouth, "his name's Taylor. I was just real drunk the night we met and slurred it into Trailer. It kinda stuck, if you know what I mean."

"Are you going to be coming out with any new movies anytime soon?" Trailer asked hopefully.

"I am retired from movies soon," Rodya said. "I'm going to be photographer now, but I need your help," he said, reaching in his coat pocket for Al's picture.

"Now why should we help you go into retirement?" Trailer demanded.

Rodya gave a tired sigh.

"Answer your fans," Evan prodded. Rodya scowled at him.

"Because," Rodya said, forcing a smile and wishing he'd gone to the bar before they'd started this conversation, "is right thing to do. It will make me happy, yes, but more important, it will make two guys just like you happy."

He then recited his oft-told tale of Al and Frank, the star-crossed lovers. He was getting to be quite an accomplished raconteur and played up the drama and pathos of the story so well that tongues were clicked disapprovingly when he described Frank's fear-driven actions, and eyes misted up when he told of current sadness and remorse.

"So will you help him?" Rodya asked, showing them Al's picture. "Have you ever seen this guy?"

Truck took the picture and examined it.

"Whoowee!" he whistled, "Wish I had seen 'im. This here's one fine-looking man!"

Trailer snatched the picture away and glared at it.

"We've never seen him before," he said, and handed the picture back to Rodya. "But," he added, giving Truck a playful punch in the stomach, "my faithful wife here will sure be on the lookout for you."

For the next half-hour Rodya circulated among the other patrons showing them the picture and asking if they'd ever seen Al. None had, so he decided to leave some of the WANTED posters and go home. He found Evan to take him home, but Evan was having far too much fun being the "new boy" and didn't want to go, so Rodya left him on his own.

The next morning, Christmas Eve, Rodya stayed in bed until almost noon. He'd been awake since seven but had resolved not to get out of bed until he had devised another strategy for finding Al. But where else could he look? he wondered. All-you-can-eat buffets? Big-and-Tall clothing stores? And it was Christmas Eve, a day most people spent with their friends and families and lovers, which was probably what Al was doing. Rodya had no family, the two aunts who had raised him having died years ago, but he did have friends, and he was expected at their house that evening, gifts in hand. Gifts he had not yet purchased because he'd been too busy hunting for Al. He knew he should forget about Al and Frank for the day and get out of bed and join all the other last-minute shoppers, but he could not stop thinking about them.

Maybe Al Whatever-His-Last-Name-Was had gone by now. Maybe he had just followed his desire, quit his job and gone to Italy. If he had,

Rodya wished him luck. And maybe, Rodya thought, he would have to do something similar—go out and find someplace else to learn, someone else to learn from. It was an idea that depressed him. He had always wanted to learn from the one he regarded as a master in his field. And even after seeing what a mess Frank Molloy was, he did not feel differently. On the contrary: the messier he discovered Frank's personal life to be, the more he admired the man's skill in creating worlds of such beauty and perfection. He wanted that apprenticeship now more than ever, but somehow he knew that if he did not find Al, he would have to abandon that dream. Frank was not the type to give points for effort. Probably he would want to bury the whole embarrassing episode, and for that, Rodya didn't really blame him. The whole hunt had been preposterous—like looking for a tiny piece of jewelry lost on a beach. Granted, this had been a large jewel, but that had not made the task of finding it any easier.

After he'd eaten something, had his coffee, and dressed, Rodya forced himself to go shopping. The thought of going to a shopping mall depressed him and he was already depressed enough so he stuck to small stores that were not conveniently bunched together. He took his camera with him and dawdled most of the day, taking pictures of the decorations and the shoppers, and by late afternoon his spirits had lifted somewhat, but he still had not finished his shopping. He put away the camera for a few hours and focused on buying gifts, finding the last one just as the shops were closing. He was happy then, and knew he should rush home, wrap the presents and go over to his friend's house, but again he dawdled, looking at all the decorations and enjoying the singing.

The singing. There was something about it. It was not one of the traditional canned Christmas songs he'd been bombarded with for the past month. No, it was one he'd not heard before and from what he could tell it was not recorded. He followed the sound down the street. An old man in a Santa suit was standing on the corner singing, a basket on the ground in front of him to collect any spare change people might throw his way.

Rodya squinted. Maybe it was, he thought. But no, it couldn't be. He got up, collected his packages and hurried down the street. He slowed down as he approached, and tried to look casual. At first, it was not easy to tell for sure that it was Al, obscured as he was behind the white wig and whiskers, but as Rodya got closer he saw that the tummy was not a prosthetic. He listened again and was able to discern that the man was singing in Italian. When he finished his song, Rodya approached. He took out one of the WANTED pamphlets and handed it to him.

"Is that you?" he asked.

Al looked at the photo, looked up at Rodya, and his whiskers drooped into a frown.

"What do you want?" Al asked, and from his tone it was clear that he remembered Rodya from the ill-fated breakfast. Rodya could not conceal his delight.

"It is you!" he cried, grabbing Al in an embrace and twirling him around on the sidewalk. "I have almost given up hope and now here you are!" Then he did a little dance on the sidewalk, pulled out his camera and began gleefully taking photographs. Al stood stiffly, while the crowd that had been listening to him sing, now stood watching the spectacle and pitying poor "Santa" for having to deal with all the downtown loonies. Once the crowd moved on, Al spoke up.

"Look, I don't know what you're doing but I wish you'd stop. If this is some way for you to gloat over last weekend, that's a pretty mean thing to do."

"No, friend, no! I have look for you for all week! Seven days I go up and around the city. I look everywhere. I am like smart men following star, except I have no star, no last name, nothing, and still I find you!"

As if in response to Bing's ceaseless repetition of what he had been dreaming about, it started to snow. Al grumbled and began collecting the bills and change from the basket.

"This will be happy Christmas," Rodya said. "for all of us!"

Excitedly, he reached in his pocket, retrieved his cell phone, and dialed his friends.

"Guess what?" he said. "Never in million years will you guess. No. No. I found him! Yes! Just now. I give up hope and then I find him! Yes. No, you're right. I forget about that. I think I'll be late. Maybe I not see you until tomorrow. Yes, yes, still work to do," he said, and hung up.

His friends, who had been privy to the saga, had raised an interesting point and one that he had, in fact, forgotten: in addition to finding Al, Rodya also needed to persuade him to see Frank and he was alarmed to realize that he really didn't have a plan to do so. He'd been so busy just trying to find him that he hadn't considered what to do once he actually did.

"There was," Rodya began, addressing Al, "how you say, misunderstanding last weekend."

Al gave a bitter laugh and began walking down the street. Rodya collected his bags and packages from the sidewalk and followed him, struggling to keep up.

"I don't think there was anything about last week that I didn't understand," Al replied. "If anything, it was all a little too clear."

"It was, and it wasn't," Rodya said. "I can explain. I didn't know anything was between you two other morning."

Al stopped abruptly and turned around. "And Frank?" he demanded. "Didn't he know?"

"Frank, uh, yes," Rodya assented. "He knowed. But he was confused in his mind. He was scared. He was coward. He's sorry."

"I bet!" Al said and began walking again. He turned the corner and approached his Subaru. Tucked under the wiper blade, beneath a fine layer of snow, a yellow traffic ticket was visible.

"Great!" Al said, grabbing the ticket and pounding the roof of the car with his fist. "Merry fucking Christmas! There goes all the money I just made."

Rodya saw an opportunity and snatched the ticket from Al's hand.

"Here, I take it. I take care of it. But please, can we go somewhere and talk? Just give me five minutes. I buy you drink."

Al looked at him over the roof of the car. The snow was falling harder.

"Fine," he said. "Get in the car."

Rodya loaded all his packages in the back seat and got in. Al started the car, revved the engine a few times and turned on the wipers to remove the snow. While they waited for the car to warm up, Rodya asked, "Why you are not at UPS anymore?"

Al groaned and said, "I got fired."

"I see."

"I got fired because I was too far behind on my route. I wasn't getting things delivered on time, and I didn't care."

"Ahh."

"You want to know why I got behind?"

"Sure."

"Because I wasted too many goddamned afternoons lying in bed with Mr. Molloy."

Rodya smiled. This was good. Al's heart was wounded, he could tell, but the wound had not scarred over yet. There was still hope.

The selection of bars open on Christmas Eve was limited, but after about fifteen minutes Al managed to find one. It was a divey place, right on Broadway, and when they entered they were assaulted with the smells of stale beer, cigarettes, popcorn, and the doubly assaulting sound of The Chipmunks Christmas album, which, they were soon to find out, was on a continuous loop on the jukebox. They both paused when they entered and assessed the surroundings. The bar took up one whole side of the room and on the other side there were some dark booths, occupied by a few sullen-looking patrons imbibing what good cheer they had on the tables in front of them. Al and Rodya took seats at the bar and waited in silence for someone to take their order.

Behind the bar there was an aquarium, equipped with the requisite shipwreck and burping plastic diver. Its sole occupant was one of those unentertaining sucking fishes that always seem to permanently adhere themselves to the underside of the shipwreck. On either side of the aquarium there were bottles of cheap liquor—the kind in plastic, shatterproof bottles that are usually seen further insulated with brown paper bags. At the far end of the bar sat an elderly couple. They were drinking and smoking and talking to a tiny, bespectacled man who was chewing and spitting tobacco. The old lady pointed at them, the bespectacled man turned, and then approached Al and Rodya, stopping along the way to scoop out a bowl of popcorn, which he set before them.

"And what's Santa drinkin' tonight?" he asked.

Al looked at the selection on display and then ordered them both a beer. The bartender reached into a small refrigerator and retrieved two cans.

"You wanna start a tab?"

"Yes, here," Rodya said, retrieving a twenty from his wallet and giving it to the man. "Maybe you could give us rest of six-pack, too."

The man obliged, reaching down and grabbing the remaining four beers. Al opened two beers and handed one to Rodya.

"I don't know what you think we have to talk about," Al said, eyeing the four unopened beers, "but since you're buying, and since we are in such charming surroundings with such delightful company, I guess I'll hear you out."

Rodya took a drink and considered how to proceed.

"He is very sorry," Rodya began. "You know that, yes?"

"Yeah, I know," Al said, his voice hard. "He's sorry every time he's horny, but once that's over, he'll go right back to being an asshole. I've seen it before. Too often."

Rodya said nothing.

"What really bothers me," Al said, "is that I thought we were in something together. But then that morning when you walked out of the bathroom I realized he wasn't in it at all. It wasn't just that you were there, that was just the icing on the cake. No, the worst part was that he didn't even invite me to his fucking party. He didn't invite me because he was too embarrassed, and don't try and tell me that's not true."

Rodya did not try, and they sat in silence for a moment.

"I really liked that guy," Al said.

"And he really like you," Rodya said. "I know he do. And I really think he change. I know you don't believe me, and maybe you shouldn't, but I think is truth."

Al sipped on his beer and stared at the aquarium.

"He is like some man," Rodya continued "who have been living in cave for many years. Finally he see some light and he go out, but it's too much, too bright, so he go back in cave to hide in shadow. You know what I mean?"

Al kept staring at the aquarium, as if waiting for the fish to move.

"Is like coming out of closet again for him," Rodya said. "You know what that's like. Scary. He is scared. Nobody make good decision when scared. Sometimes he lie about what he like, but is only because he is scared."

"Hey," Al said, "I don't deny that he likes me. I think he really does. I'm just tired of the same shit happening again and again. The only thing guys ever want me for is this," he said, leaning back from the bar and slapping his gut. "Sex is great, yeah, but I'm tired of being the object of some guy's lust and nothing else. That gets old."

Rodya nodded his agreement. "You don't think I feel same way?" he said. "Guys only want your big belly and only want my big cock. Is no different. We have big piece of body in right places."

Again, Al gave a bitter laugh. He opened another beer.

"You're only half right," Al said. "Maybe there are guys who lust after me and guys who lust after you, but there aren't any guys who envy me. Nobody wants to be fat, or worse, seen on the arm of a fat guy, anymore than they want a small dick. You're lucky for what you have. Every guy wants what you have. It's a gift."

"Maybe," Rodya said, unable to repress a slight smile. "But no gift is perfect. With all gift there is some trouble. I made money with my cock, yes, people know me because of it, yes, but that's as bad as good. Is good if I want to make sex my whole life, but I don't want. I am getting older. I need to do other thing. But now my dick get in way. People always talk, they don't take me serious. I get job, they find out about my movies and then they start whispers. Always whispers. You think people ever will know me for anything as much as my cock? No!

"Even with Frank," Rodya went on, banging his fist on the bar. "I never want to sleep with him. I want to work for him, so I try and try and try, and he never give me chance. Why? Because he think I'm dumb porno star. He never look at my portfolio, don't answer my letters. Why? Because of this!" he said, grabbing his crotch.

"So you know what I do next?" he said, taking another beer and opening it. "I decide to use my cock to get Frank. If I can't go in front door with portfolio, fine, I go in back door with cock."

Al was listening, a slight smile on his face.

"Did I succeed?" Rodya asked. "I did not. Don't try to fuck your way to top. That's my advice. Was stupid. My plan fail. And you know why? Because Frank didn't want me. He want you. He want you so bad that only way I can get him to look at my portfolio and maybe give me job, is to find you. I spend one week, every day, every night, hunting for you. Which is, how you say? pathetic. Most new workers have to make coffee for boss, take phone message for boss, maybe water boss's plants or walk his dog, but me? No. For Rodya is more difficult. I have to find boyfriend of boss he was mean to, and then I have to convince boyfriend he love him."

Al was smiling but he shook his head. "That's a very nice story," he said. "Funny. Touching. But I don't believe a word of it."

"No?" Rodya said, reaching into his coat pocket for his cell phone. "Then I prove it."

He found Frank's number in his phone and then pushed the connect button. When it started ringing, he leaned his face in close to Al's so that they could both hear.

"Hello Frank?" Rodya said, almost yelling to make himself heard over the amphetamine voices of Alvin and Theodore.

"Rodya?"

"Yes. Is me. How is your night before Christmas?"

"Oh, okay, I guess," Frank replied, his voice sounding less than cheerful. "Where are you?"

"I'm at some bar. It was place someone suggest me to look."

"Did you find him?" Frank asked, the eagerness apparent in his tone. Rodya studied Al's reaction in the mirror behind the bar, and smiled.

"No," he said. "I did not. I have one more place to check day after tomorrow. So I call you then. I think I find him soon."

"Rodya."

"Yes."

"I, well, I want to apologize and say thank you for trying. I've been a beast to everyone involved in this and I'm sorry. I spoke to Evan this morning and he told me all about how hard you've been trying to find Al. I, well, I just want to say thanks, I guess."

"Frank," Rodya said, a broad grin on his face as he watched Al's reaction, "is alright."

"No, it's not alright. Look, even if we don't find him I want to thank you for helping me to, well, for helping me to see my life a little more clearly. I also want to say that I'd be happy to look over your portfolio with you and would be honored to have you as my apprentice."

"Frank! You are serious?"

"Yes, why don't you come by day after tomorrow and we can talk about it a little more. Maybe I can even come out and help look for Al."

"I don't think you need to do that," Rodya chuckled.

"Yes. I should do it. I'm the one who chased him away. I'm the one that should find him. I should have been doing it myself from the start."

"Frank."

"Yes."

"What you do for Christmas?"

"Me? Um, I'm supposed to go to friends for dinner tomorrow night, but I think I might pass."

"Can I come by your house in hour maybe? I have present for you."

"Oh, you didn't have to do that. I feel like you've done so much already. And I've been such a shit."

"Is okay."

"Yes, I'll be home. Probably watching a movie or something."

"Okay, I see you later then."

Rodya hung up. He was about to open another beer, but Al was already headed for the door, keys in hand.

Epilogue

The flight had been booked late so they'd been forced to take three tiny seats in coach. Since Frank was the shortest he gave his aisle seat to long-legged Rodya and had squeezed himself into the one next to the window. To occupy the time Frank sat flipping through a book of Italian villas. Al sat next to him snoozing peacefully while a disk of Rossini played softly on his walkman. Next to Al sat Rodya, who was busy sorting through a pile of photos of potential soccer players.

Frank's cell phone rang. He removed it from his pocket, looked at the incoming number and smiled.

"Hello, Chapman, what can I do for you?"

"Frank! It's actually you?"

"Of course it's me."

"Jesus, every time I call I get that baby Brehznev. I never know if he's giving you my messages or not."

"Yes," Frank said, "I get them. He's very dependable."

"Maybe a little too dependable, if you ask me. It sounds like he's running the show on this book, Frank. You sure you got it under control?"

Frank looked down the row of seats at Rodya, still busy sorting the photos.

"Yes," he said, "All under control. You sound worried."

"I am a bit," he said and then paused before continuing. "I've been hearing rumors about you inking a deal with Daedalus for your little building book."

"Oh?"

"So did you?"

"Uh huh."

"You did?"

"I did."

"Well. I still think it'll tank, but if you want to risk your reputation, be my guest. I just want to make sure my book doesn't get shafted in the process."

"Don't you worry," Frank said, gazing over at Rodya. "*Your* book is in very capable hands."

Just then, Rodya's own cell phone rang.

"Hello,"

"Oh, Rodya, thank God it's you! I've been trying to reach you all morning."

"Gerald?"

"Yes, now listen. I won't beat around the bush; there's trouble. Two of the guys got into a cat fight on the set right in the middle of filming and now they're refusing to work together. It took some work but I found a replacement couple, which would be fine, except that one of them has a missing front tooth and the other one has the hiccups!"

Rodya smiled.

"The tooth's not that big a deal, we can work around it. I guess it's even kind of attractive, thuggish, but did you ever try working with someone who's got the hiccups? It's not possible. Rodya, darling, please can you help us."

"No."

"Now don't say that. How much do you want?" Gerald asked. "We can talk. We'll make it worth your trouble, I promise. We may even be able to come up with a contract, would you like that?"

"*Welcome to Alitalia flight 077 to Milan. At this time we ask that you discontinue the use of all portable cellular devices and return your tray tables and seat backs to their upright and locked position . . .*"

Both men hung up.

"Al," Frank said, gently nudging him awake. "You have to put your seat up. We're about to take off."

Al sat up sleepily, removed his headphones, and pushed the button on the arm of his seat. Then he turned, took Frank's hand and squeezed it tightly.

"Strange, isn't it," Al said, "how quickly things change. I mean who'd have thought six months ago that either one of us would be doing what we're doing now. Together."

Frank squeezed Al's hand but said nothing. He stared off into space and thought for a long time about the self he'd been before he met Al and Rodya—the poor, scared, unhappy self, who had made his personal life into one giant muddle. In retrospect, all of his plots and schemes and hiding seemed almost funny to him, but when he focused on his faint reflection in the small, dark TV screen mounted on the back of the seat in front of him, he saw that he wasn't smiling. He noticed the lines around his eyes and the gray creeping into his hair and felt only regret for all the time that had passed, all the time he had wasted. He shook his head and then turned and looked out the window at the clear sky and the mountains beneath him. There were only a few patches of snow left, high on the highest peaks, but even they were slowly melting away in the warm spring sunshine.

If You Believe

William J. Mann

Sitting here, listening to him cry, I feel guilty for the way I judged him. I don't know what to say, so I just sit here beside him, scrunching my toes in my Nikes. I knew, always knew, that it would come to this, that one or the other of them would end up crying. But I never thought it would be *me* consoling *him*.

It's Christmas Eve. Outside I can hear carolers along Evergreen Avenue, like we're part of the last reel of a Frank Capra movie or something. I mean, who *carols* anymore, especially in Hartford? Their voices seep through the door: *We wish you a merry Christmas, we wish you a merry Christmas . . .*

But the sobbing man sitting next to me doesn't seem to notice. I slip my arm around him. His head drops down onto my shoulder.

God rest ye merry gentlemen, may nothing you dismay . . .

It's been a long time since September. That's when it all started, just about four months ago, at Christopher's birthday party, the night we first met Bud. For me, of course, it goes back a long way before that, but Bud is the one who changed things, so I ought to start with him.

For weeks, Bud was all Christopher could talk about. "He's so strong," Christopher said. "So manly. So *butch.*"

James had tossed his hand at him and smirked, in the way only James can smirk. "Sugar," he said, "are we supposed to be impressed by the fact that this man engages in *posing?*"

"He's not posing," Christopher insisted. "That's just the way he is."

"Mmm hmm." James rolled his eyes. "And Mariah Carey doesn't mean to act like a diva. That's just the way she is."

He has a way about him, James does: I can't deny that. Whenever he walks into a room all attention immediately turns to him. He's tall, handsome, dark, with a cleft chin. With his looks, he could be a soap opera star. Except, of course, for his tendency to walk around with his hand on his hip and begin every sentence with "Sugar." It's as if James had been born in Alabama or someplace—instead of East Hartford, Connecticut, the son of an ironworker. It's the usual tale of so many blue-collar queens, growing up watching too many episodes of *Designing Women* to counteract their fathers' football games.

"James," Christopher was telling him, " you are *not* going to ruin this for me."

"Me, *ruin* anything?"

"I've warned Bud about you. I really have."

Christopher was trying on a shiny, silver, stretchy new shirt, modeling it in front of the full-length mirror in the hall. He was turning every which way, making sure it was tucked smoothly into his Diesel jeans. "Whaddya think, Michael?" he asked, turning to me.

When it came to Christopher and James, I didn't often manage to get a word in edgewise, so I leapt at the chance. "It's a little . . . iridescent," I offered.

"That's the whole *point* of club wear," Christopher said, making a face. "You want to be *noticed* on the dance floor."

"Oh," I said. "Where'd you get it?"

"I ordered it from International Male."

James practically spat. Until that point he'd been stretched out on the couch idly flipping through channels with the remote. Now he sat up in a hurry. "Sugar, don't tell me you actually *ordered* something from that catalog!"

"I did."

James bubbled over with laughter. "I have never known anyone who actually placed an order from that thing!"

Christopher was ignoring him. "That's it," he said, shaking his head in the mirror. "I've got to start doing crunches. Look at this tiretube around my waist."

"There's no tiretube," I told him. Christopher has always been as tight as a drum. Me—now, *I* have love handles. I grew up having pasta alfredo three times a week—for breakfast. You're not a man in my family until you have a roll of flesh hanging over your belt.

"Oh, how I hate getting old," Christopher wailed. "I just knew this would happen when I turned twenty-five."

"There's always liposuction," James called from the couch.

"I'm *serious*," Christopher said. "Come on. By twenty-five, didn't you think we'd all be rich and settled and—"

"Married with children?" James laughed.

"My parents were married when they were twenty-one," Christopher said.

"Mine were married at nineteen," James countered. "Of course, that's because dear old Dad knocked up dear old Mum and you know how Catholics are."

"I just thought I'd have some grip on life by the time I turned twenty-five," Christopher said, pouting into the mirror. "It seemed such a grown-up kind of age."

The three of us have been friends for a long time. It was freshman year of high school when we first met, at good old South Catholic, in the South End of Hartford, where James Milardo and Christopher Aresco and Michael Garafoli were drawn together by that invisible gay-dar we would only recognize and acknowledge some few years later. In so many respects the three of us were the same: queer boys from working-class families growing up in the Italian South End. Except, even when we were kids, the South End wasn't really so Italian anymore. Puerto Ricans and Vietnamese had come to outnumber the old Italian families. Most of our cousins had moved out to the suburbs and now shook their heads at the "decline" of the old neighborhood. But not us. Our families persevered. And so did we.

There were, however, significant differences in our biographical details. Both James and Christopher grew up with deadbeat dads who took off and left their broods. Neither James nor Christopher ever had anything good to say about their father. My Dad, on the other hand, held down three jobs to keep us afloat for as long as I can remember. Putting five kids through South Catholic wasn't cheap, especially after my mother died. Dad had to work his ass off, and he always did so without complaining.

Even twelve years later, it was still hard to think about my mother. She dropped dead on the kitchen floor when I was thirteen. I was sitting at the kitchen table doing algebra homework and she was standing at the stove making spaghetti sauce. All of a sudden she just keeled over and fell, the ladle still in her hand. She died on the job, so to speak. My father never really recovered from her death.

I was the last of the bunch, the only kid in my family who still lived at home. My sister, Theresa, got married the previous spring, so now it was just me and Dad. He had gotten pretty much okay with the gay stuff; we didn't talk about it much, but he was cool. Not that I ever brought anybody home. When it happened, and it happened rarely, I'd bring them to James's lover's apartment, where I was permitted to use the couch.

James's lover, Bernard, was, by far, the most successful of all of us. He held a good job and had his own apartment, and he let James live there rent-free. Bernard worked for Travelers Insurance, so he was gone all day, which allowed Christopher and me to hang out at his place with Michael, since none of us were working full time. We had a lot of time on our hands to just sit around watching *Passions* and VH-1 and MTV and consume large quantities of pizza.

"I'm going on a diet starting tomorrow," Christopher said, pulling his shiny silver shirt out of his jeans and letting it hang over his butt. "No more pizza or French fries. I do *not* want to start bulging in the wrong places." He grinned suddenly. "Actually, Bud thinks my bulge looks pretty nice in these jeans."

"Bud, Bud, Bud!" James sat up on the couch, waving his hands, Bette Davis doing "Petah, Petah, Petah!" He fell back, as if in a swoon. Christopher told him to knock it off.

"So when do we get to meet Bud?" I asked.

"At my birthday party. That way he can meet everybody at once." He shot a glare over at James. "And you'd better be on your best behavior."

"Me?" James asked innocently. "Whatever do you *mean?*"

There was a click of a key in the lock just then, and James jumped up from the couch, his feet flying through the air and landing on the floor in front of him. He quickly straightened the cushions on the couch and swiped the empty pizza box off the floor, tossing it into the trash. A quick check of his hair in the mirror and he was ready, just as the doorknob turned and Bernard walked in, briefcase in hand, paisley tie askew.

"Hello, baby," James called. "How was work?"

Bernard just shrugged, in the way only Bernard can shrug, and walked straight past us into the kitchen. I heard him set his briefcase down on the table, the *poosh* of the refrigerator door opening, and the *pop* of a twist-off beer cap.

"Christopher, Michael," he said, coming back into the living room, nodding to us before pecking James quickly on the lips, more sound than touch. Then he plopped down into an easy chair, pushing off his loafers and focusing on VH-1's "Behind the Music" on Jennifer Lopez.

"Do you like my shirt, Bernard?" Christopher asked.

He gave him one eye as he kept the other on J-Lo. "Where'd you get it," he replied snidely. "International Male?"

Christopher said nothing, just pulled the thing off. I looked at his body. Just as I said: there was no tiretube. He was still as thin as he was in high school. Alone among the three of us, Christopher was blond and blue-eyed, the after-effects of having a Swedish grandmother, I presumed. Both Michael and I were dark, with brown eyes and Roman noses. But where Michael looked like a Michelangelo sculpture, I looked like a budding Mafioso on *The Sopranos*. My hairline had—horror of gay horrors!—begun to recede just a little bit and besides being a little flabby around the middle, there was the troubling development of a minor double chin.

"Christopher had just started filling us in on *all about* his new beau," James was telling Bernard, batting his eyelashes.

"*Yes*, he certainly was," I added, trying to mimic James's campy style—unsatisfactorily, of course, but then I had yet to find a style of my own. "We are all *so* curious."

"What's his name?" Bernard asked.

"Bud," Christopher said.

"*Bud? His name is Bud?*"

"We've been told he's very *butch*," James said, sitting on the arm of Bernard's chair and putting his arm around his boyfriend's neck. "He'd *have* to be, with a name like Bud." James made a face. "Either that or he's a Rottweiler."

"James," Bernard said, finally turning away from the TV long enough to look at his boyfriend, "I've asked you not to sit on the arm of the chair."

James quickly stood up. I watched him retreat, giving Bernard the space to watch television and do whatever it was he needed to do. James just kind of pulled back, faded from view. I'd noticed a pattern with him: how, when Bernard was around, James became less queeny, less arch, less campy. Certainly not *butch*, the way we were being primed to expect Bud, but somehow toned down. Somehow not the guy I'd known all these years, the guy I grew up with, the guy on whom I'd had my first gay crush, back in sophomore year—though of course he never knew about it. I could never admit such a thing to James. How embarrassing would *that* be? We were *sisters*. It was all such a long time ago. James and I could never be lovers. Never.

Though I'd never make him tone down, pull back, fade from view. I'd never insist he act any differently than he really is, as Bernard was always seeming to do. I'd never make James get off the arm of my chair, as if it were such a *crime*—when all he was trying to do was put his arm around my neck, to show me that he loved me—*me!*—more than anyone else in the whole entire world.

"How often do you floss?" the dental hygienist asked.

It was the next day, and the spit was curling off my lip and down to my chin. There really wasn't anything I could do about it, except pretend I didn't feel absolutely mortified.

When I'd walked into my dentist's appointment that morning, I'd enjoyed some semblance of belief that I was a dignified and articulate member of the human race. Then suddenly I was flat on my back, bleeding and drooling, trying to answer the hygienist's questions while gurgling saliva and blood at the same time. Why is it hygienists only ask questions when you have sixteen tubes in your mouth?

"How often do you floss?" she asked again.

Gurgle.

"Just sometimes, huh? So you *want* this awful tartar between your teeth?"

Yeah, as a matter of fact, I do. I enjoy being stabbed through the gums and enduring lectures from frustrated spinsters with nose hairs. *Why was she torturing me?*

"Look," she said, holding out her scraper. "Some of this is still soft. *What*—were you planning to save this for lunch?"

Yeah, lady, as a matter of fact, maybe I was. Beats packing a ham sandwich and a Ring Ding in a brown paper bag.

I'd been making just that sort of lunch for myself for a couple weeks now. I was a Kelly Girl. Temp jobs were really the best I could come up with since being laid off from my job as a data-entry clerk at Fleet Bank eight months ago. This afternoon I was heading over to stuff envelopes for some financial investment group. But first I'd made this appointment to get my teeth cleaned. My insurance coverage from my last job lasted for a few more months, so I figured I might as well take advantage of what I could.

I hadn't counted on the lecture.

"Do you know studies have shown that people who floss regularly live on the average five to six years longer than those who don't?"

"Ngh," I managed to say before she stuck three of her fingers into my mouth.

I felt like a little kid being scolded. Just like Sister Margarita Mary used to do when I failed to memorize the complete list of prepositions.

"After, among, against, um, ah . . ."

"So. You *want* to speak ungrammatically for the rest of your life."

Yeah, Sister, as a matter of fact, I do, if that's the only way out of memorizing this stupid list of words.

Lying there, baking in the fluorescent light, I couldn't help but remember the time James dressed up like Sister Margarita Mary. It was hilarious. We were fourteen. How we didn't immediately clue in that we were gay I'll never know. Because James came waltzing into our student assembly wearing a nun's costume, shaking his Rosary beads the way Sister always did, challenging kids to impromptu preposition-naming contests. Sister Margarita Mary was not amused, but everyone else was.

"Rinse."

I tell you, this hygienist was as bad as a drill sergeant. When I was a kid, I never went to a dental hygienist. Back in those days, the dentist didn't care if your teeth weren't gleaming like little pearls when he stuck his nose in your mouth. "What's this?" Doc Zimmerman used to say. "An extra tooth? No, by golly, it's just a lump of hardened scrambled eggs. I'll take care of that in a jiffy."

And he'd take out his little saw and file that chunk of egg right off.

"I said *rinse*," the hygienist ordered.

I did my best to follow instructions. But with the way my mouth bleeds, I always leave a string of bloody saliva dangling from my lips when I spit into the sink. And no matter how hard I try, I can't get rid of it. If I try to wipe it away, it falls to that bib they make you wear. And then it just lays there for the rest of the visit, daring you to look at it. Real attractive, you know?

Like the time James puked on our very first night at a gay bar. Oh, man, was he a mess. Settling back for a second round of assault on my mouth, my mind spiraled back some eight years. We were seventeen, James and Christopher and I, and we snuck into the old Sanctuary Club with fake IDs. James got stinking drunk and made a fool of himself over this cute older guy who was voguing all over the dance floor. I know, it sounds tired now, but back then voguing was hot. At least it still was in Hartford. Anyway, James really liked this guy but he knew how drunk he was and correctly deduced the only way he stood even the slimmest chance with him was to somehow sober up.

"I'm going into the men's room to stick my finger down my throat," he informed Christopher and me.

I had no idea what he thought that would do, but when he came back out, there was still a drizzle of vomit on his chin. He walked right into the guy he thought was so hot who, of course, took one look at James and pronounced him "gross." The whole night was a disaster. James thought he'd forever ruined his chances of being a successful gay man. I sat with him in his mother's car until the sun was coming up, holding his hand and persuading him otherwise.

"Yow!"

The hygienist had thrust her fingers back into my mouth. What a situation. There I was, prone before her, utterly humiliated. She had forced her metal poker between my two front teeth and it *stung*. I swear she was getting off on this.

"Sorry," she said, but I didn't believe her for a second.

I tried to keep my mind on other things. I wondered if James had gotten the job he'd applied for over at the Wadsworth Atheneum. He really, *really* wanted this job, and he was supposed to find out that morning. The position wasn't much—hanging paintings and giving tours—and it paid very little, but James was tired of waiting tables at Friendly's. You see, soon after he met Bernard, James had decided he was an artist. He painted a few watercolors before deciding his medium was really sculpture, though the one piece he made cracked in the kiln. James preferred not to talk about the experience. Still, he enrolled in a couple of art classes at Greater Hartford Community College, determined to make something of his art.

I think, in truth, James was feeling less called to the artist's life than he was simply intimidated at having a successful boyfriend. Understand that Bernard was already a claims adjustor, and he was only a few years older than we were. Bernard had *ambition*, you see: he planned on becoming the manager of his policy division. He'd gone to Connecticut State University after all, and hadn't slacked off in his post-high school years the way James, Christopher and I had. James waited tables at Friendly's, I bounced around from job to job, and Christopher answered phones at a law office.

But Bernard had his eyes set on a goal even beyond his policy division: by the time he was thirty, he said, he would have moved out of Hartford. Maybe to New York, maybe to Boston. Yet, despite Bernard's frequent musings on the topic, James never referred to it. He would clam up when Bernard called Hartford a "nowhere place," a city so far past its decline it was now irretrievably *gone*. I never challenged him on such an idea—Hartford's plight was hard to refute—but such talk always pissed me off. So the city wasn't exciting like New York or Boston. So there had been no revival of the kind that had happened in nearby Providence. There were no sidewalk cafes, no bustling coffee bars, no trendy nightclubs. Downtown emptied out by six in the evening, leaving shops and office buildings dark.

But Hartford was *mine*. I was born there. I'd lived there all my life. I knew every street, every alleyway, every corner grocery. I had been an altar boy at St. Augustine's Church and attended St. Augustine's school. At South Catholic, I had supporting parts in all the school plays (James, of course, snared the leads.) I liked going to Boston and New York as much as the next guy but, truth be told, they scared me. Hartford was gray and dull, but so was I.

"Rinse."

"Are you—done?" I asked hopefully.

She moved away to wash her hands. She glanced back at me, looking somewhat weary and relieved. "We're all through," she said, and I heard her whisper to someone, "I sure earned my pay today."

Yeah, lady, but you could make better money as a dominatrix.

I stood and wiped my mouth. "Thank you very much for your efforts," I said politely.

"You start flossing regularly now, right?" she asked.

I smiled. Yeah, sure. Right after I get all of my prepositions down straight.

The problem was I couldn't think on my feet. No, that wasn't the problem. I could *think* pretty quick, I just couldn't act very quick. I could think of lots of things to say, lots of things to do, but I never said them, never did them. I just kept quiet. It was like how I never wanted to cross swords with James and so just played along with him. James was far too quick for me.

Maybe that's why in high school I never had sex with James, but I did with Christopher. Christopher was actually the *second* guy I ever had sex with, though I'm pretty sure I was Christopher's first. It happened during our senior year of high school at the Berlin Drive-In one night while we were watching some Bruce Willis actioner. *Die Hard* or one of those godawful things. We were both bored and a little stoned and Christopher whipped out his meat and started playing with it. Without saying a word, I slid across the seat and went down on him. Just like that. I'm still surprised at how ballsy I was. I'm not usually so forthright.

To be honest, I'd been hoping that exact situation would present itself with James. I still had that silly crush on him. Often I'd sit really close to James on my bed while we were watching TV and pray—I mean, actually *pray*—that something would happen between us. But it never did. Instead, it happened with Christopher, and I can actually remember imagining it was *James's* cock in my mouth instead of Christopher's. How crazy is *that*, huh?

Anyway, Christopher shot a big load, and I swallowed it, and then I came too (in my hand) and that was that. Later on, of course, I learned that swallowing wasn't really safe, but since we were both sixteen and Christopher was probably still a virgin, I doubt there was any real risk. We simply zipped up and went home before the movie was even over. The whole thing had, in fact, freaked us out enough that we hardly ever mentioned it again in nine years.

But we were horny sixteen-year-olds. What did we expect? Our gonads were ready to burst. That's what pushed me across the seat to take Christopher's cock in my mouth and that's what had allowed me to do something else really ballsy a few months before. During Christmas break, I answered a personal ad. The alternative weekly, *The Hartford Advocate*, had a "Men For Men" category, and some guy had taken out a notice that caught my eye. "Cute GWM, 19, wants to meet others my age." I left a message for him on the voicemail number listed. He called me back the next day. I remember it was Christmas Eve. My father answered the phone while my brothers and sisters were exchanging gifts. Dad thought it was James.

"Hello?" the kid said into my ear. "Can you talk?"

"Um . . . we're opening Christmas presents."

He wasn't deterred. "So do you want to meet somewhere and have sex?"

Funny how much always seemed to happen to me around Christmas. Even though he was on break, Stefan met me the next afternoon at his dorm at Trinity College. It was Christmas Day. We had the entire place to ourselves.

"So you've been with a guy before?" Stefan asked.

"Sure," I lied.

He looked at me cagily. "Are you in high school?"

I nodded.

"Cool," Stefan said. "Any of your teachers know you're gay?"

"Are you kidding?" I lauged.

"What's so unusual about that? I was out at my prep school. Two of my teachers helped me organize a gay-straight student alliance."

"Wow."

It was a world alien to my experience. At South Catholic, it might as well have been 1955. Homosexuality didn't exist except as something with which to taunt other kids. "That's so *gay*," the girls would say. "He's such a *fag*," the guys would say about anyone they didn't know, didn't like, or didn't understand.

I thought of Father Finnerty and the assignment he had given us over Christmas break. We were to write about the true meaning of the holiday, based on something we experienced in celebrating the season. "Write about what it is you truly *want* for Christmas," he said. "Write about your deepest hopes and dreams—whatever is deep down in your hearts."

Father Finnerty assured us that he wouldn't read our journals, that this was to be a personal, spiritual exercise between ourselves and God. Though he would collect our journals to make sure we had completed the assignment, Father stressed *over and over* that he would not read them. "That's so you all can feel comfortable in writing whatever you want," he said. "Be as honest as you can about what it is that really you want this Christmas."

I knew some of the students would be writing about world peace or inner harmony or a greater global acceptance of Christ's word. I wrote about having sex with Stefan. It was, after all, what I had been wanting for an awfully long time. I scrawled, in large felt-tip purple letters:

> It was like an awakening, a most beautiful revelation that came to me as we lay there on Stefan's bed staring out at the sun sinking beyond the horizon on the day Christ was born. This was my Christmas gift. This is what I was meant to do. Always. And it is somehow made even *more* wonderful because so many others would not think of this as sacred but rather as abominable and revolting. Not me. In Stefan's face I saw Jesus.

Now Father Finnerty was not a monster. The student population actually liked him—at least, the students who *fit in* liked him, the ones who were evidently straight, or going to be straight. Father Finnerty was friendly not only with the guys on the football team and the cheerleaders and the Honors Society but also the nerds in the Science Club. Even some obviously gay boys—the ones who were considering becoming brothers or priests themselves—seemed to like Father Finnerty. He was down-to-earth and friendly, with a big happy Irish face, always ready with a quick joke in the classroom.

But the kids who somehow fell between the categories had a different impression of Father Finnerty—the kids who wanted to be artists, for example, or the kids who listened to Marilyn Manson, or the ones, like me, who seemed to be a part of all groups and yet none at the same time. We weren't so sure about Father Finnerty. James said there was something underneath that crooked Irish grin that he didn't trust. What it was we couldn't quite put our fingers on, but we could spot it, lurking. Maybe it was in the way Father Finnerty began each class by making us all recite the Act of Contrition. Maybe it was in the way he smirked, rolled his eyes, and turned his head when one of the jocks called somebody a fag in class.

Like me.

On gym days, I'd skip out, counting on the astonishing obtuseness of the gym teachers. James and Christopher always seemed to get caught, but I'd slip up to the library and safely spend the hour scouring personal ads in *The Hartford Advocate*, reading about men looking for other men, men into rough sex, men into cuddling, men into long walks and candlelight dinners, men into hot sweaty action, men into BD, SM, FF, CBT, and all sorts of other initials I couldn't decipher. I would read those personals from beginning to end, memorizing them to the sounds of my classmates shouting outside on the soccer field, trapped in their own little worlds.

That's how I met Stefan.

I remember two things as being the most thrilling: holding Stefan's hand as we walked up the stairs to his room, our footsteps echoing through the hushed, empty corridors, and kissing him. *I'm kissing another guy*, I kept repeating to myself, over and over again. Stefan was a finance major, and I remember how stiff his dick was, the way a finance major's dick should be. But I couldn't get my dick to stay hard. It's not that I didn't find Stefan attractive. I did. A lot. It's just that I felt that somehow I was cheating on James. It made no sense. It was that stupid crush I had on him again. I just couldn't get it out of my head.

But still, kissing Stefan had been enough. When I got home I wrote it down in my journal.

This is what I was meant to do. Always.

Even as I wrote, I knew Father Finnerty would read it. All that talk about respecting our privacy was a crock of shit. But I didn't care. In a way, I *wanted* him to know. I wanted him and all the others who had told me that it was bad, that it was sick, to read these words. I trusted in Father Finnerty's warped sense of honor that he would never reveal that he had read the passage, that I would in fact be safe from whatever retribution he and his brethren might have in store for faggots. Perhaps it was a naive trust, but it proved to be accurate.

Father Finnerty handed me back my journal with the queerest expression on his face. Then, I perceived the look as anger. His eyes clamped onto mine, and for several seconds he wouldn't release my journal into my hands. Then he let go, giving up on his attempt to sear through my face with the power of his eyes, because it wasn't working: I simply held his glare without blinking. So he turned away, never speaking or even looking at me again.

Today I wonder about that queer look on Father Finnerty's face: was it just anger? Was it truly revulsion I saw in his eyes, or was there something else?

Stefan and I got together again a few days later. I drove out to his parents' house in Avon. It quickly became apparent to me that, despite our mutual interest in cock, I didn't have much in common with Stefan the Trinity College boy. It's a whole other world on the other side of Avon Mountain. Stefan lived in a huge stone house with a circular driveway and manicured hedges and one of those Little Black Sambo statues holding a lantern. His parents were home, and didn't seem to care that their son was boinking another boy in his room down the hall. At one point Stefan moaned really loud and I pulled back off of his dick.

"Your parents will hear," I said.

"So long as I'm safe," he insisted, "they don't care."

"That's just too weird to me," I said, thinking of my own father. Dad was cool in his own way, but I'm not sure how he'd do listening to his son get his cock sucked.

I decided not to spend the night. Thinking of my father made me think of James again for some reason, and once more I lost my wood. Walking out of Stefan's house, I was glad to be leaving. Everything was too neat here, too glossy. Not even an end table bore a speck of dust. I imagined they had a housekeeper. I drove back down his long driveway and headed back over the mountain where I was safe.

But all of that is simply leading me back to the night of Christopher's birthday party, the night last September when we first met Bud.

"Do these leather pants flatten out my ass too much?" Christopher was asking, in front of the mirror again. "Bud said he liked my ass in my Diesel jeans. Maybe I ought to wear those."

"Will you stop with Bud already?" James said. "This is *your* party, sugar."

James was in a bad mood: he hadn't gotten the job at the Atheneum. Bernard seemed as disappointed by the fact as James was. I don't think Bernard liked the idea that his boyfriend served Fribbles and Fishamajigs at Friendly's.

"But this is the first time you all are going to meet Bud," Christopher fretted.

"Why are you so nervous about us meeting him?" I asked.

"I just want you to like him."

"We'll like him."

Christopher's eyes held mine. He looked over his shoulder to make sure that James was distracted hanging crepe paper and then took me by the arm. He led me into the kitchen, where a pal of his from the law office, Oscar, was stuffing mushroom caps.

"What?" I asked Christopher. "What's wrong?"

"There's nothing wrong," Oscar interjected. "Christopher is making a molehill into a mountain, as usual."

"Michael," Christopher said, eyes fixed on me. "Bud is thirty-nine."

"Thirty-nine?"

"Yeah. Are you shocked?"

"No. It's just that you never—"

"*Bud is thirty-nine?*" James was suddenly squealing, skidding in his socks round the corner into the kitchen. "Sugar, why did you never *tell* us?"

Christopher sighed. "Precisely because of the reaction you're having right now."

"What kind of reaction am I having?" James asked innocently, eyelids fluttering, hand faintly touching his chest.

"*Bud is thirty-nine?*" Christopher mimicked James' voice and mannerisms quite well, far better than I ever could.

"Well, sugar, you have to admit, that's a considerable gap of years and life experience."

Christopher made a face. "He's a *young* thirty-nine. Besides, age doesn't matter. Not to me."

"Oh, *no*," James said, turning to Oscar and me. "This is the one who worries about turning twenty-five. He calls it a 'quarter of a century.' "

I had to suppress a smile.

James slipped an arm around Christopher's waist. "Don't worry, sugar. We'll *love* Bud. We'll make him feel right at home. Michael, run along and see if your dad has any Perry Como albums lying around."

"You're such an ass," Christopher said, pulling away.

"My first lover was forty," Bernard said all of a sudden, coming into the kitchen to grab another beer from the refrigerator. "I was seventeen. We were together almost six years."

That shut James up, for the time being at least.

"He taught me a lot," Bernard told Christopher. "He taught me about going after dreams. He helped me believe in myself."

"Yes," James purred, stroking his boyfriend's hair, "but, baby, you've also said he got just a little too possessive of you. A little too jealous. That's why it didn't last."

Bernard just grunted and walked back out into the living room.

"I don't know," James said, hands on hips. "I just couldn't date anyone that much older than me. That's why Bernard and I just fit so well. We're peers. Equals."

"Bud and I are equals!" Christopher insisted.

"Of *course* you are, sugar," James said, kissing Christopher's cheek. "I'm looking forward to meeting Bud." He followed Bernard back into the living room, but not before rolling his eyes crazily at me.

"I just hope he fits in." Christopher leaned against the sink and looked over at Oscar and me. "He's been so upset about the age thing and meeting all my friends."

"Do you know his friends?" Oscar asked, bending over to toss some scraps into the trash. I couldn't help but admire his body. Oscar had told me he worked out four times a week, and it showed—shoulders straining through his tight white shirt, his triceps gently horseshoeing as he swept the scraps from the chopping board. I admit I got a little turned on watching him. He was tall, dark and handsome—and *successful* too, even more successful than Bernard. Oscar was a paralegal. And, as far as I could tell, he was also single.

"Yes," Christopher was saying. "I know all of his friends. We get together a lot."

"What do you do when you hang out?" Oscar asked.

"I don't know. Lots of things. Go to the movies, play cards—"

"Play cards?" James' voice suddenly shot out from the living room. He'd been listening. We could hear him laughing hysterically. I bit my lip. It *was* funny—Christopher, our Christopher—sitting around playing gin rummy.

"And we go hiking," Christopher went on, ignoring James's mirth, "and swimming, and watch TV, and listen to music—"

James's face suddenly popped around the corner. "Color me Barbra!" he sang out, eyes crossing wildly.

"Fuck off, James," Christopher said.

The doorbell rang. I saw Christopher tense. He bounded out to the hallway and checked himself in the mirror, smoothing out his shirt.

"You look fine," I told him.

"Please be nice to him," he said.

"Do you know how lucky you are?" I asked. "To have found someone you like who likes you back?" My throat suddenly went tight. "You and James are *both* so lucky."

"Any boogers?" Christopher asked, tipping his head back and flaring his nostrils.

I checked. "Nope. All clean."

The doorbell rang again.

James was suddenly looming behind him. "Will you get this or do I have to?"

"I'll get it," Christopher said.

But when he opened the door it wasn't Bud. It was some guy in a ponytail and a scruffy goatee wearing baggy corduroys and a Gay Pride

T-shirt. I was about to nudge Oscar and whisper, "Get a load of the granola bar," when Oscar actually walked up, embraced the ponytail guy, and introduced him as "Edward, my lover."

I walked back into the kitchen and squished a mushroom cap between my fingers.

It was the summer after my mother died that I met the merman.

I had just turned thirteen, and all sorts of feelings were rocketing through my body. Every year since I could remember, my family had gone down to Point O'Woods Beach in Old Lyme, where my father's mother rented a cottage for the summer. We'd go down for a week or two, usually in August, and by the end of our stay Mom was usually angry at Nana for something and she'd swear we'd never go to her beach house again. But this year, with Mom being gone, Nana's cottage became a place where Dad sent us kids, just to put us somewhere, somewhere where he didn't have to be, where he didn't have to see us and hear us and think of Mom. So that whole summer I pretty much wandered the shore of Long Island Sound all by myself, not thinking about very much, just collecting shells and shiny stones. I planned to glue them to a piece of wood. I'm not sure why, and I never did get around to gluing them, but it gave me something to do.

At first, the merman was nothing more than a far-off figure, diving in and out of the waves like a dolphin. I remember watching him from the sun porch of my grandmother's cottage. He'd jump up from the surface of the water, splashing foam, diving in and out, far out beyond the limits of where I was allowed to swim.

"It's a seal," Nana told me.

"Or a whale," my sister Theresa suggested.

"It's a merman," I said.

I'd get up early in the morning—for that's when he'd most likely be seen—and I'd wait for him, sitting on the sun porch, dreaming. Dreaming of a time when I would be old enough to swim out to the place where he was now, a place I imagined where the water was always warm and filled with beautiful tropical fish.

I knew no other kids my age at my grandmother's beach, and didn't seek any out. I had no use for the games I knew they'd want to play.

Kids my age no longer held any interest for me. I seemed to myself to be old before my time, an old man who spent hours just walking up and down the beach, then turning around to marvel at the path of footprints I'd left behind. My skin burned early, by the third week of June, and it peeled painfully from my shoulders. Then it reddened, browned, and finally bronzed, deepening in color each time I took my walks along the beach.

I first spotted the merman sometime toward the end of June. It's funny how you can never pinpoint the date of those truly momentous happenings of your life. He was just there; it just happened, as if I'd always known he was out there. I spotted him one morning as I sat on the sun porch, rocking in my grandmother's white wicker rocking chair, bathed in sunlight and listening to the angry fish-fight of the gulls. I narrowed my eyes to see who would dare swim out that far, splicing in and out of the rough white waves—a daredevil swimmer, perhaps, a porpoise in human form. For the next several days I'd watch him, feeling a warm thrill take hold of my senses: a rush of sensation I'd never truly experienced before, except for those vague memories of half-forgotten dreams late at night, as I lay in bed in the far reaches of sleep—a rush that would frighten me, perplex me, fascinate me, when I'd try to remember it in the morning.

The merman swam out beyond the rocks that Nana called the end of the land. "You're not to go out there, Michael," she'd told me, in a voice that was, for her, severe. "People have been known not to return from beyond the rocks. It's treacherous, a dangerous place. Stay away from there."

Finally, one day in early July, I decided to find my grandfather's binoculars. As a child, I remembered Grampa using them to watch the ships come in over the horizon, and how he'd gallantly hold them to my tiny eyes so that I, too, could experience his thrill. Grampa had been dead for some seven years, but surely his binoculars still hung on the peg in his closet. I tiptoed into the bedroom so as not to wake my grandmother, and I slid open the old closet door. Sure enough, there they hung, and I stood on my toes to reach them and slip them off of the hook.

"Michael," came Nana's voice, "what are you doing in my closet?"

I turned to face my grandmother, her long white hair flowing around her shoulders, her pink wizened face peeking out from among its strands.

"May I use the binoculars?" I asked. "I want to watch the waves."

She raised her head a bit, as if to listen for the sound. It was there, as ever: the constant crash of water against land, the gradual wearing away of stone, the deposit of sand. It was a sound that lulled me to sleep, that woke me in the morning, that took me to places beyond reality as I strolled along the sand on my daily walks. She listened to the sound of the waves and smiled. "Yes, Michael. You may use the binoculars. Just don't break them. They're very old."

I hurried back to the sun porch, but the merman was gone. The waves crashed against the rocks in the distance with nothing to disturb them. I waited by the window all day, but he didn't return.

The next morning I woke earlier than usual, just at sunrise, when my room was suffused with blues and reds and purples. I wore nothing but my white cotton underwear, and I slung the binoculars around my neck. I scampered down the stairs and felt the heat of the day already mounting. I took my spot on the sun porch and held the binoculars to my eyes.

And there he was. Now I could see him clearly: not a dolphin, and not a man, but a merman, half-man and half-fish, throwing all restraint to the warm morning wind and diving—joyously—in and out of the waves. The sun rose higher in the sky and all his magnificence became apparent: a glistening bronzed torso, tightly muscled, a back of superb sculpture, hairless pectorals and a firm, chiseled abdomen. His hair was a mass of tangled black curls, dancing around his head each time he rose from the water and dove back down again. But most beautiful of all was his tail—a glimmering iridescent green and silver, a tail of great power that thrust him up into the air as he emerged from the waves and flapped awesomely as he descended back beneath the water's surface, sending a great splash of foam that obscured my vision until he once again burst splendidly into the air.

Overcome, I ran out the door and down the steps that led from the porch to the beach. I ran through the sand barefoot, kicking up wads of it, and then I stood at the edge of the sea, the foam swirling around my ankles. I continued to gaze at the merman through my binoculars and he continued his delirious swim until he spotted me. He rose once from the water, not in a jump but in a cautious appeal, his arms outspread, his eyes focused on the boy on the beach many yards away. I stumbled back in sudden fear—caught, discovered, exposed. My impulse was to drop the binoculars and run, hide in the security of my grandmother's cottage. But I stayed where I was, the binoculars at my face. And then I saw the merman smile, a most beautiful smile that dazzled his handsome face. And he waved. He *waved* at me.

Then he was gone. Under the waves, back to whatever magical world he came from. I waited for nearly an hour as the tide began to rise, but he did not return. Not that day.

"Nana," I asked that morning at breakfast, "do you believe in mermen?"

She was frying bacon on the old black stove. She had knotted her long hair into a tight bun on the top of her head. She wore a faded housecoat that once had been covered with bright and colorful birds. She did not turn around.

"What are mermen?" she asked.

"There are only mer*maids*," my sister Theresa said, full of air and teenage-girl cockiness. "There are no mer*men*."

"I saw one," I insisted. "He swims out beyond the rocks. Out where I'm not supposed to go."

"I told you, dumbass," Theresa said. "It was a *whale*."

"Oh, no," I said. "He swims like a dolphin. Not a whale."

"Well, you certainly didn't see a dolphin. Not up here." Nana set a plate of greasy bacon and fried eggs in front of me. "Tell me, Michael. Do you miss your friends from school?"

"No," I told her, breaking the yolks of my eggs with my fork and spreading the bright yellow over the dreary brown-whites. "I don't like kids my age."

"But maybe it would be better if you children hadn't come here for the whole summer. Do you miss your father?"

I looked at her. "I miss my old life. But it can never come back now."

Theresa started to cry and Nana wrapped her arms around her. I began eating my eggs. "Nana," I said. "I don't want to leave. Not at least until I've met the merman."

She sighed, patting my hair. She gently released Theresa, who ran outside. Nana returned to the stove where she began wiping away splattered bacon grease.

But the merman didn't reappear the next day, or the next. I began to feel panicky. Had I scared him away? What if he never came back? I *had* to meet him, I knew that for sure. I had to see where he lived. I was sorry I'd told people I'd seen him. Somehow that seemed unwise, as if I should've known they couldn't possibly understand. I didn't think there was anyone in the whole world who could understand.

Except the merman.

He returned on the third day. But this time he wasn't diving in and out of the waves. I spotted him from the sun porch again, and he was lying on the rocks. He was sunning himself in the rays of the newborn sun, and the glow made him appear as if he'd been spray-painted with gold. I walked slowly across the sand and inhaled the tangy aroma of early-morning salt water. Standing ankle-deep in the surf, I watched him with the binoculars. He'd stretch, revealing his tight, sinewy physique, and roll from his back onto his stomach. Occasionally, his tail would flap, almost as a reflex, the way a cat's tail flicks all of a sudden, with no reason, with no warning. I could hear its wet slap against the rock even from where I stood. I watched him transfixed for nearly a half hour, and then he sat up, bent his tail in front of him, leaning his arms on it as if it were his legs. He noticed me, and smiled. He waved. This time I waved back.

But he dove into the water from the rock, a graceful slicing of the air that ended with a tremendous splash, and he was gone from me again. This went on for several weeks. I'd watch him playing in the waves or sunning himself upon the rock, and he'd smile and wave, and I'd wave shyly back. I was too timid to call out to him, afraid he'd swim away or else that I'd wake my grandmother. Then he'd disappear beneath the waves. I began to give up hope that I'd ever meet him.

It was sometime toward the end of July that I woke with a start—something had awakened me, I wasn't sure what. The sun had not yet risen, but I could sense it was near morning. The world takes on an eerie calm in those moments just before the sun comes up, as night struggles in vain to hold onto the darkness. It's as if all the world holds its breath and pauses to see who will win—night or day. And, of course, day always wins. But in those quiet, still moments one is never sure, and I was terrified.

Casting a long shadow in the moonlight that cut through the deep blues of my room, I padded out into the kitchen, and I tried to discover what it was that woke me. Did something fall from a shelf? Was Nana up and walking around? But all was quiet in the house. I gradually became aware of the steady sound of the waves, and they soothed me a bit, but there *had* been something: something, I was starting to feel, had called my name.

I stepped into the sun porch and looked outside. The moonlight dappled the water, and I could see a white crest of a wave break through the darkness here and there. But everything else was total blackness. I sat in the wicker chair, and became aware that I was cold. All I wore were my white cotton briefs, and looking down, I became aware of something else: I was erect.

I sat there and watched the sun come up, my fear dissipating with every glimmer of sunlight that dissolved the night. And as I began to make out shapes and colors—the water, the sand, the rocks in the distance—I realized there was something very near shore. It looked at first as if it could be a drifting log, but then, in a sprinkling of new light, I discerned it to be the merman, floating blissfully in shallow water, near enough for me to touch.

I forgot my lingering fears and ran out onto the beach, the door to the sun porch banging behind me. I kicked through the damp sand down to the water and called out: "Please don't go! Please! I want to talk to you!"

The merman turned his head to me, drowsily, as if I'd disturbed a dream. But he smiled, an incredibly white, even smile. He used his arms to tread water and his tail disappeared under the surface. He was no more than three feet from me.

"Please," I said, suddenly aware of how my voice broke the silence of dawn. Soon it would be joined by the cawing of gulls, but for now, the beach was quiet. "What's your name?"

He only smiled. But I could sense he wasn't going to swim away. I tried again: "Your name. Do you speak English?"

I felt absurd all at once. "My name is Michael," I said.

His beautiful, full lips parted and he spoke. "Michael," he echoed, a deep, cavernous voice.

"I've been wanting to meet you for so long. Nobody believes you're real. But I've watched you every day. You've always been so far out.

Now I can see you without any doubt. You *are* real. Where do you come from?"

"Michael," was all he said, and he seemed to enjoy saying it.

I took a few steps into the surf. "Tell me where you come from. May I see it?"

The merman had drifted out a few feet into the water. He reached out his powerful arms to me, hands imploring, as if I was to follow.

"I can't go beyond the rocks," I told him.

But suddenly he was below water, his great tail crashing upwards. He emerged about a yard away, and held out his hands to me again.

I hesitated for just a moment, then plunged into the water and went after him. He swam hard, and underwater I could see him, a mighty ocean creature, cutting a path through the sea. I did my best to keep up with him. I realized we were going past the rocks, but now I didn't care. I was a good swimmer. I would be fine.

I lost him momentarily. I came to the surface, treading water with my feet, looking around in the hazy morning light. My grandmother's cottage looked very far away on land now. I spotted the merman now on the far side of the great rock, sunning himself in the new light of the breaking dawn. He looked over at me and motioned for me to join him.

I swam as hard as I could. I reached the rock and pulled myself up, scraping my knee slightly as I did. He noticed, and a look of concern passed over his face. He bent forward and pressed his warm lips to my knee, and I shivered. He raised his face and looked at me. "Michael," he said again.

I looked at his tail, glowing green and silver in the sun. Occasionally a glimmer of red or purple reflected across the silky scales. I looked at his chest: large erect brown nipples embedded in firm, rounded pectorals. I looked at his arms: strong, powerful, wet and glistening. And his hands—I noticed for the first time the translucent webbing that grew between his fingers. I looked into his face: a mature, chiseled face, full lips that drew up in a smile. But it was his eyes than transfixed me most: eyes of brown and green, big eyes, eyes accustomed to seeing both in the sun and under the water, eyes from whom no secret could possibly hide.

He pressed one wet and webbed hand to the side of my face and drew my whole slight body toward his for a long and warm kiss. I felt the fullness of his mouth and the warmth of his torso as I was crushed into his embrace. I heard the involuntary slap of his tail against the rock. My underwear was wet and clinging to my erection, and I felt a strange hardness from him, protruding into my leg. I have never been able to visualize where his penis emerged from, from what fold of his tail it came to me, but in that moment, I was beyond rational thought: his body blocked out the sun as he covered me. He slid down my underwear and I felt him enter me. No pain. Just a sting of electricity. My body shuddered. I was ecstatic.

Finally, he gently broke free. Raising himself up on his hands, he smiled down at me. "Michael," he said once again, and never before had I heard my name said in such a way. He kissed me lightly on the forehead and then dove to the right, crashing into the water, splashing so high the spray doused me completely. I pulled myself up to call after him, leaning over the side of the rock, but all I could see were the spreading ripples of his impact.

And I never saw him again.

That next day my father arrived in his red pick-up truck and said he was taking all of us kids home, that Nana had called and said she thought it was best. My father embraced me and kissed my hair lightly. "We need to be together now," he said. "Your mother would have wanted that."

My grandmother died that following winter. We never returned to the cottage. But I believe to this day that the merman still exists, and that he waits for me.

I was an imaginative kid. I used to draw pictures of fairies and goblins and elves all over the brown paper covers of my school books. But James once said I had no imagination, no hope, no faith.

"You're the most pessimistic person I know, sugar," he said. "Trust me. I know what's best. This is going to *work*."

When James met Bernard, I never expected it would last, and I told him so. Bernard was too solemn, too unsmiling. They met on Christmas night a year ago at a gay bar in New Haven. Understand that Christmas is one of those nights that's supremely popular at gay bars, with flocks of faggots descending for succor and solace after a day spent cooped up with the family. A silver Christmas tree decorated with pink triangles and rainbow ornaments stood just beside the door. The go-go boys danced in g-strings of red fur wearing Santa hats on their heads. The dance floor was crowded with queens who were already crocked, their faces pulsing with pink light.

"Merry Christmas, Michael," Christopher called, waving over to me. "Hope Santa was good to you."

I joined him with my cosmopolitan. It tasted too sweet but I didn't complain. James would have sent it back, but that's just not my way.

"Santa Claus stopped coming to our house when I was thirteen," I told Christopher, not meaning to sound wry or bitter, but I think it came out that way. "Besides, he never brings me what I really want."

Christopher just grinned and clinked his cosmo with mine.

"Where's James?" I asked.

"Off chasing some beautiful stranger." Christopher shrugged. "What else is there to do on Christmas night?"

When I was a very young boy, Christmas night was horribly depressing: the gifts all opened and put away, the cousins all gone home, the spumoni completely consumed. All the anticipation that had been building, building, building since late October suddenly dissipated at four-thirty in the afternoon, and the world went back to being ordinary and uneventful. The bright colorful paper that had protected the packages sitting under the tree was now crumpled into an enormous garbage bag. Television reverted to its usual schedule, Rudolph and Frosty and the Little Drummer Boy consigned to the network vaults for another year.

Christmas night as an adult wasn't much better. There I was, getting drunk, watching James chase that beautiful stranger who, of course, turned out to be Bernard. When James brought him over to introduce us, I could see he'd already flipped for him. Bernard barely grunted a hello. James, a little wasted, hung all over him.

"He wants a lover *soooo* bad," Christopher said after James had led Bernard back out onto the dance floor.

"He's *had* a lover," I said. "Four of them, to be exact."

Admittedly, none of James's boyfriends had lasted more than a few months, but the fact remained that James had had relationships, and I hadn't. I was twenty-four years old at the time but I'd never had a boyfriend. Not one. And James had had *four.*

"I, for one, do *not* want a lover," Christopher announced, finishing his cosmo. "Not at least until I'm thirty. I don't want to be tied down."

How things have changed since that night. That dreary Christmas night a year ago, as I stood there unsmiling as some drag queen hauled herself up onto the stage and sang "I Saw Daddy Kissing Santa Claus." Mostly, I kept my eyes on James, who was making out with Bernard on the other side of the dance floor. By last call, I was trashed.

What else is there to do on Christmas night?

I ran over a stop sign driving home. I know, it was foolish to drink and drive. Thankfully, the stop sign was the only casualty of that foolishness, that and the fender of my car. I staggered into the house and flicked on the light in the living room. My father was sitting in his chair.

"Dad," I said. "What are you still doing awake?"

"Waiting for you."

I laughed. "Dad. I'm not a kid anymore. You don't have to wait up for me."

"It's Christmas," he said simply.

"Not anymore," I said, aware that I was slurring my words. "It's one-thirty. Officially December the twenty-sixth. The whole damn holiday is over."

"Mikey, you shouldn't be drinking and driving."

I sat down opposite him on the couch. My dad is a good man. He's in his seventies, with rosy red cheeks and thin white hair and a big round belly. No wonder he played Santa Claus all those years for the PTA. How the kids used to tease me. "Mikey's dad is Santa Claus! Mikey's dad is Santa Claus!"

He was looking at me with his twinkling little eyes. "I know the holidays aren't what they used to be, Mikey."

"What did they used to be?"

"Mikey, I don't always, you know, understand about your life. But I want you to be happy. You know that, don't you?"

I made a sound, noncommital in its reply.

"You're the last of my kids," Dad said. "I've seen all the others married off and supposedly happy with their lives. What about you, Mikey?"

"I'm happy, Dad," I told him.

"I want you to be, Mikey. I want you to be happy."

I looked over at him.

He was crying.

Santa Claus was crying.

For twenty years, Dad played Santa Claus for the St. Augustine's PTA. He would don his red suit and white beard and listen to hundreds of kids recite their Christmas lists as they sat on his lap in the school cafeteria. My brothers and sisters and I all knew it was Dad under the red fur; he and my mother had told us ahead of time. Otherwise, they reasoned, our keen little ears might pick up some familiar intonation and thus shatter our always precarious belief in the *real* jolly old elf. Accordingly, Dad became Santa's special helper, and we counted our family fortunate to be so singled out by the great man himself.

At first, it was grand fun to play the game. When Santa made the rounds through the school, I knew better than to tell any of the other kids who he really was. When he'd hoist me up on his lap, he'd always mention something that would prove to the other kids that he was the Real McCoy: "Well, I'll bet this fellow wants another monster model to add to his collection this year. Will it be Dracula, Frankenstein or the creature from *Alien?*"

He'd do the same for my friends, all of whom had confided to me their secret Christmas lists, prompting wide-eyed stares and hushed questions of "How did he *know?*"

"Because he's the *real* Santa Claus," I'd tell them with a bratty, superior air.

If Dad was Santa's special helper, then I was Santa's helper's helper. At home, I assisted in the transformation. The big job was always getting the pillow to stay firm under his belt and not slip down a pant leg. Watching my then-slender, black-haired father metamorphose into Santa Claus was a thing of wonder: This, to my seven-year-old mind, was *exactly* how the real St. Nick looked.

But growing up has a way of diminishing wonder. By third grade, kids had already started scoffing at the idea of Santa Claus. By the fourth grade, they could be openly belligerent. At that age, Santa isn't cool anymore, and Dad's annual visit to my classroom was no longer something I anticipated. That my classmates would discover that it was my father in a funny red hat was something I dreaded and, of course, they did: "Hey, I recognize his voice. Hey, Mikey, that's your dad. Hey, everybody, look at Santa's son blush!"

When you're ten years old, you want nothing less than to be singled out by your peers. It's a time when you want to blend into the whole, to disappear into the comfort of conformity. I already knew I was a different kid: I couldn't keep up on the basketball court, I despised field hockey, and I had queer, confusing thoughts about Tony Petruzzi who sat next to me. I hated being singled out more than anything else in the world.

I remember it was the last day before Christmas vacation during my fifth-grade year. I told my mother I was sick. I even tried to make myself puke but, unlike James some years later in a vastly different situation, I was unsuccessful. She didn't believe me and sent me off to school to endure being called "Santa's son" and "the jolly *young* elf."

"I'm okay, Dad," I told him now, all grown up and supposedly happy. "I'm really okay."

His bloodshot eyes held me. "I know I don't understand your life very well," he said as I stood, needing to go to bed, "but if there's ever—you know—anything—"

"Yeah, Dad," I said. "I know."

The next day I had the worst hangover of my life.

The guests were arriving, all embracing Christopher with warm birthday greetings. The place was filling up, but still no sign of Bud. Christopher was frantic.

"Maybe he's not coming," he said to me. "Maybe he was just too nervous about meeting all of you."

"He'll be here," I said. "Give him time."

James was playing the grand hostess, welcoming each guest as if it were his party and not Christopher's—as if this were *his* apartment and not Bernard's. Oh, sure, he lived here, but he paid no rent, had bought none of the furniture. Most of his clothes were still at his mother's house. In fact, last year, I hadn't thought it was a good idea that James move in at all.

"Sugar, I am *stifled* at home," he'd insisted.

"But you've only known Bernard a couple months."

"Look," he said, sighing dramatically. "I know you think I'm moving too fast, and I love you for it, sugardoll, I really do. But I've told you that you just have to have more faith. Allow yourself to dream, to imagine the possibilities. This is *it*, I tell you. Bernard is the man I've been looking for. He's the *one*. He's successful, he knows what he wants, he's self-assured—"

"Fine, James," I cut him off. "I just want you to be happy."

He touched my face with my hand. I pulled away.

"Michael," he said softly. "How sweet of you to care so much."

"It's just that I've seen boyfriends come and go for you. I've seen you hurt. I only want what's best for you."

Christopher had agreed with me then, expressing concern that James was moving too fast. "We're too young to get married," he said, but that was a year ago. Now he waited anxiously for Bud's arrival— Bud, the *one*, the man he'd been looking for.

"Maybe I ought to call him," Christopher said.

"He's not going to stand you up on your birthday."

The doorbell rang again, and Christopher rushed over to the window to peer through the Venetian blinds. "It's *him*," he said, and made a beeline for the door.

I saw James arch an eyebrow over the crowd to get a good look. Christopher threw his arms around Bud in greeting, obscuring our first glimpse. But then, as they moved inside, I could see Bud's tight little smile, the wariness in his eyes. He was holding a bouquet of daisies, which Christopher accepted and clutched to his bosom.

Bud wasn't very tall, maybe five-eight, but he had a hefty build, like most gay guys of his generation. Big shoulders, big thighs. His hairline had receded considerably, though he kept his hair buzzed close, and he sported a goatee that seemed incongruously dark brown.

"Clairol makes a special dye just for mustaches and sideburns," James breathed into my ear.

I hadn't even realized he was there. "Don't be so catty," I scolded him.

"This is Oscar and Edward," Christopher was saying, making the introductions. Bud shook each of their hands. "And over here is Michael, and this is James." He paused. I realized he was using the pleasant, chirpy voice he used around my father. "They're my oldest and dearest friends."

"Nice to meet you," Bud said, and extended his hand.

"And you," I said. We shook. He had a very solid grip, one of those bone-crushers that makes you feel you're not being manly enough. He wore jeans, Levis button-fly, and a white sweatshirt. He wore those big beige workboots with leather trim so popular in the Eighties, untied, his jeans pushed down into them.

James proved utterly charming. "*Bonsoir, bonsoir, bonsoir!*" He dropped to a half-curtsy, welcoming Bud to his home, doing his very best Delta Burke. "Why, we have just heard *so* much about you, Mr. Bud!"

But after Christopher had led his new man off into the crowd, James turned to me to screech under his breath, "What catalog did he order *that* one from?"

"Someplace in the Castro, I'm sure," Oscar said with a laugh.

James giggled. "They must have been offering a special on *clones*."

It was true that I couldn't imagine our little International Male with this man. But then, I couldn't imagine James with Bernard. Or Oscar with the granola bar.

Or me with anyone.

It occurred to me, somewhere between the time we sang "Happy Birthday" and Christopher blew out his candles, that I was the only one at this little soiree not paired off. Oh, there may have been a few others, some of Bernard's straight work friends perhaps, but when I looked around, all I saw were odd little pairs.

I began collecting dirty paper cups and ashtrays into a trash bag.

I watched them all. Oscar and Edward were discussing the political situation in Afghanistan. James sat demurely at Bernard's knee, listening to his lover talk insurance policies with his work friends, his head going back and forth between them as if he were at a tennis match. And then there was Christopher, talking with Bud about music.

"No, silly, her *name* is Pink," Christopher was saying, showing Bud a CD. "Her hair changes color all the time. Sometimes it's pink, but right now she's a blonde. She's the latest diva."

"I can't keep up," Bud said. "Used to be divas hung around for a while. Now there's a new one every couple months."

"Can I make you guys another cosmo?" I asked.

Christopher nodded, handing me his empty glass, but Bud declined. "I brought some beer," he said. "That's all I drink."

"Michael, can't you see that Bud is a guy's guy?" Christopher smiled, draping his arms over Bud's beefy shoulder. "He doesn't go for girly drinks."

"So what do you do, Bud?" I asked.

"I'm a teacher," he said.

"Really? Where?"

"Bloomfield High School. History and government."

"Bud has his daughter in class this year," Christopher said, then looked immediately at Bud as if to ask if he should have revealed that.

"You have a daughter?" I asked.

Bud nodded. "She's a freshman."

"So you were married."

"Yes, very briefly. Right out of college. I've been divorced for fourteen years."

"Does your daughter know?"

"That I'm gay?"

No, that you're a hopeless fashion failure. "Yes," I said, smiling.

Bud gestured as if to keep me back. "No, not at all. She couldn't deal with that yet."

I simply sighed. If my father, a veteran of the Korean War, could deal with it, I imagined his daughter, raised in the era of *Will and Grace*, could deal with it, too. But I didn't want to judge him, even if I already had.

"Are you having fun?" I asked.

He shrugged. "Feel as if I'm the scout leader or something."

"Will you *stop?*" Christopher playfully slapped Bud's shoulder.

"Yeah," I assured him, "don't worry about it." But inside, I had determined pretty quickly that this could never last.

Bud smiled at me. "Well, I appreciate your support, Mike—or, are you like the rest of these guys here and don't use your nickname? Everybody's Bernard or James."

"I prefer Michael," I said.

"What is it with all you kids?" Bud laughed. "What's wrong with Mike, Bernie, or Jim?" He looked over at his boyfriend. "Or Chris!"

Christopher's eyes were on me. He wasn't smiling. "Michael, my cosmo?"

"Oh, right." I raised his glass and turned to head out to the kitchen. "Catch you later, Chris." Out of the corner of my eye, I saw him grimace.

The party ended late. Christopher and Bud were the first to leave— odd, given that it was Christopher's birthday party, and don't think for a minute that James didn't comment on it. Bernard's straight work friends were the last, stumbling out very loud and very drunk.

James and I cleaned up, gossiping about the guests, especially Bud.

"Age shouldn't matter," I said, "but I think it will, to Christopher, in the end."

"Of *course* age should matter," James said. "Come on, be honest, Michael. *What* do they have to talk about? When Christopher was eleven and developing his first crush on Jordan from New Kids on the Block, Bud was already married *and* divorced."

I did the math. "He was twenty-five. Christopher's age."

James nodded, stacking plates in the dishwasher. "And with a *kid* to boot." He snorted. "Like he and Christopher have *anything* in common."

"I'm going to bed," Bernard announced, appearing suddenly in the doorway. "What a night. Didn't think people would ever leave."

He pecked James on the cheek and moved off down the hall.

I thought it peculiar that Bernard wasn't helping to clean up, and said so. James bristled, saying the party had been for *our* friend, not *his*, and that Bernard shouldn't have to bear the responsibility.

"So when do *your* friends become *his* friends, too?" I asked. "Isn't that the way it's supposed to work in relationships?"

"Oh, Michael, you know what I mean."

I didn't, but kept quiet. We cleaned up the rest in silence. As I was getting ready to leave, I noticed James was setting up the couch in the living room with a pillow and blanket.

"Why aren't you sleeping with Bernard in your room?"

He looked at me. "Oh, he'll already be asleep, and he hates it when I wake him up."

Once again I held my tongue. Later, driving home, down Evergreen Avenue and all along Farmington, all the stop lights seemed to be out of sync. That night, I lay in bed awake, thinking about James and Bernard, Christopher and Bud, Oscar and Edward—all the couples I knew, all the couples in the world. I listened to the crickets, very loud, until I finally fell asleep.

So all through the fall, Bud became an uneasy member of our little group. He was always eager, always pleasant. But there was something about his eagerness and his pleasantness that I distrusted, even disliked. Christopher told me about Bud's friends—thirty- and forty-something gym queens who knew every video, *in order*, that Madonna ever made and who, after a few beers and a couple hits of X, were hot on the trail of any chicken meat that dared walk through their periphery. I met a couple of these guys, too, one Saturday night at the bar. Now, my meat might still be chicken but it's hardly lean—more like the plumped-up parts sold by Perdue. Yet Bud's friends still eyed me with a hard and desperate lust, winking and making cracks, one of them even grabbing my ass.

Please, I prayed. *Please never let me get this way.*

How must they talk about Christopher—little "Chrissy," as they called him. How Bud must brag about his pretty little twinky boyfriend. I didn't like Bud. And it became increasingly difficult to hide how I felt.

In October, James decided to start a new tradition. We would have dinner at his and Bernard's apartment every Friday night. I suspected Bernard wasn't keen on the idea, but he went along. James instructed that we'd take turns bringing the food. The first week he and Bernard would make the dinner, the next week Christopher and Bud would take over, and finally it would be my turn.

"Sure," I said, standing in the doorframe of the kitchen, watching James mix up margaritas. "All of you have partners to help you cook. I'll end up just bringing a pizza."

"Sugar," James said, "I don't cook. My talents are *not* in the kitchen."

He laughed, blowing a kiss over at Bernard, who was placing a soufflé in the oven and ignoring our conversation very well.

"Isn't my husband amazing?" James gushed. "He could have been a master chef if he hadn't become such an insurance tycoon."

"Why don't you put on some music?" Bernard suggested.

"You got it, honeycake." James practically bounded into the living room. I followed. I think Bernard just wanted us out of the kitchen. Christopher and Bud were seated on the couch, close together, holding hands. James looked over at them. "Well, maybe the lovebirds would like to pick out the music."

"I brought some, actually," Bud said.

"Oooh," James purred. "That should be interesting."

Bud stood and opened up a small leather case. There were a few CDs but most of what we could see were cassette tapes.

"Sugar," James cooed, tickling Bud under his scruffy chin. "It's time you joined the rest of us in the twenty-first century. There's no cassette player on our system."

Bud smirked. "Darn. Well, I'm glad I didn't bring all my eight-tracks then."

Christopher was immediately in James's face. "He's kidding. Tell him you're kidding, Bud. He doesn't really have any eight-tracks."

James shooed him away. "Well, let's see what CDs you do have here." He flipped through them. "Well, nothing that a self-respecting homosexual should ever be without. Cher's 'Believe.' Whitney Houston dance remixes. And, well, well, well, lookee here. The original soundtrack to *Saturday Night Fever.*"

"When I was a kid," Bud said, grinning ear to ear, "I wanted nothing more than to have a white polyester suit like John Travolta."

"Then let's play it," James said, snatching up the CD. "In honor of Bud's childhood dreams."

He popped it into the system. In moments, the Bee Gees' falsettos were bouncing off the walls of the apartment. James began doing a hilarious parody of old-fashioned disco moves, rolling his hands over each other, sticking his arm up and pointing at the ceiling, spinning around on his toes. Bud and I both laughed, but Christopher sat down sullenly on the couch.

"What year was this movie released again?" James asked, stopping suddenly. "Oh, wait, I know! The year we all were *born!*"

I saw Christopher cringe, but again Bud just smiled. "Not all of us, James. Some of us were born a few years before that."

Bernard was setting the table. "Dinner will be ready in a few minutes, you guys. You might want to sit down."

Christopher took his boyfriend's hand and led him to the table. I could see him whispering something to Bud, something hard, but I couldn't make out what it was. He was still talking to him as he fit a corkscrew over a bottle of red wine. Glasses were lined up on the table, and Christopher began pouring. But his eyes were not on his task, as he was still talking intently under his breath. As Bud moved in to take one of the glasses, Christopher bumped his arm, splashing wine all over both of their shirts.

"Now look what you made me do!" he shouted.

"I *made* you do it?" Bud asked.

"Quick," Bernard said. "Give me your shirts. I'll soak them in some seltzer water. I'll get you a couple of mine to wear for dinner."

Christopher just sighed, crossing his arms over his chest, refusing to say even that he was sorry. Bud pulled his shirt up over his head, and I was struck all at once by how hairy he was. Chest, stomach, shoulders, even some on his back. Christopher unbuttoned his shirt now, too, handing it over to Bernard who took it out to the kitchen along with Bud's. Christopher's torso was lean and smooth, with nothing more than a little trail of hair leading from his navel down into his jeans. Standing there next to each other, Bud and Christopher looked like an exhibit on evolution. I was sure Bud's hair must secretly gross Christopher out.

Once they were each secured into one of Bernard's flannel shirts, we settled down to eat. Bernard presented his soufflé with a flourish and we all gave him a little round of applause. But it wasn't long before James had picked up where he'd left off.

"I was thinking, Bud, maybe we could all take a trip to New York next month, maybe see the Christmas show at Radio City Music Hall."

What was he up to? I turned my eyes to James, trying to figure out where he was going with this.

"Sure," Bud said. "Sounds good to me."

"I was thinking maybe you could show us Stonewall," James said. "I've never been, have you, Christopher?"

"It's just like any old bar," Christopher said, still defensive.

"*Any old bar?* Bud, did you hear that? Such sacrilege." James leveled his eyes on Christopher. "Sugar, that's where people like Bud fought back so that people like you and I might sit here and drink red wine and get ready to watch *Absolutely Fabulous.*"

"Fuck you, James."

It was Bud speaking. The table fell quiet, except for James, who laughed.

"I've never been to the Stonewall," Bud told him. "I'm not even sure I know where it is."

"You weren't *there?*" James asked. "I mean, that night?"

"Like I said, James. Fuck you."

"Yes, James," Bernard said, "why don't you just eat and shut up?"

"My, my, my, everybody ganging up on me all of a sudden." James fluttered his eyelashes and stabbed his fork into Bernard's soufflé, taking a bite. "Delicious, darling. Even if it does come from a recipe from—oh, what was her name?"

"It's Philip's recipe," Bernard explained to the table. "Philip's my ex. And it's *him,* not her."

"Oh, Bernard, *please.*" This was me talking, finally. Bernard hates it when we use the female pronoun, and it pisses me off—a homophobic reaction if I ever heard one. "Lighten up," I told him.

"Now, now, Michael," James said. "Bernard has fond memories of his ex-thing. We shouldn't blaspheme."

"No, you shouldn't," Bernard said. "Especially if you want me to have fond memories of you, too."

James just stared at him. I saw his lower lip quiver a bit. Then he pushed back his chair, stood up, and stalked out of the room. I sighed. Bernard ignored him, just kept on eating. Bud sat there, just sipping his wine. Christopher's head had slumped down to his chest.

So went our first Friday night dinner. It also turned out to be our last.

I was temping at the bank where I used to work full time. It didn't make sense to me. Why had I been laid off simply to be rehired as a temporary worker? Shoshanna, a woman I used to work with and who now was in charge of explaining my routine to me, said it was simple. "They don't have to pay you benefits this way, they don't have to worry about cost-of-living salary increases, and you don't get to take personal days."

She was a tall, broad-shouldered African-American woman from Hartford's North End. "Do you ever think," I asked her, "that somehow we got gypped out of a life?"

Shoshanna scowled down at me. "*What*—do you think a life comes guaranteed when you're born?"

"I don't know." I watched as she piled copies of checks in front of me. There must have been three thousand of them, all stacked in precarious little piles across a folding table. "But I would think some sort of a life should be part of the deal."

"Michael, there's no deal. Face it. You didn't ask to be born, you just were." She points down at the checks. "Now you've got to put these all in order by check number, then separate them by the first three digits in this string of numbers here on the bottom. Michael, are you listening to me?"

"No, I'm listening to a choir of heavenly angels sing praises to God above."

She wagged a beringed finger in front of my face. "You know, I remember your mouth. When you worked here, everybody thought you were so quiet. Such a timid one. But you'd come out with zingers every once in a while, and surprise everybody."

I sighed, looking at the endless checks awaiting my efforts. "I'm always zinging people in my mind, but I keep them to myself, mostly."

"Maybe that's why you don't have a life," Shoshanna said. "Now pay attention. You've got to order these checks in three ways. First by check number, then you look down at these three digits here and put them in order. Then you have to separate them by branch . . ."

"Why? Why does all this matter in the end?"

"Michael, don't you know there's no answer to that question? Now just do your job so you can pick up your paycheck. That's the only answer you got to know." She shot me a look. "And no mouthing back."

I didn't try. I could think of nothing to say.

*   *   *

Halloween fast approached, and I set my mind on winning some cash. A bar in Waterbury was offering a thousand bucks to the first-place winner of their costume contest. A bunch of us decided to go as characters from *The Wizard of Oz*, and drew names from a hat. I really, really wanted to go as either Glinda or the Wizard, and I would've settled for the Witch or the Lion, but I got the Tin Man. I always hated the Tin Man. He always seemed so fey, so annoyingly apt to break down in tears. James, of course, got to be Glinda, and Bernard had a great time stuffing his pants with straw as the Scarecrow. Meanwhile, I stuck a funnel cup on my head and wrapped myself up in aluminum foil, but the judges didn't even notice me. The best any of us did was Christopher's honorary mention as Toto.

Bud, however, didn't get dressed up. He simply came as he was, in a T-shirt and 501s, leather jacket and, of course, those damn workboots. A couple of our friends whispered that, of course, he *was* in costume: San Francisco Clone circa 1985. I simply could not imagine what in the world Christopher *saw* in this man.

Then it turned cold: it was snowing on Thanksgiving. I didn't want to spend the holiday with my family. One of my brothers had left his wife and half of my siblings sided with him, the other half with her. I didn't care one way or the other. Accordingly, there was a lot of arguing and bitching around the turkey, and even my sister Theresa's announcement that she was pregnant failed to make for much merriment. My father said very little, just sitting there glumly at the head of the table, listening to his children bicker, staring across at my mother's empty chair. It had never been filled since her death, purposely left vacant on my father's order, so that we'd never forget what we had lost.

I couldn't wait to get out of there. James and Bernard were preparing an alternative feast, to which we all looked forward to as solace after a long day with our families.

Holidays pose a uniquely queer conundrum. At work, Shoshanna looked puzzled when I asked if she'd rather be with her friends on Christmas Eve or with her parents and siblings. "My daughter wants to see Grandma and Grandpa," she said. "And they want to see her. And she wants to play with all her cousins."

"But what about *you?*" I pressed.

She paused. "I hadn't really thought of it. I suppose what I'd really like to do is just stay home with a bottle of champagne and my boyfriend."

The difference is that many of us gay folk have already considered that latter option. Many gays have established families outside of our biological clans, and we'd rather be with *them* on the holidays. And so the juggling begins.

"Bernard is going to roast a turkey and brew up some cranberry sauce and bake some sweet potatoes," James promised. "So don't pig out at your family's table."

Our alternative celebration would consist of James and Bernard, Christopher and Bud, Oscar and Edward, and me. Not just a third wheel but a *seventh*. Oh, well.

I was the first to arrive. James was in the kitchen, crying. The place reeked of frying oil.

"What's going on?"

"Oh, Michael, Bernard isn't back from his parents' house yet! I got here and the turkey wasn't thawed!"

On the stove, hacked-off frozen turkey parts were sitting in a frying pan sizzling in olive oil. The oil popped furiously, splattering me on the arm. I yelped.

"So you're trying to *fry* it?" I asked increduously.

"I'm trying to *defrost* it. It wouldn't fit in the microwave."

"You're crazy, James."

He covered his face with his hands. "I *told* you! I'm not a cook! My talents lie *elsewhere* than the kitchen!"

I turned off the burner and opened the refrigerator door. Nothing had been started for dinner. I sighed.

"Let's start peeling some sweet potatoes," I suggested. "So we have a vegetarian Thanksgiving. There are worse situations."

James looked at me with the saddest eyes. "You always know how to fix things, don't you, Michael? Ever since we were kids, you've known how to make everything right."

I held his gaze. James has beautiful eyes. Every time he looks at me that way I'm reminded of how beautiful they are. They're deep-set, dark, hypnotic. I can remember junior year in high school, when as part of a science experiment on the effects of light, we had to stare into each other's eyes. James was my partner. We positioned ourselves opposite each other, our knees touching, and looked deeply into each other's eyes. I found the expansion and dilation of his pupils fascinating. I even popped a boner. How much I wanted to kiss him right there in front of the whole class—just like I wanted to kiss him now, standing in Bernard's kitchen.

"James," I said thickly. "You know, I—"

The door opened. Bernard walked in, and immediately berated James for forgetting to take the turkey out of the freezer. James protested meekly that Bernard had forgotten too; after all, he was the cook in the family. But Bernard would hear none of it. He just shooed us out of the kitchen so he could try to salvage something of our alternative Thanksgiving dinner.

"He's right, really," James said to me, safely out of earshot in the living room. "I was the last one out of the house this morning. I should've remembered."

"James, why do you always defer to Bernard? He should've taken the turkey out last night. Turkeys take a long time to thaw."

"Bernard has a lot on his mind, Michael. There's a whole shitload of stuff going on at work. Remember, Michael, Bernard has a *career*. Unlike us." He looked at me intently. "It's *my* fault our Thanksgiving is ruined."

I looked back at him. How handsome James was. I loved the way his face hollowed out under his cheekbones, the graceful sweep of his long, smooth, aquiline fingers. I covered my own pudgy paws, the wolf hair that covered my father's hands already creeping up toward my knuckles. I prayed to God that I wouldn't end up looking like Bud the Ape Man when I was thirty-nine.

Bud arrived with Christopher not long after that. I could see they were in the midst of a fight. Christopher's ears were red and not because of the cold. Bud, I gathered, had felt some guilt about leaving his daughter to come here, and he had communicated as much to Christopher.

"Like you *wanted* to stay any longer with your ex-wife and her husband," Christopher said, taking off his coat, revealing a new pink lycra shirt tightly encasing his torso. "Or maybe you *did*! Maybe you were just sitting there mooning over the life you threw away."

"Look, Christopher, you need to accept that I have a family," Bud said.

"*We're* your family. *I'm* your family!"

Bud sighed. "So is my daughter. And I still care about my ex-wife. You have to accept that."

"I just can't understand." Christopher looked over at me. "Can *you*, Michael?"

I just held up my hands, not wanting to get involved.

Christopher huffed. "I'm just so glad *our* generation never dabbled in heterosexuality before coming to our senses. I'm so glad *we* never got saddled with children."

Bud folded his arms across his chest. "I'm not *saddled* with my daughter."

"How about if the two of you take it outside?" James snapped. "The only thing worse than watching the two of you fight is watching the two of you make love."

Bud just snorted. Christopher sighed, scrunching up his nose. "What's that *smell?*" he asked all at once.

"Don't ask," James said.

I watched as Christopher and Bud settled into chairs on opposite sides of the room. They'd been bickering more and more these past few weeks. Christopher didn't like Bud's friends. Or his clothes. Or his taste in music. It was just as James and I had been saying all along: they were completely incompatible. We took bets on how much longer it would endure. I gave it until New Year's; James predicted the relationship wouldn't last through Christmas. However much time was left, it was definitely on its final legs. Before much longer, I was sure Christopher would give Bud the old heave-ho.

They hardly spoke all through dinner. Bernard was surly, too, being forced to serve just sweet potatoes, stuffing and cranberry sauce. We called Oscar on his cell phone and asked him to stop by on his way and pick up some Chinese food. Our alternative Thanksgiving feast turned out to consist mostly of moo-shoo pork and sweet-and-sour chicken.

And so the Christmas season found all of us, each in our own way, a little cranky.

My job at the bank was over. I trekked down to the temp agency to see what else they might have.

"Spare some change?"

It was a lady in earmuffs ringing a bell for the Salvation Army.

I could use a handout myself this year. Part of me wanted to tell her that, but I just kept my eyes downcast at the sidewalk. It had started to snow.

There's not much left in downtown Hartford. The insurance companies are still there, high above the ground in their glass and iron structures. But the businesses I remember from my childhood are nearly all gone. I paused before the boarded-up storefront of F.W. Woolworth. Even as a kid, Woolworth's was struggling to survive, unable to keep up with the malls and the Wal-Marts. But it was still my mother's favorite store, the place she'd shopped as a little kid herself, with her own mother.

For us, Woolworth's was a ritual. My sister Theresa took dancing lessons until she was thirteen. Every Wednesday, my mother would pick her up after school at St. Augustine's and drive her downtown. As I was too young to go home by myself, I had to accompany them, sitting with my mother in the waiting room listening to the tappity-tap-tap behind the door. There was never any consideration that I join Thersesa in her lessons—boys in my family definitely did *not* take dancing lessons—but in truth, gay as I already was, I wouldn't have wanted to sign up. I hated the whole experience of the dancing school. There were all these silly little girls with skinny legs and their fat older sisters who made faces at me. No one ever talked to me except my mother when I'd ask how much longer we had to sit there.

"Just a little longer. Do your homework."

But still, those afternoons with my mother resonate in my memory. What I treasure is the hour after the dancing class let out, when Mom would take Theresa and me downtown to Woolworth's. First we'd stop for milk at the Woolworth's Luncheonette, where a blue-haired lady in pink scuffed along behind the blue-green Formica counter that had red triangles embedded in it. From somewhere behind the counter there always came the clinking sound of glasses falling into a sink. My mother would specifically ask for white milk because one time, in an apparent yet unappreciated gesture on the blue-haired lady's part, we were given *chocolate* milk. Understand that Mom insisted chocolate milk wasn't nearly as healthy for us, so she always specified *white*. I remember Woolworth's milk was real cold, straight from the cooler with lots of bubbles and foam.

"Drink your milk," Mom told us. "It will help you grow."

After our milks, Theresa and I would roam through the store, her tap shoes dancing out rhythms on the old hardwood floors. I remember a salesclerk who was always peeking over the tops of aisles at us. She was very old, very wrinkled, and wore too much lipstick, thick and red, smeared over and beyond her lips. She wore a wig, too, heavy and full, tipped too far down her forehead.

"Is she bald under that wig?" I asked.

My mother shushed me and told me not to stare. I did anyway. I imagined the salesclerk at home at night, lounging around bald in her pink Woolworth's smock, leaving red lip marks on all her blue-green Woolworth's cups.

We never had a lot of money, and Mom was far more tighter with the purse strings than Dad. Still, on every trip to Woolworth's, she'd manage to buy us something. I'd pick out the latest comic books: *Superman, Justice League, X-Men.* One time my mother bought me an Etch-A-Sketch. I wrote "shit" with it on the way home and had it taken away for a week. Another time I got soap bubbles. When I started blowing them at Theresa, I got those taken away too.

Sometimes we'd get candy. My sister and I would play Holy Communion with Neco wafers as we waited in the check-out line.

"Stop being sacrilegious," Mom would scold. "We're almost through. Don't eat them all."

Woolworth's had a pet department, too, with the greatest miniature turtles, the kind with yellow-green paisley designs on their bottoms. I begged Mom for a couple turtles—begged and begged and *begged*— and finally she gave in. But when I got them home they stunk so much she made me take them down to the stream near the railroad tracks and set them free.

"But will they live through the winter down there?" I asked her.

"I don't know, Mikey, but in your heart, they'll always be alive."

One thing you could say about Mom: she didn't make false promises.

But it was Woolworth's hobby department that I loved most. As a boy, I collected monster models: The Mummy. Dracula. The Phantom of the Opera. Freddy Kreuger. Jason from *Friday the Thirteenth*. The thing from *Alien*. Some of the models glowed in the dark. One day I proudly set them all out on my dresser. When the lights went out, I could see the Mummy's hands glowing, reaching out for me. I decided all my monsters were better off kept in the closet.

Yet, for most of my childhood, I was missing one monster: the Bride of Frankenstein. I could never find her among the others on the shelves, but I knew she existed. Her picture was on the back of the package of every model I got. "I need to find her," I'd tell my parents. "I need to find her to complete my collection."

My older brothers teased me that I wanted the Bride of Frankenstein so much. "Why do you care about a girl monster?" I had no answer for them: I just wanted her, transfixed by that electrified hair, those curious eyes, that bandaged yet so obviously feminine body.

It was Christmas time, and Woolworth's was decorated with green garland and red bows tied around the poles. Every week, Mom would let me pick out one of the small wax figures for our nativity set. I went a little overboard. In our version of the Christmas story, there were sixteen wisemen and Jesus had a couple of aunts and uncles hanging around the place.

But what I really wanted was the Bride of Frankenstein, and there she finally was that Christmas, standing demurely beside Freddy Kreuger. "Too expensive," Mom said. "Pick out something else."

"Please! I really want her!"

"Not today, Mikey. Maybe for Chistmas."

But on Christmas morning, the Bride was nowhere to be found among my boxes of new Hanes underwear and that stinky baseball mitt my parents expected me to use. Dad noticed my disappointment.

"You didn't get what you wanted, Mikey?"

"It's okay," I said.

"What was it? What were you hoping for?"

Mom cut him off. "Michael, you need to learn that money doesn't grow on trees. We don't have a lot. I can't be buying you expensive toys that you will outgrow in a year."

"It's okay," I said again.

I remember my mother's eyes. How tired she looked that Christmas morning. It would be her last. Was her heart giving her trouble even then? Her eyes looked tired. Sad, too.

On our next trip to Woolworth's she bought me the Bride of Franken-stein.

"Don't tell your father," she whispered. "Just a little mad money be-tween you and me."

After my mother died, my sister stopped going to dancing school, and none of us went to Woolworth's much after that. I stopped read-ing comic books. The Etch-A-Sketch faded out so that it could only produce vertical lines. My monster models went down into the base-ment. When I noticed that the Mummy had lost one of his arms, there was an odd sadness that I couldn't quite explain. But I kept the Bride of Frankenstein on my dresser. She's still there, in fact.

Woolworth's closed a few years later. I remember once seeing the saleslady with the wig and the lipstick on the street. This time I didn't stare. I just watched her out of the corner of my eye, hobbling down the sidewalk with a cane.

"Maybe putting up a tree is too much, Dad."

He huffed, catching his breath as we dragged the blue spruce up the front steps.

"The grandkids expect it," he said. "When they come here Christmas Eve, they want a Christmas tree."

How would I tell him that I wouldn't be there myself? James had de-termined to make up for our Thanksgiving fiasco with a Christmas party. Just us, our gay family. I knew Dad would be hurt, but it was time I started living my life as I chose. Joy to the world included myself, after all.

I helped him steady the tree in the stand. It smelled fresh and tangy, the fragrance filling the room. On the floor sat the boxes from the basement. "Christmas" was written in my mother's handwriting on their sides.

Dad unwrapped an ornament from the crumbling old newspaper that protected it.

"This was one of her favorites," he said, holding the ornament out to me.

I remembered it. How could I not? Each of these little trinkets car-ried some memory with them. Mom's favorites. Gifts from relatives. Some ugly memento one of us kids had made in school. The one Dad was handing to me was old—older than I was, in fact. Delicate and gold, in the shape of a pine cone, a rusty hook hanging from its top.

"I think it was your mother's when she was a girl."

I hung it on the tree. Dad sat down on the couch and started to cry.

I felt terribly uncomfortable. My father's tears unnerved me. His grief after my mother's death had been even more unbearable than her loss. I would feel so vulnerable when he cried, so unprotected, so unsafe.

That hadn't changed.

"Dad," I said, "please don't cry."

He wiped his eyes. "Silly, huh? After all this time."

I sat beside him.

"It just sometimes comes over me. I'll think of her and just start to cry."

I sighed. I put my arm around his shoulders.

"We were supposed to be together until we both got old," he told me. "But it's just been me, by myself, watching you all grow up. Just me, getting old all by myself."

"I guess that's pretty hard," I offered.

"It's the worst thing, Mikey. You don't want to be alone when you're old."

I looked at him. He did indeed look old. Older than I'd realized. I hadn't really looked at my father in a long time. How frail he appeared sitting next to me. How small.

"So how come you never married again, Dad?"

"Your mother was my soulmate," he said plainly. "There could never be anyone else."

To love someone that much: was it possible? The next day I accompanied James and Christopher to West Farms Mall to do Christmas shopping. The Gap, Abercrombie & Fitch, Structure, Pottery Barn, Crate & Barrel—all the gay stores. James and Christopher were going on about their boyfriends, about how lucky they were.

"I think about my mother, how lonely she was every Christmas, after my father walked out on her," James said, holding up a sweater in front of him at A&F. "Do you think this looks like Bernard, Michael?"

Christopher interjected his opinion before I had the chance to answer. "It doesn't look a *thing* like Bernard, James. Don't be buying Christmas gifts for yourself now."

James smirked and tossed down the sweater. "Then why are *you* in here, Christopher? As if *Bud* would ever wear something from Abercrombie and Fitch. I suggest you head over to Sam's Army and Navy."

"My mother was the same way," Christopher said to me, ignoring James's barbs. "She'd get *sooo* depressed on Christmas Eve because she was alone."

"She had you and your sisters," I offered.

"It's not the same thing," Christopher said. "Someday, Michael, when you find a boyfriend, you'll know what I'm talking about."

He turned to the mirror to hold up a T-shirt in front of himself.

"Michael with a boyfriend?" James was saying, looking at me. "Well, that would be a novel development, wouldn't it?"

"What do you mean?" I asked. "Do you think I can't find a boyfriend?"

"Finding one is nothing compared to *keeping* one," James said. "You both are aware, aren't you, that Christmas will mark Bernard's and my *one-year anniversary?*"

Oh, I was aware of it, all right. I hadn't forgotten the night they met. I couldn't deny that a year—twelve whole months—was quite an achievement. None of our friends were ever in relationships that long. James had apparently found something that worked, even if it seemed more than a little dysfunctional to me.

But James and Bernard's dysfunction was nothing compared to Christopher and Bud's. James and I still had a wager on how soon it would fizzle out. "Before Christmas," James insisted. I thought Christopher would stick with it at least through the holiday. That way, he'd still get some Christmas presents out of the deal.

Our alternative Christmas Eve hit a snag right from the day it was planned, and the snag, as I could have predicted, was Bud. It seemed his aunt and uncle hosted a traditonal Christmas Eve gathering every year, and his daughter loved being a part of it.

"I *can't* disappoint her," Bud said. "It's *Christmas.*"

Christopher bristled. "But you can disappoint me?"

Bud just sighed.

"There's such an unchallenged assumption that blood family comes first." Christopher stood, arms akimbo, facing down his lover. "Well, in my book, gay family trumps straight aunt and uncle."

"Why don't you bring your daughter here?" I suggested to Bud, actually starting to feel a little sorry for the way Christopher was always haranguing him.

Bud blanched. "Oh, well, uh—I don't think she'd be ready for that."

Christopher was pacing the floor. "Some people simply can't see past their conditioning. They make you feel as if you're asking them to commit armed robbery if you suggest they ditch the blood relatives for a holiday."

"I've decided to try to do both," James said, putting in his two-cents' worth. "I'm not going to let my blood family determine the schedule for holidays. In fact, I'm going to do the opposite. I'll see what Bernard and I want to do, then I'll tell my mother and grandparents when I'll be able to see them. It probably won't be until Christmas night, but I'll manage to do both." He smiled over at Bernard. "Right, baby?"

But Bernard offered no reply. He was, as usual, absorbed watching MTV.

"It's very important for gay people to establish our own traditions," Christopher said, literally wagging his finger in front of Bud's face. "I admit I never knew much of a blood family, but I'll tell you one thing: I'm not going to end up alone and miserable like my mother."

I slipped on my coat, leaving them to their wrangling. I headed into town, without any real destination, just a need to walk outside while there was still some sunlight. The days were so short this time of year. Last week, in a fit of tears, James had declared he suffered from seasonal affective disorder: depression brought on by the lack of light. Maybe that's what had gotten all of us so down lately.

Yeah, that's what it was. The lack of light.

On Main Street, I spotted a knot of children.

"Ho ho ho!" came a voice from among them.

I knew that voice.

Santa Claus.

The kids were grouped around him, hopping from foot to foot as if they were standing on hot coals. He was passing out lollipops, beseiged by tiny hands.

"Sanna, I wanna Nutcracker Barbie!" one little girl shouted.

"I want a GameBoy!" called a chubby little boy who reminded me of myself at that age.

I approached them, catching Santa's eye.

"And what do *you* want for Christmas, young man?" Santa asked, eyes twinkling.

I pushed my hands deep into my pockets. "I'm not sure you could fit it down the chimney."

His smile curled under his fake beard. "Would it make you happy, Mikey?"

I laughed. The children were tugging at his red fur coat, yapping at his elbows. He turned back to them.

"Michael," came a voice behind me, "is that your *father?*"

It was James. "Yes," I told him. "That's my Dad."

James watched with amusement. "I thought he'd hung up his Santa suit a long time ago."

"I did, too." I shrugged. "I guess the Chamber of Commerce must have called him. Or maybe he just did it on his own." I turned to James. "So what brought you out of the house?"

"I just couldn't take it anymore."

"Bernard?"

He made a face. "Of course not. Christopher and Bud. Bicker, bicker, bicker."

I just nodded. I moved my eyes back to Santa. He was heading off down the street, followed by the chattering children, their mittened hands imploring. I could hear his "ho-ho-ho" rising above their voices.

We were both quiet for several minutes. Then James said, "He's pretty awesome, Michael. Your father. You know that, don't you?"

It made me pause. I knew that James's father had left his family without so much as a look over his shoulder. So had Christopher's. I suppose my dad *would* seem pretty awesome. For no financial reward, he gave up his weekend to trudge around the streets of Hartford in a heavy costume, fending off overly excited kids and the taunts of teenagers.

I looked over at James's face, his eyes still on my dad. I realized that being singled out from the crowd might not be so bad after all.

Dad was no longer just Santa's helper. He'd become the real thing.

Bernard insisted on an artificial tree. "I don't want a lot of needles all through my apartment," he said. So we headed to Wal-Mart and picked out a white and silver tree and chose to decorate it with blue lights and strung popcorn. Except we ended up eating all the popcorn and the lights didn't work, so the tree stood bare in the corner.

"It's kind of a minimalist Christmas," I said, bloated from all the popcorn.

Bud laughed.

"Oh, but we have to have *some* decorations, something!" James looked at me. "You must have something at your house, Michael. Your father's big into Christmas."

I looked at him. Yet again, he wanted me to make things better. I agreed to go see what I could find.

"Oh, Michael," James purred, "you are worth your weight in gold."

I laughed. "I don't think there's that much gold in Fort Knox."

"Oh, pooh," James said. "You're not that fat."

Key word there: *that.*

I slipped on my coat.

"I'll go with you," Bud said.

"That's not necessary."

"I'd like to."

I shrugged. Bernard's apartment was in the West End, about fifteen minutes to my father's house. I didn't relish being alone in the car with Bud for that long. We'd never done anything just the two of us, and I wasn't sure what we'd have to talk about.

"You know," Bud said, "I think we might have something in common."

I made a face. "You and me?"

"My mother died when I was eight, and I was raised by my dad."

I looked over at him but said nothing.

"My dad died a couple years ago. We were very close. I still miss him."

I didn't know what to say. "Yeah, well, my dad's been pretty . . . well, awesome."

Bud was nodding. "He ever talk to you about sex? That was the one area my dad and I never could get to."

I pulled into the driveway and shut off the ignition. I laughed. "When I was fourteen, my father handed me a book about reproduction. That was the extent of our talk about the birds and the bees. I associated sex with the mating habits of salmon. I ended up thinking I had to swim up the Columbia River if I wanted to make babies."

Bud laughed again.

"But I knew that wasn't going to be necessary," I said, enjoying making him laugh. "I was a gay kid and I'd known it from age five. When my brothers and sisters and I would play house, I always wound up playing the unmarried aunt."

Bud cracked up. "You are *very* funny, Michael. Why don't you let that part of yourself out more?"

I brushed away his comment. "Come on," I said. "Let's go find some lights."

On Christmas Eve, Dad donned the Santa suit again. How could I not be there? I'd do what James insisted was possible: I'd divide my time between blood and gay families. In Dad's bedroom, I helped him dress, my nieces and nephews gathered downstairs around the tree. I secured the pillow under his belt. I detected a little stiffness, a little pain in his back, when he lifted his legs into the black boots and later, when he hoisted the kids up onto his lap. But I was probably the only one who noticed anything. The kids were in awe, and my siblings were too busy squabbling among themselves.

"Dad," I said, whispering into his ear above the fluffy white beard, "I'm going to head out early."

His eyes shone out at me from just below the fur of his fat. "Okay, Mikey. You do what you need to do."

"There are people I want to see," I said. "You understand, don't you, Dad? They're my family, too."

He nodded. "I want you to be happy, Mikey. That's what I've always wanted."

I kissed his forehead. One of my nephews shrieked that "Unca Mike just kissed Sanna Claus!" I smiled and headed out the door.

The night was quiet, like all Christmas Eves are. It had snowed a few days earlier and patches remained on the ground, but the night was clear and not too cold. I drove through the streets of the South End, avenues I knew as well as my own heart. Better, really. Driving across town to Bernard's, I wanted to feel happy. I wanted to look forward to this gathering of my gay family. I had bought them all gifts: James some cologne, Christopher a shirt, Bernard a gift certificate to

Williams and Sonoma. I even bought Bud something: Donna Summer's greatest hits CD.

But as soon as I got there, I could see there would be no joy this yuletide.

James and Christopher were the only ones there. Both Bernard and Bud had apparently been held up at their biological family's celebrations. James and Chistopher sat at either end of the couch, a plate of Christmas cookies on the coffee table between them.

"Merry Christmas," I announced, coming in.

"Yeah, whatever," Christopher said.

"Now, sugar, don't be such a sourpuss," James said. "So they're late. They'll be here eventually."

"He promised he'd be here on time!" Christopher wailed. "He *promised!*"

"Hey," I said. "Don't you think you're being a little selfish? I mean, he has a *daughter*. He has to juggle a lot just to be here at all."

Christopher was on me as quick as a cougar, his teeth at my throat. "What do *you* know, Michael? You've never even *had* a lover."

"Now, now, children!" James called, clapping his hands. "It's Christmas."

"I am constantly being made to take second-place to his daughter and ex-wife!" Christopher's face was red and blotchy. He didn't look anything like himself. He looked like a miserable old woman. "Why am I even in a relationship if I'm going to be alone on Christmas Eve?"

"You're not alone," I told him, allowing myself to feel a little indignant. "*We're* here. Your best *friends.*"

Now James had gotten up to join us. "You don't understand, Michael," he said, nudging me away to take the distraught Christopher in his arms. "He wants his lover. His *man*. Friends just can't fill that place." He patted Christopher on the back as he pulled him close. "There, there, sugar."

The doorbell rang. It was Bud. No words were spoken. Christopher just took his hand and led him down the hall into the bedroom. We could hear angry, muffled whispers.

"Oh, dear," James said, rolling his eyes. "You'd think we'd be spared all this drama at least on Christmas."

"Of course you won't bitch out Bernard when he finally shows up."

James frowned. "No. I'm sure he—well, Bernard has a large family—"

Christopher's voice suddenly lifted in a wail from the bedroom. James and I peered down the hall. We could see him in there, pacing back and forth, in and out of the frame of the doorway. "Just like that?" he was saying, his voice loud and cracky. "*Just like that?*"

"Oh, dear," James breathed, gripping my shoulder.

"And on *Christmas Eve!*" Christopher shouted, appearing and then disappearing again. He was crying. "You'd do this to me on Christmas Eve! *Just like that!*"

"No," we could hear Bud answer calmly. "Not just like that. It's been happening, Christopher. You know that."

"*What's* been happening?" Christopher stopped pacing, suddenly turning to face us. "Just like *that* he wants to end it! He's breaking up with me on Christmas Eve!"

"Oh, sugar," James said.

"All your butch talk!" Christopher shouted, spinning back to Bud, tears flying. "All you are is a *poseur!*"

Bud appeared in the doorway now. He was looking over Christopher's shoulder down the hallway. He was talking to Christopher but looking at us. "Don't talk to *me* about posing," Bud said.

"Just like that! Just like that!" Christopher was sobbing hysterically now, a little kid in a department store denied the latest toy. "You don't really want a lover! You'd rather still be married to that bitch! You're ashamed of being gay!"

Bud snapped. I saw his forehead go green. "How *dare* you say that? You know nothing of my life, nothing of what I've been through, nothing about anybody who came before you! You little boys with your clothes and your dramas and your fucking full names!"

Christopher had moved out of the frame. All I could see were his right foot and arm. I could hear him crying into his hands.

But Bud was still staring straight ahead, at us.

"I don't want to be alone," Christopher was saying, his body heaving. "Not on Christmas Eve. I'm *twenty-five.* I want to be settled down. I don't want to be alone at twenty-five."

I saw his hands reach back into the doorway, imploring Bud to hold him. But Bud stiffened and walked past him. He brushed by us in the living room, where he sat down hard on the couch.

Christopher let out a wail, running toward us. I thought he was going to follow Bud into the living room. But instead he fled the apartment, running outside without even his coat.

"Such *drama,*" James sighed.

"We should go to him," I said. "At least bring him his coat."

"No. Just leave him alone."

"He needs us."

"He needs to be *alone.*"

My anger boiled over. "You always think you know better than me, don't you, James? But you don't even know yourself."

He smirked, in the way only James can smirk. "And you *do?*"

"I know who *you* are, anyway."

"Who?"

I faced him. "Bernard's lover," I said.

His eyes widened. James made a small sound in his throat. I took a few steps away from him, looking in at Bud in the living room.

The clock ticked loudly, the only sound in the apartment.

At last James placed a hand on my shoulder. "Michael," he said. I didn't respond.

"Okay, so you were right. We should go to Christopher. We're his best friends. After all, in the end, all we have is each other."

I looked over my shoulder at him. "No, James, you're wrong. In the end, we don't even have that."

We looked at each other for several seconds without expression. Finally James turned, snatched both his and Christopher's coats from the rack, and walked out the door.

I stepped into the living room. Bud was still on the couch, leaning forward, his big hairy hands hanging between his legs. Hands not unlike mine. Hands like I'll have fifteen years from now.

"I'm sorry," I ventured.

He didn't look up at me.

"Being alone at thirty-nine is a hell of a lot worse," he said.

I sat down next to him. I put my hand on his shoulder. From outside I could hear the carolers start their song.

Have yourself a merry little Christmas, make the yuletide gay . . .

That's when Bud started to cry.

* * *

It's an odd sound, Bud's tears. A low, hollow echo from deep within his body, so unlike Christopher's dramatic, crackly little sobs. This is different. This is how I imagine human beings were meant to cry.

"I didn't want to do it tonight," Bud tells me. "I wanted to wait. I'm not that heartless to break up with him on Christmas Eve."

His head is on my shoulder. Once more I don't know what to say.

"But he just started in on me, as soon as I walked through the door. He's always doing that. Always bitching at me. Scolding me. I just couldn't take any more."

"I understand," I say at last.

He lifts his head to look at me. "I thought you might. You alone, of all of them."

"Me?"

Bud nods. "Why do you hang out with them, Michael? They're mean, nasty, petty."

"They're my family," I tell him.

"I refuse to replace a dysfunctional blood family with a dysfunctional gay family," Bud says plainly.

I look at him. He's no longer crying. His eyes are a deep blue. Bluer than I ever noticed before. He puts his arms around me and pulls me to him.

"Merry Christmas, Michael."

I tighten my embrace of him. So tight it's like I'm hugging myself.

"Dad, this is Bud."

It's late. My siblings have all gone home, taking their kids and their gifts. My father is alone, at the kitchen table. He's drinking a cup of tea.

"Pleased to meet you, sir," Bud says, extending his hand. "Merry Christmas."

They shake. I see Dad's eyes consider him. This is the first time I've ever brought a man home to meet my father.

"Merry Christmas," Dad says in reply. "Would you boys like some tea?"

He pours us two cups. We sit down with him at the table.

"What happened to your party?" Dad asks.

"It ended early," I say, catching a look from Bud.

Dad doesn't appear to notice. "You want some coffeecake? Your sister left a plate behind."

He breaks each of us off a piece. I watch Bud. He accepts his cake, his eyes grinning over at my father. Dad had called us both "boys," as if fifteen years didn't separate us. Maybe they don't. I suppose to Dad, at seventy-four, thirty-nine isn't all that much different from twenty-five.

There had been no plan to come back here. Both Bud and I had just wanted to get out of Bernard's apartment before Christopher and James came back. We drove around a little, looking at the Christmas lights along Evergreen Avenue, then throughout the West End and Frog Hollow. The city's neighborhoods had come alive, shedding their bleakness and decay, all by just hanging out a few strings of holiday lights.

We drove into the South End.

"That's your street there, isn't it?" Bud asked, pointing.

I told him yes.

"Let's see the decorations your father put out."

I turned up my street. Dad had wrapped a strand of multicolored lights through the chain-link fence that fronted our little patch of lawn. A plastic illuminated snowman my mother had bought at Woolworth's when I was six stood with a silly grin on our front steps.

"Do you want to meet my Dad?" I asked all at once.

"Yes," Bud said, "I'd like that very much."

So we went inside, and now I sit here at the kitchen table with my father and Bud, eating coffeecake and drinking tea on Christmas Eve. They talk about the Red Sox, something I've never been able to do with my father, and about the plans to revitalize downtown Hartford. I can tell that Dad likes the fact that Bud is a teacher. He asks him lots of questions about the school system and his students. He seems struck by the fact that Bud has his daughter in class—not so much that she's in her father's classroom, but that Bud has a daughter at all.

"Here's her picture," Bud says, pulling out his wallet from his back pocket and flipping it open. Dad and I lean across the table to look down at the face of a plain teenaged girl, with glasses and mousy brown hair.

"What's her name?" Dad asks.

"Samantha," Bud tells him, and I realize as he says it that I've never known Bud's daughter's name. I'd never thought to ask. None of us had. Christopher must have known her name though. Wouldn't he?

"Did she get everything she wanted for Christmas?" Dad asks.

"I hope so." Bud smiles, looking down at the picture. "I'd give her the world if I could."

"You take good care of her," my father says—a question? a statement? a command?

Bud nods. "I do my best. I'd do anything for Samantha. I want nothing more than to give her every happiness, but . . ." He sighs. "A parent can only do so much."

I look at Dad. In the soft light of the Christmas tree, reflected even here in the kitchen, his eyes glow with moisture. He reaches across the table and pats my hand.

"I'm heading up to bed," he says thickly. "Why don't you stay the night, Bud? I'll take you boys out for Christmas breakfast in the morning."

I'm flabbergasted that Dad would suggest such a thing, but Bud just smiles. Dad stands, a little flicker of pain on his face as he puts pressure on his stiff joints. Bud and I listen without saying a word as Dad's footsteps fade out up the stairs.

"So," Bud says.

I look over at him. What's happening here? Bud is Christopher's boyfriend. What am I thinking?

"You want to see my room?" I ask.

"Sure," Bud says.

I lead him down the hall to my bedroom. I flip on the light. Bud looks around. It's a mess, as usual. My CDs strewn about the floor. My bed unmade.

"Hey, *cool*," Bud says, heading over to my dresser. "The Bride of Frankenstein."

I like that he notices her. "I've had that since I was a kid." I walk up behind him and touch the model's lithe, bandaged body. "My mom bought it for me because I was disappointed one year when I didn't get it for Christmas."

"That happen a lot?"

"What?"

His eyes smile at me. Even in the dim light of my room I'm struck by how blue they are. "Being disappointed with what you got for Christmas," he says.

I shrug. "I suppose so. But I tried never to let my parents know. They did their best with what they had."

Bud just keeps looking at me. His eyes seem to fix on me. I feel just the tiniest bit uncomfortable in his gaze. I can't tell what he's thinking.

Suddenly he leans forward. He places his hands on my shoulders and kisses me. He tastes far sweeter than I imagined. His lips are soft.

"Is this too weird?" he whispers, pulling back just a bit. "Your father upstairs?"

"No," I say, surprised at how normal that part feels. "But what *is* weird is that you're Christopher's boyfriend. Or were."

"You're not like them, Michael, " Bud tells me. "Sometimes you try to be. But you're not."

I shrug. "I'm not as cute as Christopher. I know that much. I'm not thin and defined the way he is. I'm not handsome like James."

"I like you just the way you are."

We kiss again. It's incredible. No one has ever said this to me before. No one has ever kissed me like this. Bud's mustache rubs against my upper lip. I'm surprised to discover that I like how it feels. I can't believe how much.

We make love. Here, on my childhood bed, where once I dreamed— *longed*—for such a thing, where so often have I retreated, caught up in my unresolved feelings for James. Until now this has been a bed of loneliness, of sorrow, of hopes unfulfilled. But tonight I make love to a man here. A *man*. My first, in so many ways.

He is gentle but strong. Where once I considered him unattarctive, suddenly I'm awakened to how sexy Bud is. I find that I love *everything* about him, from his strong, rough hands to his furry chest, his large Adam's apple, his soft, playful tongue. But mostly I love his whispered words in my ear: "You're beautiful, Michael. Inside and out."

It's the most shattering orgasm I've ever had.

Then we start over. And over again.

Finally, I lie in his arms, my breathing in sync with his.

"I don't know what we'll say to Christopher," I say.

"I like you, Michael. I don't want to have to lie about that."

We settle back into silence.

"Have you ever really been in love?" I ask, once more breaking the stillness. I'm not sure where the question comes from. It just pushes past my lips, surprising myself.

Bud doesn't hesitate in his reply. "Yes," he tells me.

I stir in his arms. "With who? Your wife?"

"No, Michael. With a man." He pauses. "His name was Jack."

I look up over my shoulder at him. "What happened?"

"He died."

"Oh," I say.

We fall back into the lazy quiet of the room, broken only by the ticking of my clock.

"How about you?" Bud asks. "Have you ever been in love, Michael?"

I think of James. "No," I say. "Not really."

Bud runs a hand through my hair. "It's the greatest thing, being in love. When times get tough, when I feel lonely and alone, I remember that feeling. I remember how I felt when I was in love."

"But he's not here anymore," I say. "Jack."

Bud sighs. "The day he died, I knew I had a choice. I could be miserable or I could go on. So I hit on this idea of keeping one beautiful thing in my head all the time. Just one thing. Like the memory of how I felt being with him. Or something else simple. My daughter being surprised at her birthday party. A particularly fabulous sunset. A joke that made me laugh."

I squint through the darkness at him. A thought has struck me, a crazy thought that I can't push away.

"Are you very sleepy?" I ask.

"No, not especially," he says. "Though it *is* after four o'clock."

"Will you go for a ride with me?"

Bud grins. "A ride? Where?"

"Trust me, okay?"

"Okay, Michael. I trust you."

We hurriedly dress and slip quietly out of the house. Bud thinks it's great fun, sneaking off with me in the middle of the night. We drive out of the city, its lights quickly disappearing behind us. Heading south on I-91 we see only a few other cars. There's a stillness that comes with early Christmas morning you don't experience any other time of year, not even on New Year's. It's the stillness of the world in waiting.

When we turn off 91 onto Route 9 heading toward Middletown, Bud looks over at me and makes a face. "When you said a ride, I thought we were just going around the block."

"Do you still trust me?"

"I trust you."

Middletown, Chester, Essex. Soon Long Island Sound is ahead of us, and we're passing over the Baldwin Bridge.

"Are we going to the *beach?*" Bud asks as my car turns off the main street in Old Lyme and rattles over a dirt road.

"My grandmother used to rent a cottage near here. Let me see if I can find it."

Bud grins. "Is that what you want to show me? Your grandmother's cottage?"

I don't answer. It's hard to tell where I am in the darkness, but suddenly I recognize a road, and take a sharp turn onto it. "There it is," I say. "At the end, near the water."

I park the car. The neighborhood has been upgraded since I was last here some thirteen years ago. A good number of the former seasonal cottages have been converted into year-round dwellings. Twinkling Christmas lights line the contours of several houses along the beach. But Nana's cottage, on the bluff facing out to the sea, is boarded-up and dark.

I motion for Bud to follow me. We head out of the car toward the cottage. The night air is cold but not freezing. The sky is lightening now, a soft hint of pink and gold. We can hear the steady crash of the surf, a sound that once had soothed me, that had woken me in the morning and lulled me to sleep at night, that had taken me to places beyond any reality a thirteen-year-old boy could possibly understand.

We sit up on Nana's old porch to watch the sun rise. We sit on the same old weathered wicker furniture I remember from that first lonely summer after my mother's death. Bud pulls me close to him. His warmth feels good. I push my hand down deep into the pocket of his coat. He kisses the top of my head.

Gradually the world around us brightens. Purple becomes blue becomes pink becomes gold all without us ever noticing the gradations between.

"Merry Christmas," Bud says to me.

"Merry Christmas," I say.

We kiss.

Our eyes wander out to the crashing waves ahead of us. The dawn reveals the water to be a deep azure green, the white froth of the surf startling in its contrast.

Far out on the rocks, the morning sunlight catches a figure breaking the surface of the cold sea.

"There," I whisper. "There he is."

I knew he would be here. He's been waiting for me. All this time.

"Do you see?" I ask Bud. I point with my finger. "Out there, at the very end of the land?"

Bud narrows his eyes. "Yes," he says. "What is it?"

"Look harder. What do you see?"

He squints into the new light. "Can't be a whale this time of year. A seal, maybe?"

I smile. "When I was a boy, I was convinced it was a merman."

Bud looks over at me.

"You know, like a mermaid. Only a man."

He smiles, amused.

"He was beautiful," I say. "You should've seen him, Bud. The most beautiful creature I ever laid eyes on. He was strong, and proud, and graceful. He was so sweet to me. When he kissed me his lips were so soft. He came from a place I could only imagine, a world I hoped someday to find. He was so beautiful. I wish you could have seen him."

Bud looks at me for several moments, then moves his eyes back out at the water. "I think I can see him now," he says. "I think you're right, Michael." He pulls me close. "That's a *merman* out there."

The long shadows of dawn begin to retreat as the sun inches higher in the sky.

"This year," I say in Bud's ear, "I finally got exactly what I wanted for Christmas."

He smiles.

We sit like that for some time, just watching the merman dive in and out of the waves.

Naughty or Nice

Ben Tyler

For Muriel Pollia, Ph.D.
(with devotion)

Chapter One

Polly was saying, "The Pleasure Chest. Last night. That Reese creature."

"Wither*soon*?" Tim asked, optimistically raising his eyes from Liz Smith in the morning edition of the *L.A. Times*.

"Know another?"

Tim clicked off a list. "Della. Roger. Those monkeys in research labs."

"Not *rhesus*, you boob. Reese. And it's unlikely that any of *them* would be clutching a fistful of peppermint sticks shaped like Chris McDonald's pee-pee. She claimed they were *stocking* stuffers! Snarky bit of a thing, if you ask me. *I* behaved in my uncommonly gracious manner."

"Uncommon? You?"

"I said that I thought she was darling in *Sweet Home Alabama*. Which of course was true. I should have left it there."

"Instead of gushing that Josh Lucas was a scrumptious scene-stealer?"

"I don't gush!" Polly protested. "Anyway, she pretended not to have the vaguest notion of who *I* was."

"*Was*, being the operative word." Tim rolled his eyes and shared a confidential *it's-that-time-of-the-month* look with Placenta, the maid.

Placenta was serving breakfast at the outdoor dining table by the pool.
It was a sunny morning in Bel Air, California.

"Can't be real," Polly continued.

"*Tits?*"

"Not a bad stack, really." Polly seemed to be giving serious consideration to the subject. "I suppose her twelve-year-old husband sees *something* in her."

"Please. Give it a rest. She's *adorable*," Tim said. "I refuse to hear
another of your diatribes about some perky blonde who you think is
little more than a testicle teaser, just because she was clueless about
your Hollywood pedigree. She's too young to remember you. By the
way, what in hell were you doing at the Pleasure Chest—*Mother?*"

Polly Pepper was the quintessential legend from '70s musical/com-
edy variety television. Despite receiving twelve Emmy Awards—one
for every season of her still rerun *ad infinitum* series, *The Polly Pepper
Playhouse*—as well as a Best Supporting Actress Tony Award nomina-
tion (Perma-plaqued in the trophy case) for her performance in the
short lived musical adaptation of *Thelma & Louise*, Polly's days in
front of an audience seemed to have come to a grinding halt. Like
Angela Lansbury. And with the same yawn of public apathy.

Polly pouted as she brought her eyes back to the *Daily Variety*.
"More juice, Placenta," she called out in her faux Southern drawl. She
rang a tiny tea bell, summoning her servant from the house. "And
where are my goddamned Merits?" Polly tamped out a lipstick-stained
filter in an ash-filled Waterford crystal candy dish.

Polly was in a snit. Tim could feel the tension. He recognized the
disposition—his mother feeling hung over, as well as professionally hung
out to dry.

Polly tightened the belt of her silk, salmon-colored *PP* monogrammed bathrobe. With a Baby Jane Hudson sneer she took a spiteful
swat with the paper at a humming bird that darted too close to the
juice pitcher. "Motherfucking monster!" she screeched at the thumb-
size bird, as if it were a flying Harvey Weinstein. She looked at Tim.
"And I'm not in any mood for any of your sarcasm this early in the day."

"Perfect Polly Pepper," Tim chided. "What would your adoring minions be gossiping about in your official website chat room if they could see you now?"

Mother and son sat in an uneasy silence for a moment as Placenta ambled from the kitchen to pour another glass of juice. Placenta harrumphed. She reached two inches from Polly's right hand to retrieve the pitcher and simultaneously swiped and pocketed the annoying little silver bell.

"Placenta, darling," Polly cooed as the maid began to wander away. "Jim Belushi left something icky on my pillow this morning."

Placenta merely grunted a nonverbal acknowledgment, which Tim interpreted as, *I don't do bodily fluids—yours, or your goddamn mangy mutt's!*

"Speaking of pets, my precious . . ." Polly tentatively resumed her conversation with Tim. "It's almost that time of year again." She hummed the first few bars to "Santa Claus is Coming to Town."

Tim froze in mid-swallow of his croissant. Honey and boysenberry jam pasted his lips.

"That's right, dear heart." Polly beamed. "*Our* annual Christmas party! It's only eight weeks away."

Tim pretended to choke. Christmas, like Easter, the Ides of March, and the unofficial birthday of Dorian Gray, meant having to play pre-IMClone Martha Stewart for his mother's lavish affairs. Any excuse to throw a party involved what Polly euphemistically called "Tim's magic fairy wand."

"Oh, take that pained expression off your face," Polly huffed. "It's unbecoming. You look like the Gerber babyfood baby just loaded his Pampers, for Christ sake."

Although Tim feigned antipathy, the truth was that he enjoyed the challenge of planning Polly's parties—and his mother always bumped up the work incentive package. Last year it was a new silver BMW 325 Ci convertible. This year, with the economy shot to hell, he figured he'd be lucky to get a new Rolex.

Tim vaguely protested. "I'm off to England this Christmas, Mother. We've already discussed it."

"It's sopping wet over there. As frosty as Her Majesty's German genes," Polly said. "Plus the whole damn country's a morgue at Christmas. Go later. April or May. I'll even put you up with Sir Olivier."

"I'd rather you didn't. He's dead."

"You're keeping track? Gielgud, then."

"The worms crawl in, the worms crawl out." Tim sang his response.

"Sir Ian?" Polly gave a cautious look. When Tim didn't contradict her, she smiled with self-satisfaction. "Mummy will see to everything."

It was no use arguing with the purse strings. Tim, a sandy-haired, blue-eyed, sun-bronzed California surf boy, depended on his mother for most of his income. In many ways, Tim had it made. Polly paid for his personal trainer, his gallons of Ripped Fuel, his vitamin supplements, and his Visa bills. She allocated a monthly allowance, sufficient to keep him in Dolce and Gabana. The catch, however, was that he had to be reachable by cell phone within two rings, and available 24/7 to baby-sit Jim Belushi, Polly's Bichon Frise, when she was away performing her one-woman cabaret act on the Florida Condo Circuit. Most importantly, he was also required to serve as the official party planner/co-host of her legendary soirees.

"Listen, my adorable son. The Loch Ness Monster swimming in the pool for my Scottish Stepdancing Festival was genius. Pure genius. This year, for Christmas, I want the same thing. Only different. And better, of course. You'll know what to do. Just make it brilliant. As usual."

With a deep sigh, Tim sat back in his chair. "I'm not that original," he tried to explain. "You have some weird theory that just because I'm gay, that I have a predetermined gene for decorating." He stared down his mother's look of exasperation.

"Naturally, my pet," Polly preened. "And it's not a theory. It's Masters and Johnson. Or Kinsey. Or some axiom of nature. Just name *one* of my gay friends who doesn't have more talent in their pierced nipples than any of my so-called *straight* friends. Combined. Benji's brilliant with music and lyrics. All those Oscars and Tonys prove it. I never even think about his dungeon and that fetish stuff. And dear Edmund. He has a noggin for finding cures for things that only the Nobel Prize committee and refugees in Somalia knew anyone had. Junie is the sweetest songbird this side of a convent choir loft. I know exactly what Melissa Etheridge sees in her. Humberto could sew

Brawny paper towels together and make Marsha Warfield look like Iman. And don't tell me that anybody delivers the nightly world news better than sexpot Bentley. Me? I can sing a little. Dance a little. Act a little, and tell a clever joke. Oh, wait. I'm not gay. I'm so multi-talented, that I *should* be gay. Get my point dear?"

"Should've ate him when he was young," Placenta muttered as she cleared the dishes away from the table.

"Placenta!" Polly snapped. "Don't you have a date with that deposit in my bed?"

"It's a miracle something warm besides your ass made a deposit in your bed," Placenta deadpanned.

Tim grinned at the maid. They shared an approving wink of an eye.

Looking back at his mother, Tim could tell she was considering what Placenta had said. To ease the moment, he feigned agreement with her assessment of his talent. "Yeah, yeah. I was blessed with the golden touch for set decoration, party planning and finding one hundred and one amazing combinations of uses for antique high colonic irrigation kits. It's a cliché, Mother. Not every gay man is able to name each of Judy's dress sizes. *This Old House* isn't necessarily my equivalent of *Monday Night Football*. Although," he reflected for a moment, "that hunky host, Steve Thomas, can hammer my joist anytime. And believe it or not, some of my friends do not quite get Bernadette Peters's message."

Polly reached over with her napkin to pat away croissant crumbs from Tim's lips. "I didn't mean to imply anything politically incorrect, sweetums. Just that I adore my talented son. You know I can't throw a pillow for shit, let alone a party. Mummy needs your sensitive guidance!"

Christmas at *Pepper Plantation*, as the mansion on Stone Canyon Road was affectionately known to the entertainment cognoscenti, was one of the highlights of the Hollywood holiday party season. *Beverly Hills 213*, the pretentious glossy photo collage that catered to the egos of old money from Mulholland to Rodeo, always reserved their entire year-end edition for coverage of whatever fabulous party was held at

Polly's Pit. That was the less-than-affectionate term offered by the publication's photographer and any caterer or service person who ever had the misfortune of working at Polly's over-embellished version of Versailles.

Still, from the doyennes of Doheny to the barons of Benedict Canyon, the upper crust couldn't wait for a Polly Pepper bash. It was their time to gawk at whatever grisly gown Ruta Lee had stuffed herself into. They found it an amusing diversion to study the geriatric, face-lifted smiles of Connie Stevens, Loni Anderson, Michelle Triola, and the ubiquitous Jane Withers. Half the fun of a Polly Pepper evening was trying to figure out the age and social status of whichever escort was beaming alongside such Hollywood artifacts as June Havoc or Kathryn Grayson.

Thus, an invitation to Polly Pepper's Christmas soiree was a most coveted thing. Not the least because Leeza Gibbons was always on hand with a film crew. And a Drew Carey-size Santa usually doled out halfway decent stuff from Prada, Bvlgari, Bernini, Hugo Boss or Mont-Blanc. If nothing else, the looky-loos wanted to enjoy what unique holiday theme Tim had selected for decorating the estate and surrounding grounds. Nary a Jack Skellington was ever spared.

"I'm going to England for the holidays, Mother." Tim maintained his stance. "Evan and I want a Dickensian Christmas."

"Spend the day downtown helping out at the Rescue Mission soup kitchen. It doesn't get any more Oliver Twist than that! Perhaps I'll even join you."

"Sure. Call up your publicist," Tim said wearily. "In the meantime, I'm going to the UK. End of discussion. I'll help you negotiate for Catherine the Great Caterer. She's always trying to land you as a client. Or for an extra kick, you might try Casanova Caterers. Their uniforms of bowties-only, should guarantee that all your friends, gay and straight, will be munching on more than the poo-poo platters."

"And who, Lord Almighty, is Evan?" Polly challenged. The frayed wires of her nonlinear thought process finally seemed to connect. "Some new young man you're seeing?" Polly peered over the frames of her prescription sunglasses. "Oh. A light dawns. So he's the one responsible for you turning your back on your lonely, legendary mother!"

Tim decided to break the news as delicately as possible. "I think he's the one."

"The one what? The one-calorie in a can of Diet Coke? Or the one-way ticket to Heartbreak Hotel? Timmy. Sweetie! You've said the same thing about every Polly Pepper worshiping tanktop teaser you've ever chased through this house."

"I don't chase. And they didn't all worship *you!*" Tim considered. "Well, maybe your clothes. The Bob Mackies, anyway."

"You're exaggerating, as usual," Polly dismissed. "I'm sorry if so many of your men simply wanted to be *me* when they were growing up. What does he do? Your boyfriend. In the business? Not an actor! Please dear God, spare me! Where'd you meet? I suppose you're fucking?"

"My lips are sealed."

"Well, if this Kevin . . ."

"Evan!"

"If this . . . boy . . ."

"Man."

". . . is so special, why doesn't he spend the night with you? Eh? And why hasn't he been at my table for dinner?"

Tim frowned. He had come to the disturbing conclusion that perhaps the reason that his past relationships failed as quickly as every *Seinfeld* cast members' solo sitcoms, was that men simply wanted to brag that they were banging Polly Pepper's son. As soon as they had a tour of the mansion, and got to dine with Polly and a few of her celebrity friends, the novelty wore off. They stopped calling for dates.

"I want a boyfriend for Christmas," Tim answered. "Not *for* Christmas, like a present. I mean to have around and share the holiday with."

"I hope you're not suggesting that I'm responsible . . ." Polly stopped mid-sentence. "I'm really just a simple, rich-beyond-anyone's-imagination household name, who worked her freakin' tits off to become a beloved, genuine, bigger than life, living icon. For Christ sake!"

Tim drew another deep breath. He looked up at the palm trees and tropical plants that flourished around the estate grounds. "Mother," he said, "let's be completely honest. All right? I'll always be in your shadow. There isn't anything that I will ever be able to do, that will compare to your accomplishments. Only Prince Charles, and maybe Lucie Arnaz, could understand how I feel. The truth is, I've come to the conclusion that the boys I date, for the most part, want me not for my dick but for something from *your* closet."

"That reminds me. My favorite Vera Wang scarf is missing. Find out which of those tattooed twits lifted my Wang."

"Mother, please."

"You and Jason Gould should form a support group, that's what you should do," Polly said, brandishing a butter knife just before she slathered a blueberry muffin with Fleishman's soft tub.

Tim rolled his eyes.

"Now, Timmy," Polly changed from Lauren Bacall to Jane Curtin. She leaned over and put her hand on his. "I'm a superstar, and you never will be. That's a hard fact for the offspring of God's chosen few to understand. Ask Jolie Fisher. Ask Lorna Luft. Ask Colin Hanks. But you do get all the reflected glory without ever having to spread your legs for some goddman, skinny-assed producer or middle management studio creative executive who insists that you're perfect for the role of Mona Lisa in his HBO original series about Leonardo da Vinci's greatest love, even though everybody knows he was gay—Leonardo I mean—and you believe him because you're not sure you'll ever work again, and he's not a complete turn-off, but he's married, and all he really wants is your pussy, and he's not even in charge of the production in the first place, but you don't find that out until you've put your panties back on and . . ." Polly came up for air. "Oh hell, just be thankful for what you've got!"

Polly sighed. "I did all the hard work, honey. Now you can enjoy the fruits of my labor. Hell, there's no such thing as Mr. Right anyway. Just look at your pathetic bastard father for proof, and the beards I'm stuck with."

Tim drained the remaining grapefruit juice from his glass, then looked at his mother as she tamped out another Merit butt. "I'm keeping this boyfriend. But to do so, I have to keep him away from you."

Polly's mouth dropped open. "Does he even know that I'm your mother?"

"You mean that *I'm* your son? Let's keep this about me for a change," Tim said. "But, as a matter of fact, no. I've never mentioned that we're at zero degrees of separation. So far, he seems to like me for being me."

"Of course he does, baby. Who wouldn't? But don't you think he'd like you even more if he knew that you were the son of Polly Pepper, the rich and famous movie star?"

"TV star," Tim corrected.

"I made a movie!"

"*Crawling Eyeball III: The Vision Returns?*"

Polly sniffed. "If you're serious about a relationship you shouldn't start off with a bunch of secrets and lies. Of course you'll bring him to our party! He'll get a kick out of being at a real Hollywood bash!"

Tim stood up from the table and let his white linen napkin drop beside his coffee cup. "Not only am I *not* bringing Evan home to meet you until after we're married, I'm taking him to a B&B in Yorkshire for Christmas!"

"And how do you propose to get there, dearest? England, I mean?" Polly smiled, leaning forward and resting her chin between her thumb and forefinger. "I didn't know you had any vacation time coming from . . . *unemployment.*"

Tim's hackles were raised. "You realize of course that just by giving *The Star* a first-person account of life at Pepper Plantation I could make enough dough to fly first class to Heathrow and stay at the Dorchester for a few months—with high tea service every afternoon. Don't think I haven't thought about it."

"You're a horrid son! You're being corrupted! It's the group you hang out with! I'm calling Ozzy this very moment!"

"I'm not serious!" Tim tried to lighten the moment. "But I like Evan. I like him a lot. And I don't want you spoiling my chances with him. If he knows where I live and who my mother is, I'll either get dumped, or at the very least, I'll never be able to trust that he loves me for me."

"Oh, pooh." Polly waved her hand and pushed her chair back. She stood up, adjusting the frames of her sunglasses. "We'll take this up later, dear. Right now, Mummy's got to prepare to rehearse with her new accompanist. I think you should toddle off to the mall. Or better, run along and have a massage. Use my account at The Nectar Spa."

"That cute?" Tim teased.

Polly smiled. "I don't need you to be my competition." She blew a perfunctory kiss as she left the table and padded away with small mincing steps, like the Geisha she once played in a sketch on her old show, opposite guest star Mickey Rooney.

Chapter Two

Tim hustled to shower, shave and dress. He'd scheduled lunch with one of his mother's best friends—her former assistant, Sean King. They had agreed to meet at Chin Chin on Sunset Boulevard to discuss Tim's ideas for Sean and his TV star lover's own Christmas party.

Tim had scoffed into his cell phone when he first made the date, after yawning at Sean's idea for a "Pin the tail on Michael Eisner" theme party. "This isn't some old fashioned Andy Williams Christmas world anymore," Tim said. "No cute ice sculptures of reindeer with electrical noses. Gotta crank things up about a gazillion volts. Especially for those coke-snorting, ecstasy-popping younger people in *your* crowd."

"Well, then, Mr. Macy's Fifth Avenue Storefront Window Designer, if you don't like *my* party ideas, by all means do come up with something you'd be satisfied with."

Tim was happy to help out. "For you, something totally original." He smiled. "Something as volatile as a cocktail of crystal meth and Viagra."

"Goody!" Then Sean frowned for a moment. "But if you're cheating on your mother, won't you cheat on me too?" he griped. Then he pouted. "Just promise not to break my heart. You've got to make my party the swellest of the season."

" 'Swellest,' " Tim parroted over the phone. "I don't think that's even a word."

"Of course it is!" The cell phone line crackled a little. "Thou Swell— Larry Hart. Then, thou Sweller, thou Swellest. You do the conjugation." Sean paused. "Please, please, *please*, make my party the one that will be talked about the most for months afterward. But talked about in a good way. Not talked about like Bjork's dead swan dress at the Oscars a few years back. More like the one you did for your mom's surprise birthday party for Peter Scolari. It was so evil—and inside—everybody shrieking 'surprise' behind Tom Hanks masks! For shame!"

"Mother mustn't know we're in collusion," Tim insisted. "She'd ab- solutely stuff my nuts into Placenta's Cuisinart if she knew what I was doing behind her back."

"And have all my friends think that I'm incapable of throwing the most extravagant holiday party in this whole dreary town, all by my lonesome? Not to worry your deep dish dimples, dear!"

"*Second* best party." Tim laughed. "Have to save my best ideas for Polly. Charity begins at Pepper Plantation, and if Mother gets a whiff of the fact that I'm helping anyone else with their parties, she'll with- hold my Christmas bonus."

"Baby needs a new toy? Another car?"

"A couple of weeks at Buckingham Palace will do nicely. But the way she spends her bucks, if I don't get at least some of it while she's breathing, there's liable to be little left. And she's just kooky enough to run off and marry some bimbo gold digger. She already has a new ac- companist. I hear he's a hottie. She won't let me meet him, which tells me she's itching."

Beverly Hills is a small town. Everybody knows what everybody else is doing—or they would *like* to know. Tim and Sean were taking a dan- gerous chance agreeing to meet in such a public place as Chin Chin.

The restaurant was crowded. Sean, waiting at one of the sidewalk tables, stood up when Tim approached. They exchanged a Hollywood hug—a quick embrace followed by air kisses to each cheek. "My sav- ior!" Sean cried. "Wine? Champagne? Tangueray?"

"Arnold Palmer, please," Tim said to the waitress who immediately appeared to accept his order.

"Be right back," she chirped.

"I'm too anxious to be polite and wait until after lunch to discuss business," Sean said, leaning forward. "Let me see the sketches. This whole Christmas party thing has me in a state."

"Close your eyes," Tim said. He opened up his sketchbook, peering at his first pencil drawing of the outside of a house. He turned the folio toward Sean. "Okay."

Sean opened his eyes. The expression wasn't what Tim expected. A blank stare usually meant stroke or utter incomprehension.

"What's it supposed to be?" Sean finally said.

"I told you I was amping things up. Surely you didn't expect Donner and Blitzen to be squatting on the roof!"

Sean looked at Tim again. Then he smiled. "Oh, I get it." He took the sketchbook into his own hands. "You brilliant man! Fuck you, Pat Boone! My house will beat your house in any decorating contest! And I don't even have to be a sex-starved Christian!"

"I thought you'd find it interesting," Tim boasted, as he accepted his half iced-tea/half lemonade and sipped around a mint leaf. "I guarantee, no one on your guest list has ever been to a cosmetic surgery Christmas party. Chemical peeling. Derm-abrasion. Laser resurfacing. Penile augmentation."

Sean continued to gush superlatives as he held open the sketchbook page and examined the detail. Flipping to the other illustrations of the powder rooms, the living room and even the dungeon (which Sean didn't think anyone knew about, and said so, and was red-faced when Tim laughed, "Oh, please, Stone Phillips was going to do a story on it!"), Sean said, "Something's missing. You're holding out on me."

Tim gave an expression of feigned hurt. "Holding out? On *you*?" he said. "How can you be so insensitive? I was up half the night putting the final touches on this masterpiece." Then with a grin, he said, "You're smarter than you look."

Sean smiled.

Tim said, "Trust me, it's gonna cost you."

"Hell, it's not my money." Sean rolled his eyes. "Paul's business people handle all that stuff. And if this party gets us on the super AAA+ Geffen list of the real money queens in Hollywood, it'll be worth every Euro."

"Well, since we're buddies, I'll throw in one last idea," Tim said. It was if he were offering tires and an engine to go with a used car he was selling. "Although I *was* saving this for Jodie Foster."

"Stop throwing the names of your other Johns in my face, you little perv," Sean huffed.

Taking the sketchbook, Tim flipped past a couple of blank pages. He stopped and turned the tablet back toward Sean. "Ta-da!" he announced. "With a few alterations, this can be your back yard. Tented, of course."

Sean gazed at the sketch, and his jaw dropped. "What in heaven's name? You are a genius! Or nuts."

"All stainless steel."

"This'll cost Paul a *fortune*! I love it! But can you get so many latex gloves?"

"You're right about the cost. I'd estimate at least Paul's salary for two episodes of *Think Tank*. Will he part with that much cash?"

"As easily as he parts with his wife-beater T-shirt at precisely 8:35 each Wednesday night on ABC. He won't even know the cost until it's too late. He'll hit the roof sometime in early January, at which point I'll wiggle my brand new bubble butt in a seductive tease and remind him how much fun everyone had. Basically, it's a tax write-off anyway, because half the industry will be there."

"If the IRS ever revises the tax structure for Hollywood, there'll be more meals on wheels than calimari at The Ivy," Tim sighed.

Sean studied the sketches again. He smiled then frowned. Smiled then frowned again. He turned the pages of the sketchbook and smiled some more. "When can you start?"

"I have already. But you've got a lot to do, too. The invitations have to be printed and ready to go out the first week in December. I'll take care of the rest. But you've got to promise me that you won't interfere. You're Scarlett O'Hara-Hamilton-Kennedy, and I'm the overseer you just hired to overwork the chain gang at the lumber mill. Whatever I do to make this succeed is not to be disputed. Understand?"

"Perfectly! Just as long as everybody calls me Elsa Lanchester!"

"Maxwell."

"Who?"

"Never mind," said Tim.

"You can have full control. But if my Christmas party isn't everything that's already dancing in this little sugar plum fairy's head, I'll blame it all on you."

Tim stifled a yawn. "Oh, ye of little faith," he said. "This is what I *do*. As long as you do what you do best—spending Paul's paychecks long before they're deposited into his bank account, we'll both be happy. By the by, you're picking up lunch. I've got to dash."

Sean smiled. "The new b.f.? Isn't young love grand?" He grinned. "Of course, I wouldn't know about such bliss. I married Paul 'cause he was loaded and was repped by the same agency as Justin Timberlake."

Tim shook his head. "I wouldn't trade my baby for a Justin or a Tom or even Ryan."

Sean sang out, "Merry Christmas, darling," as Tim headed for his car.

Chapter Three

Tim pulled out of the Chin Chin parking lot and turned right on Sunset Boulevard. Traffic was bumper to bumper as he headed for La Ciengega. Reaching the crowded intersection, he hung another right.

As he descended the steep hill he shifted his Beemer into second gear and cautiously made his way into the flats of West Hollywood. When he reached Santa Monica Boulevard, his cell phone rang out with "Please, Mr. Postman." Tim looked at the caller ID and smiled. "Hey, sweetie," he answered. "I'm almost there. Looks like it's jammed all the way to Melrose. It'll probably be another fifteen. See you in a few."

Tim was still smiling as he pushed the disconnect button. It was the same response he had every time he spoke to Evan on the telephone. Tim smiled a lot these days. Ever since he'd met his new lover.

Thank God for Sherwood Florist, he thought as he recalled how he and Evan met. It was a Tuesday afternoon. Tim had stopped by the flower shop to check out their Casablanca Lilies for the foyer of Pepper Plantation. The store was empty of patrons. A lone clerk was leaning into the glass door refrigerator, arranging tulips. His broad shoulders and the back of his long torso were exposed to the shop entrance. The sound of the refrigerator's motor obliterated the chime from the front door opening.

Tim couldn't help notice the man diligently working. He decided to wander around inhaling the aroma of fresh flowers. Soon, however, he was drawn to the tapered shape of the man's back. Tim stopped and leaned against a ficus tree, waiting for the shopkeeper to finish his task and turn around.

The attendant was so absorbed in what he was doing that it seemed he would never face forward. Finally, Tim cleared his throat. Tim cleared his throat again and said, "Excuse me." With that, the guy looked over his shoulder.

It was at that instant that Tim lost his heart—and his balance. He knocked over the ficus. His face immediately turned red with embarrassment. He had been caught off-guard by the wide smile, the perfect white teeth, the jet-black spiked hair, the black opal eyes, the deep dimples and the most adorable face since Parker Stevenson was a Hardy Boy. It didn't help Tim's humiliation that the guy rushed to rescue him, and the ficus. "Oh, hey, are you okay?" the Hardy Boy asked with complete sincerity and concern. Their eyes sparkled off one another's. "That tree's a real hazard. I should have moved it. I'm so sorry."

Tim smiled. "I'm cool. It was my fault. I was distracted. By all the colorful flowers, I mean."

The man smiled. "Glad you like 'em. I get distracted sometimes, too." He was still holding onto Tim's arm, absently brushing off non-existent flower petals from his shoulders and chest. "It's one of the reasons why I like working here. Sure you're okay?"

I was until I saw you, Tim wanted to say. "Just clumsy. I do that when I've got a lot of stuff on my mind." *Pull yourself together, you idiot,* Tim said to himself. "Sorry about that . . ." He looked at the guy's plastic name badge. "Evan."

Evan gave Tim another wide smile. "Not a problem. Just as long as you're not hurt."

He paused in the manner that is the universal code for *I don't know your name.*

"I'm Tim." He didn't give his last name, but he was grinning as wide as the yellow happy face on the Mylar balloon bobbing by the cash register. "What a great place to work." Tim winced inwardly. *Inane.* He may as well have said, *Any idea where I can buy flowers around here?* or something equally stupid.

"It's great." Evan was now picking dead leaves off a philodendron. "Not a lot of foot traffic though. Mostly telephone orders." He made eye contact with Tim as if letting him know that it could be a lonely job. "So what brings you in? We have a special on Birds of Paradise. Guaranteed to bring a smile to your boyfriend's lips."

Tim could be a bit moronic when it came to recognizing when another guy was hitting on him. More than a few times a friend would recall their first meeting from years ago and reveal they'd done everything but pull out their dicks to express interest. But Tim had been too obtuse to realize what was happening. Not so this time.

"No boyfriend," he said, staring into Evan's eyes.

"Me neither," Evan said.

Seldom in his life had Tim been so forward. He astounded himself when he replied, "I think that situation has just changed."

"Are you sure it's not the fragrance from the roses that has you so high," Evan practically whispered. "Like me?" He continued to gaze into Tim's eyes. "Anyway, the scent of roses don't make my heart race *this* fast."

With that, Tim took a step toward Evan and rested his hand on his chest. What Tim first felt was the hard muscle of Evan's pecks under the cotton fabric of his red T-shirt. He moved his hand to the deep cleft in Evan's chest and Tim chuckled involuntarily. Indeed, Evan's heart was racing.

He picked up Evan's hand and placed it on his own chest. "Whose is racing faster?" he asked. "Can we please have dinner tonight?"

Evan broke into a wider smile. "Is seven too early? The Cobalt?"

That was four months ago, and the bloom was still, so to speak, on the rose.

As Tim continued to drive at a parade pace down La Cienega, he thought how proud of himself he was for not sharing Evan with his mother. Although he hadn't been perfectly frank with Evan about where he lived and who his mother was, he didn't feel as though he was lying. When the subject of his family came up, Tim had told the truth—that his parents were divorced, and both lived in the area. The fact that "the area" was Bel Air was a minor fact that would eventually be revealed. He just didn't want their disparate social and economic stations to be a factor at this stage of their otherwise perfect relationship.

Not that Evan would necessarily care that Tim was Polly Pepper's son. In fact, Evan was only peripherally aware of who—or what—a Polly Pepper was. Tim had tested him one evening when they were having dinner at The Grove before heading into the theater to see Woody Allen's new film. Over the outdoor shopping center's p.a. system had come the Grammy Award-winning song "For New Kate." It had been Polly's biggest hit, an anthem for young women—and gay boys everywhere—as they set out to take on the world, after a bust-up with a man. "Nice song, don't you think?" Tim had said, cocking an ear, pretending to listen closely to the music and lyrics, which he knew by heart. "It's Polly Pepper, isn't it?"

Evan shrugged. He swallowed a bite of his enchilada. "Isn't she that one who got murdered?"

Tim nearly choked on his burrito. Then he laughed. "Many critics have tried."

Then, as Thanksgiving approached, Evan had said that since his own family lived in Upstate New York, he'd hoped Tim would invite him to one of his parents' homes for a holiday dinner. Tim had to think quickly. "Er, we always go to my grandmother's convalescent home for Thanksgiving." He felt horrible lying to Evan. But using the excuse of a depressing day spent at a stinky old folks home did the trick. It squelched any further discussion about them sharing a turkey drumstick together.

"I'll make it up to you at Christmas," Tim had promised. "That is, if you're nice."

Evan grinned back. "I'd rather be naughty." Then he pushed Tim toward the bedroom of his small apartment.

Chapter Four

Polly sighed, "If I get one more generic, computer-generated Christmas letter I'm going to hang myself by my nipples!"

Dressed in her jogging togs (although she didn't jog), Polly sat at her Michael Graves-designed desk opening the mail in her bedroom/office. She divided her attention between the annual bleeding heart correspondence from her Aunt Martha, who lived somewhere in Nebraska, and considering the guest list for her upcoming party.

Her attention divided further when she glanced out the beveled glass window.

Just past the rose bushes and night-blooming jasmine, she saw the half-naked groundskeeper who was carrying a long aluminum pole with a pool skimmer on one end.

"Wouldn't *that* be a package to unwrap at Christmas." She caught herself mid-drool, staring at the young man's bronzed skin and the mossy hair that grew up out of the waist of his cut-off jeans and spread over his hard, rippled stomach.

"Fuck youth," Polly griped in envy. She forced her attention back to the pages of the single-spaced Helvetica type that chronicled every moment of the past 365 days in the life of second or third cousins, two or three times removed. Polly was certain that she never actually met any of these people in person.

"The family's all fine. Now." The letter's introduction was a portend of one calamity after another to follow.

Reading aloud, Polly skimmed the text. "Wal-Mart's come to town. Skip, skip, skip. Law suit against Mrs. Fields cookies . . . to blame for Uncle Buck's eating disorder. Skip, skip, skip. Son Dixon dropped out of high school . . . girlfriend in labor for seventy-two excruciating hours . . . a boy . . . their third. Skip. Fourteen-year-old Emery. Skip, skip. Back yard beauty pageant for the neighbor girls. Skip, skip. Emery crowned himself Miss Morass, Nebraska. Skip. As you can see, we have just as exciting a life here, as you do out there in your Hollywood, California. By the way, we saw you on the TV selling Polly Peppermills for Kmart. Or was it Sears?"

It infuriated Polly that Aunt Martha not only didn't say that she liked the commercial, but she didn't know for which department store chain Polly was pimping. Aunt Martha couldn't complete a letter without including a jab to let Polly know that there was life beyond the red carpet of a film premiere.

Polly skipped to the postscript. As expected, Aunt Martha's Christmas letter had a thinly veiled appeal for a financial handout. This year's composition concluded with, "The Good Lord willing, we'll manage. Somehow. That is if your Uncle Buck can keep his one half-good lung drained. They say he's darn lucky to have most of his toes and a good bit of his left ear after that catastrophe at the Pizza Hut."

The letter was signed, "Yours in Christ, Martha."

"Christ is right." Polly rolled her eyes. She attached a Post-It to the letter and jotted a note reminding Placenta to iron a one hundred dollar bill to include with Aunt Martha's Christmas card. She dropped the missive into a tray marked "Today's Opportunities."

Polly swiveled her desk chair closer to her computer and signed on to AOL. One of her guilty pleasures was anonymously entering the official Polly Pepper Fan Club chat room and reading what the real world had to say about how wonderful she was. Hoping for a write-in campaign to her old network, she always tried to add fuel to a made-up rumor that Polly Pepper was considering appearing in yet another reunion show.

Using her preferred screen name, *IM8CUT4U*, she insinuated herself into a chat. "Did you all read in *Parade* that Polly might do a Christmas special?" she wrote.

Someone named *BEDRKER* wrote, "If she's smart, she'll just let us remember how she used to be."

This led Polly into a debate over how time had been extremely kind to Polly Pepper. She countered that Botox had nothing to do with her perennially youthful appearance.

Inevitably, a fan would start an argument about Polly's son's sexuality. It was common knowledge that he was gay. Tim had written a series of articles for *The Advocate* about coming out as the son of a celebrity and the effect it had on his mother's career.

That's when Polly would switch screen names. As *N2XXXDIX*, she claimed to be someone who knew someone who knew Polly Pepper's hairstylist's sister's podiatrist. She typed in the affirmation that Polly was a PFLAG mother, and had frozen margaritas with Betty DeGeneres every other Tuesday of alternating months.

"Tim's so cute, don't you think," a cyber voyeur chatted. "Saw him on *Access Hollywood*, at the premiere of *Austin Powers Twelve: Dinkwads*. Yeah, baby, yeah!"

Polly baited the fan, tapping the keys on her keyboard. "My friend, the one who knows Polly's podiatrist personally, says that Polly knows how lucky she is to have such a handsome, loving and talented son as Tim."

A response from *BONER4U*: "I heard from a friend who went to his college that Tim had the biggest Johnson in the entire graduating class at Northwestern! Anyone in the room ever have him?"

Polly, who was not the least bit uncomfortable talking about her son's sex, smiled as the testimonials for Tim's endowment began popping up. "Yeah. He's a stud, alright," *FXYFLRT* wrote.

"Had him throughout our freshman year," said *NMAPLEZ*.

Tim hadn't gone to Northwestern. He attended UCLA for one semester before dropping out of their art history program. "Heard that Polly was pleased when Tim turned out to be queer," added *EZRY-DERBOTM*.

Polly grinned, enjoying the repartee.

"Heard she only likes gay men on account of her ex-husbands were all trolls and most gay guys are cute."

"Touché," wrote *IM8CUT4U*.

"Heard she stayed married to the last one just for her image. She really is a dipshit, like that clumsy singing nurse she used to play in that comedy sketch with Robin Williams on her old show."

After that last comment, Polly decided it was time to log off and work some more on her party guest list. She exited the chat room, then withdrew a legal-size manila folder from the faux Louis Quatorze-style horizontal filing cabinet. The label on the tab read *Jingle All the Way*. When she opened it up, a sheaf of brown-edged pages nearly slipped to the floor. Polly caught them and shuffled the papers into a neat pile.

She began to look at the names and addresses typed on each page. Running alphabetically, she placed a check next to Jack Alberston then caught herself. "Surely, he's long gone. What's he still doing on this list?" She drew a black X through the dead star's entry. She continued for a only a second. "Steve Allen? Don Ameche?" She crossed off both names. "Dead. Dead. Who else is dead?" She scanned the names. "These people all have the same address. Forest Lawn!"

Polly scrunched up her face, taking another look at the heading. "How the hell did my sympathy card list get mixed in with a joyous holiday?"

She placed the pages back into the folder and called out for Placenta. She hollered again.

When there was no immediate answer, Polly left her desk and went to her bedside. Bending down on one knee, at pillow-height, she pressed the intercom *talk* button on the wall next to her reading lamp. "Placenta!" Polly barked. With her face flat against the metal grill of the intercom system, she listened intently for a response. "Placenta!" she bellowed again into the wall unit.

She was so absorbed in beckoning her maid that she didn't hear Placenta enter the room. Standing as close to Polly as a base coat of Max Factor pancake, Placenta snapped, "Whachu want?"

With a start, Polly jumped and bumped her head against the wall.

"How many years have I told you, I can't answer on that damn thing if you hold down the speaker button!" Placenta, hands on hips, watched as Polly regained her equilibrium.

Polly caught her balance and her breath. She finger-combed her dyed red hair, then reached for a package of Merits and a cigarette lighter that were on the night stand. She stood up, lit her cigarette, inhaled deeply and exhaled as nonchalantly as possible. She was not going to let Placenta think she'd really been alarmed. "I need you to help me find my Christmas guest list," she said. "You must have misfiled it last year."

"Secretary is not on my resume. If it was, I'd get a real job." Placenta huffed. "Where'd you put it?"

Polly crossed the room to the filing cabinet. She opened the drawer and turned to look at her maid. After a beat, she said, "In the folder marked *Placenta's Replacement.*"

Placenta said, with feigned intimidation, "You scare me half to death, Ms. Pepper. You've got my nerves so frayed, I think my doctor will have to prescribe a paid leave of absence. Did you hear me? *Paid leave!*" She nudged Polly to the side of the filing cabinet, looked into the drawer, and flipped through several hanging green files with clear plastic tabs. She came to one with a typed label that read "Christmas." She hunted through several folders in the slot. Then she pulled one out. She looked at the tab.

"Can you read?" Placenta asked as she turned and slapped the folder against Polly's chest. "Christmas. C-h-r-i-s-t-m-a-s. Christmas. As in, Christ, sometimes you're so stupid."

Placenta pushed the filing drawer closed with her large ass, then turned and walked out of the room. "How, in the name of Jesus, does this woman survive?" Placenta muttered as she wandered down the second floor hallway toward the staircase.

"It wasn't in the right drawer!" Polly yelled after her.

"Your brain's not in the right drawer!" Placenta called back.

Polly tamped out her cigarette, angrily crushing the half-smoked cylinder. She tossed the Christmas guest list file onto her desk. "Tim's right. This holiday sucks," she said as she plopped herself down onto her leather executive chair and opened the file.

It took her a few minutes, but soon Polly was sifting through the pages and smiling at the thought of what she would wear to out-dress Sharon Stone. Her jewelry would sparkle brighter than Josh Hartnett's eyes. Her hair would be coifed in a style that would make Gwenyth Paltrow feel as hideous as if she were wearing an Eva Gabor mail-order wig. After an hour of drawing little hearts next to names on the list of people she wanted at her party, Polly was happy again. And hungry. She closed the file folder and turned off her computer.

Polly left her bedroom and practically skipped down the stairs, completely forgetting about her irritation with Placenta. When she entered the kitchen and saw her maid squeezing lemons, she suggested that the two of them have lunch together on the patio.

"Don't let me forget to tape *Passions* for you, Ms. Polly."

Placenta smiled. "Can't miss what's happening with your Chad and Eve."

The two do-si-doed as they moved about the kitchen together, preparing their Chinese chicken salad.

Chapter Five

The Colgate Avenue duplex where Evan lived was an old, two-story, Spanish-style stucco building. It was located in a small pocket of the city where tall trees bordered both sides of the streets, and residents and landlords took pride in maintaining the properties. Gardeners could be heard working up and down the street with their leaf blowers and lawn mowers. Dog owners could be seen at all hours towed behind spunky spaniels or mellow mastiffs. They conscientiously picked up their pets' deposits as a courtesy to other neighbors and pedestrians. Evan's apartment, near the busy corner of Crescent Heights, was on the second level.

Parallel parking his BMW between a Lexus SUV and a Ford Mustang, Tim walked the short distance to Evan's residence. He noticed that a team of laborers was tenting the apartment building next door. "Termites?" he said, cocking his head toward an impossibly large black canvas cloak, as Evan greeted him at the door and ushered him into the apartment. The interior was decorated with a nursery-like abundance of green plants.

They embraced. "They're doing this place next Tuesday," Evan said as he and Tim hungrily mauled each other, and pulled their respective T-shirts over their heads.

Tim asked, "How long do you have to stay out of here?"

"Twenty-four hours," Tim said, his voice a moan of satisfaction from Tim's smothering kisses.

"Bummer. Where will you stay?"

"With you."

Tim abruptly stopped their prelude to sex. Evan backed up one step. He stared at Tim for a moment. "I knew it," he said, looking disappointed. "We've been seeing each other for how long now? All summer? And I've *never* been to your place. You're married or something. Another guy beat me to you, right? I knew you were too cute to be single."

Tim was aghast by Evan's assumption.

"I'm wrong?" Evan countered Tim's nonverbal protest. "Then why is it any big deal that I crash with you for one single night?"

Tim stuttered. "I can't have . . . I'm not supposed to . . . you'd never believe . . ."

Evan looked down in sorrow and dejection. "This'll teach me never again to fall in love at first sight," he whispered.

"Would you please just trust me for a little while?" Tim begged. "I promise to explain everything before we go to England."

Evan laughed. "England? You're not serious."

Tim was mortified. "You're not backing out, are you? No! Why?"

"Hell, I wouldn't go as far as the Santa Monica Pier with you now."

"England's our honeymoon," Tim begged. "I don't understand."

"Understand this." Evan pointed a finger at Tim's chest. "I love you. I thought you loved me."

"I *do* love . . ." Tim began to argue but was interrupted.

"I won't play games," said Even. "Not with anybody. Especially not with you. I'm not a convenience. I'm not someone to wreck the sheets with when you get bored with your other boyfriends."

"There aren't any other boyfriends!"

"I'm also not going to be the one you cheat with when there's probably somebody else who loves you as much as I do waiting for you at home."

Tim was nearly hyperventilating. "I don't love anybody else! I swear it! I'm not involved with anyone. I only want you!"

"You'll have to prove that with more than words," Evan said. "Let me stay one night with you. I don't care if you live in a dive."

"The time . . . isn't right," Tim pleaded. "Please trust me."

Evan pulled his T-shirt over his head and left the room.

Tim heard the sound of keys being picked up from a table, then the front door being opened and closed. He ran to the front picture window in time to watch as Evan unlocked the door to his ancient, rusting 280 Z. The engine started after several choking attempts. Tim saw his true love pull away from the curb and drive out of sight.

The apartment should have been vibrating from involuntary feral noises issuing from deep within Tim and Evan's rapacious bodies. Instead, the only sounds filling the rooms came from a gurgling desktop water fountain and Mariachi music wafting from a worker's boombox next door.

Tim's thoughts vacillated. One instant he was angry with himself for not revealing his true identity. A split second later he was thinking Evan was an idiot for not knowing what most of the gay population knew—that he was Polly Pepper's son. It wasn't a secret. Then he was exasperated with Polly for placing him in the absurd position where he could be open about his sexuality but had to be sensitive about revealing his pedigree. Ultimately, he was upset with himself for losing another boyfriend.

He opened the front door. As he walked through the portal, he reached behind and pushed the lock on the doorknob. He closed the door securely behind him, then drifted down the steps to the street.

Tim wasn't sure now where he'd left his car. He pushed a security button on his key ring, which caused the car to honk and blink its lights, letting Tim know where he'd parked. As he sluggishly approached the vehicle, he heard his cell phone ringing from within the car. He raced to open the door.

"Evan!" he said, fumbling for the phone, activating the answer mode. "I'm so sorry! It's all my fault! Please forgive me!"

"Darling?" It was Polly. "Honey, what's wrong? Have you and your friend had a tiff?"

Tim sighed heavily. "A tiff? You could say that."

"There, there, my pet," Polly purred. "Come home to Mummy. We'll have a little sex at sunset."

"A drink. Of course."

"Of course. Vodka was made to wash away all the unpleasantness of failed love. I haven't had a very festive day myself. Wait until I tell you about my horrid revelation."

Tim was too numb to care about Polly's dramas. He could only think about getting back together with Evan. And a martini was only good for short-term problem-solving.

"Hurry, darling," Polly continued. "Placenta's running out of lemon twists. And would you be an angel and pick up a copy of *The Enquirer?* Cher and Barbra both called me about it! All they would say was that I should pay whoever took the picture!"

Tim muttered that he was on his way. He pushed the cell phone's OFF button and resigned himself to another night in Bel Air, listening to his mother prattle on about how she had always handled her broken hearts. The more intoxicated she became the more she would start revealing her affairs with Regis Philbin, Christopher Walken, or Bob Hope. "Big balls, but selfish, unsatisfying lovers, everyone of 'em," Tim could hear her slur for the umpteenth time.

Tim inserted his key into the car's ignition and started the engine. He shifted the transmission into drive. Slowly, he eased out of his parking space, turning the wheel enough to avoid bumping into the car in front, an old Rambler that was irritatingly close. Driving robotically, he made a few turns and drove up Crescent Heights to Sunset Boulevard. There, at the signal, he turned left and then an almost immediate right, pulling in to the parking lot of The Liquor Locker. With a somnambulist's lethargy, he left his car and walked into the bright florescent-lit store.

On automatic pilot, he found the racks of celebrity rags. He picked one of them up. Calista Flockhart was on the cover. The banner headline proclaimed CALISTA'S NEW DIET SECRET: NO KITCHEN.

"You read it, you buy it." A hostile voice came from behind the cash register.

Tim ignored the old man, in no mood to be told what to do. He opened the newspaper and began looking for Polly's picture. It jumped out at him. The editors begged the question: "Polly Pepper. Dead or

Alive?" Tim skimmed the text. Supposedly, a poll had been taken. Ninety-nine percent of the average Joes who were consulted all agreed: *Alive!*

"That's a comfort," Tim said aloud.

Then, to himself, *Cher and Barbra are right.* Tim recognized the picture as one of Polly's publicity shots from the old show. It was taken more than a decade ago, when she'd been inducted into the Television Hall of Fame. Polly looked like the glamorous star she once was. Tim was impressed. He took the paper up to the counterman and paid for it.

Presently, Tim drove along the vehicle-congested Sunset Strip. When he finally reached Doheny, the traffic thinned out. He cruised on through Beverly Hills, past museum-size mansions, and the pink Beverly Hills Hotel. The serpentine street took him past UCLA to the West Gate of Bel Air. He turned right onto Stone Canyon Road, then headed through the bucolic woods toward home.

It was nearly five o'clock when he pulled up to the tall gates of Pepper Plantation and pushed the remote control that drew the famous PP monogrammed portal to open like the pages in an animated fairy-tale movie. He drove onto the estate and parked under the front portico.

Just as Tim stepped out of his car, Polly opened the front door and walked out onto the brick porch. She held two martinis. She offered him a sad smile. "My poor baby," she cooed. "Honey, we both need these," she said, handing him a drink. He took a sip even before entering the house.

Breakfast poolside was later than usual the next morning. Tim was too morose to get out of bed before ten. He'd tried calling Evan four times last night, only to get an unsympathetic answering machine.

Polly, too, was exhausted. Although she did her best to be supportive of Tim's love-life problems, in between sips from a Bloody Mary and nibbles of dry toast, she rambled on about her new accompanist, Jeb, and what a handsome and talented young man he was. "Who was I trying to fool?" she asked aloud. "He swings for your team, not mine. Still, I wouldn't mind having him in the family."

Tim couldn't conceive of being with another man. Not after Evan, who, while not the most adventurous lover Tim had ever encountered, had nonetheless given him the most satisfying sex of his life. *It's that undefinable something extra that someone brings to the experience,* Tim thought, as his mind coasted back to the times he and Tim had simply shed their clothes and held each other on the bed for hours.

Polly prattled on. "There's an old saying, my darling, 'If *they* don't want you, then you don't want *them!*' "

Tim had already made a decision. "I've changed my mind about Evan staying here. There's no good reason why he shouldn't."

"I told you that a thousand times, baby," Polly said. "You know he's welcome. But don't you dare call me a jinx when . . . er, *if,* he stops dating you!"

Tim pushed his chair away from the patio table. The wrought iron legs made a screeching sound that made Polly wince with pain. "Sorry," he said, as he saw his mother place both hands over the sides of her face to prevent her skull from exploding. "Have another Bloody. I'm going down to Evan's flower shop."

Polly flapped a hand to signal that she was saying goodbye and wishing him success.

Quickly, Tim performed his morning ablutions, then dressed in his most sexy outfit: blue jeans, tight tanktop, Nike trainers. He grabbed his wallet, cell phone and car keys and was soon seated behind the wheel of his BMW, coasting down the long driveway to the gate that let out onto Stone Canyon Road.

The traffic signal at Sunset seemed to take longer than usual to change from red to green. Then Tim had to wait for opposing traffic to glide through the Bel Air West gate before he could turn left. Finally he was on his way, but the busy street was reduced to one lane as city workers jackhammered the road in a long-term city project to widen the clogged artery. Eventually, Tim entered West Hollywood. He turned left on Larrabee Street and parked in a public metered lot.

Sherwood Florist was busy, with several customers when Tim entered the cool shop. But Evan turned to see Tim the moment he walked through the door. They both smiled, then met each other halfway into the store.

"Let me just take care of these people," Evan said. "There's tea in the back, if you'd like."

Tim was elated by Evan's cordial reception. He relaxed as he wandered through the shop, admiring bouquets and special arrangements that Evan had created. After ushering the last customer through the door, Evan approached Tim. "Good to see you," he said. "Yesterday was so stupid."

"Of course you can stay with me." Tim smiled and reached out to give Evan a hug. "I was an idiot. I'm sorry."

Evan waved a hand dismissively. "I realize that I had no right to insinuate myself into your life."

"No. I *want* you in my life." Tim smiled.

"I don't really think so," Evan said.

Tim was suddenly on faltering ground. "What?"

Evan looked down at the floor. Then he looked again into Tim's eyes. "I hope we'll always be friends, but . . ."

"More than friends!" Tim gulped, grasping for meaning to what he was hearing. "We're going to spend the rest of our lives together!"

"I'd like that," Evan said sincerely. "But I'm not mature enough to make that kind of commitment. You made me realize that yesterday. I got all huffy and jealous over what I perceived as your secret life. How lame is that? It's like IMing someone on AOL, and when they don't respond right away I automatically think they're juggling a half-dozen other guys and chatting it up with someone else. I'm just too needy. It's not fair to you."

Tim shook his head. "You've got it all backwards. It was not very grown-up of me to expect you to just trust me without any more information. Communication has to be the foundation of every relationship. It wasn't fair that I dicked you around, just because I was afraid of being honest."

"That's another thing," Evan said. "Honesty. If we don't have that, we don't have squat. Know what I'm saying?"

Tim was incredulous. "As a matter of fact, I don't know what you're saying. At least I hope you're not saying what I think you are. All I know is that I love you, and you love me. I was completely stupid not telling you everything about my personal life. As my lover, you have every right to know."

Evan shook his head. "Nobody has a right to know everything about someone else. We all have things that we need to keep private."

"But not the kind of crap that I was keeping from you," Tim asserted.

"No, Tim. You've got your reasons for not sharing certain things with me. And I've kept things from you too."

"Like what?" Tim began.

Just then the chime on the shop door sounded. Both men looked up as Bradley Whitford came into the shop. "He's a good customer. Gotta take care of him," Evan said as he walked toward the actor.

Tim was dumbfounded. He'd come to apologize to Evan, to tell him he was welcome to spend the night, any and every night if he wanted, at Pepper Plantation. But something had gone horribly wrong. Evan was brushing him off.

Famous customer or not, Tim rushed toward Evan. "Where's this conversation heading?" he interrupted Evan and Bradley Whitford. "Are you dumping me?"

Evan apologized to Whitford, then asked to be excused for a brief moment. Bradley smiled and nodded. He wandered away to give the men more privacy.

Evan pulled Tim from the Thanksgiving Day decorations toward tall buckets of iris stems. "If I wanted to dump you, I would have said so. I don't hide my feelings very well."

Tim sighed with relief.

Evan continued. "But what I was about to say, is I think we need to take a break from each other."

Tim blanched. "I can't be without you. Not even for a day. Last night was hell. I missed you so much."

"And I missed you, too," Evan said. "But I think we need to find out what we really want from each other. I know what I want, which is communication. And no dodging of issues that either of us finds important."

"But that's what I want, too!" Tim almost begged.

"Yeah, I think you do. That's why I want us to have a little time to put things into perspective. We'll talk whenever either of us feels like it. Then, maybe by Christmas, we can work something out. What do you say?"

"Give it a shot, guys," Bradley Whitford called from behind the ficus tree. "Do whatever it takes to make things work out, so you can be together."

Finally, Evan said, "I'll call you later."

With that, Tim dropped his head in defeat. He slowly walked toward the door. As he placed his hand on the knob, and just before he walked through the portal, he heard Bradley's voice call to him. "Hey, I got your mom's invitation. Tell her I'll be there."

Bradley said to Evan, "Cute stuff. I didn't know you were dating Polly Pepper's kid."

Evan looked to Bradley as Tim closed the door behind him. "That old actress? From TV?"

"Old to you, maybe," Whitford said. "She's an icon, at least to my generation. Don't tell me you didn't know?"

Evan shook his head.

"He's only the most eligible guy in the gay community. Hell, even *I* know that. Surely you've heard about Pepper Plantation? Like Harold Lloyd's Green Acres. No," he explained in advance, "not that Eva Gabor series on *Nick at Nite*. I actually got an invitation this year to their annual Christmas party. It's amazing what a little thing like an Emmy brings with it."

"He didn't tell me," Evan said.

"Like he had to?" Bradley laughed.

Even was stunned. His face turned red. Then his embarrassment turned to resentment. *I wasn't good enough to be in his world,* Evan thought. *That's why he never told me about his mother, or brought me to his home. Screw him.*

"How about those roses for Allison's birthday?" Bradley said, changing the subject.

Chapter Six

"It's beginning to look a lot like Christmas," Polly sang as she wandered through Pepper Plantation, holding her late afternoon flute of champagne, waiting for Tim to return home. He'd been away since morning.

As Polly moved about the vast house, she brushed the holiday ornaments and other decorations with the fingertips of her free hand. Her smile widened when she lifted the corners of a drop cloth and found a life-size wax figure of Fergie, the Duchess of York. Tim said he'd borrowed something from Debbie Reynolds's attic. Although Polly had no idea what the possible tie-in was to Christmas with an inanimate facsimile of the former royal, she'd long ago taken a vow never to ask questions of Tim's plans for her big holiday event. She left her son to do whatever he felt was in the best interest of his creativity—and her party-giving reputation. She also wanted to be as surprised as her guests when they first stepped into whatever netherworld Tim created for their pleasure.

Polly held up her glass and made a toast to Fergie. "Here's to you, baby! And to the not-fading-fast-enough House of Windsor. May you always make that cheap whore on the throne as nervous as her neurotic litter of corgies."

At that moment, Placenta walked into the room carrying an uncorked bottle of Dom Perignon, carefully wrapped in a white linen table napkin. Among Placenta's responsibilities was the task to ensure that Polly's glass was never empty. "You're supposed to say something nice about somebody's health when you raise a glass of this French stuff," Placenta said, responding to Polly's proposal to the wax Duchess. "Give it up. At least the Queen came to the Palladium for your dumb-ass show," she harrumphed. "*Coma: The Musical.* You musta been *in* a coma to think that turkey would fly."

Polly hated to be reminded of her flops and poor career choices. But she equally loathed and despised the perennially constipated-looking British monarch. "The bitch wouldn't even receive me!" Polly snapped. "She's nothing but a peasant!"

"A peasant with more money than God," Placenta said as she poured more champagne into Polly's Waterford crystal glass. "By the way, the mail delivery guy just carried in a tub of stuff."

Polly became euphoric. "Cards? RSVPs?"

"Do I look like Homeland Security to you? I don't commit federal crimes."

Polly ignored Placenta's remark. She took the champagne bottle away from her maid and walked briskly out of the room. She went into the kitchen. At the far end wall was the door to the laundry facility. She opened the door and reached around for the light switch. She flipped it on, and soft Christmas music issued through speakers in the ceiling.

Among the baskets of clothes and linens to be washed were white plastic bins scattered throughout the room, containing thousands of pieces of mail. In the center, on an island of utility drawers with a wide, granite countertop for folding clothes, was the new batch of en-velopes.

For the task of sorting the holiday cards and letters, Polly had hired a high school girl to open every envelope. Another hired girl then with-drew the contents and logged into a record book the postmark date on each envelope, the date received, and the contents (Christmas card with letter, Christmas card with personal inscription, Christmas card with photo, Christmas card requesting photo, party invitations, liquor bills). Anything addressed to Tim was dropped into a separate bin.

The Christmas cards were cross-referenced with a list of names of the people to whom Polly had already sent her cards. If a name and return address on an incoming envelope was not from a personal friend, or if it did not correspond with a master list of cards mailed from Pepper Plantation, the assistant would add the name and address to yet another list for possible reciprocation. The names were further pared down to those who would receive a pre-printed card with the name *Polly Pepper* stamped in red metallic ink. Occasionally Polly would personally sign a card.

Polly immediately went to the new batch of mail and began rifling through the box looking for RSVPs to her party, as well as any envelopes that appeared as if they might be inviting her to a reception. She found two dozen of the self-addressed stamped envelopes that had accompanied her mass mailing. She also dug out twelve envelopes with no sender's name. She recognized the return addresses as belonging to, among others, Nicole Kidman, David Bowie, Tiffani Thiessen, Neil Patrick Harris, Carol Burnett, Steven Webber, and Mr. and Mrs. Matthew Broderick. She smiled, pulled a tall bar stool up to the island and poured more champagne into her flute.

Finding a letter opener she wedged open the first envelope's glued flap and ripped into the paper. She withdrew the card. Polly scrunched her face as she asked aloud, "Who is John Rzeznik?"

"Someone I invited." It was Tim, standing in the doorway. "He's in a group, The Goo Goo Dolls. He's nice. Met him at Ozzy's. You'll adore him. Cute, too."

"Of course he is, precious. All your beaux are cute."

"John's not my beau. I don't have one. Remember?"

Polly drained her flute of champagne. "There's Aaron. Er, Evan."

Tim gave her a sad look. "I'll have some of that," he said, nodding toward the Dom Perignon. He picked up a Venti-size Starbucks coffee paper cup left by one of the Christmas card girls. He emptied the dark dregs of java into the sink beside the washing machine, then turned around and held it out for Polly to pour him some of her bubbly.

Polly tipped the neck of the bottle into Tim's cup. A trickle came out. "Placenta!" Polly yelled out. "More! Placenta!"

Suddenly replacing Bing Crosby over the household intercom system, the scolding voice of Placenta filled the room. "More what? Members of Congress? Flights to Maui? Hours in a day? You give me too much credit for being psychic!"

Tim walked over to the intercom unit next to the door. He pushed the TALK button. "Heya, Placenta. It's Tim." He released the button.

"Hey yourself, Mr. Tim," Placenta said sweetly. "Glad you're home. Pry a coherent thought out of your momma, would you, please?"

"I heard that!" Polly bellowed.

Tim said into the intercom, "We're in the laundry room, Placenta. I'm having a nervous breakdown, and Mother's siphoned off all the champagne. Could we please have another bottle?"

"Sure enough. Anything else? Pate? Crackers? Clorox, so your momma can make herself useful for a change?"

Tim smiled and pushed TALK. "Just another champagne flute, thanks. Oh, and of course your brilliant smile."

"Your sweet talk'll get you a date with my son's best pal. If you're ever interested."

"Thanks, Placenta. I do seem to be unexpectedly single these days. We'll talk."

Music once again filled the room. Karen Carpenter sang "Little Altar Boy." Polly rolled her eyes at Tim. "She's always liked you better. She never offered to fix me up with anybody."

"I'm not around to irritate her all the time." Placenta had been with Polly since before Tim was born. "She's probably your only real friend," he said. "She'll tell you the truth, even after you're still bloated with all the smoke that your pathetic, sycophantic publicist has blown up your ass."

Polly gave a mild sneer. "Now, tell me about Devon, er, Evan. What happened between you two?"

Tim recounted the incident at the flower shop. By the time Placenta appeared in the doorway, carrying a silver tray laden with another bottle of Dom Perignon submerged in an ice-filled silver bucket, Tim was near tears. "I keep hearing Sammy Davis, Jr. singing, 'What Kind of Fool am I?'"

"Anybody who's ever been in love is a fool," Polly said, trying to make Tim feel better.

As Placenta placed the silver tray among the stacks of cards, she said, "Tim, honey, be a fool as often as possible. It's not the heart that gets you into trouble when it comes to love. It's rationalizing about it." She left the room.

"Four husbands probably qualifies her as something of an expert,"

Polly conceded. "But, baby, now you can spend more time working on our party. And as an expression of my appreciation and love, I've arranged for you to take Sir David Frost's country house in Dorset for a month in January. I stayed there once. In the Diahann Carroll whoopee bedroom. It was heaven. And since most Englishmen have a propensity for being gay—something to do with cold showers and all-boys schools—you'll be so busy beating them off with a stick. Oh, that was a poor choice of words, wasn't it? *Beating them off,* I mean? Well, you know what I meant. You'll have fun, and you won't have time to think about this most recent low tide in the love canal."

Tim looked askance at his mother. "Is that supposed to be a simile, or a metaphor?"

"Love canal? Another poor choice?"

"Forget England. Forget love. As for the party . . ." Tim took a long pull from his champagne flute. "Fine. It's all coming together. I'm sure it'll be everything you and your guests expect."

"And much more, I hope!"

"Have you and Marvin Hamlish gone over the material you'll be singing?"

"Like England love, you can forget Marvin. He's too jealous of my new accompanist. As if he has any reason. Everybody knows that I'm devoted to him. But am I supposed to just chill while he's busy with a Broadway score? I think not." Polly nodded her head in agreement with herself. "So I'm stuck with Jeb. What kind of name is that for a piano player anyway, for Christ sake? He's actually doing a marvelous job on the new arrangements for my set. But I want you to meet with him to discuss the rest of the evening's entertainment."

"Will you be there to chaperone?"

"Jeb worships me. But not in the same way that Jimmy Brolin worships Babs." Polly held up her hands. "I've come to terms," she sighed. "How in hell did Missy Ball-Buster get so lucky to land such a handsome catch at her age? I'll bet he's a lot of laughs. Those strong silent ones always surprise. I'm still a lot of laughs, aren't I?"

Tim topped his mother's glass with more champagne. "You're nothing *but* laughs," he said. "And don't worry, love will find Polly Pepper again. It does once or twice a year." He raised his glass in a toast. "To our respective pursuits."

"Here! Here!" Polly crowed, taking another long sip from her flute. "Keep your eyes peeled for me, and I'll keep mine peeled for you."

"By the way," Tim asked, "did you ever meet Placenta's son's pal? What's he look like?"

Polly put down her glass. "He did all the tile work in the six upstairs bathrooms. Yummy. Tall. Dark. Shoulders for days, and God only knows what else. If you get my drift."

Tim made a small chuckle. He'd been through the routine of being dumped before, and he knew the resulting Kubler-Ross emotional stages. He'd been stuck all day somewhere in between denial, anger, and bargaining. Now, aware of himself sitting in a laundry room getting drunk on champagne with his mother, who was toying with him about a sexy tile mason—as well as her stupid Christmas party—he automatically jumped straight to the depression stage. But he knew that eventually he'd face acceptance. Then maybe he'd be ready for Jeb. Or even Placenta's son's pal.

Chapter Seven

For the next two weeks, Tim tried to focus all of his attention and energy on his party planning work. It was difficult. But with friends/clients like Sean, there was little time left for Tim to dwell on his personal issues.

Sean was becoming a pain in the ass. He worried about everything, especially Tim's party theme. "You don't think it's too avant garde?" Sean looked freaked. "My social status and well-deserved and inordinately extravagant Christmas present from Paul are riding on the success of this affair!" Sean nearly hyperventilated, watching a construction crew build an aluminum scaffold in the backyard. "What's that for?" he asked, alarmed. "No. Don't tell me!" He scampered away toward the safety of his house, his fist in his mouth.

The nonstop whirl, which required the organizational skills of a building contractor and the diplomacy of a police hostage negotiator, filled up most of the time that Tim would have had to dwell on his unhappiness over not seeing Evan. At least there was Jeb; a flicker of light in an otherwise dreary world.

Tim and Polly had similar tastes in men, so it wasn't surprising that Tim found himself vaguely attracted to his mother's accompanist. Although he didn't want to be. Soon after Tim and Jeb met for a discussion about the entertainment at Pepper Plantation, Tim realized why Polly had been captivated—and ultimately dejected—by the handsome piano man.

Although Tim and Polly were enticed by more than Jeb's physical attributes, it didn't hurt that he had luxurious blond hair, a flawless pink complexion, a wide Ultrabright toothpaste smile, and strong, rounded shoulders, which he often advertised in a tanktop. Jeb was also intelligent and genuinely talented. Tim and Polly had always agreed that the combination of those two qualities was at least seventy-five percent of what made a man seductive.

"Two talented men should be together," Polly affirmed over break-fast the morning after Tim's first dinner date with Jeb. "I knew from the moment that Cher recommended him, that we'd adore him. However, knowing Cher—and you know I do—I pretty much figured I wouldn't be the type to whom he'd be writing serenades. My beautiful son, maybe."

"You've never shied from borrowing a chapter from *Lolita*."

"I suspected that darling Jeb would be more likely to be swept away by Justin Timberlake, than a living legend, like me."

"Justin's a legend too," Tim affirmed. "Anyway, Jeb's just a friend. I don't have the time or inclination for anything more." Tim wanted to dismiss any idea of romantic interest. "He's a nice guy. He fills a space."

Polly peered over her sunglasses.

Tim shook his head. "He's simply a diversion. He has lots of fun stories about all the divas he's worked for."

Polly looked up from Army Archerd in *Daily Variety* and sniggered. "Did he tell you the one about rehearsing Pamela Lee for her cabaret act? Wish I'd been a fly on their sheet music. Or how about the fun he had with Robert Goulet and Victoria Principal, preparing for a national tour of *Old Folks at Home*? Jeb's a riot. He has something on everybody."

Polly twisted her mouth in contemplation. A look of panic crossed her face. "He didn't say anything about me, did he?"

Tim smiled. "What could he possibly say about everybody's favorite comedienne?"

Polly smiled back. Then her expression became one of suspicion. "That wasn't an answer to my question. If he's making small talk with you about our friends, who's to say he isn't babbling to them about us?" Polly slapped her paper onto the glass tabletop. "He wouldn't be a beast and repeat my Steve and Edie story, would he?"

"Wouldn't he?"

"They're my dearest friends!" Polly cried. "Anyway, I only told the part that practically everybody else already knows!"

Placenta had come out to the patio with a plate of peeled and separated tangerines. "Nobody knew anything about that until you and your conga line of rumor-mongers conference-called each other," she interjected.

"When was the last time you spoke to Edie?" Tim asked his mother.

Polly thought for a moment. "It's been . . . Well, it was when she and Steve . . . They're on the road, I think. Aren't they always? Oh, shit! You don't think he believed that Kim Cattrall rumor? Oh Christ! Marlo Thomas told that to me in confidence! It's Phil's fault for telling her! Crap! What if Jeb misinterpreted that little nugget about Heather Graham and Britney? What if he got the impression that they were . . ."

Placenta cackled as she watched Polly sweat about the possible consequences of the gossip she recycled. Polly threw up her hands. "Okay. I'm fucked! There should be a diva/accompanist confidentiality law! What the hell else are we supposed to do during rehearsals?" Polly picked up her *Daily Variety* and returned to Army.

Tim continued his breakfast. In between bites of bagel and sips of juice or coffee, he poked his Palm Pilot with its stylus, checking his daily activity list.

As he was calculating the number of gurneys he needed to accommodate Sean's party guests, his concentration was shattered by the sudden shrill ring of an incoming call on his cell phone.

Although two weeks had elapsed since his last conversation with Evan, Tim still jumped with hopeful expectation whenever a call came through. He looked at the digital display screen. Sean's number appeared. Tim ignored the theme to "The Lone Ranger" and let it go to voice mail.

His action was not lost on Polly. "Darling," she cooed, "if you don't mind my being observant, I think you've been more than a little distracted lately. I'm starting to get anxiety attacks. Is my party going to be the best ever? You know that I have every confidence in you, but the truth is, I'm getting a wee-bit jittery."

"Everything's under control," Tim said, returning to his Palm Pilot.

Polly took out her own daily planner, checking dates and items on a list. She hardly registered that Placenta was still standing by her chair. Polly frowned. "Honey," she said to Tim, "I see that we're three short ones out. Can we take a meeting to talk about my fitting at Elizabeth Courtney? I really should see what Bob and Ray have whipped up. And I think another pow-wow with Jeb is in order. I don't want to interfere with his program, but I'm not sure I was entirely clear when I suggested that Krystle Carrington—what's her real name?—should *not* attempt to sing again if she's going to do her usual repertoire of 'Push, Push, in the Bush,' and her completely unfunny parody of 'The Twelve Days of Christmas.' And are we really going to chance letting John Tesh get anywhere near a synthesizer?"

"What *Lola* here is trying to tell you, is that if you need anything baby, we're never too busy to help," Placenta said, knuckles resting on her hips.

Tim stopped jotting notes. He looked up at Placenta with a wide smile. For a moment there was only the slurping sound of water being sucked into the pool filter, and the whining of Jim Belushi, demanding a piece of Polly's blueberry muffin.

Polly looked down at her dog. Then she looked up and saw Tim and their maid sharing a moment. "But of course, darling. Anything that needs attention, we'll be happy to take care of for you. But it does seem to me that you must be on the fast track and going hog wild with our affair this year. I've never seen you so busy. Perhaps you need an assistant. I can ring up the agency, if you'd like."

Tim's thoughts whirled. He wondered how in the hell he ever imagined that he could juggle creating two huge parties simultaneously, all by himself. *And where in hell am I going to find a dozen CAT scan machines and technicians for the Life Sciences tent at Sean's?* Tim sighed. He unintentionally ignored his mother, who was saying something about taking over buying all the floral arrangements.

Chapter Eight

"Alright, Missy, spill it!" Polly planted herself behind Placenta in the kitchen. "I want to know what *you* know."

Placenta's ample body was wedged deep into the subzero freezer as she reached for a brick of leftover lasagna behind a half-dozen bottles of Stoly. "One thing I know for sure," Placenta returned over the muting sound of the freezer's cooling vent, "your people should haul their butts back here from that galaxy far, far away and drag you home."

"Did you hear me in there?" Polly challenged. "What's with the agitation every time Tim's phone rings?" Polly drummed her fingers on her folded arms. "Why is he so distracted? My PSA for Actors and Others for Animals aired three times last night, and he didn't pay any attention. Didn't you think I was convincing as I begged for neutering."

"Praise the Lord, you're finally getting fixed!"

Polly ignored the jibe. "That's not like my ever-supportive Timmy. He embraces all of my humanitarian causes. He's sleeping with Jeb, isn't he?"

Placenta found the foil-wrapped food, and she withdrew the item and herself from inside the custom-made appliance. As she closed the door she tossed the anvil-solid pasta onto the pink Italian granite countertop. "Don't ask questions if you're not prepared to hear the answers," Placenta said as she set the microwave to defrost.

"Pooh." Polly dismissed her maid's warning. "I'm a grown-up. I can take the news that my son's making babies with Jeb. They're both better looking than anything on *American Idol*. I'm just glad he's getting some. As long as he doesn't run out of tinsel for my party."

Placenta made a grunt of incredulity as she unwrapped the meal and placed it in a Corning Ware dish in preparation for nuking.

Polly raised her hands. "Sorry. That didn't come out right," she apologized. "It was trivial of me to think only of the decorations. I just meant that I'd rather hear that he and Jeb are having man-to-man noogie, instead of something important like . . ."

Placenta cocked her head and waited a beat.

". . . like Brad and Jennifer having their party on the same night as mine!"

"Yes, ma'am. You certainly know from comedy and tragedy," Placenta said.

"That is the business I'm in." Polly nodded in agreement. "So, what are you holding back from me about my Timmy? Just tell me he's jumping Jeb's bones and I'll chalk up his behavior to puppy lust."

Placenta closed the microwave oven door more loudly than necessary. She turned around and faced Polly. "I don't know anything that I'm not supposed to. That's what I tell those spies for the *Enquirer* when they see me cleaning out the aisles at The Liquor Locker, and it's what I'm telling you."

"Remind me to give you your Christmas gift early. A two-for-one coupon for Mop 'n Glow."

"And remind me to give you an egg nog enema." Placenta turned away with more grace than one might expect from a woman of her weight. "And don't forget your *Crystal Lite* audition this afternoon," she called cheerily.

"Joan Rivers is an alien!"

As Tim cruised his Beemer east along Sunset Boulevard, he listened to Danny Bonaduce, his favorite morning drive-time shock jock. Danny was venting about a televised awards program from the previous night. "She reminds me of that thing in the movie *Signs*," he grumbled. "Hey, stay out of the cornfield, kiddies. Mom and Melissa may be lurking among the stalks!"

The morning was bright and relatively smog-free. The city seemed immersed in winter coolness. It was the type of morning that usually reminded Tim of how blessed he was to live in Southern California. While news headlines were filled with stories about twelve-foot-high drifts of snow in the Midwest, and chill factors of minus 40 snapping power lines and reducing hundreds of thousands of homes to virtual ice boxes, Tim drove along the wide Beverly Hills Boulevard with the top down on his convertible.

However, Tim's thoughts about his overwhelming workload were mixed with a feeling of emptiness for Evan and a curious twinge in his navel when he formed a mental picture of Jeb. The collision of job anxiety and the confusion of thoughts and emotions about two men made him nearly oblivious to the cloudless blue sky, palm trees and the center median planted with a profusion of colorful flowers. Which he almost ran into when his cell phone suddenly rang.

Tim made an involuntary lunge for the phone. "Tim," he announced, simultaneously pushing his cell's keypad, and breaking for a SUV with a bumper sticker that read: "Jesus. Don't Leave Earth Without Him."

"Had a thought." It was Jeb. "Your mom bitches about Carol Burnett finding a young husband at her age, and MTM having the same—a doctor, no less! How cool would it be if you gave her a stud for Christmas?"

"Polly Pepper doesn't bitch," Tim said. "Polly Pepper protests. Polly Pepper laments. Polly Pepper frets."

"You're talking to her shoulder," Jeb said. "She's lonely. My ears get used a lot around her. And not just talking about making arrangements to 'For New Kate.' "

Tim always smiled when someone rapidly spoke that title. He often wondered if it wasn't the most clever joke ever perpetrated against his mother's well-crafted Julie Andrews/Ingrid Bergman (before Rossellini) image. "She'll never seriously date," Tim said. "She thinks she's too old and too famous. Every man would only be interested in basking in re-flected glory. Anyway, there isn't anyone left in the BH edition of *Who's Who* that she hasn't gone out with."

"How about Glendale?" Jeb asked. "He doesn't have your blue eyes and dimples. But he is, as they say, a man of a certain age—like your mother. He takes care of himself—like your mother. He's bright. Cheerful. He's never rude to busboys or service people. We'll meet at *Pane e Vino*. Your mom loves that place."

Tim was curious. "Trust me, she'll dismiss an actor or a sycophant. She needs somebody independent. He'd have to be strong yet sensitive. You know how vulnerable she actually is. The ideal man for Polly is self-assured but not arrogant. Articulate but doesn't throw around polysyllabic words to impress and intimidate others."

"Like you're doing with . . . what was that word you just used that sounded like something mean about your mother? Or a disease?"

"The ideal man is a guy whose nature is kindness. And he doesn't fuss over the sommelier's presentation of a bottle of wine at restaurants. I'll make sure that the next man she hooks up with is someone that she wouldn't mind being stranded with on a desert island."

"Oh sure, the impossible dream," Jeb said. "But I can tell you from experience that this one is strong when he has to be. But he's also intuitive about others' feelings, and he would never step on anyone's ego. And he's done a great job raising his kids. I'm one of 'em."

Tim was taken aback. "I didn't know you had a father."

"I wouldn't know you had one either, if I hadn't saved all the *People* magazines about their divorce trial, and all the loot she had to dump on him," Jeb said. "Believe it or not, I also have a mother. But she's out of the picture. Didn't appreciate what she had in my dad."

This new information intrigued Tim. As he crawled along Sunset, heading toward La Cienega, he agreed that it might be worth the time to double-date with Jeb and his father. "Does your dad know about this idea?" Tim asked.

"He knows that I've been working with Polly Pepper, but I haven't mentioned anything about a date. I think if we get them together, nature will just take its course."

Tim nodded his head. "But I can't tell Polly this is a date. It's gotta seem perfectly natural, like this dinner is your Christmas gift to her and me."

"How's Friday night?" Jeb asked.

Tim made a mental reminder to call Polly right after his meeting to confirm her schedule.

"And speaking of nature . . ." Jeb paused. "When do I get to see you again?"

Tim cleared his throat. "We'll see each other at dinner." He smiled as he disconnected the call.

Immediately, Tim's cell phone rang again. His heart raced as he took his eyes off the road for a quick glance at the caller ID. He rolled his eyes and pushed a number on the keypad. "I still don't have an answer on whether or not the UCLA gymnastics team will perform at the party without their shirts," he said wearily.

"And good morning to you, too," Sean said, unfazed by Tim's response. "I have a much bigger issue to deal with than a skin show for me and my guests who want to look young and fit," he said. "Paul's getting ugly."

"Retouch his headshots!" Tim jested.

"He's starting to reign me in. He's slashing the party budget."

"You could save a bundle by eliminating the Malibu beach fantasy tent," Tim deadpanned. "I still haven't come up with enough body oil for all the lifeguards you want."

"Forget the lifeguards. He's talking crazy talk. Something about no money because there aren't enough episodes of his show for syndication. He doesn't understand how important this party is to me. And to his career."

"One less station at the party isn't going to make any difference." Tim sighed. "Your guests won't miss what they didn't expect in the first place. Besides, you've still got your wet T-shirt waiters."

Sean made a noise that Tim interpreted to mean, *Big whoop.* Sean wouldn't let the subject die. "That's not all," he said. "He thinks we could have done this party without you, and saved a fortune."

"Don't make me laugh," Tim said, feeling offended by Sean's remark. "You and Paul make great atmosphere at parties but . . ."

"We do, don't we?"

". . . but you're hardly equipped—and I mean that in a non-sexual way—to please people in your natural habitat. What I can accomplish in three weeks would take you six months, and it would cost you five times as much. Don't you see, that's why people hire a pro. With me at the helm, all you have to do is sit back and enjoy the raves from your friends. You want to be a guest at your own party, don't you?"

Sean was silent.

Tim went on. "Then I suggest you tell your stiff b/f—and I don't mean that in a sexual way—to either pay the bills and stop squawking, or cancel the affair altogether. Or . . ."

"Or what?" Sean asked.

"Or, do the rest yourselves. I'd like to see you guys try. Frankly, I could do with one less headache. In fact . . ."

"No! No!" Sean anticipated Tim's announcement.

"I want you to hang up, talk to Paul, and call me back in no more than one hour. You'll tell me I have *carte blanche* to finish this job—without interference—or I resign."

"I didn't realize you were such a prima donna!"

"One hour, Sean. Whatever you guys decide will be cool with me." Tim pushed the disconnect button on his telephone and rounded the corner of La Cienega and Melrose. He wasn't angry. In fact, he felt empowered. When it came to pleasing friends, he rarely responded to inequitable situations, such as the one presented by Sean, with such firm resolve. The altercation with Sean gave Tim a rush of adrenaline, a sudden sense that he was indomitable; that if he felt a certain way about something, he could be bold enough to stand his ground. With that thought, he pulled into the Sherwood Florist parking lot.

It was too early for the shop to be open. However, Tim knew that Evan would have already been to the downtown Los Angeles Flower Mart by 5:30 A.M., and most likely he would be in the back room preparing his procurement of lilies, anthuriums, gardenias and amaryllis. His heart beating rapidly in anticipation of seeing Evan for the first time in weeks, Tim stepped out of his car and walked to the flower shop door. He pushed, although a sign said PULL. Then he followed the instructions. Still the door did not budge.

Tim put his face against the glass. He cupped his hands around his eyes to eliminate a glare of light and peered through the smoked glass door. There was no sign of activity, but he could see a light emanating from a crack in the back room. Then a silhouette moved and disappeared. Presently, the shadow reappeared. Tim knew that it had to be Evan.

He knocked on the door. Again the shadow moved and disappeared. Tim stood in place. Then he saw Evan's face peer around the corner, toward the front door.

It took a moment, then recognition was displayed on Evan's face. He moved out of the back and into the main room of the shop, coming to the door. He smiled, quickly unlocking the door. "Hey," Evan said as Tim stepped into the shop.

"Hey yourself," Tim replied. "I was driving by and . . ."

Evan gave a soft laugh. "Every time the door chimes I hope it's you walking in."

"Then why haven't you called me?" Tim implored. "I've been Vikki Carr for weeks!"

Evan smiled. "I was kind of hoping that you'd call *me*. I was going to impress you with my newfound knowledge of pop culture. Or at least some trivia."

Tim gave Evan a quizzical look.

Evan stepped back and hung his head as if timid about where he was going with the conversation. Without looking directly at Tim he said, "Let's play twenty questions." He didn't wait for a reply. "What famous woman, other than Cher and Carol Burnett, dominated musical/variety television? Ding! Ding! Ding! That's right! Polly Pepper!"

Tim blinked.

"Okay, Round Two! What famous comedienne topped the Billboard pop charts in the 1970s with a string of hit records, including 'For New Kate'? Right again! Polly Pepper! Ding! Ding! Ding! Bonus round. Who is the only legendary television star with a gay son named Tim? I know this is a tough category. But try to guess."

Tim nodded. "Polly Pepper."

"Ding! Ding! Ding! You've just won our grand prize! You and a guest are going to . . . drum roll . . . *Pleasure Island*. That's right, where wicked boys are turned into donkeys!"

"I'm not wicked," Tim insisted. "Okay, I know I should have told you a very long time ago."

Evan said, "It's not a crime. I don't hold it against you. I was just a little disappointed. Okay, a lot disappointed. I just read the signals wrong. I kind of thought that you were considering me marriage material."

"I was! I do!" Tim stammered. "Please don't mock me!"

"I'm mocking the situation," Evan said. "I guess it's kind of funny that I was dating the son of somebody really famous and my expensive education at Yale didn't prevent me from being an idiot."

"You never told me that you went to an Ivy League school," Tim said.

"I'm a little embarrassed that my undergrad degree in ethics, politics and economics can't get me a decent job, okay?"

Tim straightened. "So, it's like me being self-conscious about being Polly Pepper's son. What's the difference?"

"You never asked me about my education, but I asked you about your family. And you lied to me."

"Evaded the issue, maybe. But I didn't really lie."

"Semantics."

"Whatever. Can we please put all of this behind us and get back to being lovers?"

Evan thought for a long moment. "I've really missed you, Tim."

Tim moved forward, standing close enough to feel the warmth of Evan's body and smell the fragrance of flowers on his clothes. "I've never loved anyone as much as I love you." Tim wrapped his arms around Evan. They kissed each other with all the passion that had been repressed from weeks of not being able to see and touch.

Chapter Nine

Tim was filled with euphoria as he drove back toward Bel Air. Although he was inching along in the congestion of street traffic, he couldn't help smiling. This time when the telephone rang, he wasn't startled. Tim blissfully inserted the earpiece of his headset and pushed the keypad. "And a pleasant howdy-do to you."

"Yo!" It was Paul Rosewood, using his tough-guy TV show character's one-word catchphrase. It meant *Dude, I'm in a bad mood.* The bark of his voice further prepared Tim for castigation. "Man, I'm so disappointed in you. Sean's an idiot, especially when it comes to money. *My* money. And I'm stupefied that you, of all people, would take advantage of a half-wit. I thought you were supposed to be his friend."

Tim came out of his Evan reverie. *Even a half-wit would know better than to marry you.*

Paul was saying, "Charging him—*me*—a freakin' mint for a Christmas party? Hell, I could put in a new pool for what this thing is costing."

"You've already got a pool." Tim tried to sound lighthearted. "Anyway, you are the family's cash cow."

"A cow?" Paul demanded. "I'm down to three-percent body fat! That's why I get plenty of mail from fans who'd like to milk my udder!"

Tim had always suspected that to be trapped in an elevator with the hunky star, and to try to make conversation between floors of a high-rise, would be his worst nightmare come true. After this swipe at his character, and his events planning qualifications, Tim gave up his pacifist disposition. "I'll save you something . . . money . . . *and* the effort of continuing to find new ways to insult me," he said to Paul. "You don't have to like or trust me. That's cool. But I'm a busy man and you're wasting the tick, tick, ticking on my watch. I can't afford to squander my time and creativity on someone who can't appreciate my services."

"You make it sound as though it's my fault," Paul said.

"It is your fault. I'm resigning. Expect your guests—all those hotshot network *programming* execs that Sean invited—to snore through your party. If the caterers don't pack up before the hors d'oeuvres get cold I'll be surprised. I won't even have to read about it. The news of your disaster will be all over town. Oh, and if Sean doesn't blow you for six months, remember that you personally initiated the chain of events."

Tim pushed the disconnect button on his cell phone and pulled the headset out of his ear. His smile immediately returned. Another feeling of power washed over him. He realized that in the space of a couple of hours he had determined to get his boyfriend back, and he made it happen. Then, for one of the rare times in his life, he didn't kowtow to bully clients—first Sean, then Sean's lover. He was pleased with himself. He thought about how much fun it would be telling Evan about the moronic actor who didn't know the first law of networking in Hollywood: give a boring party, expect to eat alone at the studio commissary.

Within seconds, "The Lone Ranger" issued again from the ring alert. Tim replaced his headset and answered.

"He didn't mean it! He didn't! I promise! Take me back! Please finish my party!" It was a sniveling Sean. "I can't face Leonardo, Toby, Giovanni, and Matt if you're not responsible for how it all turns out!"

Tim hadn't heard such bootlicking since Polly's former business manager was in court, being sentenced to three hundred hours of community service in Compton for pilfering tip money left on a table at Orso.

"I am *so* getting divorced!" Sean ranted. "I can do heaps better than that muscle-bound, bleach-blond, cheap-ass ex-hustler!" Sean must have covered the mouthpiece of his telephone, but Tim could still hear him screaming to Paul. "You heard me, Mister Never-Made-It-As-Feature-Film Star-Hack! I said hustler! Cheap, West Hollywood, hustler! Hustler! Hustler! Hustler!" Sean chanted.

Tim once again pushed the disconnect button. He would handle Sean and his party dilemma later. For now, he wanted to return to basking in the glow of being in love.

Thoughts of Evan's long, lean, cream-colored, naturally defined body, his crown of thick black hair, his dark eyes and sweet smile, made Tim's navel ache. "God, I can't wait to taste him again," Tim sighed aloud.

Then the phone rang out.

"Later, Sean!" Tim addressed the caller. But this time it was Jeb.

"Dad's fine with dinner Friday. And, as an early Christmas gift to you, I've got tickets for us to see Bette's concert at the Amphitheater tonight. It's sold out, but your mom and Bette are like this . . . from Bette being a guest on *Pepper Playhouse* that time, I guess. Polly got us house seats. Not bad, huh? I thought that afterwards we could maybe . . ."

Jeb's voice left a trail of seduction.

For an instant, Tim forgot about Evan. He immediately gushed an acceptance to Jeb's offer.

But then he just as quickly checked himself. "Oh, hell, I can't," Tim whined with sincere grief.

"Sean?" Jeb asked.

"No, Evan."

"I have a confession," Jeb continued. "Your mom bought the tickets from a broker. Bette's office never returned her calls. She paid three times the face value for these seats. She's pissed at Bette *and* the broker, but this is her way of trying to bring you out of what she called your 'post-partner depression.' "

Tim sighed. "You and I have to talk."

"Yeah," Jeb said. "Tonight? Dinner before the show?"

Tim didn't even try to protest. "Pick me up at seven."

He sat at a traffic light at the intersection of Sunset and Beverly Boulevards, and dragged his fingers through his hair. "The Lord giveth and the Lord taketh away! How the hell do I get into these messes?"

He picked up his phone and called Evan.

"Never complain. Never explain," Evan graciously said, when Tim began to offer his reason for changing their plans. "Isn't that what Joan Crawford had stitched in a satin pillow or something? I can wait until . . . well, whenever."

Disappointment rode with Tim the remaining twenty minutes to Pepper Plantation. Lying to Evan that they couldn't meet that night because of a forgotten previous engagement mortified Tim. He pounded the steering wheel, castigating himself for not being forthright, conceding that his mother had spent a small fortune on theater tickets. He felt obligated to accept the invitation to go with "a family friend," which was true enough. He argued with himself over why he didn't simply call Jeb and cancel their date.

As Tim approached the estate he shook his head sadly. "One minute I've got the balls to tell a client where he could shove his job and how deep. The next minute I'm a sniveling idiot, afraid of offending a friend and then not getting what I really want—and need." He was still wrestling with the contradictions when he arrived at the Pepper Plantation gates.

As arranged, his floral designer had adorned the tall iron bars with two enormous, flocked, fir Christmas wreaths. A silvery glittered banner ribbon across the first one announced *Naughty*. It's mate said *& Nice!* "Too traditional?" Tim screwed up his face in momentary doubt. "So next year I'll do *Give it up for Kwanzaa.*"

The electronic mechanism parted the gates and Tim drove up the long driveway to the front portico.

"Sweetie!" Polly called from the second floor landing as she spied Tim entering the foyer. "The Beverly Hills chapter of the ASPCA just called. They asked for you personally." Polly descended the staircase dressed in a silk chinoiserie pants suit, her ear lobes clipped with jade. "Some tiresome woman. Ranting about *bears* being illegal in Bel Air. I should hope so. We have enough beasts living here as neighbors."

Tim met his mother at the bottom step of the staircase. "We can't have just any sort of creature wandering the estates," Polly continued. "I told the woman, 'Forget the bears. Do something about Marilyn Beck.' Bears? Why on earth would she be calling *you* about bears?"

Tim wagged a finger at Polly. "Don't be nosy. You like surprises, don't you? Especially at your parties?"

Polly cringed. "You're not having some sort of fusty menagerie—besides Ozzy and his brood—are you?" She thought about it for no more than half a second, then smiled broadly. "You've got a party theme!" She just as quickly frowned. "Bears. Nothing to do with Wall Street, I hope? Too many of our friends have gone bust. Even bulls would be such an ugly reminder of portfolios gone by."

Tim dismissed the idea that he'd do anything that might insult the newly insolvent. "But I'll keep that idea in mind for your April 15th boogie night."

Polly flexed her limp cat's paws wrists up and down. "A theme! I knew it! My baby's back in the stirrups!" She clapped. "I'm so relieved! No more questions—or worries—about our big night, I promise! This calls for a mimosa!"

Tim looked at his wristwatch, then gave his mother a look of objection. He shook his head.

"Just a wee celebratory sip?" Polly maintained. "One should always thank the Gods when they send us wet kisses."

"Vishnu? Rama? Shiva?"

"Whomever. And you, my adorable son, are worth untold thanks to all of them. You should light a candle or throw some coins in a fountain. Especially now that your sex problems are over."

"I never had sex problems," Tim retorted.

"Placenta always says, 'Sex is like air. It's only a problem if you aren't getting any.' "

Tim was surprised by how quickly word got around that he and Evan were a couple again. "It's great, isn't it?" Tim smiled. "I'm on a different path this time. No more subterfuge."

Polly clapped again. "I'm very relieved. He's already practically part of the family. I know he's the right one."

"You didn't think so before," Tim reminded.

Polly kissed him on the cheek. "All I want is for my baby to be happy. You give a good party when you're happy. That makes me happy, too."

"By the by, Jeb and his father want to take us to dinner Friday night," Tim said. "A Christmas gift."

"Is Daddy cute?"

"We've never met. But Jeb certainly got his genes from someone. I'm willing to bet they're paternal."

Polly smiled. "Aren't we progressive. Mother and son double-dating!" She practically skipped away toward the kitchen.

Tim began to ascend the stairs. From the distance he heard his mother calling back, "By the by, I asked Placenta to put the black satin sheets on your bed!"

"What's wrong with the flannel?" Tim asked.

"For *after* the concert!" Polly called back. "But try not to shoot on the fabric. Stains, you know! Warn Jeb as well!"

Chapter Ten

Being Polly Pepper's son came with many more advantages than disadvantages. For one, Tim never had to wait in line at a restaurant or club. Gladstones at Universal City Walk was where Tim and Jeb chose to dine before the concert. They sidled past patrons who were standing in a queue of several dozen. Crossing the floor, which was covered in wood shavings, they were escorted by a bubbly high school girl to a secluded table. She didn't have a clue who these handsome men were, but the fact that her manager didn't make them cool their heels for forty-five minutes told her that she had VIPs in tow.

As soon as the waiter brought their drinks and withdrew from their table, Jeb raised his glass. "To friendship," he said.

Tim smiled weakly. "Am I that transparent?"

Jeb nodded. "I'm not as quick on the uptake as some. But I'd have to be as thick as Loni Anderson's lips not to realize that your Christmas Wish List doesn't include the Jeb action figure doll."

The two men stared into each other's eyes for a long moment. "He's taken my heart," Tim whispered. "Polly thinks it's you I'm about to marry."

Jeb smiled. "She's been very excited about us. It's infectious. She had me eager, too. She was so enthusiastic I started to imagine that maybe I was wrong. Perhaps she knew something that I didn't. Even though I knew that we'd never really get beyond the stage of sex." Jeb gave a weak chuckle. "Looks like we won't even get that far."

"Her one-track mind," Tim explained. "It's why she's so successful. Polly may not be the most talented star in the cosmos, but she's among the brightest. When she believes in something—especially herself—she makes everybody else believe it too. That's why she got a hit TV show and Lydia Shorofsky didn't."

"Who's Lydia . . . ?"

"Exactly. There are a million Lydia Shorofskys and Greta Gubers out there, but only one Polly Pepper. Self-delusion is a major factor in every showbiz success. Just look at all the divas you work with."

Jeb nodded in agreement. "You got Polly's genes," he said. "From what I've seen these past few weeks, if you find something—or someone—that you want, you stay focused. It obviously worked with Evan."

Tim smiled and raised his glass again. "Not only are you a brilliant musician, who looks stunning in a tank, you're a cool guy. I'm glad we're friends."

"Yeah. I'm running on cool a lot these days." Jeb spoke in a sardonic tone. "I've sort of lost my appetite. Let's just have the wine and some nibbles. Then on to our last 'date.' "

"We're still on for Friday?" Tim asked.

"Perhaps we'll become step-brothers," Jeb said.

The Universal Amphitheater—which hasn't been a real amphitheater for decades—was jammed with fans. Concession stands with barkers hawking colorful souvenir programs, T-shirts, CDs, and posters were set up outside each doorway entrance. They were taking in money, literally hand over fist. After waiting ten minutes in line at one of the kiosks, Tim returned to Jeb with the gift of a program and a bag full of CDs. They presented their tickets to an usher and were guided to the most enviable section of the venue. Their seats were only a few feet from the stage.

Tim and Jeb knew many of the other fans in their reserved area. Tim waved and said hello to Warren and Annette, Doris Roberts, David Hyde Pierce, Steve Martin, Tyne Daly, and many of his mother's other friends. Jeb meanwhile caught the attention of some of the stars he knew from being a rehearsal pianist—Alicia Keys, Megan Mullally, Mary J. Blige, Mary Hart. Surrounded by a swarm of people, Tim and Jeb were too busy bestowing air kisses to the over-privileged, that they didn't notice they had a rapt audience of one man quietly standing beside their seats.

Then Tim caught the sound of a familiar sounding voice imitating Bette. "So, Ernie says to Soph, 'Soph? Don't ya know, my doctor warned me about the sexual side effects of taking too many *stupid* pills . . . ' "

Tim turned to hear the punch line—and locked eyes with Evan's.

"Don't ya know, Soph? He already had me on *idiot* pills," Evan said, dropping the imitation.

Tim was stunned. "Please, Evan," he begged. "*I'm* the idiot. Let me explain. These are my mother's tickets."

"She's a little more butch than her picture on the web," Evan said, looking at Jeb, who was looking at Tim and Evan.

"She bought the tickets for me. 'Cause I'm a big fan."

"So am I." Evan held out a stub and an unused ticket. "If I'd known, I could have saved myself a small fortune."

Tim realized he wasn't making himself clear. "Jeb's just a friend. Of my mother's. I mean, he's my friend too, but that's all we are. Just friends."

"Lovely. For all of you." Evan looked at his wristwatch. "If you see Jenifer Lewis anywhere around here, tell her I'm a huge fan." With that, Evan slowly pivoted on his heel and walked away.

Tim's eyes followed Evan up the steps as he left the arena. "Oh, Christ! I blew it!" Tim cried.

The house lights began to dim. As the orchestra began its overture Jeb leaned over. "Wanna go?" he asked.

Tim shook his head. The curtain parted. The Harlettes appeared. And Bette came down from the ceiling perched on a swing.

Chapter Eleven

Jeb and his father, Harry, could watch Polly and Tim enter *Pane e
Vino*. En route to her reserved table, Polly stopped to receive com-
pliments on her Marc Jacobs dress. "Beaded silver!" Shirley Jones exclaimed, running her fingertips over the fabric, pretending to care.
Carol Channing and Mandy Patankin, flanking Shirley to the left and
right respectively, forced smiles.

Moving farther into the room: "Yellow skirt and matching scarf! It's
so *you*," Alana Hamilton babbled. She failed to introduce her sullen,
nondescript escort who occupied the other seat at her table.

Ten minutes later, validated that she could still make an entrance
and turn the right—if has-been—heads, Polly at last arrived at her
table.

As Tim and his mother approached, Jeb's father stood up from his
chair. "The famous Polly Pepper," he said. "Lovely to meet you. I'm an
ardent admirer."

"Pashaw!" Polly smiled good-naturedly. "Not so famous, really.
Legendary, perhaps." Polly laid a limp hand in Harry's strong one, siz-
ing him up. *Bet he's got a thick one*. She mentally tallied the sum of his
parts: eyes, nose, mustache, and full head of silver/gray hair. *Nice
shoulders*, she said to herself. *If they're anything like Jeb's* . . . "Heaven
to meet you," she bubbled.

Polly greeted her accompanist and leaned in for a kiss on the cheek. "Jeb, my precious."

As she accepted the chair that Tim held out for her, next to Harry's, she surreptitiously whispered into her son's ear, "Nice choice. The restaurant's acceptable, too."

Before the first bottle of Cristal had been imbibed, Polly was emphasizing the punch lines of her anecdotes with light taps to Harry's arm. ". . . That's when I told Rosie. I said, 'Dear, ix-nay the Little Suzies!' The crumbcakes, I mean." She laughed at her own story. "Have you seen her lately? She's obviously on the Hindenberg diet! I don't want to be at ground zero when she detonates!"

Polly switched gears. "Remember Timmy, when your Aunt Demi stayed in the guest house after one of her little tiffs with Uncle Brucey? We had to find a new poolboy and gardener while she was there." She faced Harry. "As if they'd never before seen a naked movie star swimming laps!"

Polly's jolly laugh encouraged the others. "Another time I'll tell you about my altercation on the set of *Pepper Playhouse* with Betty Buckley. Thank God she has talent, otherwise I know of at least a dozen actors and stage hands who would have raced to pull her mustache! 'Children Should Listen,' indeed! Oh, but you must think me such a terrible gossip."

"Not at all," said Harry.

"I'm really quite shy. Isn't that true Timmy?" Polly smiled and took another sip of champagne. "You know, we named our son after Lassie. Rather, we named him after that cutie who played Lassie's little boy. Timmy's down the well!" She flailed her hands. "Timmy's kidnapped by bandits! Timmy's grounded for life for sniffing airplane glue from a brown paper lunch sack! The kid was too good to be true. That's what I wanted for a son. And that's what I got." Polly tickled the bottom of Tim's chin. "He'll make an excellent mate."

She smiled warmly at Jeb, then turned and offered a conspiratorial wink to let Harry know that she knew he was someone who would appreciate her son's character. By the time the second bottle was placed upside down in the ice bucket, Polly had insisted that Harry be a guest at her Christmas party. "You're not afraid of bears, are you?" she asked.

Harry arched an eyebrow.

"Now that the boys are so cozy, we have to get to know each other better," said Polly.

Jeb looked at Tim. His body language said: *Have things changed?* With a small grimace and shake of his head, Tim conveyed, *She's crazy.*

"It's settled then," Polly announced triumphantly. "I'll send an invitation so you'll remember the date. Shall we squeeze you in . . . plus one?" she asked.

"I wouldn't think of imposing by bringing another guest," said Harry.

"Timmy, when's that date again?"

"Two weeks from tomorrow, Mom."

"Christ on crack!" Heads at nearby tables pivoted toward the sound of Polly's sudden outburst. She shrugged and apologized to her table. "Are we ready for the unwashed masses?" she asked.

The impact of realizing that her grandest annual social event was a mere fourteen days away sobered Polly for a moment. She smiled at Harry and retreated to her demure persona. "Why do I worry about trivial things? My Timmy comes through year in and year out. I think he does Christmas best of all. Gay Pride being a close second. Are you a PFLAG father?"

The moment Polly was buckled into the passenger seat of her Park Ward Rolls Royce, Tim pulled away from the valet. "I'm a little apprehensive," Polly said, staring out through the windshield.

"About?" Tim was making a right-hand turn toward Sweetzer Avenue.

"I had no idea that our event was a mere tick away."

Tim could tell that Polly was reeling from too much champagne, and too little *Carpaccio*, *Lombata Di Vitello Al Rosmarino*, and *Bacche Di Stagione*. "Perhaps you should be seeing less of Jeb, and devoting your undivided attention to Christmas." Polly yawned.

Driving along North Canon Drive, toward Sunset, Tim toyed with the CD player. "Things aren't always as they appear," he finally said. "Did I ever actually tell you that I was dating Jeb?"

"You didn't have to. It's obvious." Polly made her case. "The dinners together. The Bette concert. The sexy silk sheets."

Tim interrupted. "The silk sheets were your idea. Ask Placenta. She'll tell you they were never used."

"Did you get dumped *again*? Jeez, I'm beginning to think you're heading toward the 'Fifty Ways to Leave Your Lover,' benchmark."

Tim huffed. "It only seems like I'm homing in there. I confess, Jeb's adorable. But I haven't gotten over Evan."

"Evan!" Polly snorted. "Honey, I thought that thing was in the distant past. It's so unlike you to pine for someone who dumped you."

"He's not a *thing*." Tim turned right onto Bel Air Road. He made another right onto Copa De Oro, then drove straight to Belagio, which became Stone Canyon Road. Continuing in a quieter tone, Tim said, "Evan didn't dump me. Not exactly."

"He'd be a fool to, honey." Polly reached out and placed her hand on Tim's thigh. "Just a big misunderstanding, eh?"

"Sort of."

"Just don't blame me for not having enough time to keep a lover satisfied," Polly said. "I happen to know all about your sneaking around behind my back with Sean! So please don't pretend that Pepper Plantation takes up all your time."

Tim was mortified. "Sean? That son-of-a-bitch!"

"Retribution, he called it." Polly sniffed. "He said that Colin Cowie had agreed to finish where you left off."

"Colin Cowie!"

"For Christ sake, Timmy! What were you thinking, alienating a friend that way? You know how our nearest and dearest are in this town. They sharpen their shivs when your back is turned! How can my party possibly compete with a Colin Cowie affair? Honey, you're brilliant, but jeez, Colin! You don't have a TV show!"

As Tim pulled up to the estate's gates and pushed the remote control entry, he suddenly felt the entire weight of his personal and professional life beginning to suffocate him. He rolled the car onto the Pepper Plantation grounds, then sat for a long silent moment just inside the gates as he waited for them to close. Finally, he whispered, "Your party will be fine. I promise, Mother."

Polly made a face. "Fine? Yes, I have every confidence that it will be *fine*. But dearest, *fine* isn't exactly . . ." She stopped herself. "Let's get to the house. Mummy's head has a hatchet buried between her frontal and temporal lobes. Is this car spinning?"

Chapter Twelve

The morning sun seeped into Tim's room. Slowly he stirred to consciousness. Semi-awake, he lay on his stomach, clutching a body pillow and imagining that it was Evan he was holding. Eventually, thoughts of Sean's vindictiveness pushed through his reverie. One moment Tim was happily simulating sex with his pillow. The next he was plotting retribution against Sean for squealing to Polly about his extracurricular activities. *Bad caviar to make everyone sick.* He thought about various party disaster scenarios he could orchestrate. *Swans that get pissed off and attack the guests. Plumbing that backs up and dribbles down the staircase.*

A tap on the door was followed by Placenta's whisper. "Mister Tim? Are you awake?"

She opened the door before Tim could answer. Tim turned over and dragged the body pillow up parallel with his headboard. He pulled the top sheet up to cover the lower half of his body.

Placenta smiled at Tim's modesty as she entered his room. "Glad the good Lord gave you what you've got, and gave me the eyes to see."

Tim propped himself up with another pillow. "I was just having a very nice dream."

"No fooling." Placenta stole a glance at the tent pole under Tim's sheet. "Don't look so shocked. I washed your butt when you were a baby. And speaking of butts, are the folks in this house just going to sleep time away?"

"Sorry," Tim answered. He rolled to his side to hide his erection. "I didn't set my alarm. Did I miss breakfast?"

Placenta waved away his apology. "I just thought you should know that the workers are here to begin the installation."

It took Tim a moment to catch on. "Oh, God, the dance floor. The tent. The snowmaking machines on the roof. Polly's probably not in any condition to tolerate all the racket."

Placenta smiled again. "This is the weekend your helpers begin all the interior decorations, too. I already got a head start. I replaced the light bulbs in the foyer chandelier with red and green ones. Just like you asked. Where are those mirror balls going?"

"Up in the tree branches, outside. When they're hit with strobes it'll look like it's snowing." Tim sat upright. The bed sheet dropped to his waist.

Placenta said, "Your Evan is certainly missing a nice piece of work."

"Evan?"

"Oh, please!" Placenta pretended to be offended that she could be judged as ignorant. "Don't be coy with me, mister. You've been a wreck for months!"

"Am I that much of an open book?"

"You always have been, at least to me," Placenta said. "Your momma's head—bless her heart—may be as empty as a condemned theater, but that doesn't mean the rest of us who adore you don't catch on quick enough."

Tim fell back against his body pillow. "I've been a good boy all year," he whined. "Why can't Santa Claus give me the one thing on my to-beg-for list? I don't want a G.I. Joe or Sponge Bob doll. I want Evan."

"Lordy, we've got the same wish list. Only mine is named Mel Gibson. If you were to come to me for advice, I'd say go back to that flower store where your Evan works and pick him like he was a bouquet of posies."

Tim hugged his pillow tighter. "I tried. It backfired." Then he added, "Anyway, all this party stuff is taking up the bulk of my time now. Polly's right, I shouldn't be distracted. Not if I want my event to succeed. And if I'm going to ruin Sean's party."

"Tweedle Dee'll ruin his own affair without any help from you." Placenta turned to leave the room. "Concentrate on this bash, and you'll be fine."

Tim made a small laugh. "I'm afraid to ask you how much you know about every other aspect of my life."

"You know I'm a clam, Mister Tim," Polly said. "Half of my job is keeping your momma semi-sober. The other half is keeping her secrets from those wicked spy nurses over at Cedars."

"You're a good friend, Placenta," Tim said as she walked out of the room and closed the door behind her. "I'll be down in a flash!" he called.

After one last thought of having Evan's naked body pressed against his, Tim gave a deep sigh and pushed the sheet away with his legs. He got out of bed naked, then dropped down to the plush carpet to perform his routine of push-ups and stomach crunches. Then he hit the shower.

By the time Polly appeared at the garden breakfast table, the sun was melting the votive candles in the centerpiece. The celery stalk in her Bloody Mary was turning pink. Polly, wearing a scarf over her matted hair and Jackie O. shades, steadied herself with one hand on the back of her chair. She knocked back her drink with the other hand.

She looked around and scrutinized the activity. The laborers' noisy sawing and hammering was abrasive to Polly's nerves. A pickup truck was parked in the yard. Its bed was jammed with birch trees, the roots of which were encased in burlap. "Christ, what part of *poinsettia* doesn't Julio comprendo!" Polly complained aloud.

Placenta, who was serving a tray laden with a bowl of fruit cocktail, yogurt and buttered toast, answered, "The gardener is Jesus. He *comprendos* just fine. These are Mister Tim's people. They're putting a temporary addition on the house."

Polly clapped her hands together. "It's like the chaos of rehearsals, but without that son-of-a-bitch Jerry Robbins riding my ass." For a moment, she almost forgot her hangover. "I always adore behind-the-scenes activity. Is Timmy videotaping the before and after?"

Placenta picked up Polly's empty old-fashioned glass. She pivoted and headed for the house. "Knowing Tim, he's probably got *In Style* magazine covering the installation," she said. "You want a splash of tomato juice to go with the vodka?"

"Light on the Worcestshire, please," Polly said absently. She was paying little attention to her maid, admiring instead the pumped chest, thick arms and tight abs of a sweating worker who had removed his shirt. "Timmy certainly knows how to pick 'em," she said, followed by a deep sigh.

"It's all about presentation. Or so I tell my clients."

Polly was startled to hear her son's voice, absorbed with admiring the eye candy. She hadn't realized he'd joined her on the patio. "Some meaty menu," she acknowledged. "For starters, I'll take the one in the red bandana with the jeans that keep sliding down his hips. An inny, too! Pity to think that he'll have a gut in a few years. That is, if he's straight."

"It's 'Be Nice to Breeders Month,'" Tim cautioned playfully. "Remember, you married a couple of them."

"My foolish heart." She turned toward the house and bellowed, "Placenta! My breakfast drink!"

"Talk about performance art, eh?" Tim said, indicating the brawn on the lawn. "A hint of what's to follow at the party."

Polly perked up. "Hell, we have a ballroom in the basement." She scowled. "Why all the fuss with an addition? Just for fun, give me a hint about the set decoration theme."

Tim folded his arms across his chest and stared her down. "Ye of little faith," he mocked. "I think I'll just let you be surprised along with your guests."

"Oh, just a teensy hint, Timmy. It'll calm my nerves. It's your fault that they're shot in the first place. All the anxiety."

"Isn't that what the vodka is for?" he said as Placenta arrived with Polly's drink on a tray. "Think, *From Russia with Love*."

Polly frowned. "James Bond?" she said with distaste on her tongue. "I'm sure that Bushie has spies in Hollywood, but let's not aggrandize them!"

Placenta spoke out. "Better example: *Doctor Zhivago*."

Tim smiled.

"A mass exodus of staring Slavs? For a party? Are you nuts?" Polly was more concerned than ever.

Above the din from the workers pounding their hammers and calling orders back and forth from one another, Placenta offered, "Imperial Russia? All that Bolshevik and Romanov decadence? We'll have our very own ice palace, right here in Bel Air!" She stopped for a moment, then said to Tim, "Your mother and I hereby volunteer to pick out the flowers. Everything in white. Don't you think?"

Tim said, "As a matter of fact, it would be cool if you both could help out with just that little thing. Our affair will still be the talk of the country club, I guarantee it Mother."

"What about Sean and his Colin."

"The town will be talking about his soiree too. But Sean'll never be able to hold his head up among the movers and shakers he's so desperate to please."

Placenta sniggered. She gave Tim a knowing wink. "You just give me a list of the types of flowers you want, and we'll handle the rest," she said.

"Way ahead of you." Tim opened a leather folder and withdrew a printed page. As he handed the sheaf to Placenta, he said, "Pepper Plantation will become Tivoli Gardens!"

Polly snatched the paper from Placenta. After scanning the list, she handed it back to her maid. "It's the least we can do."

Tim looked at his wristwatch. "Have to dash. I have an appointment with the caterer. I'm thinking a caviar station. Imperial, Royal Blue, Beluga."

"Trying to bankrupt me?" Polly asked.

Placenta added, "Over at Lisa Marie's they had a grilled cheese station. Seems to be the gimmick of the moment."

"Already have that planned," Tim said. "I've ordered a ton of Brie, mozzarella, provolone, and gouda. And of course there's the vodka station."

Polly perked up. "Dear me. You've thought of everything."

"More than everything," Tim said proudly. "How does this sound—the bar will be made completely of ice. And there's a vodka luge. I'll fill you in more later but basically . . ." Tim gesticulated. "See, they pour vodka in these little tubes, which are built on ice blocks, and it spins through the ice. This not only chills the vodka, but when you put your mouth up against the base of it, the vodka shoots down! Very fun!"

Polly was ecstatic. "Run along and do your chores!" she said. "Placenta and I will handle the floral arrangements. Trust us."

Tim made a small bow. "Okay ladies. I'm off. Take care of my boys here with some ice water or lemonade every once in awhile. Keep 'em hydrated and sweaty. I'll be back for dinner."

As Tim walked out through the garden gate, he stopped to speak to some of the men. One by one they all gave him a slap on the butt. The activity wasn't lost on Polly. "Does Tim like straight men too?" she asked Placenta.

"Do you see a straight man on this entire property?" Placenta looked askance at Polly. "Now, take some Tylenol and get dressed. We've got errands."

Chapter Thirteen

Polly appeared on the front portico of Pepper Plantation wearing a cowl-neck, glimmering, metallic thread blouse with a leather taupe-colored skirt and matching handbag. She checked her makeup in a small compact mirror as she waited for Placenta to drive the Rolls from the garage. The car arrived, and Polly slipped into the front passenger seat.

Placenta seemed impressed with how well Polly had put herself back together. She said, "What's that smell?"

"Tabu. Only $2.50 at Marshall's." Polly gave a triumphant nod.

The car moved down the Pepper Plantation driveway and stopped at the end, waiting for the gates to part. Although Placenta had driven the car for years, Polly gave her oft-repeated instructions on how to manage the vehicle. It wasn't until the car was moving along Melrose Avenue that Polly looked around and asked where they were going.

"Tahiti. Where do you think?" Placenta asked testily. "Flowers from a place Tim likes. A lot."

Polly was placated, until Placenta pulled into the parking lot of Sherwood Florist and turned off the ignition. "What's so special about this place?" Polly asked, while again checking her face in the vanity mirror of the window visor and patting her hair.

Placenta turned to Polly. "Okay, listen up. This is the place where Tim's Evan works."

Polly's jaw dropped. "Are you out of your mind?"

Placenta was resolute. "We're going to give him the Christmas present he wants and deserves."

Polly was flustered. She agreed that Tim deserved to have a boyfriend, and she wanted him to have a great Christmas present. But she also knew that Tim had been in love so many times, there had to be a good reason why none of his relationships worked out. Including the one with Evan.

Placenta said, "We'll just go in and check the boy out. Nothing ventured, and all."

"He'll think we're spying for Tim," Polly said.

Placenta sighed. "Tim said he wasn't going to tell this guy about you until after the holidays. Selective memory?"

"I'm highly recognizable. He'd have to have been living in a cave not to know Polly Pepper, for Christ sake!"

Placenta opened her door. Polly gave in and pulled on her handle. She stepped out of the car, unable to resist reminding Placenta not to forget to activate the alarm.

The women walked to the entrance. Inside the shop, Polly and Placenta were met with cool air and the heavy fragrance of flowers. Classical music wafted from speakers mounted on the wall behind the cash register counter. The store appeared to be empty.

They waited for a moment, then Polly sang out a greeting. "Yoo-hoo?"

She repeated her call a second time. This summoned a young man who came out from a back room.

"Sorry," Evan said, "I was on the telephone. I didn't hear the doorbell. Hope I didn't keep you ladies waiting too long."

"I'm not accustomed to cooling my heels," Polly said in a crisp tone.

"You were highly recommended," Placenta said to Evan to help thaw the nippy atmosphere created by Polly's temperament.

Evan nodded. "Word of mouth is the best advertising. My name is Evan."

"Big party," Polly said, coming to the point of their presence. "Can you handle this?" She removed Tim's list of flowers from her purse and handed it to Evan.

"We do a lot of events, I'm sure we can help make . . ." Evan's voice trailed off as he studied the list. He made a quizzical face. "Orchids, hydrangea, Casablanca lilies, evening primrose, lady tresses, tulips." He harrumphed. Then he said, "Not sure about the Alpine Phlox. Everything's white. Part of a theme or something?"

"*From Russia with Love*," Polly said.

Evan smiled. "A lot of Russians have moved to this part of town." He scanned the page again. "This is quite an order, but I'm sure we can handle it. Let's sit down and talk about the particulars."

He motioned toward a round, redwood patio table and pulled out two chairs for the ladies. He offered tea. Both women accepted. "I'll pour," he said and excused himself.

When Evan disappeared into the back room, Polly and Placenta bent their heads together. "Cute!" Polly exclaimed in a whisper. "And so polite."

"Knowledgeable, too," Placenta added.

"Tim's got a good eye, I'll give him that much!" Polly was about to comment on Evan's dimples, when Placenta nudged her into silence.

"Here we go," Evan said, placing two mugs on the table. "Cream? Sugar?"

"This is so lovely," Polly said.

Evan placed a clipboard with an order blank attached to it onto the table in front of him. He took the cap off of a ballpoint pen. "Let's get a few details. May I have your name, please?"

"I need delivery on December 21st," Polly answered. "Early afternoon. And you can't be a moment late."

"We're highly professional." Evan smiled. "Name?"

"Stone Canyon Road. Number 92750."

"Got it," Evan said as he wrote the address. "And your name?"

"The telephone number is area three-one-oh, five, five, five, two, seven, three, five."

"I can take a charge card, if you prefer."

Polly removed her American Express card from her purse. She handed it to Evan and in just that instant she cringed realizing that she had unintentionally given away her identity.

"This is only the second black AmEx I've ever seen," Evan said, impressed by the novelty of such a highly regarded credit status. "*Pepper*," he read the name on the card to himself. "Polly Pepper," he said and suddenly turned bright red. *Shit, Tim's mother! What's she doing here?*

Evan thought, spiraling into crisis mode. He tried to recover and hide his anxiety by focusing on the business at hand. "Sorry if this sounds indelicate," Evan said, "but we should discuss the budget."

"Never mind that," Polly said blithely as she stood up to leave. "My son, *Tim*, will be in touch. You do know Tim, don't you?" Polly asked. "Intimately?"

Evan said, "It's been a while."

"Young man, you should brush up on your pop culture. Or are you pretending not to know who I am?" Polly looked down her powdered nose.

"Your name's come up a lot lately. I apologize for not having seen your movies."

"Mostly television," Polly corrected. "Classic musical variety. You've heard of Cher?"

"Of course." Evan smiled.

"She had Chastity. I had Timmy. Otherwise we're practically the same diva."

"We've taken up enough of Evan's time," Placenta said to Polly.

"We'll gather our posies elsewhere, thank you." Polly turned to leave, but she stopped midway to the door.

"How is Tim?" Evan asked.

Polly turned around. "Busy."

Evan nodded. "Christmas can get pretty nuts." He was silent for a moment. "Look," he finally said, "even though Tim is obviously too swamped to see me, I'd still like to handle your floral business. My boss'll kill me if he finds out I blew a big order like this. Also . . ." He stopped himself.

"Give *you* my business?" Polly snapped. "Do I look like the FTD sprite?" Polly was hands-on-hips incredulous. "Every boss is a dinkwad. Get used to it. Timmy's happiness is my priority."

Placenta looked at Polly, then turned to Evan. "Finish your thought. You said 'Also . . . ' You want to see Tim, don't you?"

"It's no secret. I'm in love with him." Evan turned a deeper shade of red as he looked at Polly.

Polly pursed her lips. She straightened her back. "Get over it." Then with a smile she added, "Your embarrassment, I mean. Timmy's my pride and joy. If you make him happy, then you make me happy. Besides, you aren't entirely unattractive."

Placenta sidled up beside Polly, then said sternly to Evan, "What are we going to do about you and Tim? You're both working your cute tails off. He's got an annoying client . . . her," she cocked her head toward Polly. "Where is there time for any social life?"

Evan sighed. "Tell me about it. I've got a freak client too. Not that *you're* a freak or anything." He looked at Polly and backtracked. "It's that TV actor, Paul Rosewood, and his insane boyfriend, Sean something. They're never satisfied. They constantly change their order. As a matter of fact, they're no longer my clients. That Paul guy fired me just before you walked in. Which is really fine by me."

Placenta laughed. "You had Sean? My heart goes out. That was supposed to be Tim's party to create. They didn't appreciate him either. Now Tim and Sean aren't speaking."

Evan emitted a little laugh. "So Sean told me. Their new event guy, someone big in society, decided they weren't worth his time and effort. Now they're on their own and sweating like they're going to the guillotine."

Polly showed a wide smile. "And they *should* be terrified. I own my own rumor mill. It churns and spews and incites, and the whole town adores it. My news gets embellished out of all proportion before it leaks out and practically becomes instant urban legend."

"Isn't she poetic," Placenta deadpanned.

Polly continued, "After all that Timmy put in to prepping Sean's party, the b/f, Paul, fired him." Her eyes took on a faraway cast. "I was just thinking," she said.

Placenta said, "What are you hatching in your tiny brain? Sick doves released over the crowd at Sean's party? A plumbing sabotage? A bottle of Xenadrin in the coffee pot?"

"There's only one conclusion," Polly continued.

Evan's eyes went from Polly to Placenta and back to Polly. "It will solve *everyone's* problems." Polly snapped her fingers and pointed to the clipboard. Then she signed her name at the bottom of the order form.

Chapter Fourteen

When Polly arrived home, she found the foyer of Pepper Plantation filled with bare-chested calendar-model-perfect men. Taken aback by her sudden immersion in a sea of half-naked muscled torsos, Polly feigned a swoon.

"There really is a Santa Claus," Polly cooed as she wended her way, as slowly as possible, through the crowd. She imagined herself as Dietrich, reviewing her troops in an old black-and-white film. She absently but seductively patted her coif as her eyes connected with a particularly magnetic brawny brunette who had a deep cleft between his pecs and pierced right nipple. She felt a flutter in her stomach when she spied his red and green dragon wrapping its scaly body around the man's forearm and breathing fire on to his veined biceps.

"Mother."

Tim's voice broke Polly's reverie. "Impeccable timing. You can help me choose the wait staff."

"Is it of any relevance whether or not they've read Emily Post?" she quipped.

"Will Miss Manners do?" said a young peaches 'n' cream blonde with shoulder-length hair.

"You're hired, sweetheart," Polly shot back, admiring his tight abs and small waist.

"He was already on my list," Tim said *sotto voce* as Polly arrived at his side. "Where's Placenta? This'll give her a kick."

"If I'd known that we were entertaining. I would have dressed . . . more appropriately." She grinned at the sea of anatomy.

"You're not here to sleep with them," Tim reminded. "Did you take care of the flowers?"

"They are positively in full bloom. The men, I mean. The buds'll be here next Saturday. Just as you requested."

"I know you like them fresh. The flowers, I mean," Tim parried. "Trust me, these guys are only interested in each other—and that picture of you and John Davidson in the hallway."

"You have a talent for ruining a moment," Polly pouted. "I'll find Placenta. Don't hire anyone else until we've returned."

By seven P.M. Polly and Tim were seated in the music room. Placenta served champagne. "Something to take the edge off, after our oh-so-arduous task," Placenta said.

"I felt slightly bad letting even one of those precious men go home without a job," Polly said after her first sip of Cristal.

"I hired all of them," Tim explained. "The ones who didn't make the cut for working inside will be driving the sleighs or running valet. We need all the boys we can get."

"That's my mantra, too," Polly said.

The liquid voice of Nat King Cole poured out through hidden speakers, singing, "Chestnuts roasting on an open fire." Placenta cleared her throat. She looked at Polly with a steely arch of an eyebrow. "Get on with it."

"*You* get on with it!" Polly huffed at her maid. "It was *your* idea!"

Tim cocked his head. "What?" he asked.

"I need a glass of champagne myself," Placenta said as she stood up and walked to the bar.

Tim sat forward on the sofa facing his mother. He placed his glass on the marble-top coffee table. Placenta returned. She poured bubbly into her flute and positioned herself next to Polly. She looked straight at Tim. "Honey," she said, "who loves you more than me and your momma?"

Tim shook his head. "No one. I guess."

"Then you can't be angry with people whose hearts are in the right place, despite their actions. Right?"

"Sure I can," Tim said. "Try me."

"Oh, shit." Polly sat forward and placed her flute on the table. "Did you like any of those men today, honey?" she asked. "I mean . . . would you sleep with any of them?"

"That's a waste of two of your twenty questions," Placenta scolded Polly. "He's young. He's horny. They were young and horny. What adds up? And this is not even the subject."

Tim blushed. "Probably. Most of them. Yeah, for sure. In a heartbeat. Why? Did one of them ask about me?" He smiled, hopefully.

Placenta drained her glass and reached for the bottle for a refill. She took a long pull. She genuflected then gave a quick glance heavenward. "Ignore your dumb momma," she said as she poured another round for Polly. "You know Forrest Gump scripts all of her lines."

Polly asked Tim, "Could any of those boys have replaced your friend Evan?"

"Evan?" Tim shook his head. "No one could replace Evan. But he doesn't want me. He's probably moved on anyway. Just as I should do." Tim was quiet for a moment. "Except that I can't." After a long swallow of champagne, he asked, "What's your point?"

Placenta was matter-of-fact. "Do you, or do you not love Evan?"

"I vote, yes," Polly said.

Tim tapped his index finger to the tip of his nose.

Placenta plowed ahead. "What's more important? Friends or gym talent? The thing is, your friend Sean has a major problem."

"Just being Sean is a calamity unto itself," Tim agreed.

"Get this: He hired your Evan . . ."

"He's not *my* Evan."

". . . to do the flowers for his party. Then he fired him."

Tim snorted. "He'll never find a better floral arranger in all of Los Angeles."

"Get to the point, old maid," Polly nudged Placenta. "Tell him that Sean begged us to ask Tim to come back and help him out."

Tim looked perplexed.

"Sean's been dumped by Colin," Placenta continued.

"Serves him right, after the way he treated my baby," Polly added. "Placenta all but offered you to help clean up his mess."

Tim grimaced, thinking. "And what does this have to do with how I felt about the studs gracing our little abode this afternoon?"

Polly said, "If you fancied one of those boys, I wouldn't expect you to still want Evan. Which might change my mind to go along with Placenta's idea of farming you out to help Sean."

"Sean was a real jerk to me," Tim said. "And if he fired Evan, he's an even bigger idiot than I suspected. But Placenta's right. If he needs help, someone should see what can be done."

"Let him drown on his own," Polly suggested. "He'll be destroyed when his bash is the shower room talk at Crunch, or he winds up as a monologue joke on *Leno*. He won't appreciate you until the post-party word on the street rivals the reviews for *Freddy Got Fingered*."

"How mean can you get?" Tim asked.

"Pretty mean," Polly stated honestly. "Now, if I were you, I'd put away any idea of racing over to Sean's to bail him out."

"I never had such an idea," Tim said.

Polly continued, "Instead, perhaps you should run to the fridge for another bottle, then drive over to Evan's and cheer him up. Being fired is no fun." She thought for a moment. "I fired Vicki Lawrence once. That actually *was* fun. Surely you can take the night off from your events planning. It's Saturday. Date night, for Christ sake!"

Tim shook his head. "I'm just an old thorny rose to Evan. Maybe I should call up Jeb? He's the man you think I should marry."

Polly flipped away his remark. "Changed my mind. He's sexy and talented, but he doesn't have *it*."

Tim said, "As for Evan, I still sometimes think about kidnapping him and running off to England. But I'd be busted at airport security for carrying a mind-altering drug." He paused. "I'm going to ring up Sean and Paul and offer the grand gesture," he announced. "Catch you before I go to bed."

"That's my unselfish Tim." Placenta smiled.

"Timmy always knows best," Polly stated.

*　*　*

The moment Tim left the room, Polly and Placenta both broke into wide smiles. They began playfully pinching one another. "I told you so!" Polly giggled as she tickled Placenta's belly.

"I told *you* so!" Placenta laughed. "He got scooped right into our trap. Now I think I finally understand what that critic from the *Times* meant when he wrote, 'Polly Pepper skillfully deceives an audience into thinking that she's capable of a multi-dimensional performance.' You were awesome, the way you played dumb."

"It comes natural to me," Polly said, wrapping her arm around Placenta's shoulder. "Now we're certain where Tim and Evan stand with each other. We'll have 'em back together in no time."

Placenta prepared a late meal of lentil soup and brie on crackers for Polly. The scent of food cooking wafted to the second floor and aroused Tim. He wandered down the stairs and into the kitchen, where he found his mother and Placenta sitting at the granite-top bar counter. They were noisily slurping their soup. They looked up when he came into the room.

"And?" Polly asked, not needing to preface the question.

"Got an earful from Paul," he said. "My services are so *not* required. His mother is flying in from Nebraska to help."

Polly smiled. "Those sturdy farm women can be so handy at Hollywood parties."

"Less work for me. And at least I tried to be a friend." Tim looked at his mother. "Think their party really will be a joke on *Leno?*"

"Jay and I go way back," she said. A perverse smile formed on her lips. "I can practically guarantee it."

Chapter Fifteen

Although the night sky over Southern California was clear and revealed a crescent moon and unusually bright stars, snow was
falling on Pepper Plantation. The air temperature was sixty-five degrees, but the mansion in Bel Air appeared to have been transported to
winter in Siberia.

Along the shoulders of the serpentine street that meandered past
Polly Pepper's home, several hundred cars were parked in tandem.
Behind a cortege of Mercedes, BMWs, Hummvies, Lexus and Rolls
Royces, Sean and Paul waited in their red, two-door Carrera to arrive at
a platoon of valets dressed—with a few liberties taken—in the costume of guards from Imperial Russia. The retinue wore white vests finished with braided gold piping over their otherwise bare, muscled
chests. The valets were further accessorized with faux mink fez hats
and gold sabers sheathed in bejeweled scabbards.

Sean and Paul, still recovering from the ego-bruising fiasco of their
own Christmas party the night before, had accepted Tim's invitation
to his mother's blow-out. Primarily, they needed to get out of the
house to be able to use a toilet that wasn't broken from negligent party
guests. But they also were intrigued to determine what they had done
wrong.

"Christ!" Sean exclaimed. "Those smelly valets we hired wore those stupid Acme Parking restaurant vests! Look what these guys are wearing!"

"*Half* wearing," Paul corrected. His jaw had dropped in amazement, envy and lust.

The driver and passenger side doors of their car were simultaneously opened by attendant foot-servants. The moment that Sean and Paul stepped out of their vehicle, they felt conspicuous. They couldn't help noticing that the other arriving guests were dressed as if they were attending the opening of the opera season at La Scala.

"The Empress will be disheartened," said one of the valets in a thick, phony Russian accent. He looked Sean up and down. "Black tie for men, no blue jean. Say so on invitation. Sure you at right party?"

"Actor?" Paul snapped a wad of gum. "Your accent sucks."

Sean and his lover had not bothered to read the invitation, which had been delivered via messenger to their home that morning. Thus, they dressed as one ordinarily dresses for most events in Los Angeles: grunge, mixed with Rolex and Cartier. Flipping their invitation at the snooty guard, they were escorted by another member of the Imperial regiment through the gates at the entrance to the estate. Awaiting them was an elaborately decorated gold swan sleigh, hitched to a pair of midnight-black, satin-coated stallions. Another hunky guard assisted the men as they climbed into the plush burgundy velour seats of the sleigh. Their laps were then draped with a faux mink throw. Then they were off, following closely behind an identical chariot.

The sleigh, riding up the drive on casters over wet pavement, passed under the boughs of flocked evergreens. Snow, blowing out from a dozen camouflaged machines that dotted the lawn, drifted down and covered their hair and shoulders.

The house was dazzling, with multicolored lights radiating through the innumerable windows. The music from an orchestra was audible. They found out later that Jeb had convinced Polly Pepper fanatic Keith Lockhart, conductor of the Boston Pops orchestra, to fly in for the weekend and assume the baton. He was leading his musicians to an all-Russian evening. Sean thought he identified the music as "Swan Lake."

When the sleigh arrived at the front portico, a contingent of guards, dressed as Cossacks, stood at military attention on the steps leading to the house. As the two men were assisted out of the sleigh, they looked at the banners and elaborately decorated wreaths on the façade of the mansion. Wide-eyed, they marveled at the decadence and attention to detail.

As they began to ascend the red-carpeted steps, the soldiers, in unison, withdrew their swords and created a canopy of curved blades for them to walk beneath. Sean whined. "You and your tight-ass wallet! We had to hire that cheap security team. I'll bet these guys wouldn't feel up Ethel Kennedy, for Christ sake!"

"Ethel Kennedy came to your party?"

The voice was Tim's. He was standing at the doorway, greeting each guest. Dressed in a dark green uniform with gold epaulets and ribboned medals, he suggested noble lineage.

"The bouncer who was checking invitations wouldn't know Ethel Kennedy from ethanol," Sean complained. "Thought the old bag was too on in years to be anybody vaguely important. The idiot asked her for three forms of picture ID." Sean stopped himself and put on a smiley face. "She missed an altogether unforgettable night!" he boasted as if he'd just jumped Oscar de la Hoya's bones. Sean gave a small push against Paul's thick arm. "It was all your fault."

"I'm an important star. We had to have security, fool."

"That Neanderthal who works the door at Matrix Baths? Condom police, maybe. But security? You're the fool, fool."

Tim intervened. "You can forget all about the horrors of the past for a few hours." He smiled. "Tonight you're far away from Hollywood. Think Ural Mountains. You're guests at the Winter Palace of the Czar Nicholas and Empress Alexandra. And we will not let in that Bolshevik, Cindy Adams. Who, I hear, is not so secretly reveling in your misery."

Tim bowed, clicked his heels, and motioned for the two men to enter a lavish recreation of an early twentieth-century Russian royal residence at Christmastime. As the three continued into the foyer, they walked a receiving line. Ahead of Tim was Placenta, followed by Jim Belushi on a taut leash, then life-like wax figures of Omar Sharif, Julie Christie and Rod Steiger, dressed in tattered costumes from *Doctor Zhivago*—borrowed, like Fergie, from Debbie Reynolds.

*   *   *

When they were finally a safe distance into the house, Paul said, "A little inappropriate for the maid to be in the receiving line, don't you think?"

"Better the smiling maid, than your fat, blubber lips mother!" Sean retorted.

They moved along under a chandelier whose tapered bulbs had been changed to red and green. "Polly's probably having an affair with her. That's the rumor," Paul sniggered.

Tim came up behind Sean and Paul. "I think that Placenta can handle the stragglers. I'll take you to where the fun people are hanging."

He walked them through the cavernous living room, which was dominated by an ornately decorated Christmas tree. The sound of applause filtered through the house. "Must be the bears."

"Bears?" Sean asked.

"Yup," Tim exclaimed as they arrived in what had only recently been the enormous patio gardens and which was now an elegant throne room. "Look, Ma, no muzzle! Grrr!"

At the far end of the patio, in front of the orchestra, surrounded by tables draped in heavy brocade fabrics, was an oval ice rink. The surface was painted with a pattern of Russian lace. At the center of everybody's rapt attention was the Russian circus. Tim pointed to a man in a tight thong, which revealed his powerful upper body. "Vladimir Putin's sexy brother. And those are Dimitri and Svetlana." Two bears in tu-tus were performing an ice ballet. The audience was enraptured.

Tim turned to his mortified friends. "Run along and enjoy all the food and entertainment. Dance and mingle with the overprivileged. You're bound to know dozens of people." He pointed. "Check out the guy with Lauren Ambrose. I'm sort of eager to talk to Edward Norton, myself. And if you accidentally on purpose walk into the Anastasia Powder Room, you might catch Reese and Ryan changing the baby's diapers."

Sean reached out for a glass of champagne on a tray being passed among the crowd. Snidely, he said to Tim, "Unlike we common folk, you obviously spared no expense. The jewel-colored glasses. The orchestra. The Russian soldiers. Bears on ice who fox trot like a freakin' Torvil and Dean, for God's sake. I even noticed gold leaf artichokes in the table centerpieces."

"This was probably not much more expensive than your party," Tim assessed. "I always pass on my professional discounts to my clients."

Sean's depression loomed larger. His gaze drifted past Tim to take in the opulence. "Even used What's-His-Name's overpriced floral arrangements," Sean acknowledged.

"Aren't they stunning?" Tim agreed. "Everbody's commented. What *is* his name?" Tim shrugged. "Some delicious new floral designer Polly and Placenta discovered on their own. After tonight, the guy is going to be the busiest florist in Beverly Hills, if he isn't already." Tim indicated a sumptuous, tall arrangement of Casablanca lilies on a bed of white roses. "But I'm sure your decorations were as glorious as these. I heard that you hired the best. That cutie Evan, from over at Sherwood?"

From behind Tim, a familiar male voice spoke out. "And who are *you* calling cutie? Cutie."

Tim turned around.

"Am I Trotsky enough for you?" Evan opened his arms to display his costume. "Your mom had a pal in wardrobe at Television City put it together for me."

"You look amazing!" Tim said. "My mom? She . . . I mean, does she know . . ." His confusion was obvious.

Evan bowed graciously. "She hired me to do the flowers. I'm just checking up to make sure you're satisfied."

Paul caught Evan's eye with a look that he reserved for low-life criminals on his TV show. "Glad my mother doesn't have to buy my boyfriends for me," he said.

Evan took in his former clients. "And I'm *so* sorry about Liz Taylor's hip. Jeez. What a tough break. For you guys, I mean. But heck, she's probably used to dislocations. I wouldn't worry too much. Electrical things always go wrong at nighttime parties. I'm sure the next time you want to backlight an ice sculpture and need a cord to the outlet, you'll run it *under* the carpet. Ambulance lights can certainly be festive!"

Sean burst into tears and ran away. Paul ran after him.

Tim stifled a snigger at the retelling of what had made headline news in the Saturday morning edition of the *Los Angeles Times*. Liz was reported as doing exceptionally well—which was more than could be said for the television actor named on every news station and on *ET*.

Tim said to Evan, "So, what's the real deal? Polly hired you to do these amazing flowers? I should have guessed. They're beautiful. Like you."

Even blushed. "Your mother has amazing decorating instincts," he said. "She's been in my shop every day for the past week, making suggestions . . ."

"Suggestions?" Tim interrupted with a laugh. "You mean demands."

Evan smiled. "Her only demand was that I come to the party. She said there would be a huge surprise. I guess I'm it. And I hope it's true what she said, that you were planning to call me as soon as this is history."

"She actually listened to something I said?" To Tim, it was an unthinkable idea. "Fortunately, this is my only job of the season."

Suddenly, the entire assembly broke out into thunderous applause. Tim and Evan, along with every other guest, turned to watch as Polly, on the arm of Jeb's father, made her entrance to an orchestral arrangement of the theme to her old musical variety show. Passing through the crowd, stopping along the way to chat with friends, Polly played up her role as a monarch. Then she spied Evan. "Darling!" she wailed as she made her way through the crowd of friends. "The petals are yummy! You are a divine genius! Just like my Timmy!"

She transitioned to her son. "Honey," she called over the din of a joyful crowd, "you've outdone yourself, as usual! Barbecuing the Pillsbury Dough Boy last summer doesn't even come close! And isn't it just perfect that both Evan and Henry could join us?" She leaned into Tim's ear and cupped a hand around the side of her mouth. "He's adorable!" she whispered.

Tim whispered back, "I'm glad you finally approve of one of my boyfriends!"

"I was talking about Harry!" Polly replied. "But Evan's scrumptious too."

She returned her attention to the swirl of activity around her. "Jeb's a busy bee getting the singers ready for their set," she said, loudly enough for the guests in her immediate area to hear. "He says they're a little nervous because Barbra's here."

Evan was suddenly attentive. "Barbra?" he stammered with excitement.

Photographers from *Beverly Hills 213* snapped candid pictures of old celebrities and the town's young Turks. Jeb spoke, acknowledging the legend and talents of their hostess and host, saying flattering things about the wait staff and Evan's flower arrangements. "Now, enough of this Shostikovitch shit," he said, looking at Keith Lockhart. The maestro smiled and nodded his agreement. "Let's all boogie to a dance remix of *For New Kate!*" Jeb demanded.

As a recording of the song blared through the house audio system, Jeb jumped down from the bandstand and worked his way toward Tim and Evan. Coming up on the pair, he said, "A little toast to you guys." Jeb gently picked up glasses of bubbly from the champagne pyramid. "Hey," he said, looking at Evan. "That night at Bette's? I swear that Tim and I were just there because Polly gave me tickets."

Evan nodded in understanding. "Polly's generous about giving away tickets."

Tim felt a tightening in his throat.

"So, going away for the holidays?" Jeb asked.

Evan nodded. "Polly's Christmas present."

"Family? Or someplace exotic and crawling with wild and untamed men?" Jeb asked.

"Pretty exotic. At least to me. And just *one* man."

"How about you?" Evan asked Tim.

"Anyone I know?" asked Jeb.

Tim was puzzled. "Me?"

"I meant, are you all packed? Man, you have had too much bubbly." Evan laughed.

Tim looked askance at Evan.

At that moment, with a loud drumroll, Polly walked up a couple of steps to the bandstand. She gave a peck to Keith Lockhart's cheek. Then she picked the microphone up off of the bench of the grand piano.

A pink spotlight illuminated her glittering Vera Wang as she shaded her eyes from the light. "So, there were these three wise men and a

baby," Polly began. "Oh, God, I can't go there! Can you stand me? I'm
such a Pagan. I haven't a clue what the true meaning of Christmas is.
But I do worship. Thank you, Jesus, for that blessed monk, Dom
Perignon!" Polly grinned at the throng who sent a tidal wave of laughter at her.

"Jesus was right when he said 'Give a man a fish, and he'll eat for a
day. Teach a man to fish, and he'll discover caviar!' "

As she was waiting for the laughter to die down, Polly raised a gold
goblet to the crowd and then took a long sip. She waited another moment, until silence once again filled the huge room. "It's goddamned
Christmas again!" she exclaimed. "Didn't we just do this like twelve
months ago? Christ, how time flies when you're outta work!" Again peals
of laughter from her audience. "But speaking of work, I want to sincerely thank the man responsible for this altogether groovy evening.
The handsome. The talented."

She paused for a beat. "Before this little speech turns into a monologue from my act, I've gotta let you all in on a little secret. It's about
the key to my success. It's that unheralded man who takes a kernel of
an idea for a party and turns it into a freakin' Imperial Russian palace,
and me into a dead empress." Polly paused again. "It's obviously a
poorly kept secret, considering that some of you have been cheating
with my man. But I can't blame you. He's so gifted."

Tim was smiling at his mother's speech, knowing that the spotlight
would soon fall on him. He would take a quick appreciative bow, throw
Polly a kiss and then throw another kiss at the crowd. It was routine.

Polly continued, "I also want you to know, for all of your Actors and
Others for Animals fanatics, and PETA freaks out there, that no animals were harmed in the making of this shindig. The bears put their
paws into those freakin' tight skates and did those funny tricks because they really like to do it. A lot. Yeah. Ah huh. Really. Sure."

Polly knew when to quit while she was ahead. "Hell, I want to party,
so I'm throwing this microphone back to Jeb and Keith. But before I
do, I want to say Merry Christmas, Happy Chanukah, be at peace for
Kwanza, do a nice fast for Ramadan, or have a cup of wine for Our
Lady of Guadeloupe. However you celebrate the end of a sucky year,
do so with as much joy as you can muster.

"And speaking of joy," she continued, "please help me thank my brilliant event planner. I'm the luckiest legend in the universe to have such a divine man in my life. My very own pride and joy. My son, Tim!"

Applause exploded. Tim graciously accepted the commendation from his mother. Polly blew a kiss to him. "Just one more thing," she said, "because I've gotta go to the bathroom. I want to give my precious Timmy his Christmas bonus right now. Timmy," she said, gesturing for him to join her. "And bring your adorable b/f, Evan. That's *boyfriend*," she stage-whispered to the crowd.

Tim and Evan hustled to the bandstand. They took the steps to the platform, momentarily taken aback by the bright lights that blinded them to the audience. Placenta followed them up the steps holding a silver tray on which a manila envelope was placed.

Tim looked at Polly. "Your Last Will and Testament?" he joked, as his mother picked up the envelope.

"As a gesture of my love and appreciation, this is for you." She handed the mailer to Tim.

"Open it now?" he asked.

"Immediately, please. Otherwise you're liable to miss your flight."

Tim looked at his mother again, then opened the envelope. He removed the contents and studied them for a moment. He could hear whispers from the crowd.

With pure shock and joy, Tim shouted, "Mother!" He looked at Evan, then out into the audience. "Gotta say goodnight right now, people. By this time tomorrow, I'll be, that is Evan and I, will be at . . ." He looked at the itinerary again, "at Ashwickshire Castle in England!"

Thunderous applause from the crowd. The orchestra began playing "God Save the Queen."

Tim hugged his mother. Then he hugged Placenta, who said, "You're all packed. The bags are by the front door. But please, change out of that tacky costume!" She hugged Tim again, then gave a squeeze to Evan. "You boys give my love to Ewan McGregor! And Robbie Williams!"

Chapter Sixteen

On Christmas Day, the telephone hardly stopped ringing. Polly was becoming weary of trying to remember what presents she received from Elton, Reba, Regis, Oprah, and Calista. She found herself cheating by simply telling them, "You are the most thoughtful, loving, and generous friend I have!" Fortunately, Placenta had carefully catalogued all the presents and Polly would send formal notes in a few days when her head stopped throbbing.

Placenta came into the family room dressed in comfortable clothes, holding a bottle of champagne. "Refill?" she asked.

"Christmas certainly doesn't suck this year," Polly exclaimed, pasting a small amount of brie on a Carrs cracker and hand-feeding it to Harry who was seated by Polly's side. "We probably should have gone to Katie Couric's, but this is so cozy."

"I'm hitting the movies," Placenta offered.

"With the Cossack, again?" Polly asked.

"Mmm." Placenta smiled. "Derek. The Woody Allen at the Sunset Five. Horrid reviews, so we shouldn't have to wait in any line. By the way, Jim Belushi is still angry about having to sleep in the laundry room the past few nights."

Polly picked up her flute of champagne. "He'll survive," she said. Just then, the telephone rang again. "Will they stop already. I know everybody loves me. Christ, they just want to hear me gush about how the world would be uninhabitable without The Sharper Image."

Polly picked up the phone and pushed the receive button. "Hello?" she asked, as brightly as she could.

Her umbrage instantly vanished. "Well, Merry Christmas to you, too, dear!" she chirped into the mouthpiece. She covered it for a split second and announced, "It's Tim!"

Placenta put down the bottle of Cristal and moved in close enough to hear the conversation.

Tim was saying, "This is so wonderful, Mother! Even though you were right about this place being as wet as a bog! But I love it! We love it! We're having a fantastic holiday! The castle is to die for! And we have it all to ourselves! Practically! There's a cook, a butler and a couple of maids! It's awesome! And so romantic!"

"Oh, my dearest, *you're* awesome! You thought to call your poor old internationally-renowned mother whose party—*our* party—will, this afternoon, be the lead story on *Access Hollywood!*"

"Hiya Mr. Timmy!" Placenta yelled into Polly's ear. "Merry Christmas! And thanks for the slippers."

Polly handed the phone to Placenta. "There's no need to scream. That's why we have MCI!"

Placenta continued her conversation with Tim. ". . . the bathrobe, the TiVo. And the gift certificate for piano lessons! I'm going to drive your mother crazier than she already is. You're so thoughtful. I love you. Here's your mother again. Bye-bye, honey."

Polly accepted the telephone. "As if the nude photographic study of Josh Hartnett wasn't enough. You outdid yourself, with all the other stuff sweetie. You must have read my mind to know what I really wanted."

Before disconnecting, Polly and Tim both announced that they had important personal news. "I may have another party for you to plan," Polly practically sang.

"I still think you're asking for trouble if you insist on a combination Botox-and-Tupperware party."

"I confess, I've been a little naughty lately," she offered.

"Me too," Tim conceded. "Still, Santa's been a doll to me. By the way, Evan sends hugs and kisses."

"Does this mean you're actually getting some?"

"Are you?"

Polly glanced at Harry and blushed.

"I get your message." Tim paused. "Bye, Mum. It's late here and I have a present to unwrap. If you know what I mean. Hope you're doing the same."

"Back at ya, son," Polly said.

"Merry Christmas!" Placenta yelled from across the room. "Happy New Year!"

Polly pushed the disconnect button on her phone and placed it on the coffee table before her. She smiled at Placenta. "Have a lovely time with *Woody*," she said as Placenta walked out of the room.

Then she leaned in and put her arm around Harry. "Want to give this angel another set of wings?" She giggled, then took him by the hand. "It's your turn to play Santa's workshop. What'll it be this time? Naughty? Or nice?"